Other Voices, Darker Rooms

Eight Grim Tales

H. A. Covington

Writers Club Press
San Jose New York Lincoln Shanghai

Other Voices, Darker Rooms
Eight Grim Tales

Writers Club Press
an imprint of iUniverse.com, Inc.

For information address:
iUniverse.com, Inc.
5220 S 16th, Ste. 200
Lincoln, NE 68512
www.iuniverse.com

The stories in this book are entirely fictional.

ISBN: 0-595-19762-0

Printed in the United States of America

This book is for my Dark Lady.

"I slept, and dreamed that life was beauty.
I woke, and found that life was duty."

Contents

Cold Earth

(Translated from a fragmentary Latin manuscript believed to be of monastic origin, dated circa 1100 A. D., now held in the Rigsarkiv at Viborg, Denmark.)

*I*t is told in the Isle of Man that in the days when Harald Fairhair was king of Norway, a sea-rover named Ketil came down into that island from Stavanger, bringing with him all his housecarles and goods and servants in three ships. This Ketil was renowned as a hardy and adventurous captain, fearless and bold. He sailed on many voyages and always returned with great wealth, which he shared generously among his followers. Yet withal he was a grim and bloodthirsty man, an inflexible tyrant to those he mastered and a cruel enemy who never forgot or forgave an injury. He was always seeking vengeance for this or that, and in Norway he finally went too far and killed a kinsman of the king, for which he was outlawed.

Whereat he betook himself and his people to Mann, where he had a foster brother named Olaf Eirikson, who was one of the foremost jarls and landowners of the island. Jarl Olaf welcomed his foster brother and granted him a markland on the wild western shore of the island, some leagues south of the bishop's dun at St. Patrick's Isle, which lies above a village called Peel. There was good grazing there for Ketil's stock and a small sheltered cove for his ships to beach during the winter, while from the plenteous timber he built himself a capacious wooden steading. He apportioned land among his housecarles and retainers, and for a time he settled down peacefully enough among his new neighbors.

This Ketil, however, persisted in following the old heathen gods of his ancestors, whereas the bulk of the Manxmen both Gael and Norse were Christians. Ketil was often wont to mock the Whitechrist in his mead-hall saying, "What good is the Christian faith save for slaves and women? What use is this Whitechrist to a warrior such as myself? Will he lend strength to my sword-arm and cunning to my designs? Will he bring down the mist and storm among my foemen's vessels and sink them in the sea? And where is this insipid Heaven that the priests prattle of? How can it compare with Valhall and the eternal company of the heroes of antiquity and the gods of the Aesir? Christ hung upon his cross for only three days, yet Odin the All-Father hung upon the tree Ygdrassil and gave up one of his eyes in order that he might gain wisdom!" He uttered many more such blasphemies, but his long sword of Moorish steel hung over his seat at the high table and he was wont to use it in theological debate, so after a time few cared to dispute with him on matters of eternal truth.

Many of Ketil's men settled down in their yardlands with Manx women both Gael and Norse, wife and concubine, but although Ketil dallied with slave girls he seemed cool to all womanhood until a maiden of surpassing beauty and virtue filled his eye and seemed to take away his reason, as reluctant as she was thus to become the object of his ferocious lust. She was called Shona, and she was of the old Manx race who had formerly inhabited the island before the coming of the Norse and even before the coming of the Gael from Ireland. Her hair was long and black, her eyes blue and slanting, her form slender and graceful. She was the daughter of a crofter who lived in an isolated valley, and despite her beauty the young men of the district shunned her because her family was reputed to have uncanny powers and dealings with the fairies. So besotted was Ketil with her that he even offered to take her in marriage, yet she would have none of him. She said she could not give herself to one who was not of her faith. Ketil cursed and swore that no woman, be she ever so comely, would compel him to embrace the Whitechrist he despised, although later events cast some doubt as to whether it was indeed the Christian faith that Shona referred to.

Finally the turbulent lover lost patience, and descended upon her father's croft at Michaelmas with a party of housecarles at his back full armed with sword and spear. Ketil slew Shona's father and her brothers and carried the maiden off to his hall by the sea, where he used her as one might expect. Yet she refused to accept her abduction and enthrall-ment, and she was by turns cold and distant to him or else she wept and cursed him. Ketil's fury grew black, and his love for her turned to ashes in his heart, and finally he determined that Shona should die in the most abominable manner he might contrive.

During that autumn Ketil had set masons and thralls to the task of building him a new stone mead-hall at a better site some short distance from his wooden one. The foundation trenches were dug and the foun-dation stones laid save for the southwest corner, where according to old custom a cockerel or a goat would be sacrificed and entombed therein, despite the oft-repeated admonitions of God's priests against this hea-then practice. Now Ketil said, "In the old days in the Northland before we were most of us Christians, a living thrall was buried in the founda-tions of the chief's hall or mill that his soul might keep watch and drive away evil spirits, trolls, and the great worms from the deep caverns beneath the ground. I am no Christian, and I shall have all done in the manner of my forefathers to the honor of the gods of Asgard. This woman thrall of mine gives me no pleasure. She is sullen and unpleasing even when I flog her and her constant lamentation disturbs my sleep. We shall see if cold earth cannot muffle her complaint."

Had Jarl Olaf Eirikson been in Mann at the time he might have prevented this detestable crime, but he was away on a voyage to the Orkneys. The priest of the parish railed at Ketil and promised his soul's damnation for it, but Ketil cut out the priest's tongue and carried out his wicked design over even the protests of some of his own men. He stood the violated maiden Shona in the foundation trench, tightly bound, and he buried her alive with his own hands. She screamed until the soil covered her face.

In a few more days the stone mead-hall was completed, roofed and thatched, and the walls hung with hides and shields while fresh rushes crackled underfoot. Ketil ordered a great feasting for which he slaughtered a whole ox and numberless pigs and sheep, with fowls and every variety of fish and eels from the sea as well as many casks of ale and mead and skins of wine from Frankland. It was a merry and exuberant feast, and yet late at night when the fire burned low to glowing embers there was a terrible interruption.

Those who were not too fuddled to see anything at all started up and stared at their lord in horror where he sat at the high table, as well they might, for behind Ketil's oaken bench stood a frightful apparition, the image of the entombed maiden Shona. The spectre wore the same coarse linen kirtle in which she had been put to death, but her limbs were encrusted with clay that dripped from her fingers. Her face was a mask of clay from which her eyes started horribly and her tongue protruded, bright blue from suffocation. On seeing the horror-struck faces of his retainers Ketil demanded to know why they stared at him so. But even as he spake he heard a thick whisper in his ear saying, "It is cold here, my lord. The earth wherein you buried me is cold and heavy, and the stones over my head weigh me down."

Yet when he whirled about there was no one there, only some cool earth which had dropped from her lips.

Thereafter as the season progressed into winter, the dread spectre of Shona was seen often around the steading. Sometimes she appeared in the hall or walked along the roof beam, sometimes she was seen in the fields or by the byres, sometimes on the strand or by the smoking sheds where the herring catch hung to cure, and sometimes she was seen walking along the fells against the sunset. The haunting grew notorious in Mann, and folk began to shun Ketil and his lands as accursed. His retainers found cause to move north to Ramsey or else to take ship on some enterprise over the seas. On market days in Peel men shunned Ketil and said to one another as he passed, "I see there a man whose luck has left him!"

Yet strangely, Ketil himself never actually saw this terrible spectre, although he often heard footsteps behind him and felt clammy breath upon the back of his neck, and once in the night he heard a whisper that said, "The earth where I lie is cold and the stones of your fine hall are heavy, my lord. Will you not come down and warm me? In life you were not so unwilling to come to my side."

Ketil even sought help from the Church to rid himself of the visitation, but his own priest could speak no exorcisms as he had no tongue, and the bishop merely cursed Ketil and threw offal down at him from the stockade on St. Patrick's Isle, although he prudently ensured that the tide was in and the gate barred before responding in this uncharitable manner.

By Yulefest none remained with Ketil save a handful of his oldest and most loyal housecarles, men who had sailed and fought with him and eaten his meat from the Baltic to the Pillars of Hercules, and to give them due credit would not desert their chieftain now that he was fey. On Midwinter's Night they sat morosely by the hall fire drinking ale and eating such ill-prepared fare as they could fetch for themselves, since the cooks and the kitchen thralls had run away. Their mark-lord sat alone at the high table, drinking heavily and speaking to no one.

Then in the darkest hour of midnight Ketil suddenly leaped from his seat with a hideous scream of terror and rage. "I see! At last, I see!" he shrieked, pointing to the shadows beyond the fire at the end of the hall, although one else could see ought. "Dog my footsteps no more, devil woman! Do you still complain that the earth wherein you lie is cold? Then together we shall journey to Hell, where you shall be colder still!" Whereupon he drew his sword and charged out into the freezing rain and darkness, slashing at empty shadows and cursing like a madman.

His body was found two days later in the ocean nearby, tangled in seaweed among the rocks that line that perilous Manx shore. When his men pulled him from the water they noticed that his corpse was curiously heavy, and when they slit him open in order that he might appear before the gods of Asgard bearing the wounds of blades upon his body as a hero should, they found that his lungs and belly were filled not with sea water as one might expect, but with dry cold earth.

Old Asgrim

Squire Theophilus Asgrim lived about a mile outside the village of Ballyfell in County Leitrim, in a huge stone mansion with half the roof gone. The grounds were overgrown with weeds and brambles. The old man was reputed to be ninety years old if he was a day and more than half-mad. He was the last of the district's former Anglo-Irish Ascendancy families, and Ballyfell's people still referred to him as "the Squire", when they referred to him at all, and to the house as "the Hall."

It might be expected that the younger residents of Ballyfell would be free of this diffidence, that the young boys would sneak over the tumbled-down walls of Asgrim Hall to steal apples from the gnarled trees in the garden, that teenagers would enter the grounds at night to drink cider from plastic bottles, smoke cigarettes and cuddle members of the opposite sex. Yet this was never the case. There was something so ineffably sinister about the place that everyone young or old simply stayed away. Old Asgrim presumably bought his victuals and supplies elsewhere, for he was never seen in the village. He had no telephone, neither received nor sent any letters, and was only glimpsed at odd hours in unusual places such as graveyards. It would therefore easy for the folk of Ballyfell to forget that he existed, yet somehow they always knew that he was there.

Part of this reticence must be laid to ancestral memory. The "half-mounted gentry" and drunken squireens of the Ascendancy were seldom a saintly crew, but the Asgrims had been a curse and a horror to this little corner of Ireland for over three centuries. There was something about them, a sort of calculated cruelty, that went beyond the mere swinishness and callous brutality of their contemporaries. The first Asgrim was a colonel in the New Model Army who came in the wake of Cromwell's invasion with a troop of Roundhead musketeers at his back. He eliminated all local opposition to his Parliamentary land grant by impaling the last Gaelic chieftain of the area, his entire family, and the parish priest on wooden stakes. Then he herded every man above the age of twelve into the church, bolted the doors, and burned it down. He set the women, the girls, and the young boys to work hauling stone and timber for his fine new house. By day they toiled in leg irons beneath the barrels of smoking matchlocks, and by night they entertained the troops in orgies of mass rape. By the time the house was finished those who weren't dead were pregnant, and thus was Ballyfell repopulated in the next generation.

But no local maiden was good enough for Colonel Asgrim. He brought from England a lovely young girl of sixteen to be his bride. One of the few local youths who had been spared from the massacre to be a stable boy had developed a way with horses and became a groom at the Hall, where he grew tall and handsome. One day the Colonel caught the groom and his young wife together. Whether they were actually lovers, whether Asgrim was insane with jealousy, or simply insane was never determined. He had the soldiers seize them both. What was left of the boy was found in a field a week or so later and was buried in a closed coffin. The wife was locked in an upstairs chamber. There followed a long night of screaming, so horrible that hardened wretches though they were half of Asgrim's troop of mercenaries deserted him the next day, and afterwards she was never seen again. The time and the place being what it was, no inquiry was made into the matter by anyone in authority. Asgrim *was* the authority.

There was never another lady of the manor. The Squires of the line took to spending long periods of time in England, leaving behind agents as bad as themselves to squeeze the rents from the people of Ballyfell, wine-sodden English clerks or brutal Ulster Scots-Irishmen who squeezed the last coin and the last piglet from the village. As bad as these periods of absentee ownership were, they were the common lot in Ireland during the eighteenth and nineteenth centuries and there was nothing remarkable about them. But every twenty-five or thirty years another Asgrim heir would arrive at the hall to take up residence. The Asgrim men apparently bred true to their line, for each new Squire would so resemble his father that the older villagers who remembered the previous master would cross themselves in fear and wonder. They also bred true to their evil genius, for when an Asgrim was *in situ* they ruled with an iron hand. Sometimes there would be resistance, but the hall was always staffed with a crew of burly and violent men, the sweepings of the London gutters or dark-visaged foreigners who spoke neither Irish nor English. The least refusal of rent, labor, or service from man or woman led them to the whipping post, the gallows, or the stinking hulks bound for Botany Bay. Sometimes daring poachers took pheasants or rabbits from the estate's lands or Ribbonmen burned a hayrick; they were always caught and punished with atrocity. The Land League passed Ballyfell by after two organizers were found hanging dead by their heels at a crossroads. One night in 1921 a heavily armed I. R. A. squad set out to burn the Hall. They vanished. Leaving Asgrim Hall alone was something that became indelibly stamped into the soul of Ballyfell.

Little was known about the present tenant of the Hall save that he was ancient, eccentric, and a total recluse. He was seen only rarely, and then only at a distance, generally around dusk or else at night, walking through the deserted country behind the Hall. On certain nights of the year there were fires visible out in the hills and odd sounds could be heard. Sometimes local farmers would venture out to certain ill-regarded "fairy rings" in search of lost cattle or sheep, and they would find blackened spots and evidence that someone had been up to no good. In the mid-1980s there was talk of getting Theophilus Asgrim committed on grounds of evident senility, and a doctor from the Midlands Health Board went out to interview the old man. He came back dazed and puzzled. He could not remember very clearly what had been said, or even what the old man looked like, but he certainly wasn't certifiable. No, certainly not. The doctor suffered some kind of break-down later and was taken away to one of his own sanitoria. The idea of committal went with him.

Then Annie Malone disappeared.

           *   *   *

"It has to be foul play, I tell you!" cried Michael Malone to the three friends who sat with him in O'Neill's pub. "Annie was never one of these flighty kind of girls who'd just take up and run off. We'd have heard something from her. It's been four whole days and her mother and all of us out of our minds with worry!"

"What do the Guards say?" asked his friend Charlie McDonnell.

"Ah, what do them lousers know?" growled Michael Malone in disgust, knocking back the remnants of his pint of Guinness. "Makin' enquiries, they says! My daughter probably lyin' dead in her blood out at that place, and they're making bloody enquiries, is it?"

"But did they talk to the oul' fella at all, Michael?" asked Tim O'Flaherty. "What did he tell them?"

"Who knows?" exploded Malone. "Sean, four more pints and large Paddies with. Oh to be sure, they went out to see the oul' blackguard, our local Keystone cops the pair of 'em, Casey and McNally. I can't get a bloody thing out of 'em. You know, I'm of the opinion they can't even remember what he told them! I ask and they mutter and mumble and look embarrassed like they'd just walked into church and clean forgot their trousers! Disgustin', I call it! After almost seventy years of freedom we're still tuggin' our forelocks to that sort. Oh, he done it all right. Didn't your own sister see Annie going up the lane that runs by the Hall?"

"Just the once," said O'Flaherty anxiously.

"Aye, the night she disappeared from home!" snapped Malone. "Well, I'm not going to just sit around and do nothin' about it! I'm after going out there tonight, and by Heaven I'll get some answers from him! Are you lads for coming with?"

"Blessed saints, don't do that!" spoke up the fourth toper, aghast. He was a very old and wrinkled little man in a cloth cap and a dirty Aran jumper, and now he crossed himself fervently. "For your very soul's sake, Michael, don't do that!"

"And why shouldn't I, *à Phadraig?*" demanded Michael. Normally old Padraig would have sewn his own lips together rather than discuss Theophilus Asgrim or anything to do with Asgrim Hall, but he was on his third round of Paddy and black and his friends were talking wildly and dangerously.

"Have ye never heard the truth about *him?*" whispered Padraig intensely. "Me oul' granny told me long ago. Has no one ever told yez just *what he is?*"

"What in blazes are you blathering about?" asked Malone.

"It's *him* out there!" hissed Padraig urgently. "The very first one! All these centuries, there has never been more than one of him!"

"Codswallop," said Charlie McDonnell succinctly.

"No, no, it's true, on me life!" wailed Padraig. "Oul' Asgrim made a pact with the very devil himself all those years gone, right out there in that accursed house! Satan promised a hundred years of life for every human soul he could seize upon and sacrifice to the Powers of Darkness! But there's a catch in it, as 'tis always with the devil and his works. The sacrificin' has to be done right there in the very room where Colonel Asgrim first saw the devil and made the pact, signed it in his own blood after he made his first sacrifice, which was his own poor young wife! That's why every twenty or thirty years he goes away and then comes back pretending to be his own son. He's tied to this place!"

"Paddy," said Michael in a calm, reasonable voice, "Did you catch the nine o'clock news on the telly up there over the bar? They showed two American blokes wearin' space suits repairing a satellite in orbit around the earth, after which they got back into their space ship and now they're headed for home. My children go to the same national school I went to as a boy, but now they've got computers and videos and they're learning things as chiselers that blokes in universities didn't know when I was their age. I've got no time at all for this mad talk of the devil. The only devil out there is that soddin' ould pervert. I'm going out there tonight, and if I find my daughter has been hurt in any way I promise you he'll not live out the night, never mind another hundred years. Now who's with me?"

After much argument, more whiskey and stout, and an adjournment at closing time to Charlie McDonnell's kitchen where a bottle of poitin was broached, it turned out that two of the three were with him. Under no circumstances drunk or sober would old Padraig set foot anywhere near Asgrim Hall, especially after midnight. Michael Malone slipped into his house down the street and fetched his shotgun, while McConnell and O'Flaherty armed themselves with hurley sticks and the poitin bottle.

The moon was out and it was a warm spring night; they walked out to the Hall with only the occasional stagger. They halted at the gate and stared up at the grim pile from which their ancestors had for genera-tions been pillaged and terrorized. The eerie silence of the place affected their nerves, but Annie Malone had been a popular and pretty girl, and for all their vague disquieting fears all three were convinced that the strange old man who lived in the house was responsible for her disap-pearance. It was a pity they didn't wait one more day before embarking on this expedition, for the very next morning Mrs. Malone would receive a letter from Annie, who had taken a short cut up the lane which ran by the Hall four nights earlier so she could catch the Dublin bus without going through the village. She had left without telling anyone in order to avoid the inevitable argument with her father. He did not care what she did in life so long as she did it in Ballyfell, but she wanted out of the parental nest. She was now living in a flat in Rathmines with two other Leitrim girls and going to secretarial school.

A single light burned in a room at the top of the house. The three men crept up the weed-choked walkway and up the broad steps to the portico with the huge fanlight over the doorway. The panes in the fan-light were missing and it yawned like the black maw of a ghoul. Malone turned the latch, and the unlocked door swung open. An indescribable odor met their nostrils and they entered the house, fetid and dank. Michael drew an electric torch from his pocket and shined it over the several rooms on the ground floor, all of them filled with dust and cob-webs and piles of rotting furniture. The walls were damp and in more than one place they were encrusted with fungus. Over all was an unearthly stillness. The alcoholic courage of the trio was rapidly evapo-rating. "Let's get out of here!" whispered O'Flaherty in a tremulous voice.

"We're going to find Annie!" grated Malone. "He's upstairs. Come on, follow me." They mounted the stairs carefully clutching their weapons. The ancient woodwork might have been expected to creak under their weight, but there was never a sound. It was unnatural and unnerving. At the top of the stairs was a long corridor, with black oak doors and alcoves containing busts and cupboards along the length of the hallway. The wallpaper was peeling and the carpet beneath their feet stank of decay. At the far end of the hall a light shone from under a door. The men approached it carefully. Michael Malone reached out his hand and touched the latch when a voice from within called out, "Come in, good sirs! I pray you to come in! You are expected!" The voice was dry and harsh, as if long disused.

"Mother of God, let's get out of here!" croaked Charlie McConnell. He would have fled but his feet seemed rooted to the floor. Michael Malone shoved the door open and all three of them pushed convulsively into the room, crowding into the center of the large, high chamber. It was a study or library furnished in an antique baroque style, the walls lined with shelves containing many books, some of them of great age. More books and papers from eighteenth century works to last week's Irish *Times* were stacked on the floors, in the corners, on tables, and in alcoves. A chandelier of crystal holding a good fifty candles lighted the room. Facing them was a slim, spare figure in the costume of the Restoration period. He wore a periwig, gartered satin knee breeches, hose and shoes with silver buckles, lace cuffs, and at his side hung a rapier. The face was a mass of seams and wrinkles in which two watery eyes glittered and two wide, wet lips glistened. The lips stretched into an insane grin. *"Three hundred more years, Your Majesty!"* the creature cackled.

The door slammed shut behind them, and something at their backs moved with a dry rustling sound. All three whirled around to see what it was, and then the screaming began.

Mick The Cutler

 *T*he computer system went down at the Plastica Perfecto plant in Colonia Suarez about ten thirty in the morning, all four production lines ground to a halt shortly after that, and the manager Señor Portillo went into hysterics.

The IT, the manufacturing process and quality control servers were the responsibility of two young Americans, aged twenty-four and twenty-five respectively, who drove across the sewage-filled Rio Grande from Brownsville every day wearing Calvin Kleins and tie-dyed T-shirts. They were each paid the sum of $80,000 per year by Plastica Perfecto, a salary roughly equivalent to the annual pay of all 200 workers on both shifts of any one of the four production lines. They were also warned not to eat the local food; both young men always brought in their lunches from the Wendy's or the H.E.B. deli counter in Brownsville. Usually the two techies hid behind the steel doors of the computer room, in the cooling blast of its four roaring air conditioners, where they played video games and foosball all day, but now both cyber-kids were actually called upon to earn their pay. They tapped maniacally on their keyboards at the admin terminals trying to identify and fix the software glitch that had crashed the system, while Portillo cowered in his office on the telephone to his *abogado,* making some panicky last minute changes to his will, which would quite possibly need to be probated if he did not get the factory producing again very soon. The workers on the line were told via the loudspeakers on the intercom that out of the kindness of the management's hearts, they would be paid up until eleven o'clock for the day and they'd go back on the clock when the line came up again. In the meantime, they were graciously granted permission to go into the parking lot and smoke.

The Colonia Suarez *maquiladora* was run by a clique of PRI-connected businessmen out of Vera Cruz who were also known to deal in exotic pharmaceuticals and certain sporting goods of heavy caliber. With its twelve hundred workers and its own fleet of double-trailered Kenworth trucks to haul the product north, Plastica Perfecto was the NAFTA jewel in the Colonia's crown, not to mention providing the grandees from Vera Cruz with a legal and publicly demonstrable source for their wealth. Plastica Perfecto manufactured a wide variety of small plastic items such as cheap childrens' toys, combs, plastic wristwatches, throwaway soft drink bottles, even plastic shoes which were shipped southward to the even more impoverished lands of Honduras, Guyana and El Salvador. The factory was a huge building constructed mostly of garish yellow cinderblock and roofed with corrugated iron, but the conveyors, the trimming machinery, the molding and pouring tanks, the cutting lines and the robotics were the state of the art from the U. S., Taiwan and Japan. The workers were paid a princely forty cents per hour per twelve-hour shift, and every day people came from as far away as Yucatan to line up and beg at the gates for a trickle from the Niagara of NAFTA wealth. The factory owners periodically drove up from Vera Cruz in their Cadillacs and their flashy Armani suits. They strolled leisurely down the lines with a regal air, and then went into the manager's air-conditioned office, where God help Señor Portillo if profits were down by so much as a peso, never mind a dollar. On one occasion, the owners had been accompanied into the office by a huge greasy-haired Indio in a sweat-stained yellow pastel shirt with a loud flowered tie wrapped around his bulging neck. At the conclusion of the conference this man had applied an electric stun gun to sensitive parts of Señor Portillo's body until the plant manager's screams could be heard on the factory floor. Profits had leaped magically after this episode.

It was a warm spring morning, not yet hot. The employees' lounge consisted of some battered lawn furniture and upturned crates under a tall and gnarled live oak beside the graveled parking lot's chain link fence. About seventy men and women now milled around beneath the tree, mostly young, mostly wearing baseball caps and knock-off denim jeans manufactured in Guatemala and cheap cotton shirts and blouses, crunching a carpet of cigarette butts beneath their feet as they laughed and joked and smoked Marlboros and a few hand-rolled cigars. An enterprising *madrugadore* driving a battered van hauled an ice cooler out to the tree and started selling cold cans of Coca-Cola and Dr. Pepper. The factory workers were half pleased at the unexpected and extended break in their tedious day, and half angry at what promised to be the loss of at least several hours of pay while the two American whizz kids tinkered with the computers.

Fabio Sotelo sat apart from the rest on a wooden bench about thirty yards down the chain link fence, smoking a hand-rolled cigarette of strong Chiapas leaf. He was entitled to such aloofness by virtue of his supervisory status as head bookkeeper in the warehouse. Most of the workers were various shades of mestizo brown, but Fabio's light complexion, along with the chiseled bone structure and light freckles and green eyes he had inherited from his Irish mother, proclaimed his *criollo* class status. So did the short-sleeved white shirt and the black tie he wore, and the plastic pocket protector containing three Bic pens, the ultimate badge of the Mexican white-collar worker. One of the great sources of gossip at the company was why such an educated and personable young man was working in a *maquiladora* at all; with his looks and upbringing he should have been an army officer or a government official in any Latin American country. But to be sure, young Fabio did have some occasional odd and eccentric habits. Like right now, for instance. Fabio was sitting on the bench and trembling like a leaf, his face as white as a sheet. The hand-rolled cigarette was so low it was in danger of burning his lips, yet Sotelo seemed not to notice.

Fabio Sotelo was staring after a strikingly lovely young woman who had walked past him on the dirt path running from the parking lot down to the side gate of the factory. Her name was Maria, and Fabio loved her to the point of madness. Like Fabio, Maria as well was possessed of the old Spanish beauty, wherein the original European genetic heritage was not yet totally extinguished. Her shoulder length hair was dark and glowing brown rather than black, with occasional reddish gleams. She was noticeably tall for a Mexican girl, tall and lissome and clean-limbed, and when she walked down the line with an easy and natural grace every male eye on the floor followed her. Today she was wearing battered denim overalls and a patched but clean T-shirt underneath, yet her bare shoulders and arms seemed to cry out for a black lace mantilla even as her hair thirsted for a flower. Her oval face should have been draped into the folds of a veil and her enigmatic, fathomless dark eyes should have been glimpsed over a fan or a through the iron grille of a hacienda window as she whispered to a highborn lover, the lover that Fabio so desperately wanted to be. As she passed him, the girl pointedly looked away from him with a cold toss of her shoulders, but it was not that had turned the young man who watched her so white. Fabio sat on the bench, the fire on the cigarette finally touching his lips and making him spit out the butt, trembling like a leaf, convinced that he was going raving mad.

As Maria walked down the long sloping hill to the side entrance, something was following her. It seemed to be a man crawling on his hands and knees, or at least a human-like figure crawling on all fours, except the figure was horribly thin, almost skeletal. The sun was high and bright overhead, and yet the figure seemed to move in a constant shadow almost as if it was night in the few square feet of space that it occupied. Like something glimpsed at night by an occasional flash of lightning, Fabio could only see it dimly against the undulating darkness. The figure crawled sometimes on its belly and sometimes with a kind of heaving flop, following a few feet behind the girl like some hideous, deformed pet. From what little Fabio could actually glimpse of it within its bubble of murk, the man or the figure seemed to be wrapped in a kind of cloak or drapery, and Fabio thought he could glimpse the outline of beads or feathers. The girl opened the side gate and went inside, her strange companion crawling in swiftly behind her, and both were gone.

Fabio buried his face in his hands and moaned, sick with horror and fear for his beloved, knowing that no one else could see the thing. He alone possessed a terrible knowledge that was past all bearing and which could never be shared. For the hundredth time he considered walking into the parking lot, getting into his Peruvian-made Toyota Camry, and simply fleeing. Back to Durango, to his sister in San Antonio, anywhere to be away from the horror of that black crawling figure.

"That's a bad one," said a voice above him. Fabio looked up and saw the old gringo trucker lighting up one of his cheap Optimo cigars with a Zippo. The American's face was weathered and beaten beneath his battered, almost shapeless Stetson. His handlebar moustache was grizzled brown and gray like a rat's muzzle. He was wearing Levi jeans, boots, and a gray twill work shirt. He stuck the cardboard box of Optimo Sports into his shirt box. Sotelo decided he had not heard the American correctly. He started to roll another cigarette. His hands were trembling so badly that he spilled the tobacco on the ground. *"Buenos dias,* Fabio."

"Hello, Jack," said Fabio. "When did you get in?"

Jack flipped the Zippo alight and Fabio inhaled almost half the cigarette in one drag. "Last night. Brought some generator and conveyor parts down from Dallas and I'll be hauling a load of plastic crap back up to Arkansas to Wal-Mart." His Spanish was almost perfect and unaccented. "Yep, that's a bad one. Almost near-about the worst one of them thangs I've ever seen. How long has she had it with her?" asked Jack conversationally. Fabio stared at him in shock.

"You see it too?" he gasped in horrified disbelief.

"Been seeing 'em for a long time, son," said Jack. He seated himself on the bench. "Since I was a very young child, I been seeing 'em. Just like you probably have since you was a *pocito*."

Fabio stared at the ground for a while. "I never knew there was anyone else," he said after a while.

"Probably more of us than anyone suspects. It's not the sort of thing one discusses in public," said the American, puffing on his cigar.

"No, it is not."

"Any idea what it's all about?" asked the older man quietly, exhaling cigar smoke.

"Her name is Maria. She's going to be murdered!" said Fabio, almost weeping.

"Yeah, I figured it was something like that," said the American sadly. "It's a damned shame. She looks like a lovely girl. I only see the bad stuff. It's always been that way for me."

"Sometimes it's been good for me," Fabio told him. "When I was four years old in Durango, I would have long conversations with my grandmother, who died before I was born," said Fabio. "She was a wonderful old lady and she loved me. I would tell my parents at breakfast things she had said. It terrified them. My mother said it was a curse from the devil. She wanted to have me exorcised by the priest."

"So you learned to keep quiet?" asked the old gringo.

"Yes. You?"

"My folks just thought I was crazy and wanted to send me to a kiddie shrink," said the old man. "It all came to a head when I was in the first grade in back home."

"Where was home?" asked Fabio.

"Oxford, Mississippi," Jack told him. "I was six years old. There was this old man dressed in a dark suit, probably the one he was buried in. I would see him hanging around the edge of the schoolyard, looking through the fence from the street, sometimes under a chinaberry tree way at the back. He'd be looking at all the children real bad, real nasty. I could see in my own mind what was running through his, what he wanted to do to the little girls. I didn't understand it, but I knew it was a terrible thing he wanted, that he was a terrible thing who should not be there. I called him a school criminal, which was the only thing I could think of at that age to call him. I ran to the teachers and told on him, but after a while I came to realize that only I could see him. There was a big conference with my folks and they were about to send me down to Jackson to some child psychiatrist to have my noggin tuned and my brain washed squeaky clean, but I was able to talk my way out of it by sayin' I'd just been makin' the whole thang up. From that day to this, I have never spoken of any of these...episodes to any living soul, except for once. I made the mistake of trying to help someone. Just the once."

"What happened?" asked Fabio.

"She died. What's worse, she died hating me and fearing me because she couldn't understand. " said the old man. "Reckon that's what you're thinking about trying, eh? Don't. You can't change anything, and it will only make things worse. Trust me on this one, Fabio. I know."

"I've already tried," whispered Fabio in agony. "I tried to warn her."

"And it didn't go well," responded Jack, a statement rather than a question.

"It went terribly. I couldn't tell her everything, not the whole truth. Even as shaken as I was, I had enough sense to realize that, but still I tried to talk to her. You're right. It did no good. All I accomplished was to convince her that I am insane."

"Does she know that you love her?" asked the American. Fabio didn't even bother to ask Jack how he knew.

"Yes. I've told her in a few ridiculous, stumbling ways, but I never pushed things because it was obvious she didn't want to deal with it. She has a boyfriend, a real low-life. Ramon Saldivar, the foreman of the trimming line. God knows what she sees him. Maria's very intellectual, she's been to college in Mexico City, and she's working here to raise money to finish getting her degree. Psychology of all the damned subjects. I sure wish she could apply some psychology to herself. The only thing I can figure is Ramon's got a motorcycle."

"Motorcycles will get 'em every time," agreed Jack, chewing on his cigar.

"Saldivar isn't even a real Mexican. He's just a Tejano punk from San Angelo. He does a classy Antonio Banderas act to her face, smooth as silk, all smiles and bows and jolly jokes and *te amo,* and all the while he's chasing everything in tight jeans on the factory floor, sometimes literally behind Maria's back. I've seen him cop a feel of another girl's ass ten feet behind her while she worked the line. He's a mean drunk, a bully who picks fights with little guys in the cantina but falls all over himself backing away when anyone stands up to him. Some of the girls from up north knew him before he came down here. He's a woman-beater as well, apparently, and he's down here because he's got some warrants or something on him in Texas. God, I hate yellow dog bullies who beat women! They don't have the courage to fight other men."

"Yeah, I know Saldivar," Jack told him. "Seen him on that chopped hog of his. I had a little run-in with him once on the loading dock out back. He tried to play hombre with me, Viva La Raza and all that crap, but when it came down to it he decided that the better part of valor was discretion. All of a sudden he remembered he had something real important to do back on the floor, a lot more important than getting his face shoved into the damned concrete. He's a wannabe cholo. Likes to build his rep by dropping hints that he's down with the Puente Rojo, although he's discreet about making any such claim where any of Cabral's real people might hear about it. José doesn't like his name being taken in vain."

Sotelo looked at Jack oddly. "You know Cabral? I heard something, that you used to be a Texas Ranger?"

"Among other things," chuckled Jack. "Long ago and not germane to the present topic of discussion, amigo. So it's Saldivar?"

"Yes," moaned Fabio. "He's going to kill her. Maybe tomorrow, maybe next week, maybe next year, hell, maybe ten years from now. But he's going to murder her."

"Might as well give it to me from the top, son," said Jack. "How long has she had that thing on her?"

"I've had some, well, twinges I guess you'd call them, ever since I've known her. I've always been worried for her, especially since I started quietly asking around and heard some things about Saldivar that gave me cause for concern. But *that?* About a week. It happened one night that I was leaving and I had to drop off some work at the front office, so I cut through the floor just after shift change. I looked through the window into the cafeteria and Maria was sitting right in front of me at one of the tables. She had one of her books. She actually reads books, you know. Real books. Cervantes, Borges, José Martì. Saldivar was teasing her over it, trying to grab it, the kind of childish thing you and I got out of doing to little girls when we were ten years old, but he does it all very Antonio Banderas and she just eats it up."

"He has a gift for appearing non-threatening to her, no matter how he comes across to others?" suggested Jack.

"Yes. You put it very well."

"Men of his kind often have that knack. So what happened then?" prompted Jack.

"They ended up with her sitting down and him leaning over and stroking her, nuzzling her like a porcupine, and then...." Fabio leaned over, gasping for breath, almost vomiting from the remembered terror.

"Go on," prodded Jack gently.

"I can't really describe it. Everything kind of flashed, black was white and white was black, like looking at a photographic negative, and then all of a sudden it wasn't Ramon Saldivar leaning over Maria it was...it was...oh, may Christ have mercy on her! It was *that!* I saw it plainly. It was a rotting corpse, the face a horned skull half human and half snake, wrapped in a long cloak or gown of feathers, and it was slipping its fingers around Maria's face and grinning, I don't mean like skulls usually look like they grin but really grinning, and laughing high in the sky in mad lust for blood and pain, lifting up her gentle smiling face with fingers of bone and the teeth coming down like a kiss to sink into her throat....." Fabio was trying to roll another cigarette, without success. Jack took the works from him and rolled it himself. "And then I *knew.* I just knew then what it was trying to show me, trying to tell me. What it mocked me with. What it wanted me to know so I would suffer. Ramon Saldivar is going to murder her some day."

"Probably happen when she finally wises up and tries to leave him. That's usually when it turns from mental and physical abuse to murder. Of course that may be a few years and a few kids from now, God pity them." He stuck the cigarette in Fabio's mouth and lit it. "And then you were faced with the worst part of being in love. The time had come when you had to tell her something she didn't want to hear. How did she react when you tried to talk to her?" asked Jack.

"After I ran to the men's room and dry-heaved for five minutes? She told me gently but firmly to mind my own business, how I don't know anything about him or her, how she knows him better than anybody and he is just this most wonderful *muchacho* in the world, how I am just a friend and I have no right to any say in her life. Go away, funny little man, and take your heart and your soul with you, for you are no longer amusing and the motorcycle calls. You get the idea."

"You sure she's worth it, son?" asked Jack softly.

"Quite positive, yes. She just doesn't know she's worth it. She told me she was a big girl and she could take care of herself."

"She can't take care of herself against *that!*" replied Jack morosely.

"Mother of God, don't you think I know that?" moaned Fabio. "What the hell am I going to do, Jack?"

"Nothing," said the older man kindly. "You're going to do nothing. I'm sorry, amigo, but you must now face up to one of the most cruel and agonizing lessons in all of life. That lesson is that you cannot save people from themselves."

"I can try!" responded Fabio with spirit.

"Yes, you can try, because you are a brave and noble young man and you love her. And you will thereby cause yourself nothing but misery and a pain you cannot imagine. One of the hardest things on earth for any human being to do, Fabio, but especially for a woman, is to admit to themselves, much less to anyone else, that they just might not know everything in the world there is to know. That someone outside their own situation might be able to see what she cannot see, as indeed you do so terribly see. Almost no one on earth has the intelligence and humility truly to listen to someone else who genuinely has their best interests to heart. It took me thirty years to acquire that ability, in such small measure as I possess it. You can't accept it even now, with me, as I tell you all this, can you? Don't blame Maria if she can't do it. I don't think anyone your age can.

"Let me tell you something else, something that applies to most women I've ever known. Even if Maria could somehow be brought to understand and accept what is happening to her, my guess is that she would quite literally rather die than do what has to be done to save herself. Because to do that would be to admit that in a matter of her own innermost heart she really couldn't take care of herself, that she needs you, that you were right and she was wrong. Again, it's only one woman in a thousand who can admit to making the kind of mistake that she has made. It's not Maria's fault she's one of the nine hundred and ninety-nine. She'll only admit it when the truth is forced upon her in some way she cannot possibly fail to understand. Give a woman an out, any out, any excuse to cut a man like Saldivar a single inch of slack, and she'll do it. Oh, they do wise up eventually, sometimes at a mortal cost. Eventually he'll turn on Antonio Banderas once too often and all of a sudden the scales will fall from her eyes. She'll finally understand, she'll try to leave, he'll kill her, and there is not one goddamned thing on the face of this earth that you can do to stop it. Because *she will not listen to you!* And on her tombstone will be written the epitaph of God alone knows how many women since time began."

"What epitaph?" asked the younger man.

"These words: *'She did not know who her friends were.'* Those words will say it all. There is no way, none, that you can make that girl understand that you are her friend and that the man whom she believes to be her lover is not. Burn this into your brain, Fabio: *she will not listen to you!* She will never admit that you might have some knowledge, some truth about her life that she cannot discern herself. There is only one man that she has chosen to let that close, and you are not that man."

"You saw what she has chosen to let that close!" growled Fabio.

"Yes, I saw, and my heart and my soul cry out for her," Jack told him compassionately. "But you have no part in this. You are an outsider and you cannot force your way in. You see what you see only because of this gift or curse which has been our lifelong misfortune. I don't pretend to understand it. But I know that if you do not walk away from this, you'll tear yourself apart."

"I will not accept that there is nothing I can do!" cried Fabio heatedly. "And I'm not trying to save her from herself, I am trying to save her from that woman-beating bastard Ramon Saldivar!"

"This ain't the nineteenth century, young 'un, and she ain't a slave," Jack reminded him. "She is with him because she wants to be. It is her choice, however stupid and dangerous a choice that is. She will not let you choose otherwise for her, and she will willingly run the risk of death or injury at that man's hands rather than admit that you know better in this matter than she does. It looks as if she will pay a heavy price for that choice. But *there is nothing you can do!* You cannot help people and you cannot save them from themselves. You can see that damned thing that's on her, but you can't save her. All I can suggest is that you leave this place so you don't have to watch, and try to forget her."

"There is one way I can save her," said Fabio, his voice quiet with deadly hate. "Macho man Ramon and his motorcycle may just ride off into the sunset and disappear into the desert one night. You said it yourself, Cabral doesn't like people using his name without permission. The cops will look at his people, not me."

"You can't do that son," said the older man quietly.

"I think you would be amazed at how easily I can do that, *compadre*," snarled Fabio.

"No, you can't, for three reasons." Jack ticked them off on his fingers. "First off, you ain't smart enough to do it and not get caught. No, you ain't. If Ramon disappears and the *Federales* come nosing around, who do you think is going to be the first person to run to them and point her finger right at you? Your beloved Maria, that's who. You would leave a trail of evidence a blind heel hound could follow, and you'll end up rotting for the next forty years in Matamoros State Prison. You would destroy yourself and you wouldn't save her, and that's the second reason you need to drop homicide from your menu. Have you noticed that our creepy-crawly whatsit is following *her*, not him? If you waste Ramon Saldivar, you think she's suddenly gone come to her senses and turn to you? Like hell she will! Ramon's brothers in spirit Juan and Pedro and Jésus are waiting for her right down the road, just as charming and mean and lying and cheating with fists at the ready for her. If this girl wanted what you had to offer she would had chosen you in the first place. She didn't. Learn to live with that or you will go completely *loco*, I guarantee. The third reason you can't kill him is because he isn't a murderer, at least not that we know of. At least not yet. This is Mexico, not Israel, and you can't murder a man for what he *might* do in the future. That puts the black hat squarely on your head, Fabio. Ever heard of karma?"

The loudspeakers boomed. "The processing lines will be back up in five minutes! All employees return to your work stations!"

"You are a true friend to say these things to me, Jack," said Fabio with a sigh as he stood up. "I thank you for it most gratefully."

"Have I made a dent?" asked Jack grimly.

"I can't stand by and do nothing," responded Fabio quietly but firmly. "I can't do it, Jack. I can't just leave her to *that!*"

"No, you can't," responded Jack with a tired smile. "Not and still be the man you are. A pity you and your father don't speak any more. I think Alejandro would be proud of you now."

The two friends walked down to the factory and along the side of the main building, back towards the loading dock where Fabio had his small cubbyhole with the computer terminal and the adding machine, and where Jack's truck was backed into one of the bays. "She's on Line Three, light molding, and Ramon runs Line Four, trimming," said Fabio. "I suppose it could be worse. He could be in a position of actual authority over her." He looked into one of the dusty windows at the men and women lining up along the conveyor. He saw Maria at her station, stacking small molds high beside her in preparation for the imminent start up of the line and adjusting the long metal arm with the steel stamping and shaping plate above her. Fabio peered into the window. "I don't see it. Where the hell is it?" he wondered aloud. Jack joined him at the window, shading his eyes, and they both scanned the cavernous interior of the factory hangar.

The thing leaped up at them, its horned skull-face staring inches from theirs behind the glass, wearing a weird feathered headdress, sockets in bone burning fiery red, crocodile teeth that dripped rotten meat grinning and slavering, mad chattering laughter gibbering a Name into their brains behind their horrified eyes. Both men screamed like animals being torn apart limb from limb, collapsing and cowering in the dust. Fortunately the line started just then and the noise drowned out their shrieks. Finally they staggered to their feet, leaning on one another. "Mick the Cutler!" gasped Jack. "Mick the Cutler! Mick the Cutler!"

"Jack, it's worse than ever I imagined! I beg you, on my knees, help me!" wept Fabio. "Jack, we can't let it have Maria! We know even if she doesn't! If we let it have her it will mean the damnation of our souls, Jack! She's human, we're human, and we can't turn away from her! God is watching us! I can't turn away from her now that I know what it is! You can't turn away from Maria now! In the name of God, help me!"

"I take it back, what I said earlier. That really is the worst one I've ever seen, bar none," whispered Jack, trembling.

"What was the worst up until today?" asked Fabio, curious even in his battered emotional state.

"My grandparents' house down by the sea, in Pass Christian," said Jack in a low voice. "Things used to walk there at night. Try to picture in your mind a six or seven year-old child who wakes up in the night and has to go to the bathroom, and opens the door and sees things walking up and down the hall. Things with the bodies of men and the heads of animals. Think of your father and your mother and your grandfather and your grandmother asking you to explain why you pissed on the floor in the corner of your bedroom instead of going to the toilet. Try lying awake at night in the darkness and hearing the doorknob turn and seeing a seven foot tall thing dressed in rotten cloth with the head of a pig or a rabbit looking into your room and speaking your name."

"Oh, Jesus, Jack, I'm sorry! God, it must have been hell for you! I never saw anything that bad."

"My situation was kind of different, You had a good birth and a good upbringing. Your mom especially was a good woman. My family has had some strange things going on for the past couple of centuries. Long story. What the hell does Mick the Cutler mean?" muttered Jack, dazed.

"You didn't hear it right," replied Sotelo, leaning against the wall and retching up bile from his stomach.

"Huh?"

"You still think in English, so you heard it in your mind in English," explained Fabio.

"It doesn't make any sense in Spanish either!" protested Jack.

"Not Spanish. Nahuatl. The language of the ancient Aztecs. Believe it or not there's still a few hundred thousand people in central Mexico who still speak some fragments of it," said Fabio, breathing deeply.

"So what does Mick the Cutler mean in Aztec?" asked Jack, his face white.

"Not Mick the Cutler. Mictlantecutli." Fabio stared at Jack with all the horror of the abyss in his eyes. "Mictlantecutli. The Aztec god of the dead."

            *   *   *

Midnight was long past when the Luna Azul cantina finally closed. Ramon Saldivar strode out the door and mounted his motorcycle.

Ramon was doing fine. Ten Dos Equis and five double José Cuervos and he was barely staggering. Ramon was twenty-five years old, thickset and well-muscled although the beer-fat was finally starting to pile up around his waist. His face was brown and square and handsome enough, although his eyes were often puffy now and the odd fold and wattle of beer-fat was starting to ripple and quiver in cheek and under the chin there as well. In another year the liquid bloating would start and become visible. But tonight Ramon Saldivar was a man on top of his game, as strong and as stupid as a young bull. He'd finally gotten that little black-haired minx Marisol from Packing out behind the cantina and fucked her against the wall, not just that but with her blouse and her bra both down to her waist so he could actually see her tits by the streetlight *Not bad, muchacho, not bad!* Ramon congratulated himself. A daring plan was taking shape in Ramon's mind. A weekend with Maria in Brownsville in the Motel 6, two rooms paid for and an evening's entertainment, a gallant kiss good night and a "sleep well, *querida*" as he left her in her own room to show how much he respected his Madonna, and then off to the third room where Marisol would await him…what a coup! What an *hombre!* He, Ramon Saldivar, would pull it off! He would need a fair amount of cash, but that he could get easily enough from the temporary workers, the *madrugadores,* when he took half their pay in kickbacks over the next few days, for the privilege of choosing them at the early morning shape-up outside the factory gates. *Fucking Indio peasants from Yucatan don't need money anyway. They should be paid in yams,* Ramon thought. He eased his bike over the railroad crossing and he was about to turn left down the dirt road, back to the men's hostel where he enjoyed the privilege of a room all to himself, when he heard a yell to his right. *"Hola! Ramon el cabron!"*

Ramon looked to his right and in the moonlight he saw the old gringo truck driver Jack sitting at the top of an embankment over the railroad tracks. Jack was waving a bottle in the air and apparently drunk out of his gourd. Ramon was reminded of the fact that he had some unfinished business with Jack. He noticed that there were neither witnesses nor concrete floors present, and in any case Jack seemed to be in no condition to push Ramon's face into anything, concrete or not. A drunken old man was his for the taking. Ramon grinned, killed the bike, parked it on the kickstand, and started climbing up to where Jack sat swigging from the bottle. "Gringo, you think I forgot you?" he snarled menacingly.

"Hey there, *Ramon el cabron!*" shouted Jack cheerily, waving the bottle again. "Beat up any women tonight? Or maybe you been playin' cards? Find any jokers in your deck? The game ain't really worth playing lessen you got a joker or two in the deck. Wanna drink?"

"Sure, I'll drink. After I kick your ass," said Ramon, grinning.

"Hey Ramon, how much do you know about Mexican history?" babbled Jack as Ramon towered over the old man seated cross-legged on the ground. "You maybe know what a *Diablo del Rio* is?"

"No, *viejo*. Tell me what that is."

"During the Mexican War from 1846 to 1848, most of the American troops who came down here and bitch-slapped you greaseballs were from Mississippi," cackled Jack in inebriated glee. "You *campesinos* couldn't pronounce the name, but you knew it was the same name as the biggest river in the whole fucking world, so you called us the Devils from the River. Now you know the origin of one of your country's folk sayin's. And guess what, *Ramon el cabron?* I'm from Missi-goddamned-ssippi!"

"We got a folk saying here in Mexico too, you gringo dog," hissed Ramon. "*Huevos revueltos*. Scrambled eggs. But it don't mean scrambled eggs like the kind you eat. You gonna find out what it means right now, old fool." He leaned down and jerked the whiskey-reeking Jack to his feet by his shirt.

"Yeah, well, I got an even better *Yanqui* folk saying for you, Ray my man!" crooned the semi-comatose trucker.

"And what's that saying?" laughed Ramon, drawing back his fist to smash Jack's face in.

Jack spoke. His voice was suddenly calm, deep, and stone cold sober. He spoke in English. "Youth and enthusiasm will always be vanquished by age and treachery."

Ramon felt the icepick sliding through his left ear and into his brain. It was cold and it tickled slightly, and then he felt nothing more, ever again. He did not even feel himself hit the ground as he died.

*   *   *

Jack arrived back in Colonia Suarez ten days later with a load of steel pipe from Mobile. Fabio stood outside on the cracked asphalt street and smoked with him while the truck was being unloaded. "The cops said the way he'd been drinking that night they were amazed he could even balance himself on the motorcycle," said Fabio. "They had to scrape him and the bike both up off the railroad tracks with shovels."

"Getting run over by fifty freight cars don't leave much," agreed Jack.

"Not much in the way of evidence, no." They puffed for a while, Fabio on his Chiapas hand roll and Jack on his cheap Optimo. "What about karma, Jack?" asked Fabio softly.

Jack shrugged. "Hell, my karma has been in pretty bad shape for a long time."

"Maria is leaving. She's going back to Mexico City. You didn't save her, you know," said Fabio with terrible sadness. "It's still with her."

Jack spoke carefully. "If I had any idea what you were talking about, which I categorically deny, I would say that what was done wasn't done to save her, Fabio. It was done to save you. I meant what I said, son. You have so many better things ahead of you than being buried alive up there in Matamoros."

"I thought you told me no one can save someone else from themselves?" Fabio reminded him archly.

"Did I say that? Let's just say I'm old fashioned. I owe your daddy and your mama a debt that means much more than money, and I'm kind of partial to you too, if the truth be known."

"I know that. I just wish you could have saved Maria as well," said Fabio. "Did you really want to marry my mother all those years ago?"

"More than anything," said Jack bleakly. "Just my tough luck she found a better man than me."

"I have to get back to work. Stop by when I get off and we'll go out for a *cerveza* or two."

"Be thar with bells on," said Jack. After Fabio left Jack leaned against the wall smoking his cigar meditatively for a while. He looked to his right and about fifty yards away he saw the girl Maria, standing at the bus stop. She was wearing a green skirt and linen blouse, and she had a suitcase with her. A few yards behind her the strange feathery figure of shadow sat slumped back against the wall like a wino. Quietly Jack strolled down to the bus stop. Maria did not turn to look at him. Jack squatted down by the dark one. "Look at me," he commanded.

The half man, half-serpent skull stared into Jack's eyes. *You're doing it again*, the thing thought at him. *You're meddling with my schedule. Ramon wasn't due for a while and now she's going to be late. We've had this discussion before, Jack.*

"That was long ago," said Jack. "Long ago and we both had different names. I don't suppose there's any chance you'd let me cut in line and take her place?"

It doesn't work like that, Jack. You of all people should know this.

"I know it. Just thought I'd inquire." He stood up and walked over to the girl. She looked at him with pain and fear and horror in her eyes.

"Is it still there?" she whispered.

"Yes," he told her.

"You spoke with it. It won't talk to me. What did it say?" she pleaded.

"Nothing of any importance."

"Is there anything at all I can do, *señor?*" she asked, her face pale and haggard.

"Down that road, another Ramon awaits you. But if you're lucky, maybe another Fabio as well. You have eyes and ears and a mind. Use them. Never close them, and when a man who loves you speaks, never refuse to listen to him no matter how much you may not want to hear what he says. That's all I can advise you. *Vaya con Dios, señorita. Espero que algun dia sepas quienes son tus amigos.* May you come to know who your friends are."

Jack waited until she was on the bus and it had pulled out into the street, on its was southward. Until it turned the corner and disappeared from view, he could still see something black and feathered sitting cross-legged on the roof of the bus like a wise old sage in meditation, ancient and patient and terrible.

The Wheelbarrow

I have been investigating paranormal phenomena and unusual occur-rences in Ireland for many years. The bulk of my cases turn out to be explicable in very ordinary ways, but about one third of the cases in my files do have paranormal aspects to them. That is to say that they cannot be explained away as sincere observer error, neurosis, hoax, or misinter-pretation of some natural occurrence. In these cases something has occurred which is contrary to the laws of physics and the accepted processes of nature as we understand those processes.

The most frustrating thing about many of these manifestations is that they appear to be so completely *pointless*. For example, there is an office in Dublin's Merrion Square where once a month a pool of water appears, about three inches deep, at the same spot on the floor. Successive tenants of the office have done everything conceivable to determine the source of the water and stop these regular inundations, but without success. There are no pipes or plumbing in the floor, the ceiling, or the walls of that particular room, Condensation of any sort is a ridiculous explanation; we are talking about thirty or forty gallons of water that appear out of nowhere while people watch. I myself have the entire process recorded on videotape.

I checked with as many previous tenants as I could run down, and I found out that the solicitors who presently rent the chambers are by no means the first to experience this problem. It has been happening for as long as anyone can remember, and a friend of mine in An Taisce located a reference to the phenomenon dated 1819, when the great Georgian townhouse was a private residence for the Lord Mayor of Dublin. I discovered that the pool appears exactly two hours after the completion of each month's lunar cycle, when the moon has just turned full. Since it there is a variation of some odd minutes in this, the moment of the materialization has varied and up until now no one has thought of connecting it with the moon. I had the water analyzed and the results confirmed the verdict of my nostrils. It was sea water, salt and plankton and all.

There the matter rests to this day. No one has a clue as to why on earth this thing happens. Once a month the janitor gets in an hour's overtime with mop and squeegee, the solicitors have quit trying to keep that floor carpeted, and like preceding generations who have lived in that house we have simply given up attempting to figure out the whys and the wherefores. We simply accept it as something that *is*.

What does this tell us about the moon? About the earth? About the Creator who made the entire universe and yet finds it desirable or necessary that a large pool of water should appear on the third floor of a human habitation twelve times a year when the moon turns full? What would happen if something were to prevent this from occurring? What will happen when the building is torn down? How was this situation dealt with before human hands built that house in the eighteenth century? The questions posed by this one very minor, unspectacular paranormal phenomenon cut very deep, which I believe to be one reason the Catholic Church and other organized Western religions deplore and condemn systematic research into paranormal phenomena. No one likes being asked questions they are unable to answer.

Some of my bona fide paranormal cases are mildly amusing. Some are horrific, and some are so bad I keep them in a special black file box. The horrific ones I may write about one day should I hearken to the pleasing sounds of a publisher riffling his checkbook; the ones in my black box will never see the light of day. But some other incidents in my collection are neither amusing nor horrible nor edifying, but merely odd. The story of the wheelbarrow is one of the odd ones.

In January of 1982 I was called to a private boys' school in the south Dublin suburb of Rathfarnham. I'll call this place St. Anthony's, although any Dublin resident will quickly figure out the institution I'm talking about. It is one of the most exclusive and high standard Catholic private schools in the world, and receives students from all over Europe, Canada, and the United States. For this reason their Christmas holiday lasted a week longer than normal, given the distances that many of the students had to travel. The students were away when I called on the headmaster that day. He was Dr. Andrew O'Regan, B.A. (Hons.), M.A., Ph. D., and Lit. D., name an academic distinction and it hung on his wall. O'Regan looked the part of a university don to a T, tall and distinguished, study lined with massive tomes on equally massive shelving of polished oak and mahogany. The classrooms, the dormitories and science lab, and the offices formed an ivy-covered square around a huge quad big as a rugby field. Diamond paned windows, immaculately trimmed verges and graveled walks, all very Eton-ish. Can we take all the Tom Brown clichés as read? It was that kind of place.

After I was seated in Dr. O'Regan's office and handed an excellent cup of tea, he got right to the point. "I'll tell you why I asked to see you, Mr. Carter. I've got an unusual problem. My office, this room where we are now sitting, appears to be haunted. I suppose that would be the word. At any rate, it's driving me around the twist. Is there anything you can do about it?"

"Probably not," I told him frankly. "It's usually impossible actually to *do* anything about any paranormal phenomenon. They are something that occur according to laws of supernature which we understand only very dimly and human ability to affect their course is limited at best and often non-existent. Very occasionally a skilled medium can contact a disembodied human spirit or soul or ghost or whatever you want to call them, and persuade it to depart, but that's the exception rather than the rule. What type of manifestation are we talking about here?"

"Well, I'm afraid this is a bit different than your usual Grey Lady or chain-rattling specter," he replied with a tired smile. "Not even your good oul' Irish banshee, I'm afraid. Mr. Carter, my office is haunted by a material object. A bloody garden tool. A wheelbarrow, to be precise, which is at the present moment hanging in a shed down at the other end of the quad."

"Now that *is* unusual," I agreed. "You'd better start at the beginning."

"For almost ten years now, ever since the school took over these premises, I have sometimes come into work on exceptionally cold mornings, such as this morning in fact, and I have found this bloody great wheelbarrow here in my office. Doors locked, windows locked, no forced entry, nothing stolen or out of place, no sign on earth as to how it got here or who brought it. Just a wheelbarrow in front of the fireplace or leaned up against my desk. No one could possibly have any motive for doing something like this as a practical joke, even if I could see how it was done. Only the head custodian and myself have been here for the entire ten years this has been going on, and when you meet Paddy you'll understand it's really absurd to suspect him of doing such a thing. What possible motive could he have?"

"Who else knows about the phenomenon?" I asked.

"Only Paddy and myself. I didn't even tell our mutual friend who conveyed my invitation that I wanted to meet you."

"Has no one else noticed the wheelbarrow in here during all that time?" I asked.

"Oh, on several occasions the staff and the boys who have been up and about early on winter mornings have seen me trundling that damned thing down the hall to put it back in the shed where it belongs, which has given me something of a reputation for eccentricity, but then that's a headmasterly tradition. Thirty years from now St. Anthony's boys will meet in their clubs and at cocktail parties and ask one another if they remember Old Andy and his wheelbarrow. I called the gardai once, years ago, but they wrote it off as a prank because nothing was stolen. At any rate, I found the festering thing in here again this morning, and that's the straw that broke the camel's back. Even if I can't stop it, Mr. Carter, I want to get some idea of how and why this bizarre business is happening."

"Hmm. Just appears, you say?" I asked. "Any track marks, footprints?"

"No. Sometimes there is snow on the ground outside and still I can't find any tracks of the wheel or footprints from anyone pushing the barrow here from the shed."

"Always the same wheelbarrow?" I asked, making notes on a pad.

"Yes. It's an old wooden one, large and heavy. The gardeners have several others, but this one was here when we bought this place from the Church of Ireland."

"Is the wheelbarrow empty when you find it in the morning?" I inquired, growing more intrigued by the mystery every moment.

"Most times yes, but on rare occasions not. I have checked through my diaries for the past ten years ever since we arrived here." Dr. O'Regan turned and pointed to a series of leather bound volumes on a shelf behind him. "All my appointments, staff meetings, finance committee meetings, so forth and so on, but I've also made a note of every time the wheelbarrow has appeared, which is forty-six times since the autumn of 1971. It always comes on very cold winter mornings, often with snow or sleet. It has been empty on all but three occasions. In 1976 there was a load of turf in it, which I burned in my grate here with no ill effects. It was just turf. In 1980 there was a load of horse dung that had been dumped all over the floor. That was when I lost my temper and called the Guards and made a fool of myself. They called it simple vandalism and I didn't argue. Then this morning the whole barrow was quite full of fresh, new-fallen snow."

"Snow?" I remarked. "It hasn't snowed yet this year." (As an aside, this incident occurred several weeks before the great blizzard of '82.)

"Yes, I know. Don't ask me where the stuff came from. Maybe the sprite that brought the wheelbarrow stopped off at the North Pole for a load of the white stuff before he came. But you can still see the stain on the carpet where the stuff had half melted when I arrived. Come to think of it, where did the turf or the horse manure come from? We have no stables or horses anywhere near and we use oil-fired central heating. I am absolutely convinced that no human agency is responsible for this visitation, Mr. Carter. The whole thing is so petty, so pointless, and so silly. Why on earth would even the most demented practical joker keep it up for ten years? And how on earth would he get a wheelbarrow out of a locked shed past three locked doors and into this room? I've sounded the floorboards and tapped on the walls and I will swear there's no secret entrance of any kind."

"Sounds to me like a very pronounced case of spontaneous bi-location," I said. "Otherwise known as OOPTHS."

"I beg your pardon?"

"O-O-P-T-H-S. Out Of Place Things. Actually it's the most common paranormal phenomenon outside of *deja vu*. Small objects disappear, generally re-appearing elsewhere although sometimes they stay gone for good. You've probably had it happen before to yourself, but you put it down to carelessness or forgetfulness. Pens, pencils, scissors, single sheets of paper or documents, keys, cigarette lighters, small items of clothing, rings or other jewelry, coins. The sort of things a monkey or a mischievous child might take, generally metallic and shiny or brightly colored, generally something we are about to use or need to find. We find it later in the pockets of another suit, or in the bathroom, or on the desk where we *know* perfectly well we looked before. Sometimes it is in a ludicrous place like the butter dish or the letter box. But who are we going to tell? Who will believe us? We'll simply end up making ourselves look and feel ridiculous over something completely trivial. And so we say nothing, and after a while we decide that it *was* just our own care-lessness or a bad memory after all. And of course sometimes that really is the explanation. I'm not saying that gremlins are responsible for every lost pencil or toothbrush. And yet this sort of thing does happen quite often, although like most paranormal phenomena it tends to happen more to some people than to others. This is the first time I've ever heard of a recurring bi-location of something as large as a wheelbarrow, how-ever. Is it out in this shed of yours right now?"

"Yes," said O'Regan. "That's the weird part about it. It is an entirely tangible object. It doesn't turn into a pumpkin at midnight or vanish into a puff of smoke in the light of dawn. No one sees it rolling by itself or dancing in the moonlight, nothing like that. The grounds crew use it regularly and it doesn't groan in spectral protest when they load it with dirt or gravel. Would you like to see it?"

The tool shed was off to one side of the building, next to the wing containing the offices but about two hundred yards down the wall. O'Regan brought his keys, but they weren't needed. "Ah, I see Paddy is working this afternoon," he said, pointing out a man in a fur-lined anorak and wool cap who was loading scrap timber onto a flatbed lorry. "Paddy is our senior custodian, the one I told you about. He's been here for twenty-five years. We more or less inherited him from the C. of I., although he's a Catholic himself. He tells me that the wheelbarrow was here when he came and that it has always rocked up in that office peri-odically, always on cold mornings, ever since he's been here. When he opens up the shed and he finds the wheelbarrow missing he just toddles up, collects it, and wheels it back down to the shed or wherever he wants to use it. I suppose once can get used to something as bizarre as this if it keeps up for a quarter century."

Paddy turned out to be a typical Dublin character, but I won't try to turn this narrative into an Irish joke by reproducing his dialect. Nothing loath, he pointed out the wheelbarrow in question to me and at my request he took it down from its hook on the wall and showed it to me. It was a large barrow, sturdily if roughly made of tough, seasoned wood. The single wheel was rimmed in rusty iron It was hand crafted and of some age, unquestionably nineteenth century vintage, and it was unusual for a simple hand tool like this still to be serviceable after a century. From the size of it one might have assumed it was quite heavy, but it lifted quite easily and turned handily as I pushed it about on the frozen lawn. "See here," I told O'Regan, "Quite frankly I doubt there's anything I can do to interdict this manifestation, fascinating as it is. Why not just break the thing up and burn it?"

"Shame to waste a perfectly good piece of equipment," remarked Paddy reasonably enough. "A replacement would cost forty, fifty pound at least."

"And?" I detected a sardonic humor in the caretaker's voice.

"The fact is, we've tried to get rid of the thing," said O'Regan uncomfortably. "After the horse dung incident. It won't burn. Not at all. It won't break up, either. Paddy and several of his helpers built a bonfire and broke several bow saw blades trying to do what you just suggested. One of them dislocated his shoulder by pounding on the damned thing with an axe."

"That there wood is petry-fied," interjected Paddy.

"He and I took the wheelbarrow up into the Wicklow Mountains in a lorry," continued Dr. O'Regan. "Dumped it out in the middle of the Featherbed. It was here in the shed hanging on its hook when we got back. I took it out on the Isle of Man ferry, weighted it down, and sank it into the sea. Same result. Wasn't even wet when Paddy found it back here."

"You don't mind if I have a go?" I asked. I eschewed the saw but took a number of lusty whacks at the wheelbarrow with a hatchet, striking sparks and getting a sore right arm for my trouble and not inflicting the smallest mark on the thing. I went so far as to wheel the barrow out onto the gravel walk, douse it with paraffin, and set it alight. The paraffin burned, the wheelbarrow didn't. We returned it to its hook in the shed. "See here, Paddy," I asked him, "You've been here a long time. Can you shed any light on this at all? When you first came to work here, what was the status of this wheelbarrow?"

"Ah, the Protestants still owned this place then, but they hadn't used it for years," said Paddy.

"It was a Church of Ireland seminary for over a hundred years, but it was closed down for lack of students," explained Dr. O'Regan. "That was sometime in the 1930s. The C. of I. used it for conferences, storage, and various other functions but they always kept a man here as combination caretaker and watchman."

"That was oul' Mr. Crawford when I came," said Paddy, swigging hot coffee from a thermos flask and wiping his unshaven chin with his sleeve. "He told me about that wheelbarra. He said just leave it alone, it was here before he himself came, it was nothin' to do with Christian people either Protestant or Catholic. When I came in of a cold morning and it wasn't there I'd foind it right up in the big study where the Doctor has his office now. He said just go get it, put it back, and get on with yer work, which is what I've always done."

Back in the office I asked O'Regan, "Did you ever query anyone in the Church of Ireland over this?"

"No," he said. "I'm broad-minded and all that, Mr. Carter, but the fact is that I have a deep aversion to making a fool of myself in front of our separated brethren. It would give them grist for their mill, those petty little needlings over tea in the rectory about Papist superstition among the wild Irish."

"I'll see what I can find out," I promised. "Would you object to my spending the night in your office? I believe the weather report predicts it is heading to below zero degrees Celsius tonight."

"I was going to suggest that myself," said O'Regan. "I would have done it before this, but to be perfectly frank, I was too bloody scared. I know it's utterly absurd to be afraid of a wheelbarrow, of all things, but I still don't want to be alone in this office in the dead of night when whatever brings it here rocks up, and that's the long and the short of it."

"Nothing to be ashamed of," I assured him. "Only a fool fails to treat the unknown with respect. I'd tell you some of my experiences, but that might put you off the idea entirely."

That night we both sat up in the office. Dr. O'Regan had a very comfortable couch where we could both take turns cat-napping, and we loaded up on sandwich material and brought the coffee maker from the faculty lounge into the study to make a sort of buffet on the sideboard. We built up the fire and turned the heat up high. It was frigid with a whistling wind outside. "You're going to feel awfully put out if nothing happens," O'Regan said to me.

"Not at all," I replied cheerily. "I've been on scores of night vigils like this one, in places all across Europe, many of them much more uncomfortable than this. More often than not absolutely nothing happens on the first night, or any other. I won't be disappointed. Paranormal phenomena are not performing dogs that will jump through a hoop on command. But the conditions seem to be right. RTE weather said we were headed for sleet tonight." We talked and listened to a Brahms concerto on RTE radio. O'Regan had a short wave and at midnight we switched to BBC World Service for the news and then to Radio Moscow for some Prokofiev. We were about to try to track down the Voice of America for some comic relief when I heard something and snapped off the radio. "Sshhh!" I hissed. We both heard it now.

There was a low rumbling sound approaching us down the tiled corridor outside. It was unmistakably the sound of a wheelbarrow. It came on, very slowly, and is it got closer I could hear the sound of muffled, shuffling footfalls. "Someone or something is pushing it," I told Dr. O'Regan. All the electric lights were on and the fire was bright and cheery, and yet O'Regan's teeth were chattering.

"For God's sake, open the door and let's see it!" he whispered.

"No need," I said. "It's coming right here, remember?" The low rumbling hiss of the iron-shod wheel and the dragging, muffled footfalls stopped just outside the double doors to the office. I leaped to the doors and threw them open, and simultaneously every electric light in the room went out, in the best Hollywood tradition. O'Regan gave a mixed yell of fear and excitement. I rushed into the darkened corridor and was enveloped in a cold so icy and sharp and penetrating that I could not breathe, psychic cold, not the natural cold of the winter night outside. Then it was gone and O'Regan blundered into me in the dim firelight, and he damned near brained me with a heavy candlestick before I could calm him down.

The lights suddenly were on again, and looking through the door we saw the wheelbarrow, quite empty, sitting squarely on top of O'Regan's mahogany desk.

*   *   *

About a week later I spent a day in Wicklow with a retired Church of Ireland minister who is probably the greatest living authority on the history of that church now resident in the island. "Mmmm…" he said over tea. "Yes, I do recall that there were some rather unsavory stories connected with those grounds at one time, something about a wheelbarrow…seems to me I read it somewhere…let's have a look, shall we?" After an hour of digging around in his priceless library of rare and obscure books on his church, he found what I was looking for. It was in *Memoirs From An Irish Manse,* by (wait for it!) The Right Reverend

Junius Harbottle Thrope, D. D., "…privately printed at Dublin through the subscriptions of a few kind friends" in 1895.

Victorian clergymen had a horrible habit of inflicting upon the world the most abominable drivel in the guise of literature, and for the most part their memoirs are particularly leprous. Suffice it to say that out of respect for Dr. Thrope's one ray of illumination on my problem, I borrowed the book and forced myself to read the whole thing, which was considerably above and beyond the call, believe me. It was absolutely dreadful; a railroad timetable from 1895 would have been less boring. But the excerpt on the wheelbarrow was interesting indeed.

"I received my ordination into holy orders after having taken my degree from the small but stimulating and spiritually intense seminary of our blessed faith, St. Anthony's at Rathfarnham, set in the lovely foothills of Dublin-shire." (I will here omit about twenty pages of twaddle. "Dublin-shire" will give you some idea of what you are missing.) "In the years before my arrival at dear old St. Anthony's, the student of modern history may recall that the dreaded Second Horseman of the Apocalypse, *Famine*, had stricken the tragic Emerald Isle and caused great havoc and wretchedness among the peasant classes, almost all of whom stubbornly adhered to the Romish faith despite the effort of our own Church and the better class of people in Ireland to wean them away from their ancestral creed. Nonetheless, in the time of crisis the Protestant faith did not show itself by any means lacking in Christian charity towards our suffering Catholic countrymen, and our Church may pride itself that it stinted no reasonable expenditure to relieve the intense destitution which prevailed among the lower orders.

"The seminarians at dear old St. Anthony's had by private subscription raised among themselves and various alumni a fund, whereby a number of men were employed upon the grounds doing renovation, stonemasonry, carpentry, landscape work, and so on, each destitute person thus relieved being emolulated at the generous stipend of sevenpence per day. Most of these unhappy paupers were well content at the bounty thus provided, but as in any group of Irish peasants there were the ill-disposed, the grumblers, and the disaffected who complained that the wages offered were too low to buy bread for their families starving in the countryside around, that they had no warm clothing or fire in the winter by which they might warm themselves, that their hours from dawn to dusk were too long even though the winter days were short, and all of the usual niggling complaints through which the Irishman all too often seeks to avoid honest labour.

"One such was a man named Davy M'Keever or M'Geever, who was described to me once by an older acquaintance who saw him as being tall and gaunt of figure, his body stooped and weakened by hunger and privation. Yet despite his condition he gave much trouble to the good rector of the time, Dr. Henry Lysander Carruthers (1801-1877). Finally, in an uncharacteristic fit of irritation, the reverend gentleman told M'Keever he should find a task to his liking or else lose his position. The labour Dr. Carruthers assigned him was that he should cart a wheelbarrow full of the heaviest stones which might be found, around and around the seminary grounds from sunup to sundown with only the normal interlude of one half hour to break his fast at noonday which all the others received. Rebellious as he was, M'Keever had a wife and a number of children living in a ditch near Tallaght, and for their sakes he dared not refuse the reverend's uncharitable order.

"One day in mid-winter, very cold and with snow upon the ground, as the sun was near setting M'Keever passed beneath the rector's window with his wheelbarrow full of stones, and he called up to the good minister that his wages were due that evening to the sum of three shillings and eightpence, and that he (the rector) should have them ready for him sharp on time. Angered at this interruption while he was reading, Dr. Carruthers shouted down from the window that since M'Keever had so much vigor remaining that he could offer insolent badinage to his betters, he might continue to push the wheelbarrow around the grounds until he was told to stop, and only then might he collect his wages. Doctor Carruthers then resumed his interrupted reading before the fire, and after a while arose and went to the refectory for his supper. He admitted later that he completely forgot about the wretched man who still trundled the heavy wheelbarrow full of stones in endless circles around the buildings. Dr. Carruthers returned to his study after dinner and fell asleep by the fire, while outside a terrible storm of sleet blew up and the night grew frigid. He was awakened at about midnight by the sound of a wheelbarrow approaching his study down the corridor, and then he heard a knock on the door and the voice of M'Keever saying quite plainly, 'Minister, I have come for my wages.' Suddenly recalling his victim, the conscience-stricken Dr. Carruthers immediately arose and opened the door, fully intending to apologize and give the man a hot toddy after giving him his wages in full. But to his amazement, the corridor outside the door was empty. A search of the grounds located the wretched peasant, dead of hunger and exhaustion, his hands still frozen to the cruel wheelbarrow full of stones.

"Every school in Britain ought by right to boast its own resident ghost, and at dear old St. Anthony's this spectral requirement was filled by Davy M'Keever and his wheelbarrow. The good Doctor Carruthers is said to have changed his accommodation after inexplicably finding a wooden wheelbarrow in his study on several chilly mornings. There are even those who claim to have seen old Davy's ghost on cold winter nights, glowing with St. Elmo's fire while trundling his wheelbarrow across the moonlit grounds waiting for permission to stop from a rector long dead."

I photocopied the relevant pages from Dr. Thrope's *magnum opus* and showed them to Dr. O'Regan, who turned white and signed himself with the Stations. "My God, do you think that's it?" he whispered in horror. "Davy M'Keever coming for his wages? Is such a thing possible, Carter?"

"It's a bit more melodramatic than most paranormal phenomena, but yes, it's possible," I told him. "Sometimes human emotions are so strong that they imbue or imprint themselves on the very matter of their surroundings, the woodwork and stone of a house, or quite probably in this case a wheelbarrow. Unfortunately it's usually the negative emotions that reach this level of intensity. Hate, fear, anger, misery, revenge, lust, madness. Davy M'Keever must have hated long and hard as he pushed that damnable wheelbarrow full of stones in the freezing cold. Hard enough so that even death hasn't stopped him from attempting to attain his final goal in life, after a hundred and thirty odd years. I wish we could find some way to destroy or remove that wheelbarrow."

"I've got a better idea," said O'Regan quietly. "I think it's time Davy M'Keever was paid what he is owed."

O'Regan went to a Dublin coin shop and purchased the sum of three shillings and eightpence in early Victorian coinage, carefully selecting pre-1845 specimens. "It cost me about a hundred pounds," he told me. "An average week's wage for pushing a wheelbarrow nowadays." On the night of the great blizzard of 1982, he left the coins prominently out on his desk in his locked office. Two days later when he fought his way through the snowy streets and returned, the coins were gone and the wheelbarrow hung on its peg in the shed, only now it was heavy and pocked and dry. It splintered easily beneath Paddy's hatchet and burned hot and fast in the fireplace of the room it had haunted so long. The iron wheel rim hangs on Dr. O'Regan's wall to this day as a reminder that ancient wrongs sometimes do not die with the men who committed them. As the last of the wheelbarrow turned to ash Paddy and O'Regan and I drank a solemn toast, and the headmaster added a short prayer for the soul of David M'Keever, that he might now find rest with his wages paid in full.

I do not pretend to know where Davy M'Keever is now. Presumably someplace where some of us, at least, may chance to meet him someday, and I hope I have that privilege. I'm very curious to know how he spent that three shillings and eightpence.

Whisper Her Name On The Wind

*T*he residents of Beit Efrat would set a visitor straight very quickly: theirs was not a *shtetl*, nor even a village, but a proper small town of a thousand devout Jewish souls. Beit Efrat did not wallow in some God-forsaken bog in Galicia or huddle out on some windy Ukrainian steppe, but stood strong and solid in a pretty wooded valley in a bend of the River Vistula in eastern Poland. There were five synagogues, each with a yeshiva and a House of Study attached, as well as a *mikvah* ritual bath for the women. The institutions were all of the Vilna school and imported the most erudite and eloquent Litvaker rabbis for their congregations. There was a bookseller, Nathan Halter. There were a dozen kosher butchers and a dozen dairies and cheesemakers, and a small but vibrant weaving and leatherworking industry that brought buyers from as far away as Cracow and Danzig. The High Street, two parallel streets and two cross streets were paved with cobblestones, and there were street lamps that were lit every night and extinguished every morning by Herzl the lamplighter and his sons. There were shops and a market square and a guildhall where the rabbis and prosperous heads of household gathered to do business. It was the only guildhall in Poland bearing the Star of David rather than a cross over its doors. Preserved in a fine silver casket in that town hall was a charter from Catherine the Great, graciously granting the Jews of Beit Efrat permission to live outside the Pale of Settlement, and even more treasured, permission for their town to bear a Hebrew name. No *shtetl* at all was Beit Efrat!

Next to the town's biggest synagogue, fronting right onto the market square, lived the holy rabbi Shlomo Shmulevitz, his wife Hannah, and his four daughters. The rabbi was a man of impressive girth and resonant voice when he read aloud from the Torah on the sabbath, and he was reputed to have the most magnificent white beard of any holy man in Poland. His oldest daughter was actually a distant niece whom the rabbi had adopted out of duty and charity on the death of her parents in a scarlet fever epidemic many years before. Her name was Hadass. She was a tall and languid girl of deep dark eyes and gentle voice. She was also something of a scandal in the town because she remained unmarried at the ripe old age of twenty-five. There were problems with her dowry, since if the truth be told the holy rabbi Shlomo Shmulevitz was somewhat inclined to the sin of parsimony, and had reserved most of his wealth to dower his three younger daughters by blood. These three were beautiful and vivacious, and would make good matches if only a husband could be found for Hadass, or else if Rabbi Shmulevitz could be persuaded to depart from the ancient custom that daughters must marry in precedence of age.

There was also a problem in that Hadass had some very un-womanly attributes. She was not only highly intelligent, but she was tactless enough to show it. Instead of sewing and baking and washing she was known to while away her time reading books as if she were a man in the

House of Study. Not just holy *seforim* either, but works of pagan *goyim* like Herodotus, Abelard, Machiavelli, and Horace Walpole. She spent her allowance from her father not on scarves and belts and gloves or earrings, but in Nathan Halter's bookshop. She repeatedly turned down a series of men whom her father and the local matchmaker put forward as candidates for her hand, including a *shochet* or kosher slaughterman and a wealthy glazier who employed five glassblowers and fitters in his shop and whose only fault was to be thirty years older than she. The attitude of the younger Shmulevitz girls towards their older sister became somewhat strained as the years went by and Hadass remained unattached in her adopted father's house, while the holy rabbi bore his tribulation bravely and earned the respect of his congregants as a patient and saintly man.

But in the spring of 1813, there were other topics of interest for the Beit Efrat folk to wag their tongues about. The year before, the historic year of 1812, the armies of Napoleon had surged eastwards across Europe and into Russia. The merchants and weavers, the cobblers and butchers and dairymen of Beit Efrat had grown affluent off the sale of cloth and leather and cordage and meat and cheese and bread and wine to the long blue columns of marching men. After Bonaparte's Pyrrhic victory at Borodino and the subsequent fall and then the evacuation of Moscow, all through the terrible winter the blue-coated grenadiers and *tirailleurs* and *Chausseurs* on their spavined horses had straggled and stumbled back through the snow and down the muddy roads, staggering back bleeding and starving and exhausted towards the dream of *La Belle France* in the west. The businessmen of Beit Efrat had grown wealthier still, as desperate Frenchmen gave over their last coins, their watches, their rings, the silver lockets of their wives and mothers and lovers, anything for a bowl of hot soup or a place to rest by a fire for a single night before resuming their long nightmare retreat. But just as in the time of Israel's Egyptian captivity there had been seven fat years, the people of Beit Efrat knew that they now faced a lean and dangerous time. They had never feared the French. Even in defeat, Bonaparte ruled his troops with an iron hand, and God help the French soldier who ever took so much as a needle and thread or a single sausage without paying for it. But the French were gone, and now would come their victors and pursuers, terrible and ancient enemies of Israel...the Russians. The Russians were a different kettle of fish altogether. The citizens of the town of Beit Efrat stashed their valuables in wells and under garden stones, swept out cellars and set up cots wherein to hide their daughters, and waited.

The spring came and there was some news of local interest to enliven the tense waiting. Would wonders never cease, that high-nosed maiden Hadass Luria had finally accepted a suitor! At Passover she had agreed that she and the wool factor Yossele Lipshits would marry on the holiday of Tisha B'av in June. Rumor had it that the holy rabbi Shlomo Shmulevitz had finally come to accept that getting Hadass off his hands was going to cost him, and at the importunings of his wife and younger daughters he had loosened his purse strings considerably in the matter of a dowry for his oldest girl. Yossele Lipshits was squat and ugly, with a face like a monkey, and his reputation in the town was not of the best. His business practices were reputed to be sharp, not only with the *goyim* but also with his fellow Jews, nor was he known for charity despite his relative wealth. Yossele spent rather too much time drinking schnapps and playing cards in Shmuel Butman's tavern on the market square, and he was reputed to engage in even worse dissipations with the *shiksa* prostitutes of Cracow on his frequent business trips. But what, at twenty-five she should expect Prince Charming, already? decreed the community consensus. A collective sigh of relief went up from the more eligible young men of Beit Efrat, for now they would be free to court the younger and much more personable daughters of the holy rabbi themselves. The lovely Shulamit was the next up in age, and after her came the fetching Simcha and the blossoming fifteen year-old Naomi, prizes indeed!

The odd thing was that Hadass herself seemed quite happy with the match. To everyone's surprise the gnome-like Yossele exhibited a sudden flowering of almost debonair charm. He did not lack a certain sprightly if somewhat infantile sense of humor, and for the first time in her drab and dreary life Hadass found herself courted, cozened, and paid attention to by a man of her own age who showed her interest and affection. The old yentas gossiping by the well and on the wooden stoops shrugged. "She'll see through him soon enough, the *shlumpf*," they assured one another. "But she'll be married by then. Isn't that always the way of it?"

As the eldest child, adopted or not, Hadass was able to command a small garret room of her own below the eaves of the rabbi's house, while her three sisters shared a large room on the first floor among themselves. This arrangement emphasized her position in the household as fostered, not quite part of the family. It also enabled the younger girls to engage in their favorite pastime after lights out, which was gossiping and spitefully criticizing and maligning Hadass in whispers and giggles beneath the bedclothes, sometimes loudly enough for Hadass to hear when the weather was warm and the windows open. The wedding plans for Tisha B'av were well afoot when Hadass awoke one night late in April to the sound of clattering hooves, creaking cart wheels and low voices on the square beneath her window. She rose quietly in her shift and peered out the small diamond-paned window. Beneath the flickering oil lamps of which the town was so proud she saw two mule-drawn carts drawn up against the wall of the house, and a number of men were lugging heavy wooden boxes or crates off the cart, two men per crate. Rabbi Shmulevitz himself was at the door with a lanthorn in his hand, urging the men to greater speed in frantic whispers. Hadass recognized one of the men who sweated as he unloaded the carts as her betrothed, Yossele Lipshits. Hadass shrugged and went back to bed. Jews did what they had to do in order to survive in a hostile world, and sometimes that included a spot of smuggling, or anything moving in the shade to generate a bit of income that could be concealed from the rapacious tax collectors of the Czar.

Hadass would not even have mentioned the incident to her intended had Yossele not done so first. Although generally it was considered licentious for betrothed couples to be too familiar or spend much time in one another's company prior to the nuptials, the next day Yossele met Hadass on the street as she was on her way home from bringing a cake from the rebbetzin's kitchen to a sick woman neighbor, and he pulled her aside excitedly. He was overwhelmed and bursting to tell someone his secret. "Hadass, I can't reveal much to you, but there are great tidings! Real wealth has come to Beit Efrat at last! We will be able to expand every synagogue and yeshiva in town, buy hundreds more *seforim* until we have libraries to rival Vilna and Cracow, endow any number of poor students so they need not toil for a living and can spend their time studying Torah! And because I am part of this secret windfall, all our own problems are over as well! After you and I are married I will be able to expand my business and undercut every wool and leather producer in the province on my prices, and eventually corner the market! With this capital we will create the greatest center of Torah and the greatest nexus of business and finance in Europe right here in our town! I will become a great man in Israel, and you shall be a great man's wife! We'll have servants and a coach and I will dress you in silk!" he boasted.

"What are you talking about, Yossele?" asked Hadass curiously, catching some of his excitement. "I saw you and father and those other men unloading those carts last night. What are you smuggling? Isn't it dangerous? What if you get caught?"

"You saw us?" asked Lipshits, alarmed. "Hadass, you must say nothing! You must never say anything to anyone about what you saw!"

"Yossele, what are you talking about?" she asked again. "What on earth are you involved in?"

"It could get us all hanged or sent to Siberia!" hissed Yossele.

"And what is worth making me a widow when I am not yet even wed?" she demanded with some spirit. Yossele looked around furtively and took something out of his pocket, which he pressed into the young woman's hand. It was cool and hard and round. She looked down and her eyes widened as she saw in her palm the reverse side of a gleaming heavy coin of yellow gold, bearing a fasces and the words "*Liberté, egalité, fraternité.*" She turned the coin over and on the obverse side she saw the profiled head of the Emperor Napoleon. "We have thousands of these in those boxes in your father's cellar!" whispered Lipshits in an ecstasy of excitement. "Thousands, I tell you!"

"In heaven's name, where did you get such a vast treasure?" asked Hadass, gasping in shock. "And how can we hope to spend French gold without anyone asking where it came from?"

"I can't tell you where we got it, but it won't be French gold for long," said Yossele. "I have written to my cousin in Vienna who has contacts with the Rothschilds. You know our merchants picked up quite a bit of French specie when the army was coming through, selling them supplies and services, and the Vienna Rothschilds handled the exchange at a good discount, giving us rubles or Prussian marks that don't attract so much attention. I know they will be willing to take on a transaction of this size, and there's a dozen different ways they can conceal it all using bank drafts and letters of credit that will be as good as coin in Cracow or St. Petersburg or Danzig. It will take a few weeks, but once that's done then a whole new way of life will be ours!"

But the people of Beit Efrat did not have a few weeks. The next day the Russians entered the town.

*   *   *

The word flashed through the streets before the echoes of the enemy's iron-shod hooves on the cobblestones reached the square. Gabbling in terror, Hannah the rabbi's wife snatched up Shulamit and

Simcha and Naomi by their collars and shoved them down into the cellar. "Where's Hadass? *Where's Hadass?*" cried the rebbetzin distractedly.

"Mother, leave Hadass! What if the soldiers take *you?*" called one of the terrified girls from the darkness below. Suddenly remembering that she was female herself, Hannah shrieked in terror and fled into the cellar, slamming the door behind her.

Hadass was in fact browsing in Nathan Halter's bookshop and was so engrossed in the book she was reading that she didn't even hear the horses in the street until the old bookseller grabbed her arm and she saw his stricken face. She looked out the front window of the shop, and it was filled with rippling horseflesh and saddle leather and men's legs and waists, clattering sabers and pistols in belts and musket butts leaning on hips. "Hadass, hide under the counter!" pleaded Halter.

"I'd feel very foolish hiding until I at least know there is a threat, Reb Nathan," the young woman chided him gently. "We are after all subjects of the Czar, and those are the Czar's soldiers. They're supposed to be on our side."

"No, you don't understand!" pleaded the old man, his face a mask of horror. "Those aren't Russian soldiers, at least not regular ones!"

"Then they are...?" prodded Hadass.

"*Cossacks!*" whispered Halter, quaking. "May God have mercy on us all, *those are Cossacks!*" Hadass turned pale. She was a gentle and loving soul who always tried to see the good in all people, but even she had sense enough to be afraid of Cossacks. She gripped herself.

"I won't run away or hide," she said. "I will go to the square and see what is happening."

"Are you mad, girl?" demanded Halter.

"How can I come to harm?" she asked with a wan smile. "I will have you to protect me." Humbled and proud, the old man bowed and gallantly offered her his arm.

The holy rabbi Shlomo Shmulevitz stood on the steps of the town hall, wearing his finest suit of clothes and his kipa, his prayer shawl and his phylacteries, while his fellow rabbis and the town's most prominent men gathered around him in a knot. Cold fear twisted in all their guts as the mounted column filled the square. The riders were a motley crew, most wearing double-breasted tunics of goat's wool, but some in leather vests, and others wearing shirts of bearskin or wolf pelts. Most wore cylindrical hats of fur or wool or felt, but some wore ancient pointed helmets with nasal guards and some had leather hoods. A few were fully bearded, but most wore long curved moustaches above jutting, stubbled chins. Their cross-hilted, wickedly curved sabers of Damascus steel hung not on their belts as a European gentleman would carry his sword, but rode in their scabbards high and to the left of their saddle pommels. Some of the men rode with long steel-headed lances resting against their stirrups, with horsetail pennons. Short carbines were slung on their backs, and their torsos and belts were garlanded with brace after brace of flintlock pistols. At least every third man carried a rolled and looped whip of braided leather, twelve feet in length. Over them all floated two standards, the double-eagled Imperial Ensign of the Czar of All the Russias and a blue banner of the Archangel Michael, whom the Cossacks venerated on a par with Christ and His Virgin Mother. "What are they?" demanded Shmulevitz in panic. "What Horde? Does any one recognize them? Donets? Zaporozhia?"

"Kuban, I think," muttered Rabbi Yaacov Feldman. "The ones with the helmets are Circassians. I have heard they are cannibals."

"Watch those whips!" whispered the jeweler Ariel Goldstein in fear. "They can pop a man's eyeball right out of his head and leave the rest of his face untouched, or tap him on the brow light as a feather so he drops stone dead. And if they aim lower..." All the men shuddered.

At the head of the cavalry brigade rode three figures. The first was a heavy-set man in a resplendent and finely embroidered scarlet Cossack jacket and black fez, with a huge curving red moustache and blue eyes that seemed to burn in a perpetual rage. The second was a tall and elegant, blond moustachioed man in European dress, wearing a bicorne hat with a cockade and a whitish uniform that looked almost like a frock coat, and sporting a rapier by his side. But the third figure struck the most terror into the townsmen, for he was known to them by description and reputation. He was tall and well built; his face pale and handsome but marred on his left cheek by two saber scars, souvenirs of his dueling days as a student at Heidelberg. His hair and his neatly trimmed beard were black, his eyes green and as cold as the Arctic seas. He wore a short burred shako on his head, as well as the gold-braided green jacket, demi-cape and white trousers of the Preobrazhensky Regiment of the Russian Imperial Guards. "*Barmine!*" whispered Goldstein. "It's Prince Barmine, the man who once ordered a thousand French prisoners put to death in a single afternoon."

"And this town holds a thousand Jewish souls," replied Shmulevitz. "*Am Yisrael chai.* Israel must live. My friends, we must find some way out of this."

The three leaders dismounted. The red-moustached Cossack commander looked at them like he wanted to vomit. "Jews," he said in a flat disgusted voice. "We should kill them all, Prince my brother."

Rabbi Shmulevitz bowed low, trying not to shake. "Welcome to Beit Efrat, Your Excellencies!" he boomed in a mellifluous voice. "Our town's poor amenities are at your command. Please, step into our council chambers and we shall..."

"Is that a tavern?" asked the man in the green uniform. "I should far prefer to step in there." Without waiting for any further comment he walked down the street a few steps and into Shmuel Butman's public house, the man in the bicorne and the Cossack officer stalking after him. Their high riding boots made the plank floor shake. The town dignitaries followed after them in confusion. So did a couple who had quietly sidled up the street and into the square, Nathan Halter and Hadass Luria. The young woman had not entered a tavern more than twice in her life, but she practically dragged the old bookseller inside in the wake of the town leaders, and her father was too distracted and busy concentrating on the town's unwelcome visitors to notice his oldest daughter tagging along behind them with her ancient escort. The Cossack with the red moustache went behind the bar, shoving aside the stunned innkeeper Butman, where he rooted around and pulled out several bottles which he tossed to the other two. Then he picked up a small keg of ale, bashed in the head with his fist and began drinking from it, holding it with both hands.

The man in green uncorked his bottle, sniffed it, and took a long pull. "A passable Rhenish," he said conversationally to Butman. He dumped a small handful of silver onto the bar. "You are Rabbi Shmulevitz, I take it?" he asked. Shmulevitz bowed again. "I am General Prince Barmine, Ilya Aleksandrovitch. My colleague here is Colonel Fyodor Petrovitch Koltsov, of the Imperial Gendarmerie. Third Section." A shudder went through the assembly at the mention of the Czar's dreaded secret police, originally established by Potemkin under Catherine's reign. "Colonel Koltsov is here to keep me honest. This third comrade in arms of ours, who is inhaling this establishment's ale behind the bar there, is the Hetman Basaraba. He is here to keep Koltsov honest."

"And who keeps him honest?" quipped Yossele irresistably. The barbarian lowered the ale keg and looked at him, a tiger ready to spring and crush and rip flesh from bone. Yossele suddenly understood what he should have understood from the beginning, and he froze in hideous fear. Barmine raised his hand and glanced over at Basaraba sharply, shaking his head, then looked at Yossele.

"Don't do that again, any of you," warned the general quietly. "I will not save you a second time." He took another drink out of the wine bottle. "Do you know why I have come here?" he asked Shmulevitz. "I am looking for someone."

"Please, tell us who, Your Excellency," begged Rabbi Shmulevitz, his bowels turning to water.

"I am looking for this man." Barmine held up a gold coin, the duplicate of the one Yossele had shown to Hadass. "I have reason to believe I will find him here."

"But Your Excellency, everyone knows that Bonaparte is back in Paris by now!" protested Shmulevitz.

"Yet I think I will find him here," said Barmine. "I think I will find him twenty thousand times, because I am firmly of the opinion that somewhere concealed around this town are a number of boxes containing twenty thousand *Napoleons d'Or*. Attend, my Mosaic friends," he continued, seating himself on a table and swigging his wine. "When Bonaparte invaded the Motherland last year, you may have heard how Russia responded. We scorched the earth. We burned our own fields and our own homes and slaughtered our own livestock, burned our forests, poisoned our own wells and wrecked every wagon, smashed every stick of furniture, chopped down and burned every orchard, laid poison for the very deer in the woodlands and the birds of the air lest the French kill them and eat them. My childhood home I torched with my own hands lest a single Frenchman defile the floors where I crawled as a baby, or sit on a chair once occupied by the sanctified presence of my father or my mother.

"Napoleon didn't expect that. He expected to live off the land and buy his foodstuffs and his supplies from people who did not care that he came as an invader and a destroyer of our religion and our culture. He brought with him an immense amount of money to pay for the supplies he expected to buy from traitors, gold cast in his own image. This gold." Barmine flipped the coin in the air. "During the retreat from Moscow, our Cossacks captured one of the enemy's straggling supply trains. The French troops were tired and demoralized and weak from hunger, many of them wounded, but they still fought like lions to defend those wagons, and before they were wiped out they killed a number of Cossacks, brothers to the men outside," he informed them, jerking his head at the door. "The gold we found in that wagon train will go far towards rebuilding a shattered Russia, after it is melted down and re-coined as good Russian rubles. It would have gone even farther, had someone not decided to help themselves to a hefty chunk of it. When the wagons arrived in St. Petersburg, we found many cases were full of stones instead of golden Napoleons. My esteemed colleague Colonel Koltsov here was called in for consultation. Fyodor Petrovitch has a nose for human duplicity and chicanery, and he eventually figured out how that exchange was accomplished right under the noses of five hundred soldiers, by two clerks in our army commissary department. One Avigdor Fischer and one Chaim Lipshits. I will not comment on exactly how it was done, except to say that it formidably augments the well-deserved reputation that the Jewish people bear for high intelligence and brilliant planning, combined with a complete lack of anything remotely resembling moral scruple where the rights or the property of non-Jews are concerned. I believe you all knew the late Monsieurs Fischer and Lipshits, since they hale from here and their families still reside in this town?"

"The...the late...?" stammered Shmulevitz.

"They weren't quite as clever as they thought they were, and they underestimated their opponents' determination to avenge robbery and insult," said Barmine gently. "Again, rabbi, a situation not unknown in the long and fascinating history of your people. Colonel Koltsov deduced what they did and how they had done it far more quickly than they thought he would, and then they got careless. They stopped at an inn outside Minsk for a night in a soft feather bed in pleasant company. They should have kept on riding. We questioned them, quite sternly. I think everyone here knows quite well what we were told. There is a large oak tree at a crossroads outside Minsk. I suspect that the ravens and the vultures have gotten them both stripped down to their ribs by now."

There was a shudder and a moan through the gathered townsfolk. "May God have mercy on their souls..." muttered Shmulevitz.

Rabbi Feldman spoke up. "Your Excellency, you cannot mean that you suspect us of having anything to do with this tragic and ill-advised crime? We are loyal subjects of His Imperial Majesty, and we would never..."

Barmine held up his hand. "Don't," he advised calmly. "Whatever you do, rabbi, do not insult my intelligence. That would make me angry. You don't want me to become angry, rabbi. Believe me, you don't. Because if I get angry, Basaraba gets angry, and if Basaraba gets angry..." He nodded his head towards the square full of lowering Cossacks and stamping, blowing horses. "Listen to me now. Within the next twenty-four hours, one of two things is going to happen in the town of Beit Efrat. The first thing that might happen is that you will take counsel among yourselves, and tomorrow morning when I step out onto that square, I will find boxes containing the sum of twenty thousand gold Napoleons. Alongside those boxes will stand the men who were involved in this. Whether they will necessarily be all of the men who are involved in this I do not care, nor will I care if a few of the men I find standing behind those boxes are not involved and willing substitutes for the guilty. Yes, I know some of your people possess that kind of courage and nobility of character, when needs must. You have proven it often enough down through the centuries, and I respect that. If tomorrow I should find nothing but elderly men who are at the end of their lives in any case, then I will understand and will overlook that incongruent circumstance. But there should be enough to lade a gallows amply, at least eight or ten...no, ten, definitely ten men. A *minyan*. We will count the gold, and if all twenty thousand Napoleons are there, then I promise you that there will be no exuberance with whips or red-heated gun barrels, no beards ripped out in handfuls by the roots, no such flamboyant embellishments. I shall swing the ten of them gentle and artistic from a single tree. I saw one coming into town that will do nicely. We shall depart to return to the Czar his property, and the matter will henceforth be considered closed. I will trust in the well-renowned perspicacity of your people, rabbi, to ensure that none of you ever again allow the thought of stealing from the Emperor to cross your minds for a single, fleeting moment. That is the first possibility for tomorrow."

Barmine smiled beatifically and went on as his listeners sank to their knees, trembling. "The second possibility is that you will try something else besides producing those twenty thousand gold coins and those ten men for punishment. Anything else. It might be a trick of some kind, a lie, a denial, a plea for mercy, some attempt to stall and buy time. If we are exceptionally fortunate, you might even try to fight us. We would enjoy that immensely. But to continue. If I step out upon that square tomorrow morning and see anything other than what I wish to see, then my company and I will go in search of the gold ourselves. We will search every house, every barn, every shop, every stable, every shed, every privy. We will indeed dig up the privies in search of that gold, or shall I say that all your rabbinical pastors and your yeshiva students shall dig them up. With their bare hands. My lads will need light while they search in the dark corners, and so they will be carrying lamps and lanthorns, possibly even torches. Open flames of any kind always invite accidents. Any gold or silver we find may well be part of this stolen hoard, and so we would have to confiscate it until its legal ownership is determined, and possession is nine tenths of the law. Some of you may have pretty wives or daughters or sisters, and since my troops are rough-hewn boys from the steppes and the forests they may become somewhat overly enthusiastic in expressing their admiration for such dainty damsels. There is a language problem as well. If you try to address them in Yiddish some of my good fellows may think you are mocking them. Cossacks intensely dislike being mocked, and they have a number of ways of ensuring that no one repeats the offense. Do you begin to see how fraught with peril it would be for you to do anything other than turn over to me the twenty thousand, and the ten?"

Shlomo Shmulevitz was slumping to the floor on his knees by now, palsied with fear. He looked up. "How do we know you won't just slaughter us all no matter what we do?" he moaned.

"You don't," said Barmine. "But know this. Among the Cossacks a man always, let me repeat that, *always* keeps his word, for good or for ill. Even when given to a Jew. If I were to break my word and start a pogrom after you obeyed my command and handed over to me the gold and the culprits, those men out there would participate most gleefully, no doubt of it. But they would also remember that Prince Barmine broke his word, and that is by no means a reputation I wish to bear among them. That would not be in my long-term interest at all." He turned to the Cossack chief. "Basaraba, my brother, bring the baggage train in and set up the tents at both ends of the High Street and at the northern and southern boundaries of the town. For today, the men are not to come into the town. Only officers with necessary business. They are not to molest or harm anyone in Beit Efrat. There is one exception to this order. If anyone, man or woman, tries to escape from this place then catch them, take them to the campfires, strip them and peel their skin from their body. Slowly. Inch by inch, so that everyone in town can hear their screams as they die." Basaraba grinned, showing two missing front teeth. "As for myself, I think Colonel Koltsov and I will take advantage of such civilized amenities as Beit Efrat has to offer. Who is the town's richest man?" he asked conversationally.

"Why...why I suppose I am," spoke up Gershon Avitan the banker.

"Where is your house?" asked Barmine.

"Across the square there, Excellency, with the portico and the red stucco roof," said Avitan.

"It will do. I presume you will not object to a couple of guests for the night?" said Barmine. "If you find our presence to be objectionable, perhaps you and your family might stay with friends this evening. In fact, I insist that you do so."

"Certainly, Your Excellency," said Avitan with defeated resignation.

"I think Colonel Koltsov and I and our orderlies can rough it for a night in your abode, sir," said the general. "By the by, Basaraba my brother, perhaps you might explain to these gentlemen what will happen tomorrow if any harm should befall Colonel Koltsov or myself tonight?"

"We will kill all the Jews. Burn the town. Tear down every brick and stone and smash them to powder. Sow the ground with salt," said Basaraba with another gap-toothed grin.

"I suddenly feel as safe as if I were in my mother's arms," said Barmine gaily. "Now get out, all of you. I am going to have a few drinks with my friends." The group of Beit Efrat dignitaries stumbled to the door in a shocked daze, Nathan Halter the bookseller with them. Hadass began to sidle for the door herself, trembling with horror and consternation at what she had heard. Suddenly Barmine glanced over and saw her, and their eyes met for a long moment. He raised his hand. "You. Girl. Come here."

Hadass lowered her eyes, stepped forward, and curtseyed, but she was so stunned she forgot she had a book in her hand from Halter's shop, and it dropped to the floor. She froze. "What are you reading, girl?" asked Barmine. He held out his hand peremptorily. She picked up the book, handed it to him, and again curtseyed low, her eyes downcast. "*Fundamental Legal Reform In The Russian Judiciary 1798 to 1805*, by Mikhail Mikhailovitch Speransky, Doctor of Law, Jurisconsult, published at St. Petersburg in 1810?" asked Barmine, caught off guard. "You're not studying to be a lawyer, are you girl?" he said with a chuckle.

"No, Excellency," replied Hadass quietly but firmly. "I was reading that book in Reb Nathan Halter's bookshop, and then I saw your troops riding in and I came here to see what was happening. I absent-mindedly brought it with me. But with the greatest of respect, Excellency, I am not a girl. I am twenty-five years of age." There was a barely suppressed gasp among the Jewish men present. Was she mad to bait this powerful and dangerous nobleman?

"I know Speransky. He is a high-minded man but rather naïve in the realities of life," replied Barmine. He tossed the book onto the table. "But a woman who reads law books interests me. Your name?"

"Hadass Luria, Excellency."

"Your patronymic? Ah, sorry, I forgot, you Jews don't use them, do you?" said Barmine.

"No, Excellency. I am the daughter of the physician Isaac Luria, who is now dead. I am proud and honored to say that my adopted father is the most holy and learned rebbe, Shlomo Shmulevitz, who stands before you." Her soft yet firm voice impressed the general.

"I hope your father appreciates your obvious accomplishments. You intrigue me. I am curious as to just how accomplished you are. Stay a while and converse with me, mistress. The rest of you, out!" Once more the Jewish men surged towards the door.

"Excellency, the book?" spoke up Hadass.

"What about it?" asked Barmine, unsure what she meant.

"I unthinkingly removed it from Reb Halter's premises without paying for it, a transgression for which I hope he will forgive me. It should therefore be returned to him. It is part of his inventory and belongs in his shop. It is not my property," she said.

"Nor mine?" replied Barmine with a laugh. "Very diplomatically put, mistress. You are quite correct. In view of the purpose of my visit here it would indeed be inappropriate for me to retain something that is not mine. Thank you for pointing that out. Which of you is Halter?" The old bookman timidly raised his hand. Barmine tossed him the volume and jerked his thumb towards the door. The Jews nearly fell over themselves leaving. "Basaraba, send in my orderly Stepan and then get the men bivouacked. Do you play chess?" he asked her.

"Yes, Excellency," replied Hadass. "My father taught me to play when I was a child."

"I see the tavern's board over there on that table. Bring it to me, please," ordered Barmine. She calmly rose and did so. "Put it on the table and set up the pieces," he commanded, and she complied. "Do you want Black or White?" he asked.

"I will leave that to Your Excellency," replied Hadass.

"I will be White, then, since I am a by nature a man of attack," said Barmine. "Mistress Luria, you will play me a game now, and you will do everything you possibly can in order to win. I will do the same. Because the stake we play for is your father's life. If I win, then he takes his share of tomorrow's events as they would in any event transpire, no more, no less. If you beat me, then you have my word that no matter what happens tomorrow, I will spare him."

Hadass looked up at him. In her dark eyes was a fire that burned to Barmine's soul, and he knew he was lost to her forever. "My mother and my three sisters as well, and my betrothed Joseph Lipshits," she said. "Otherwise I will not play against you, Excellency, and you must punish me as you think fit."

"Done," said Barmine.

Barmine won the game, but it took him four hours to do so. By the end every officer in the troop both Russian and Cossack was standing around them in a circle, silent and fascinated. When Barmine checkmated her Hadass let out one dry sob of agony and then asked softly, "Have I your permission to go home now, Excellency?"

"Yes," he said. "Thank you for the game, mistress. Your father taught you well, but I discern that he had in you a student of brilliance." She rose and curtseyed. As she left the tavern, as one man all the soldiers rose and bowed to her.

Koltsov leaned over to him. "I have eyes that see into men's hearts, Ilya Aleksandrovitch. I have to, in my job. Don't go insane at your time of life. She is magnificent beyond words, that I grant you. But you *cannot* have a Jewess, at least not in the way you want this woman. What if the Czar were to come to hear of it? Heed me, my friend. She is not worth losing everything you have."

"She is worth any price that a man can pay," said Barmine.

"If any man touches her, I will kill him with my own hands, be he my own blood brother," said Basaraba in awe. "She is an angel."

*   *   *

Hadass should have realized that every Jewish eye in the town had been glued to the front door of Shmuel Butman's tavern during the four hours of her ghoulish game. By now the rumors regarding what was transpiring inside had reached heights of erotic and homicidal fantasy that would soon elevate the incident, already sufficiently bizarre in fact, into the realm of legend. When Hadass crossed the square and got back to her father's house she found the front room full of people. The holy rabbi Shlomo Shmulevitz arose anxiously from his seat. "Hadass! Have you been with…with *him* all this time?" he asked. "Why? What did he say? What did he want of you? In God's name, daughter, speak!"

"I tried to win your life from him," said Hadass, emotionally exhausted. "I tried to win all your lives from him. I failed. I am so sorry, Father, please, I couldn't, I just couldn't…" She did not have the strength to explain that she had spent the past four hours trying to win a chess game against an eccentric mass murderer with human lives as the stake, and no one in the room could be blamed if they misunderstood what she meant. Her father came to her and embraced her.

"Hadass, I must ask you this. Did you…what did you do to persuade him not to kill us?" he asked. "Do not fear to speak the truth. You are a daughter of Israel and there is no shame in doing what Jewish women have done in the past when this terrible necessity has arisen." Hadass comprehended then, and laughed wearily.

"Oh, so you think it was *that*? No. You and Yossele need have no fear. I am still undefiled, Father," she told him. "It could hardly be otherwise with all his officers and men around him all the time." She wasn't thinking clearly and still did not perceive the implications, the direction that the conversation was taking.

"So you have found favor in his eyes? So you still…you might still persuade him to spare us? Later on tonight when he is alone?" asked Rabbi Feldman in a low voice. "He finds you fair? He wants you? Have we a true Hadass in our midst? A biblical Queen Esther?" Then she understood.

"I don't know," she whispered, stunned. "You…you *want* me to do such a thing? How could you?"

"*Am Yisrael chai,*" said Shlomo Shmulevitz in a dead voice. "Israel must live."

"Reb Shlomo, I know I am not your daughter by blood, and I have always been grateful to you and to Hannah for all the kindness you have shown to me since the death of my parents," she said slowly. "I have also understood that you have never loved me as you have loved the daughters of your own flesh. That is natural and human, and I have never begrudged my sisters that love. But what have I ever done that was so wrong that you would now make me into a whore?" she cried bitterly.

"*We want to live!*" screamed Hannah, falling on her knees in terror before the stunned young woman. "Forgive me, Hadass, forgive me for every slight, for every unkind and thoughtless word, for every time I showed favoritism to your sisters, forgive! Forgive and let us live!"

"Hadass?" spoke up the teenaged Naomi, black-haired and pretty, tears on her face. "Let me speak for all us three, Shulamit and Simcha and me. We've been absolutely rotten to you for years now, and you must hate us for it. God knows I would if I had been you. But we beg you, give us a chance, let us repay you for those wrongs for the rest of our lives, as sisters…don't make us pay for it all tomorrow! Hadass, I'm afraid. Tomorrow those…those men will come and you know what's going to happen to me, and to Shulamit and Simcha when they find us down in the cellar with those crates. Hadass…I'm so scared…Hadass, *please!*" The girl began to weep.

Hadass looked at her betrothed. "Yossele?" she asked. "Have you agreed to this as well?"

Lipshits looked down at the floor and shuffled his feet. After a time he muttered *"Am Yisrael chai."* Quietly and without fanfare, Hadass's heart died within her forever.

"Israel must live. So be it," she said calmly. "Please wait here, Father. I must clean myself up, dress my hair and attire myself in my finest garments so that I can perform this holy duty that you command of me for the sake of our people, although I presume I will be wearing them for but a short while. I just want one thing from you."

"What is that?" asked Shmulevitz anxiously.

"Walk with me to his door. Look at him, and look at me, and give me to him as you should have given me to my husband on Tisha B'av," said Hadass, bitter tears streaming from her eyes. Shmulevitz recoiled.

"I...I can't do such a thing!" he jabbered in revulsion.

"She has the right to ask that of you, Reb Shlomo," said Yaacov Feldman. Feldman looked at Hadass. "If your father will not do this, daughter of Israel, then I will do it."

"Hadass, if you want, I will...." put in Yossele timidly. Hadass turned on him like a she-wolf.

"You will do nothing!" she cried in rage and agony. "How dare you? After this night, you will never, ever speak to me again!"

*   *   *

She wore a gown of white cotton and linen that her mother and sisters had made for her wedding dress, and on her head was a long lace veil. She crossed the square alone and knocked at the door of the house of Gershon Avitan the banker. The door was opened by the prince's orderly, who seemed unsurprised and did not even ask her why she had come. He simply pointed and said, "Upstairs." As she entered the house she heard a cry from someone across the square, *"Queen Esther!"*

Barmine was in the master bedroom upstairs. He opened the door at her knock. He had taken off his hat and uniform jacket and was wearing a rich velvet dressing down, a long Cuban cheroot smoking in his hand. Hadass stepped into the room and looked at him. "Excellency, I have come to beg for your favor, and for your mercy to all who dwell here. Do no harm to the people of this town tomorrow, no matter what you may find as you search, and in payment for that mercy do with me whatever you wish, tonight and for as long afterward as you wish. I ask only one thing, that when you ride out of here, you take me with you. Leave me by the roadside somewhere when you tire of my company. I don't want to have to look at them again, and I don't want them looking at me."

Barmine stared at her. "Sit down," he ordered, indicating a chair. She sat. "Whose idea was this? Yours or your father's?"

"It is the wish of all of us, Excellency. We all understand that we must pay tribute to the Czar."

"You are a very bad liar, Mistress Luria," said Barmine compassionately. Suddenly Hadass was overcome by it all and she broke down, weeping vehemently, rocking back in the chair with her head in her hands. "*I thought he loved me!*" she cried in agony. "*I was so sure, so sure he loved me!*"

"You mean that monkey-faced woolmonger?" said Barmine. "I'm sure he does love you in his own weak way. Holy Peter, how can any man *not* love you? But men who are afraid for their lives are not always able to overcome that fear, and sometimes they do disgraceful things in order to save the lives that they themselves have already rendered worthless. I told those cowering rag-peddlers this afternoon that I understand your people can show great courage at times. Your presence here tonight proves that. It's just a different kind of courage from ours, a survival instinct to be called upon only at direst need, just as any rat will fight when he is cornered."

"Whereas you fight among one another like rabid dogs, all the time, and when you're not savaging one another you come here to butcher us like animals for sport?" snapped Hadass, still rocking back and forth in the chair in her misery.

"No. We value courage for its own sake, because it uplifts the human spirit and breeds a higher human character by forcing men to undergo danger, privation and death for the sake of others, for our comrades in arms, to keep enemies from our families' hearths, and for ideals of the mind and the heart. There is more to life than simply staying alive, mistress."

"You can afford the luxury of such bloody high-mindedness," said Hadass. "We can't."

"I know. Here," he said, handing her a brandy snifter. "Your town banker keeps a fine cellar and has excellent taste in cognac." Hadass swallowed the fiery liquid in one gulp.

"Thank you, Excellency. Can I have some more? Would you mind if I was at least partly drunk before we proceed?" she asked.

"There are many things you have to fear, Mistress Luria, but that is not one of them," said the general. "Put your mind at rest on that score. I don't rape women."

"You just kill men," she said bitterly.

"Yes. That is our peculiar Christian idea of honor," he said with a smile.

"Your Excellency is pleased to make a jest out of something that is horrible beyond thought. You mean it? You really will not harm me?" she said, looking up at him in sudden hope.

"I didn't say that," replied Barmine, puffing on his cheroot. "I will quite possibly do you great harm. Do not mistake me, demoiselle. I have a duty to perform here, and although I hold you in high regard, I can be very cruel. I will be very cruel to you if you compel me to be so. That is a very fine bed. You will sleep in it tonight, alone. This armchair is quite comfortable and I can easily take a long nap in it. You will leave at dawn. You may if you wish tell everyone in town how the chivalrous Prince Barmine let you spend the night alone and unmolested in the banker Avitan's fine feather bed. Out of kindness, your family and your friends and your simian affianced may even pretend to believe you."

"But no one will ever really believe it," said Hadass in a dull voice.

"No. Human nature being what it is, they will have no desire to believe it. A beautiful captive spending the night alone in such a bed? How disappointing and dull! The alternative is so much juicier and lends itself to so much more prurient imagination, so many forbidden pictures in the mind. The story of this night will follow you all your life here. I know what your name means, Hadass. It is the Hebrew for Esther. I heard someone call out Queen Esther on the square a while ago. If you feel you can live the rest of your life here as this small town's Queen Esther, then do so. If you really want me to take you out of here when I leave, then you may come, and I won't leave you by the roadside. I'll leave you in Minsk or St. Petersburg with enough money to start life over. I give you my word that you, at least, will be safe from whatever happens tomorrow. But I must have the Emperor's gold back, and I will not allow the theft to go unpunished. There is another alternative, if you will agree, but it must be agreed upon between us quickly in order to be convincing. I can enhance your reputation for the good, by hurling your lovely body out that door and chasing you back to your father's house in a rage, possibly wearing only my nightshirt for comic effect, all the time shouting that I would rather sleep with the devil's granddaughter than that fiery Jewish bitch Hadass Luria. I'll even let you sink your teeth into my arm and leave a nice big bite mark on me. That way you are not only Queen Esther, you also are a kind of Polish Judith to my Holofernes. Tomorrow will still be bloody and bad, but when the smoke clears away you will emerge as the heroine of this whole episode. It will be your passionate refusal to yield to my horrible lecherous advances that will be remembered. Every Jewish household in Europe will honor your name."

"And may I inquire as to your price for elevating me onto this pedestal, Excellency?" asked Hadass, smiling slightly in spite of herself.

"Tell me where the gold is hidden!" he urged her.

"Not unless you agree not to harm anyone in the town," she said. "I don't care about my own reputation any more. That ended the moment I stepped inside this house. If you make me sleep here in that bed tonight, then to the Jews I'm a whore for the rest of my life, whether or not you lie beside me. But I don't care. All I care about is that you depart this place without shedding blood. Tell me what I must do for that to happen."

"You know I can't do that. What am I supposed to tell the Czar? That I found his twenty thousand gold Napoleons under a cabbage leaf?" asked Barmine in exasperation.

"It is not my concern what you tell the Czar," she told him. "Just now I spoke for my father and the people of Beit Efrat. Now hear me speak for myself, Excellency! If I can save the life of one single human being through any action of mine, then tell me what you want me to do and I shall do it. But do not ask me to be satisfied with a mere ten deaths as opposed to a hundred. Murder is murder, and I beg of you to leave this place having done no murder! I'll give you anything you want, do anything you want, be anything you want me to be, but my price for that is no death, no blood, none at all! And if you agree falsely tonight, and then you betray me tomorrow, if you hurt any of my friends or my neighbors, then I swear to you before God I will punish you with death. My death! I'll cut my own throat or hang myself from these rafters by my belt, and before the throne of God I will cry out that my blood is on your hands and not mine!" She knelt before him. "Please hear me! Let me do this! I want to do it if it will stop violence and murder! Let me turn your anger from my people. Whatever you want in your heart to do to Jews, do it to just one Jew. Do it to me, and not to anyone else here!"

"Noblest of women, now hear me," Barmine whispered in awe, taking her hands in his and raising her. "I did not come here in search of Jews. I am here to deal with thieves and traitors. Can you not understand that of me? Hadass, do you have any idea what I would give to hear such words from you in any other time, any other place than this? Do you have any idea what I would do for you if you could come to me with your head held high and tell me that you truly wanted me? But you have wounded me now in the one place where I must refuse you, in my duty to my king and to my country. Hadass, I would give you anything in the world I have to give, but my duty and my honor do not belong to me that I may give them away. They belong to Russia."

"What will you do?" she whispered dismally.

"What I said. I never believed that your father and his people would voluntarily surrender the gold, never mind hand over ten Jews to me for execution. I expected them to try something, a trick, an escape, a bribe. I am terribly sorry that you turned out to be the bribe. Tomorrow morning we start tossing this town inch by inch and we find the gold, and after we find it there must be punishment."

"But you won't hang the right person," she said.

"Probably not," sighed Barmine. "But appearances must be maintained."

"It won't be very good for appearances when the Czar reads my confession," said Hadass.

Barmine's blood cold. "You can't..." he stuttered. "Oh, Mother of God! Hadass, *no!* I beg you! Not for me, for like you I no longer care about my reputation where you are concerned! You don't understand. The Czar and his army have been made to look foolish by Jews, and you can have no idea how angry they are!"

She looked up at him. "Tomorrow, you will harm no one. Take the gold. But leave here with no one injured or slain. If you punish anyone for this I will walk to St. Petersburg if I have to, and I will pound on every official door I can find until someone will listen to my detailed confession as to how I helped rob the Czar of twenty thousand *Napoleons d'Or* in concert with whoever you have already executed here. I will name them, for the dead will be beyond harm, and I think I can concoct a story that will convince. I don't care what they do to me afterwards, but whatever it is you will live the rest of your life knowing you could have prevented it. Choose, Excellency. Take your gold and leave here with no blood on your hands, or you shall spill mine as well whether you will or no."

"I can't do that," said Barmine wearily. "Hadass, just as I will not dishonor you tonight, neither will I lie to you. I must do my duty, and I will do it. All I can ask is that in return you do not destroy yourself, not by suicide, and not by confessing to a crime you did not commit. If you choose to do so out of a desire for revenge or hatred for me, then yes, you will inflict upon me a lifetime of grief and remorse. That power you have, lady. Before you use it, make sure you really do hate me that much." He stood and pointed to the bed. "I think you must be exhausted. Go to bed, my honored guest, and sleep well. You need fear no harm from me this night."

Hadass was indeed exhausted. She curtseyed to Barmine, took off her shoes and lay down on the rich satin counterpane in her wedding dress, and she was asleep almost as soon as her eyes closed. Her sleep was deep and mercifully dreamless, until she awoke hours later. The first blue light of dawn was faintly visible through the cracks in the shutters, and for a moment she did not realize where she was until she remembered. *"Why did I have to awaken?"* she whispered to herself. Barmine was not there; she was alone in the room. The ashes in the fireplace still smoldered. She arose and put on her shoes and wrapped her wedding veil around her head. Now she would leave, cross the square to her father's house, and begin her lifetime to come of unspoken shame and sidelong looks on the street and whispers behind her back. Eventually, when it got too unbearable, she believed she could work up the courage to kill herself. She wondered how long it would take.

The woman descended the stairs. There was no sign of the orderly Stepan. She was about to open the front door and leave the house when she heard low voices in the parlor. She touched the door and it moved slightly beneath her hand. She slid it open just a crack and carefully put her eye to the aperture. She could just see the white-shirted back and suspenders of Barmine as he sat at a small table, smoking one of his Cuban cheroots. There was a mirror above the mantelpiece, and in it she could see Colonel Koltsov standing with one foot up on a chair, a sardonic smile on his face, both hands resting on his rapier grip. A third man was seated at the table, dressed in somber Hasidic broadcloth, but his face was cut off by the top of the mirror and she could not see who it was. Koltsov was speaking. "Fifty per cent is ridiculous, of course, and I am amazed at his impudence, but then he always was a cheeky little bugger. I confess he amuses me, especially since no one would blame you at all if you rewarded him with nine feet of rope, Ilya Aleksandrovitch. But then one of mine would have to be rather special in the effrontery department, eh? That's what makes mine the best. I choose and groom my rats for the cleverness of their character as well as for their tales." Koltsov laughed at his own pun.

"If I hear the phrase 'fifty per cent' fall from his lips again, he will get one hundred per cent of that nine feet rope you mentioned," said Barmine grimly. "Can this...gentleman be trusted, Fyodor Petrovitch? Are you of that opinion?"

"I believe he is over last year's little flirtation with the French, Ilya Aleksandrovitch," chuckled Koltsov.

"Please, Your Honors mistake me!" protested the third man in a fawning voice, spreading his hands deprecatingly with palms upward. "The dangerous associations I undertook with the French invaders of the Motherland were all in Your Honors' service, I swear to you! Why, did I not turn over to Your Honors my own cousin Chaim when, to my shock and horror I discovered him to be a thief and a traitor? How more loyal can one of the Emperor's servants be?" A knife stabbed Hadass to the heart, for she recognized the voice.

The third man was Yossele Lipshits.

"Horse dung!" said Barmine succinctly. "You betrayed Colonel Koltsov to a higher bidder, and you betrayed your cousin because you had just enough rudimentary intelligence to understand that you were in over your head stealing that much money from the army, and you'd best look to your own worthless skin!"

"Oh, la, Ilya Aleksandrovitch, such are the vagaries of the profession," said the secret policeman. "Spies are whores, and who ever expects a whore to be entirely faithful when someone else comes along with a fat purse? Especially a purse fat with these?" Koltsov flipped a gold Napoleon in the air.

"Give me the other nineteen thousand, nine hundred and ninety-nine of them and you will not go unrewarded, Lipshits," growled Barmine.

"Thirty per cent!" wheedled Yossele eagerly.

"Twelve feet of rope," replied Barmine. "And the highest perch on the tree. That's my final offer."

"Don't push it, you idiot!" said Koltsov softly. "Come to me in Cracow in a month's time. Meet me at Mother Gertrude's place and you'll have enough to spend three days and nights there, tup all the girls and then tip them, and still leave with a purse heavy enough to pull down your belt. Be content with that and speak now, before we lose patience and ask the Hetman Basaraba to join us."

"There is one thing, Your Excellency, that I must ask of you," said Yossele. "I ask that you spare the lives of Reb Shlomo Shmulevitz and his family. I am to marry his daughter."

"I see," said Barmine calmly, his voice unreadable. "And you think that Hadass will still wed you after you sent her here last night? You think most highly of yourself, or else very little of her."

"Well, actually, before she came over here she did tell me I was never to speak to her again," said Yossele with a self-deprecating chuckle. "But no, of course not, I couldn't marry Hadass now even if she still wanted me. No, Excellency, I mean that I am to marry the rabbi's daughter Shulamit on Tisha B'av. It was agreed upon last night. The rebbe feels I should have some recompense for the sacrifice I have made for the honor of Israel."

"The…sacrifice…you…have…made?" repeated Barmine slowly. "Koltsov, get him out of here. Take him somewhere and get the necessary information from him, before I kill him. I swear I will kill him if I have to look at him for another minute."

"Marry Shulamit!" whispered Hadass desolately, leaning against the door frame, and she could not repress a wracking sob of devastation. The men in the room heard her. Koltsov's sword was out and he leaped to the door, threw it open, and dragged Hadass a short way into the room. Yossele leaped to his feet and they stared at one another, both horrified by what they saw. "I almost loved you," she said to him. Then she turned and walked back upstairs to the bedroom.

She sat on the bed staring at the floor, her mind blank. After a while the door opened and Barmine came in and knelt beside her. "I won't say I am sorry."

"I know. Your duty," she said tonelessly.

"No. I won't say I am sorry because some injuries are beyond any apology. Your own people did you one such last night, and I have done you another this morning. I have come to offer what little reparation I can make. This isn't a command on my part, it's not even a suggestion. It's just something I'd like you to think about. Outside St. Petersburg I have a mansion of seventy-five rooms overlooking the River Neva. Behind it are parks and gardens and a menagerie. There is a library of something like eight thousand books, if I recall correctly. There are musical instruments and musicians to play them, there is a laboratory where scientists from all over Russia come to study and experiment. There is learning, and culture, and a life of peace there, if you will accept it from me. I do not offer you these things to buy you, Hadass. I do not suggest for one instant that you could ever be bought. I offer you these things because they are all I have to give you in exchange for the pain you have suffered over this last day. There is one more thing I can offer you, Hadass, if you are willing to make one more sacrifice, a terrible one for you. There are some things that even a prince cannot do, and one of them is to marry a Jewess. But if you will convert to Christianity and be baptised, upon my oath as a *boyar* I will marry you. In our church, before God and before the eyes of all men, I will say that you are the woman I want for my partner in life, and I will defy anyone from the Czar himself on down who objects."

"You would destroy your career!" she protested in amazement.

"Yes. And I would gain my life. Will you come with me from this place?" he asked gently.

"I know you mean this honorably, Ilya Aleksandrovitch, and from the bottom of my heart I thank you," she whispered. "As to conversion, no, never, it can never be. One cannot choose one's God. One's God chooses you. As to living with you, then I would be what the world already thinks me to be."

"Then why not? Who would know the difference?" demanded Barmine.

"I would know," she told him. He rose and bowed to her. "Go do you your duty, Ilya Aleksandrovitch," she told him. "If you feel you owe me a debt, you know how I want it repaid."

The prince took up his jacket and his shako, turned, bowed to her deeply once again, and left the room. After a time she heard the horses' hooves clattering in the square outside, the creak of the leather saddlery and the gutteral talk of the Cossacks. Then there was some shouting and pounding, then the rumble of a wagon. She arose and opened the shutters and looked out. The wagon stood before the door of her father's house, and a chain of dismounted Cossack soldiers were passing out the wooden crates containing the stolen treasure and stacking them into the wagon bed, lashing them down with ropes and covering them with canvas. Knots of people watched from the side streets, but there were no gunshots or shouts or screams or smoke, and it seemed to be an orderly process. Hadass closed the window and went and sat down again on a stool by the dead ashes of the fire. The noises in the square outside rose and fell, and there were more horses, this time moving out down the street. The door of the room opened. It was Barmine again. He came to her side. He held out his hand to her. "Hadass? We are leaving now. No one has been hurt or punished. Please. Please come with me."

"This place and these people are all I have ever known," she said. "They hated and feared you so much that they threw me to you like the peasants in the folk tale who threw their children off the sleigh to the pursuing wolves."

"And in the tale, when the parents got to the church, no one would look at them, for they all knew what had been done. Do you want them looking at you like that for the rest of your life, lady?" asked Barmine.

"If I were guilty, then as I told you last night, I would go with you. But I am innocent, thanks to your kindness and chivalry. Ironic, isn't it, Your Excellency?" she said with a wan smile. "The very nobility of your own nature has deprived you of what you desire."

"Life is full of irony," agreed Barmine. "Will you not come with me anyway?"

"I won't run away for a sin I did not commit." She rose and curtseyed to him. "For your mercy to my friends and my family, Excellency, and for your kindness and your courtesy to me, I humbly thank you. God speed."

"Goodbye, noble lady," said Barmine.

"Goodbye, Excellency," she replied, her eyes downcast. He left the room and she sat down again. The sound of the horses' hooves receded, and then there was an eerie silence over the town, except for voices she could hear coming from her father's synagogue across the square. Presumably the community was gathered there doing a post-mortem on the Cossacks' visitation and giving thanks to the God of Abraham that the dark angel of death had passed over the Jews of Beit Efrat. Hadass knew she should get up and go home, but she couldn't seem to move, to focus her thoughts.

The sun had risen high in the sky outside when the door crashed open and the grim, bearded, black-coated men with shirt collars and cuffs decently buttoned came into the room. They grabbed Hadass by her arms, and dragged her down the stairs while she cried out questions and protests. They pulled her out the door and into the market square where hundreds of people surrounded her, to the center of the plaza, and there she saw the piles of stones awaiting her. The holy rabbi Shlomo Shmulevitz stood by the biggest pile, his face livid and ghastly. The earth seemed to open beneath her feet. *"Father! Why?"* his daughter screamed. *"You sent me to him! You told me to do it!* Now they're gone and no one has died, and yet I must be stoned? How can you be so cruel and unjust? Why, Father, *why?"*

"It is not for your fornication, but for your falsehood," rumbled Shmulevitz in his deepest and most resonant preaching voice. "The treasure trove of gold that was taken from us by the *goyim* this morning on foot of your vile betrayal would have built a dozen shuls and Houses of Study, bought a thousand *seforim,* endowed hundreds of poor scholars each one of whom might have grown to be a Torah light unto the nations of man. That gold would have fed and clothed the Jewish destitute through the coldest winters, placed menorahs and Torah arks of silver and gold on the high altars in honor of God. You were sent into that house to save the Jewish people of this town, woman. Not to rob them! I can only guess, to my shame, that you were unable to do your duty without taking blasphemous and sinful pleasure in it. You convinced yourself that tyrant was your lover, that you traded the secret of this town's wealth because of some promise he made to you to take you away with him to a life of whoredom. Was that it, Hadass? If so, then you see how your Gentile lover of last night has kept his promise. He has left you here among the people whom you betrayed to suffer for your sin!"

"You think *I* told them...?" Hadass was stunned. She looked at Yossele, pale and trembling beside the rabbi. "Yossele? Will you let me die? Will you not speak?"

"Don't appeal to Yossele of all men!" snapped Shmulevitz. "He has already spoken, may God pity him! He told us of how he went to Avitan's house in the dawn this morning, hoping to get you away from that scarred devil, longing to beg your forgiveness for what he saw as his shame and weakness last night. He has also told us what you were...he told us how he found you. Right before the whole congregation he told us. Every filthy detail."

"I can imagine," said Hadass, her voice icy with contempt. "He learned much of such things in Cracow. Does my sister Shulamit know that on Tisha B'av she is to be married to a dog?"

With a hoarse shout of rage Yossele ran forward and hurled the first stone into her mouth full force, splintering her teeth and making sure she could speak no more. Hadass could taste her own blood in her mouth, and felt it running over her chin as she closed her eyes and drew her wedding veil over her face, but not before she saw her father hurl the second stone that knocked her to the ground. She tried to rise, felt more blows, then surrendered and let the soft dark peace of the end enfold her.

*   *   *

""Never thought I'd say it, but today Basaraba would be better company. Are you going to be like this all the way back to St. Petersburg?" asked Fyodor Petrovich Koltsov in irritation as he and Barmine rode at the head of the column. They were near the river now, and a cool breeze whispered through the bright apple blossoms and green buds of spring, dancing through the grass.

"Probably," sighed Barmine. "I'm probably not wholly sane right now, you know. I hear her name in the wind. Can't you?" The trees swayed in the breeze and did indeed seem in a sense to whisper *Hadass…Hadass…*

"When a man starts hearing a woman's name whispered on the wind he'd better do something about it," said Koltsov practically. "You are a very fortunate lover, Ilya Aleksandrovitch, in that you *can* do something about it. You are a general and a nobleman and she's a girl from a Jewish *shtetl*. She's only a couple of miles back, for Christ's sake! Go back there and just take her! Arrest her for something if the legalities bother you, or if you like I'll arrest her for crimes against the state and you can make yourself a hero in her eyes by saving her from me. You'll be doing her a favor in the long run. She doesn't belong in that shithole, and if she's as intelligent as she showed herself yesterday over that chess board she will come to understand that. Jewess or not, that lady was born for silks and a salon. Get her up to St. Petersburg and then worry about wooing her favor. She'll come around when she sees the city lights." Barmine looked around him at the trees that shivered in the wind with her name.

Hadass…Hadass…

"You know, I think you're right, Fyodor Petrovich," he said. "What is the point in being a prince if one cannot engage in the odd princely gesture like carrying off a beautiful girl on one's saddle bow? Basaraba! Leave the first troop here to guard the treasure wagon. Bring the second troop and come with me. We're going back to Beit Efrat!"

But before they reached Beit Efrat they came to a tall tree within sight of the rooftops of the town, the very one that the prince had earlier earmarked for his gallows tree. There they found a mule cart and the holy rabbi Shlomo Shmulevitz, who was digging a grave beneath the tree with a mattock and sobbing his heart out. On the ground nearby lay a silent form, covered with a cloth shroud that was soaked through with blood, fresh and wet and crimson. Stricken with sudden horror, Barmine leaped from his saddle and ripped the cloth from the body. He stared at the shattered remnants of his beloved for a long moment, and then looked up at the rabbi. "What have you done, old man?" he roared in a voice like thunder. The white-bearded rabbi stared at him for a moment with wild eyes, then ignored him and went on digging. Barmine went to his mount and pulled a long flintlock horse pistol from the saddle holster, and cocked it. He went up to Shmulevitz. "Old man, do you know who I am?" he asked, not with a raised or angry voice, yet something in his tone made Shmulevitz stop his work and look up.

"Yes, I know who you are. You are Esau," said the rabbi. "You had your mess of pottage from us long ago. We paid our bargain and your birthright is now ours, even though you withhold it from us. Now leave me to bury my child."

"No, I am not Esau," replied Barmine.

"Who are you, then, ignoramus?" muttered Shmulevitz as he dug.

"*I am the wrath of God!*" came the prince's reply, ringing like iron. Out of the corner of his eye the old rabbi caught the motion of the pistol being raised, and he turned and screamed in a high falsetto, putting up his hands to protect his face. The muzzle vomited flame and smoke and noise, and the heavy lead ball smashed through the rabbi's upraised palms and into his skull, splattering sixty years of Torah over the trunk of the tree in a bloody, white-ropey mess. The old man fell into the grave he had been digging for his daughter and flopped for a bit, then was still. In the leaves above the wind stirred and whispered the dead girl's name sadly over her murdered body into Barmine's ear.

Hadass…Hadass…

Basaraba rode forward. "That's one," he said. "A good start. And now, Prince my brother?"

Hadass…Hadass…

"I am the wrath of God," said Barmine again. He pointed towards the rooftops of the town. "Now go and kill them. Kill them all." He heard her name whispered again, this time not from the leaves above him, but from behind him where the Cossacks sat on their horses.

Hadass…Hadass…

It was the sound of two hundred sabers drawing from their sheaths.

Bringing Mary Home

From sweet Londonderry to fair London Town,
There is no other like her at all to be found.
Where the children are smiling and play 'round the shore,
There the joy bells are ringing for the maid of Coolmore.
-Traditional

"Is this where he killed her?" asked the big man softly.

"This is where she was found, Mr. Donovan," replied the SBI agent. The state cop was a thickset middle-aged man in a rakish fedora, with a long Dominican cigar in his teeth, named Matt Redmond. Redmond's badge hung from a leather case on his belt, and he carried a .357 Magnum Colt Python with a six-inch barrel in his shoulder holster. All of the men were wearing jackets against the autumn nip in the sunny air.

"The actual assault occurred up there, just below the wooden bridge over this little creek. Then he dragged her body down here to conceal her. We know that because there was a lot of blood on the ground and on the rocks of the creek up there, and the drag marks leading down here," Redmond went on. "It had been dry for a couple of weeks before and we weren't able to get any usable footprints, worse luck. It was summer then, and this area was a lot more grown over. We were lucky the body was discovered as quickly as it was by some early morning joggers in the park. That way the medical examiner was able to get a fairly good estimate of the time of death, somewhere between midnight and two in the morning. The killer tried to cover her up with branches and leaves, but it was dark and he didn't do a very good job. The joggers saw her foot sticking out, they took a closer look and then called the Carrboro police. This is a Carrboro city park, but the actual city limits stop at the embankment by the pond up there, and so the Orange County Sheriff's Department has jurisdiction. Lonnie here is actually the primary while I'm the North Carolina State Bureau of Investigation agent assigned to the case."

The three men were standing in a small dell or depression in the woods. The afternoon air was chill even though the sun shone brightly, and the leaves were drooping and falling around them, the last bright orange foliage of late November. Sheriff's detective Lonnie Jacobs lit a Marlboro and offered one to the big Irishman. Jacobs was a tall and lanky man of about fifty with a permanently soured look and a droopy moustache. He wore a sports jacket, a shoestring tie and no hat. "Ta," said Donovan. Jacobs lit the smoke with a Bic lighter. The red-headed Irishman had on a brown tweed suit of an oddly lumpish looking cut, tight on a tall and bulky body built on potatoes and Guinness and thick greasy Ulster fry-ups. The suit was worn and had seen better days. Somehow both men sensed it was the only suit the Irishman owned. "How bad was it?"

"You sure you wanna know that, sir?" asked Jacobs. "I have to tell you, the details are pretty gruesome."

"I'm a big lad. I can take it." Donovan's accent wasn't mock-Kerry stage-Irish, but the harder and more flat speech of Northern Ireland. Every vowel seemed to snarl. Jacobs looked at Matt, and the SBI agent responded.

"It was a brutal and frenzied attack," Redmond told him bluntly. "Your sister was stabbed and cut over seventy times and her face was slashed beyond recognition. The ME tells us the weapon was a long, straight, heavy blade with a very sharp point, possibly a butcher knife or a dagger or a bayonet of some kind. It did not have any serrated edges and the blade was about nine inches in length. Many of the stab wounds were defensive injuries on her arms. She knew what was happening and tried to fight back, but the man who attacked her was berserk. Most likely she screamed and called for help, but by then the company party back at the picnic area must have broken up, everyone had gone home, and there was no one to hear her. She never had a chance. She died from massive internal trauma and loss of blood, but it took some minutes, and her suffering during that time is something best not dwelled upon. I'm sorry, but you asked."

"I did so. Rape?" Donovan might have been talking about the weather.

"No. Neither actual, nor so far as we could tell attempted. No exterior seminal discharge either. Mr. Donovan, while we are on the subject, I have to ask you a question you may find painful. The medical examiner was able to tell us that Mary gave birth to at least one child in the past. Can you shed any light on that?"

"Your medical examiner is right. A piece of teenaged carelessness. She has a chiseler. A son named Brendan. He's seven years old now. He lives with the father's parents in Belfast," said Donovan.

"Where is the boy's father now?" asked Matt. "I'm sorry, but you never know what might turn out to be relevant."

"Dead," replied Donovan.

"What happened to him?" asked Jacobs.

"He went down the wrong street one day and a bomb went off. It was before Brendan was born. Any flesh or skin or blood from the bastard who killed her under her fingernails?" asked Donovan. "Any chance of a DNA match?" The two American policemen looked at him curiously. "I never miss an episode of *Crimewatch UK,*" explained Donovan tonelessly. "It's the Brit version of *America's Most Wanted.*"

"No, there was no foreign tissue or DNA material obtainable," said Matt. "We did get some fibers of blue wool. That is very unusual fabric for anyone to be wearing in the muggy heat of a Carolina summer night. I have a theory about that. I think the killer was wearing blue wool winter gloves or mittens, or else a balaclava type ski mask over his face. Or both."

"If he came dressed like that, it would indicate premeditation," said Jacobs.

"It would so," agreed Donovan, dragging on the Marlboro. "He knew he'd be doing bloody work and he came prepared to cover his entire body so as to leave no trace of himself behind. He came here that night planning to murder Mary."

"That's the way I scope it, yes," said Matt. "The problem is that the blue wool fibers are the only physical evidence we have. We have none of the garments, we don't have the weapon, we can place the suspect here at the scene but so were twenty-odd other people at the party, and no one saw David Cross or anyone else wearing any garment of blue wool. Nor do we really have a motive, at least nothing a D. A. will accept, never mind a jury. Mary Donovan and David Cross were officially considered to be an item, and although they weren't formally engaged as yet, supposedly it was in the cards. So far as everyone knew they had a stable and loving relationship."

"But you still think it was Cross?" asked Donovan. "Why? I'm not asking for sensitive information, I know you can't tell me everything. I never met the man meself and Mary wasn't very forthcoming about that part of her life. Or any part."

"Just when was the last time you saw your sister, Mr. Donovan?" asked Lonnie Jacobs.

"Six years ago, just before she came to America. She was nineteen and over the moon to be getting the hell out of Belfast, coming here to your university. She swore she'd never come back. I told her I'd wager she would so. I was right, she'll be after coming home now. I've come to bring her home in her coffin, so she can lie forever beneath the pelting rain of a land she came to hate."

"She left her child behind in Ireland?" asked Matt.

"The baby had a loving home, and everyone agreed that there was no reason for Mary to lose this opportunity and end up spending her life as a single mammy in a two-up-two-down in the Ardoyne," replied Donovan. "She was meant for better things, we always knew that. It was the hardest thing she ever did, but she was right to do it. She had a chance to get out and make something of herself, and everyone wanted her to take it. Including me. There was no bad blood at all, at all over her decision. When she got her master's degree and got a good job here in the States so she could support a child, she was going to send for Brendan."

"And what do you do in Belfast, sir?" asked Jacobs.

"I run a panel beater's shop. What you'd call an auto body shop, on the Falls Road."

"That's heavy I.R.A. country, I've heard," said Redmond.

"You heard right. You didn't answer my question. Why do you suspect this fella Cross?"

"Several reasons that make cop-sense but which don't constitute legal proof, or even legal evidence," said Redmond. "Statistics for one. Sixty percent of all female homicide victims are murdered by their husbands or boyfriends. Then there's logic. We are assuming she was murdered just after the party broke up, so why did she stay? How did she come to be down here in these woods three hundred yards away from the picnic area? She must have come down here with someone she trusted, or to meet someone she trusted. There is also the complete and total lack of anyone else who even remotely resembles a suspect. One thing I have learned in this investigation is that everyone who ever met your sister loved her and admired her. Her student friends, including my own daughter Tori, her professors, her fellow employees and her supervisors out at Cybertel, the staff at Duke Hospital in Durham and Memorial Hospital here where she did her volunteer work. The word I have heard most used to describe her is angel. I don't say it's impossible that Mary Donovan stepped out here for a nature break, or just for a walk under the stars, and through sheer bad luck she ran into a homicidal maniac who was lurking in this park dressed to kill. Things like that do happen. One of the more charming aspects of modern American society under the Love Generation is that at any given time, there are thirty or forty nomadic serial killers wandering around the country hunting people for sport. But we have no evidence at all that any such thing *did* happen, and there have been no similar crimes in any time frame or sufficiently geographically close to be meaningful. We're back to the statistical near-certainty that she was killed by someone she knew.

"There are some other telltale signs that make my ass twitch," Redmond went on as they mounted the small wooden bridge. The SBI man leaned on the railing and puffed on his cigar. "David Cross is real piece of work, as phony as a three dollar bill. He made a really theatrical show of grief and bereavement, breaking down and weeping in front of us and his top-dollar lawyer when we first questioned him, even did the old throw-yourself-on-the-coffin trick at her funeral. But when we looked into him in depth, we found out that the guy is a Grade A asshole. He is a pathological liar and a compulsive womanizer. He was stepping out on Ms. Donovan right, left, and center with anything female, with his fellow employees out there at Cybertel, college girls, waitresses, even a couple of underage girls from Chapel Hill High

School who could get him in trouble if their parents decided to make an issue of it.

"We also dug up some rather disturbing information from our boy's past. It seems that Mr. Cross doesn't take rejection from a lady very well. He likes to use his fists to express his displeasure. He had a couple of arrests for stalking and domestic violence out in California, where he's from, and also an arrest for unlawful carnal with a minor. The actual case wasn't much. He was caught kissing a fifteen year-old girl. In theory we could try to make him register as a sex offender here in North Carolina, but he's got a really sharp lawyer in Raleigh named Mack Terry who could probably beat it. That's another thing that sets my antennae to quivering. How does it come about that an ostensible RTP techie geek who's just had his fiancée murdered doesn't wait for us to come to him in his home or at work, but instead he shows up unannounced at the sheriff's office in Hillsborough for his first interview with Mack Terry in tow? Terry specializes in heavy organized crime and felony cases, and he defends the sleaziest clients imaginable, porno shop owners, drug mules, major league embezzlers and con men, SOBS who dump toxic chemicals along the state's roadsides. This suit charges two hundred dollars an hour and his initial consultation fee is five hundred dollars. That's half a grand just to plunk your butt down into his office chair. Cybertel pays their computer whizz kids well, but that's a lot of shekels for an evil Beavis like Dave Cross to have to cough up. When someone feels they need that kind of legal firepower just to talk to the police, we start wondering why. Finally, Mr. C. categorically refuses to take a polygraph test, or at any rate one of ours. In this country he has that legal right, but then he tried to palm us off with a polygraph arranged by Mack Terry, through a private security agency we have suspected in the past of not being totally on the up and up, and finding what their employers pay them to find. Needless to say, he passed that one."

"And?" prompted Donovan. "Something else?"

"I just think he did it," said Matt firmly. "I know that is unprofessional and prejudicial, and I would never say anything like that in court. But there is such a thing as copper's instinct, Mr. Donovan. You can size people up." Matt looked steadily at him.

"When can I have Mary?" the Irishman asked.

"I'll speak to Judge Simmons today and get you your exhumation order. Then you'll have to arrange for her to be removed from her present interment site in Parkway Memorial. Gregg Funeral Home can help you with all the arrangements and the paperwork," said Jacobs. "They told me the best way to go would be Raleigh-Durham to Atlanta, then Delta to Dublin. Would you like for me to drive you out there? To the cemetery, I mean."

"Ta, mate, but I have a map. I can find it. I'd like to go alone, if you don't mind."

"Certainly, sir," said Jacobs.

"Thanks for the fag," said Donovan, and he walked up to the embankment and off around the pond full of ducks and geese, towards the picnic area where his sister had spent her last hours on earth, to the parking lot beyond where his rental car was parked.

"You got a feelin' about that feller, Matt?" asked Jacobs, lighting another Marlboro. "I do."

"Yes. After all these years on the job you learn to know the type, the ones who stand out one way or the other. The ones who aren't afraid of a policeman. He's either one of us or he's one of them."

"You gone check him out?" asked Jacobs.

"Oh, yes," said Matt.

*   *   *

The first time that I met her, she passéd me by.
The next time that I met her she bade me goodbye.
But the last time that I met her, she grieved my heart sore,
For she sailed out of Ireland, away from Coolmore.

"I'm here, Mary," said Michael Donovan tenderly as he knelt by the grave in Parkway Cemetery. A simple temporary steel plate nailed into the ground recorded her name, the date of her birth, and the date of her death. "I know that I am the last man on earth that you would want to be here. But needs must, lass, needs must. You wouldn't let me atone for the wrong that I did to you in Belfast, although I offered you me very life for it. You ran away rather than accept anything I tried to do to earn your forgiveness. You would never let me show you how sorry I was when you were alive, so I have to show you now. I know who betrayed you, Mary. They won't escape me." He wept quietly for a while, then he stood up stood and returned to his rental car. He left a sheaf of white lilies on her grave, noting with gratitude that other fresh floral offerings also lay there on the chilly autumn earth, from friends at UNC and the company where she had worked. He saw with surprise that one of them carried the card "From Matt, Heather, and Tori."

        *   *   *

Agent Matt Redmond arrived home at his house on Boundary Street in Chapel Hill at about six o'clock that night. His wife Heather, who was an accountant at the University of North Carolina, was in the kitchen laying out two place settings. "Beef stew out of a can tonight, I'm afraid," she said with a wry smile. She was a tall and slender woman who had refined aging gracefully into an art form. At 46 she looked to be in her mid-thirties max, and the white in her long silky hair was blending neatly and cleanly with the ash blond.

"Hey, whatever's going is fine so long as it has your magic touch. You can work miracles with Spam," said Matt fondly, taking off his hat and his gun and laying them in a corner on the counter. He looked at her for a while.

"What?" she asked, blushing.

"Just remembering. Four years ago last month. That evening when you came charging out that door pointing an empty gun at me," he recalled with a fond laugh. "I still can't believe how lucky I am." She simply smiled.

"You should have gotten home a few minutes ago. I just got off the phone with Tori," she told Matt.

"Jeez, it's what time now in Florence? Midnight?"

"Thereabouts. Sounded like she was just coming in from throwing three coins in the fountain."

"I think that's supposed to be Rome."

"She hated missing Thanksgiving dinner with us."

"We missed her at the Pizza Hut, too," laughed Matt. He and Heather had agreed to skip the traditional Thanksgiving dinner, the first one Heather had ever spent without Tori since her daughter's birth. They had celebrated by splitting a pitcher and a large beef and mushroom with anchovies at the one place in Chapel Hill that was open on Thanksgiving day.

"She really loves it over there, her classes and her professors are great, and she says she can already ask her way around and order in restaurants in Italian," said Heather.

"I suppose she practices with Tony?" said Matt with a sigh.

"I don't know. I didn't ask and she didn't mention him. You know the arrangement."

"I know. Having made our feelings clear, to put it mildly, bottom line is it's her life and her decision. But in view of the incompatibility between Tony's profession and mine, she keeps *omertà* unless something major happens, one she breaks up with him, two she shacks up with him, three she marries him, God forbid. Lovely arrangement to have with one's daughter. Hi, honey, how's school, and are you Married To The Mob yet? Damn, I wish I didn't actually *like* that cocky little hoodlum!" [See *Slow Coming Dark* by the same author.]

"Are we going to spend the rest of the evening beating our heads on that particular brick wall? Again?" asked Heather ruefully.

"No, no, I think both our noggins are sufficiently bloody from that one. I'm afraid I'm still hammering my bruised and krovvy rookers on another, though. I talked with Phil Hightower this afternoon, and he can only give me another couple of weeks on the Mary Donovan case. Then we have to feather it. There are other crimes being committed in North Carolina, after all. Looks like there goes my 100% clearance rate, finally."

"Then we leave Blockbuster for another night and we go over it again, Holmes. From the top," said Heather.

"Thanks, Watson."

After dinner Matt cleared the table and put the dirty dishes in the dishwasher, and then he took down the Donovan case files and laid them in order onto the kitchen table. There were the initial incident reports, forensic and pathology reports and crime scene photos in a plain manila envelope which Heather had declined to look at, witness interview reports, raw leads and rumors and speculation, background on the victim. Matt wrestled one file away from a huge orange cat named Trumpeldor who seemed determined to eat it, and put the animal on the floor. The cat slugged Matt viciously in the ankle a couple of time with a closed paw to let him know who was boss, and then stalked away. "Mary Eileen Donovan. Female Caucasian, twenty-five years old, green-eyed beauty and green card immigrant, born in Belfast, Northern Ireland. Bachelor's degree from UNC in psychology and working on her master's degree in business administration so she could join the great capitalist rat race and someday have the Great American Dream, the split level ranch house, the two point five cars in the garage, fifty grand in debt on twenty credit cards, one or two divorces and maybe a little alcoholism and drug abuse, and the two point five latchkey kids growing up to be psychos...."

"Matt!" said Heather warningly.

"Sorry, honey, you're right," said her husband with a sigh. "The girl was murdered and I shouldn't turn her into one of my paleoconservative homilies. It's disrespectful. I might add that she was loved by all who knew her, with one obvious exception, and will be sorely missed."

"Tori cried at her funeral," said Heather in sad recollection.

"She also asked me to make sure I got the bastard," said Matt in a low voice. "I promised her I would. Oh Christ, Heather, I hate to break that promise!"

"You once took twenty-six years to keep another such promise, but you kept it," his wife reminded him. [See *Fire and Rain* by the same author.] "You'll keep this one. Tori won't be disappointed."

"Thanks, Watson. To continue, Ms. Donovan was employed as an accounting and management intern by Cybertel in the Research Triangle Park on a full time basis, but with a flexible schedule that allowed her to attend her classes. In her second year she would have been allowed to serve a business internship in Europe if she qualified. I wonder if she would have chosen Ireland? On the night of Friday, August the fifth, Ms. Donovan attended a kind of combination picnic and kegger in the Carrboro Municipal Park picnic area. She arrived with her main man, David Cross, also an employee in the Cybertel electronic engineering department, research and development to be specific. She spent the entire evening in his company. They both, however, arrived in separate vehicles, which I have always believed to be significant. Why?"

"It seems to have been a departure from their usual practice," agreed Heather. "Most couples do go to social functions and on dates in the same car. From what you learned, Mary and David usually did as well?"

"Correct."

"You never got a straight answer out of Cross as to why that one night they arrived in separate cars?" asked Heather.

"He claims she told him she had some errands to run after she left work and instead of him picking her up at her apartment she would meet him at the park," said Matt. "We have been completely unable to trace her movements during the three hours or so from the time she left Cybertel and the time she arrived at the party. Whatever she was doing, it wasn't picking up her dry cleaning or grocery shopping or any everyday errand. I really would like to reconstruct how she spent that time, that missing segment from the last few hours of her life. We'll most likely never be able to prove it, but I think Cross somehow persuaded Mary to bring her own car, so that he could explain why he would leave later on without her. His separation from her at the onset of the critical time period is very convenient for him."

"That implies premeditation," suggested Heather.

"I am as convinced as I sit here that this was a premeditated crime," said Matt flatly. "I always have been, from day one. Don't ask me why. I just know. Real Sherlockian ratiocination there, eh?."

"They got there at what time?" asked Heather.

"Both about eight P. M. No one really noticed the exact time. Dave and Mary were an accepted item at these functions, they drifted in and out, and no one thought anything about it or clocked them. Why should they?"

"You told me these get-togethers are held every Friday by Cybertel as a kind of semi-official, morale building and bonding type company function. Sometimes they are at a bar or restaurant, sometimes outdoors if the weather is favorable. The Cybertel employees had special permission to remain in the park after the usual closing time."

"You got it," said Matt. "The cookout ended at midnight and the remaining employees went off home or to dissipations elsewhere. It appears to have been a fairly standard hot dog, hamburger and brewski bash attended by mid-twentysomethings of both the UNC grad student

and RTP yuppie-techie variety. In other words, animated but not
Animal House. The first hints of adult maturity beginning to set in, no
longer cool to chase the ducks naked or vomit all over the barbecue
grill. Music was provided by a CD boom box but not too loud, there was
some dancing, a fair amount of drinking but nothing too wild and
woolly and in any case there were a sufficient number designated driv-
ers to go round, which is important to remember, because it means
we've got six or eight witnesses who were sober the whole night, damn
their eyes! They saw nothing at all in any way suspicious or odd. Mary
Donovan was there with David Cross and no one observed anything
untoward in their interaction with one another or with anyone else at
the gathering. On the contrary, towards the end of the evening the pair
of them were observed sitting on one of the farther picnic table benches
billing and cooing, nuzzling and canoodling, and no, Heather I'm not
being calloused or disrespectful again. You know darn well what I am
talking about, and it's relevant to the investigation. It will be one of the
main points in Cross's defense if it ever gets that far, that they were
being physically affectionate and demonstrative right up until the
moment she disappeared from the gathering. In fact, I have even known
you and I to indulge in the odd canoodle on a summer evening out on
the deck there, despite the ripeness of our years.

"About midnight the remaining attendees noticed that Cross and
Donovan were no longer present. Everyone simply assumed they had
left together. The party broke up and we now run into one of the most
infuriating aspects of the case. Despite grilling by myself and Lonnie,
intensive to the point of breaking out the rubber hoses, none of the witnesses present, drunk or sober, can swear absolutely one way or the
other whether or not Mary Donovan's blue Hyundai or David Cross's
white Bronco were in the parking lot still when they left. Mary's car
especially is important. Some say they are sure the Hyundai was there
and some say it wasn't, but it was a dark color and it was a dark night.
Of course, no one was looking, but the fact is that we simply don't know

whether either vehicle was left behind when everyone else left. Then at eight the next morning the body of Mary Donovan is found chopped up into hamburger beneath a pile of woodland rubbish, her car sitting in the parking lot with no indication as to how long it was there. Cross's fingerprints were in the car but he often rode in it and drove it as well when he was out with Mary."

"Cross's alibi?" asked Heather.

"The hardest of all to break. No alibi at all. He says he kissed Mary goodnight at around midnight, got in his car, drove to his apartment on the 54 Bypass, and went to bed. He has a long distance call from his home number on his phone bill to a friend in California lasting from 12:20 A.M. to 12:50, although of course anyone can dial a telephone."

"And he also has his kicker," sighed Heather.

"His kicker, yes," growled Matt. "His kicker is he gets pulled over by a Highway Patrol officer at 12:09 A.M. on August the sixth, right at the turn-off on Highway 54, only a few hundred yards from the entrance to Carrboro Municipal Park. Going right where he should be going, home. Trooper Jeff Puntis spots him weaving a little, figures he's got a Friday night drunk, and pops the bubble gum machine on him. Cross is pulled over in his 1999 Ford Bronco. He is respectful and a little shamefaced, admits he's had a few more beers at the party than he should, obediently walks the line and blows into the bag. He breathalyzes at .08, which is right at the legal limit but not staggering drunk. Puntis runs him and the truck, finds no outstanding wants or warrants or tickets, decides to give the guy a break and writes him not for DWI but for reckless operation, which he is allowed to do for someone right at .08. Puntis told me that Cross was feeling no pain but was by no means incoherent or incapable, and since he only lived a mile down the road he looked OK to drive that far. Puntis gave Cross the ticket, read him the standard riot act, and told Cross to get his ass home and get to bed. Cross was wearing a white UNC t-shirt and jeans and a baseball cap. There was not a sign of blue wool or bloodstains, although Puntis didn't search the vehicle. He couldn't have, no probable cause."

"So why couldn't Cross have doubled back and met Mary in the woods and killed her?" asked Heather.

"I think he did, or something like that. I think Mary Donovan was already dead, but Cross gave no indication at all to the eye of an experienced police officer that he had just come from hacking his girl friend to pieces. In court Mack Terry will take that traffic ticket, and before that jury's very eyes he will elevate it into a piece of the True Cross, no pun intended, a holy document which will render forever stainless and sanctified the legend of Saint David the Persecuted." Redmond opened the file folder and slapped down the Highway Patrolman's report in disgust. "Behold, I give you David Cross's Get Out of Jail Free Card," he went on mournfully. "On the morning of August the sixth, we had a woman slashed to ribbons Friday the Thirteenth style. A day later we had some minute strands of commercially dyed dark blue wool. Not light Tar Heel blue, by the by. Dark Navy. And in the past three and a half months that's as far as we've gotten. We're dead in the water."

"Except that you know who the killer is," said Heather.

"I *think* I know who the killer is," said Matt. "I'm honest enough to admit that my so-called copper's gut instinct may be simple dislike of the man and a desire to find the woman-beating son of a bitch guilty of something. But if not Cross, then *who*, for crying out loud? Like I told her brother this afternoon, a wandering maniac is always a possibility, given the kind of society we live in. Ted Bundys do exist. But in this case it just doesn't ring true, Heather! It was either someone who knew her, or it was a stranger, and there is no indication at all of any stranger. That leaves someone she knew. Men kill for three reasons, passion, profit, and protection. We have not uncovered a single scrap of evidence that anyone was involved with Mary Donovan within any of those three dynamics, with the exception of David Cross. We have not come up with one single individual other than Cross who could even remotely be described as a suspect. Everyone who knew the girl practically worshipped the ground she walked on."

"Any chance she was about to break up with him or leave him? That's usually when abusive men become homicidal," suggested Heather. "Especially with someone as special as Mary. A man who believed he had a permanent thing going with this angelic woman, as she has been described, could really go off the rails if he thought he was about to lose her. Especially if he was unstable and inclined to violence against women anyway, as Cross's previous record indicates."

"I agree. But our interviews with all their friends at Cybertel indicate the exact opposite. The relationship was in fact moving in the other direction. Cross was already cruising the jewelers shopping around for a ring. He said so when we talked to him and apparently he mentioned this to others before her death."

"She came from one of the most violent and dangerous parts of the world, Matt," said Heather. "Is it possible that something followed her from Belfast? Although I know the Provos generally run more to guns and explosives than knives."

"That possibility did occur to me. I ran her with the British and Irish embassies both, even made a call to the Garda Special Branch in Dublin, and she had no I. R. A. or political background at all. She came to this country because she grew up surrounded by the Troubles and she wanted nothing to do with them. She came here find peace and instead she found a nine-inch blade waiting for her in the dark. Oh damn, damn, *God damn!*" Matt shuddered and rested his face on his fists. Heather reached over and took one of his hands in hers.

"I think that's always been one of the things that has most impressed me about you," she told him. "The way you've been doing this all your life and yet you have never stopped caring."

"Southerners have a sense of place that only a few other people like the Irish might understand," said Matt. "I love Carolina and I take it as a personal offense, a personal insult, when someone comes to harm here.

She was by every account a gentle and damned near saintly person, although I confess I found out something today from her brother that somewhat disturbs me. Possibly the first tarnish on Saint Mary's halo, may her spirit forgive me for putting it that way."

"What is that?" asked Heather curiously.

"We knew she had a child in the past, as I told you before. The medical examiner told us that. Her brother confirmed it was a baby boy. This occurred when she was about eighteen, and when the baby was a year old Mary came here to UNC and left him in Ireland with the father's family. She never mentioned the child to any of her American friends and from what I gather from the brother, she never had much if any contact with the child or his foster parents since. Kid's seven years old now."

"How odd," mused Heather. "That's so out of character for her, Matt! All those people who knew her can't be wrong, surely? She loved children so much she volunteered to work with them in the hospitals as a nurse's aide and a physical therapist. Yet she abandoned her own child? There's a story there, mark my words. Can you get the whole skinny from the brother, do you think?"

"I have some reservations about Mr. Michael Donovan. Not sure, but I think he's a bit of a hard case. I asked Phil to have an Interpol and Scotland Yard workup done on him. I think he's not being entirely frank with us about some things, although I'm not sure what. I agree, there's something in that situation we need to know about. I sensed it."

"Matt," spoke up Heather, the Highway Patrolman's report open in front of her. "Matt, let me be clear on something. The entrance to the park is just a few hundred yards past the turnoff onto the bypass on the Carrboro town side, right? That's east of the turnoff."

"Yes," replied Matt. "You got something, Watson?"

"I never actually read Trooper Puntis's report before this," she said. "He says that he observed the Bronco at 12:09 A.M. proceeding eastbound on Highway 54, crossing over the yellow dividing line, etcetera, and pulled said vehicle over as a possible DWI. Cross was proceeding *eastbound*, Matt. So, if David Cross was just coming from the party, toward the turnoff to go home to his own apartment, why wasn't he proceeding *west*?"

Redmond snatched the papers from her and stared. "My God!" he whispered. "Christ on a raft, Heather, I am a fool! I ought to be sitting in your cubicle every day crunching numbers and you should be wearing this badge and doing my job. In three and a half months, I never noticed this! Cross wasn't coming from the park when he was pulled over! He was coming from somewhere up Highway 54, from the direction of Burlington!" He looked at his wife, laid the papers on the table, and kissed her hand. "You did it!" he whispered in awe and admiration.

"I haven't done jack, Holmes," warned Heather. "All he has to say is hey, I was drunk and I missed the turn-off and I had to turn around and come back."

"But that's not what he told Puntis and not what he told us!" cackled Matt triumphantly. "Cross lied to us! Heather, do you know where the first break in a case usually comes? It comes when we catch our suspect telling his first lie. We take that one lie, like the loose end of thread on a garment, and we pull on it. Eventually it all unravels. I'll get hold of Puntis tomorrow and make sure he's got his directions straight."

The phone rang. Matt picked it up. "This the Southern Sherlock Holmes?" snarled a voice on the other end.

"A very humbled Sherlock Holmes, Phil," laughed Matt. "Doctor Watson just rubbed my nose right in it."

"You know, Heather breaks your cases so often I'm kind of surprised she doesn't start sending us a bill," said the director of the North Carolina State Bureau of Investigation.

"If she does, for Pete's sake, pay it!" urged Matt with a chuckle.

"What's that fine lady of yours come up with now?" Matt described the newly discovered discrepancy in Cross's midnight traffic stop.

"Hmmm..it ain't much," said Phil warningly. "It may not mean any-thing at all, Matt."

"It means that David Cross went somewhere and did something he hasn't told us about, right in the middle of the crucial time window," said Matt. "It means that right about the time Mary Donovan was being murdered or waiting down by that little plank bridge to be murdered, David Cross was not where he told us he was. That's our loose end, Phil, and tomorrow Lonnie Jacobs and I start pulling on it. Did you have something for me?"

"Your hunch about Donovan was right," said Hightower. "I got so curious that I got on the horn to your old buddy Special Agent Frank Hardesty at the FBI in Washington and got him to go in to his basement cubbyhole at the Bureau and get on the computer. He still has clearance for the FBI's counter-terrorism classifieds, even if they have booted him out of the field for political incorrectness. It's all legit, by the by; I faxed him an official assistance request. In view of the way you are regarded in the corridors of power due to your habit of shooting assistant directors and cutting off Senators' ears, I kind of forgot to mention your name on the paperwork."

"Oh, hell, yes!" said Matt. "If they figure out Frank and I are close he'll end up floating in the Potomac or going out a window like the Divine Miss A. What did he come up with?"

"Michael Donovan is Provisional I. R. A. Or was. He is now listed by the R.U.C. and the Yard as inactive, for whatever that may be worth."

"I knew he was either one of us or one of them," said Matt grimly.

"Now, here's where it gets weird. The man we have down here is Michael Donovan, but he is not Mary Donovan's brother," said the director. "Mary Donovan's immigration file mentions only one grand-mother as immediate family, parents deceased. There's nothing on file about Mary in the Bureau's counterterrorism database, but quite a bit on Mike the Mick, and he does not have a sister named Mary. Two brothers named Gerald and Seumas and three sisters all of whom have lovely-looking exotic Gaelic names I won't try to pronounce, and all in their 30s and 40s. Donovan himself is 42, by the way. No sister named Mary, aged twenty-five, so he's lying to us about that."

"Then he's using a false British passport," said Matt. "He had to identify himself when he filled out the paperwork to take possession of the girl's remains. His passport says Michael Patrick Donovan."

"No, that's what's odd. His passport is legit. I say again, the Feds know this guy. His name is Michael Patrick Donovan, all right, just no relation to the vic or else very distant. Do you know how many Donovans there would be in the Belfast telephone directory, Matt? Maybe he just happens to have the same name as the deceased. But I am very interested to know what he's doing here pretending to be the brother of a North Carolina murder victim, even going so far as to try and shanghai the poor girl's mortal remains back to the Emerald Isle. He's on an immigration watch list. That's how Hardesty picked up on him. When Donovan entered the country his passport ding-a-linged the computer. Donovan is C-Category, not actually wanted for a crime, so when he arrives the drill is don't arrest him or deport him, just follow him and see where he goes and who he meets. He made several trips to the States in the late '80s and early '90s, each about six weeks in duration. He usually hangs around up in New England and New York, presumably because that's where all the good Irish pubs are. The FBI suspects that these were shopping trips on behalf of The Lads."

"Guns?" asked Matt keenly.

"Maybe. He's a slippery customer. No one seems to have been able to figure out exactly what the hell he has been doing here, but MI5 in London claims that Donovan was at one stage one of the Provos' master bomb makers."

"At one stage?"

"Like I said, Donovan is now officially considered inactive, since about '93 or so. That makes no never mind to me. Do me a favor, will you, Matt? Grip this son of a bitch tomorrow. I don't like people who make bombs wandering around in my state."

"Consider him gripped," said Matt. "Thanks, Phil." He hung up.

"Who are you going to grip?" asked Heather.

"I'll tell you right after I grip you," said Matt, catching his wife up in his arms and carrying her up the stairs in the manner of Rhett Butler.

*   *   *

The next morning Redmond, Jacobs, and the big Irishman sat in an interrogation room in the Chapel Hill Public Safety building. "I knew you were either one of us or one of them. You're one of them, in spades. I don't appreciate being lied to, Donovan," said Matt Redmond coldly. "And I damned sure don't appreciate being lied to by terrorists!"

"And have you no heard of the Peace of Good Friday?" said Donovan with an ironic smile. "Sure all of that carry-on is behind us now as Ireland greets the dawn of a new century, turns into a high-tech Celtic Tiger and every Irish man and woman stands proud and tall with e-mail and a cellular phone in their hand, courtesy of the New World Order."

"Aw, crikey, Matt, don't the *both* of you start goin' on about the god-damned New World Order!" begged Jacobs in alarm.

Matt fought to repress a smile. "Why are you here?" he demanded of the Irishman.

"I told you why. I'm here to return the body of Mary Donovan to Ireland for burial alongside her own."

"Since you're not a blood relative, you have no legal right to remove Ms. Donovan's remains," said Matt.

"I do, actually," said Donovan. "I'm the most immediate family possible." He pulled two papers from his pocket and tossed them on the table in front of the two detectives. "I brought these along with me, in the hope I'd never have to use them. The top one is a certified extract of a marriage license from the public registry office in Belfast, and the second is a marriage certificate signed by Father James McGowan, P. P. Mary Donovan was my wife. Mary Byrne, she was, but she kept her married name when she came here, even though she left everything else behind. I never expected she'd do that. I had no right to expect it."

Matt stared down at the documents and handed them to Jacobs. "Mr. Donovan, are you familiar with an American expression to the effect that we are now in a whole new ball game?"

"We're not, you know," said Donovan with a sigh. "The first week in August I was at work at my place of business every day, including the Saturday. You can ring the R.U.C. in Belfast if you like and ask them. They still keep track of me and if I disappeared for even a few days they'd have been interested and made a note of it. They're probably wondering where I've got to now and they'll appreciate your telling them. And just how could I have done a shufty into this country and out again after I allegedly killed Mary, without leaving any record of the fact with immigration? That's what you're thinking, isn't it? That I crept over here and murdered her? I was home in Ireland, Redmond, but go ahead and waste your time checking it out if you like."

"The taxpayers of this great state give me plenty of time to waste on such matters," said Redmond. "They even pay me for it. You'd better believe we will indeed check with the R.U.C. as to your whereabouts on August the fifth and sixth of this year."

"Why the lying, Donovan?" asked Jacobs. "If you're the dead woman's husband, why pretend to be her brother?"

"Coupla reasons. I told you, I haven't seen her in six years, and that was the truth. I didn't kill her, but I know yez don't know that and being coppers you'd get suspicious, understandably enough. Why not just avoid the whole problem? I didn't want you getting ideas about me and letting this Cross fella off the hook. I just came to collect Mary's remains and take her home, so she'll have a grave Brendan and I can visit and lay flowers on. What happened in Belfast between me and her has not got a bloody thing to do with her murder here and it's not a good memory at all, at all. I just wanted to come and collect her without poking up sleeping dogs."

"And maybe do a little duty-free shopping for the Provos while you're here?" asked Matt.

Donovan shook his head. "No. That's all behind me now, although I know yez won't believe that. See here, if I tell yez the whole horrible story will yez not let yeselves get dragged into a dead end tryin' to pound me square head into a round hole? I didn't do her in, dammit! From what yez tell me it was most likely that bastard Cross."

"I won't forget Mr. Cross, rest assured," said Matt. "Start at the beginning. Are you the father of Mary Donovan's child?"

"No," said Donovan. "I'm quite a bit older than Mary, as I'm sure you've noticed. She grew up on my housing estate just off the Falls. When I got out of Long Kesh I came back and there was this tall lovely lass next door where there'd just been a chiseler when I left. I loved her at first sight, but I was too old for her and I was a Volunteer besides. She hated the bloodshed and the violence around her with all her being. Her father was murdered by the U.D.R. and her ma died of cancer. She lived with her gran. She could never have gone with anyone who was involved in the fighting, and I knew it. Brendan's father was a fella named Kevin Connolly. A good lad, steady and sober, not involved in the Troubles at all. I knew him, I was envious of him, but I liked him and couldn't find it in my heart to be jealous. She wasn't for me. I understood that. Unemployment was always bad in Belfast, but he and Mary were both working and saving up for a house before they got married. They were a lot more responsible than American kids of that age would be, no offense meant."

"None taken," said Matt. "You're quite correct. I wouldn't wish Belfast on us, but Americans have had things entirely too easy for entirely too long. A little deprivation, hardship and desperation would do us all a world of good. Go on."

"Kevin Connolly had his own business, a food van, what ye'd call a roach coach over here, sold fish and chips and bacon butties and sausage rolls, that kind of thing to workers on their lunch or tea breaks. He had a regular route, but every now and then he'd just pull over to the kerb in some likely spot and start selling nosh to the passersby. One day he parked on Sorley Street and was getting set up to do some business, about fifty yards away from an army checkpoint. A Provo car bomb detonated and he was killed, along with a U.D.R. man and another bystander. Mary was eighteen years old, seven months pregnant and shattered to the point of total mental and emotional collapse. She actually spent some time in a psychiatric ward. When she came home with Brendan I did something that was either very noble or very despicable, and I myself am not sure which it was to this day. I paid court to her and I practically strong-armed her into marrying me. It wasn't hard. She was a single mother with an infant in arms all alone in Belfast except for an old woman, and I offered strength and support for her and a father for her child. We were wed, I broke with the Provos and made it clear to them that if they tried to force me back I'd take some of them with me, and for six months...oh, those six months when I saw how me life might have been! Dear God, but it almost worked! It almost worked!" Tears glistened in the big man's eyes.

"Then she found out that you were the one who set the bomb that killed her lover," said Redmond flatly.

"How in the name of God could you know that?" gasped Donovan.

"Educated guess," replied Redmond. "It would have to be something on that level for a Catholic girl of Mary's known integrity and character to flee from her husband and her child and never try to even see the boy. That's the part I don't understand. I can see her leaving you, but why in the name of heaven did she leave her child in the hands of the man who murdered his father?"

"To make sure I never went back," replied Donovan quietly. There was a long silence. "She knew if I lost them both I would have turned

into a monster in my grief and my rage at all the world. She couldn't
bear to stay with me herself, but she left me Brendan so that I might
remain a human being. I murdered the man she loved, and she repaid
me with that kind of mercy and compassion." There was a long silence.

"Christ!" whispered Jacobs, shaken. "I think she really was an angel."

"She was that," agreed Donovan, taking the proffered Marlboro from
Jacobs and lighting it himself. "Let me take her home, Redmond.
Please."

"When you give me the rest of it," said Redmond. Donovan looked at
him.

"What makes you think there is any more?" he asked steadily.

"The murder of Mary Donovan was a premeditated act. I have no
evidence of that except negative evidence, i.e. we haven't caught the guy
yet. Policemen aren't perfect, but we're not fools and we have a well
tried and tested by-the-numbers drill that catches the overwhelming
majority of all perpetrators of serious crimes. When a felon evades
detection by our standard procedures he is either cosmically lucky or
else he planned carefully. Despite the terrible nature of the assault
against your wife, to my trained eye and experience this whole thing has
reeked of meticulous planning since the get-go. An unpremeditated
passion killing by David Cross or anyone else would have left more evidence, or more likely the horrified killer would have broken down and
confessed. That hasn't happened. A sex crime or serial killing would fit
into an overall pattern of similar crimes. There is none here. One of two
things happened to Mary Donovan. Either David Cross decided to take
her life for reasons of sexual jealousy or rejection, and did so in a very
cold and calculating way, or else she was murdered for some reason having nothing to do with passion but related to profit or protection. You
have now provided us with the first thin link to either of those other
two motives. You lied to us about the nature of your relationship
because you didn't want us to find out who and what you were, and for
all your protestations maybe you still are. You didn't want us to find out

about this Provisional I.R.A. link. You say that's all over for you? For your sake, I hope it is, because those men do things I would never want on my conscience. Prove it. You're holding something back. What is it?"

Donovan stared at him. "Bloody hell, you *are* Sherlock Holmes!"

"Well?" asked Redmond.

Donovan sighed. "It's a *maybe* something. I don't know for sure meself. It may just be a terrible and ghoulish coincidence, but I had to come here and check it out. You're right, I used to do some shopping over here on this side for The Lads. Not guns. Specialty stuff. Electronic parts for remote controlled bomb detonators, mostly, but also computer gear, surveillance equipment, that kind of thing. Back in June, I was approached by one of my old contacts in Belfast. Fella named Tommy O'Hara. He's with the Real I.R.A. now, the faction that doesn't accept Good Friday and wants to keep on fighting. They wanted to know if now Mary was out of the picture I'd be willing to come over here and look over a new toy they were interested in. A special circuit card for laptop and desktop computers both. It provides a satellite communications uplink that will access a cellular phone grid anywhere in the world, with the right configuration. It's supposed to be used for beepers, so you can sit at your computer here in Chapel Hill and beep yer man in Amsterdam, if ye loike, or send him a message for his palm-top pocket computer, whatever. It sends an electronic signal within a wide radius in the targeted area, in other words, but remotely, from anywhere in the world. You see the possibilities?"

"Ghastly possibilities," whispered Matt in horror.

"Ou, aye. No need any longer to muck about with timing devices at all, at all. The Lads can plant a dozen packages in London with remote controlled radio transponders you can buy in any hobby shop that sells toy airplanes or race cars for kiddies, all wired to a detonator cap and tuned to the right pager signal, then get clean out of the country at their leisure. A few days later, or even weeks later, the top man can sit down in his lounge in Dundalk, pull himself a pint, open his laptop, and blow all twelve packages at once by hitting a few function keys. Or all fifty. Or all hundred. Or pop them off two by two or ten by ten loike a daisy chain of party crackers from Brighton to Buckingham Palace. The Lads were no end keen, let me tell you."

"Why did you have to buy these gadgets under the table if they're going to be commercially available soon?" asked Matt.

"The New World Order spook types at MI5, the CIA, the Mossad and so on are just as aware of the possibilities for politically incorrect usage as you and I," said Donovan. "They made the designers put a marker on each card. It's series of slight sine wave blips in the signal that will leave a log of each page on the satellite's database that can be read from the ground. Here we get into the top secret stuff, I don't know all the details meself and it would probably be beyond me if I did, but basically it's like a fingerprint that gives the manufacturer's batch number and individual hardware identifier for each signal and records the time and the source grid of each page. After the fireworks the high-tech boffins could get an approximate fix on the location of the computer that sent the detonation command. That can be beat by using a laptop from someplace and then easin' yer body on out of the area quick before they figure out what hit them, but that batch number would enable the cops to begin tracing down where the card was sold over the counter, in what machine, so forth and so on. It also means that if they find the card in someone's possession it can be matched and used as evidence, so each card would have to be removed and destroyed after use. The Lads needed a good initial supply of cards that weren't in the tracking system yet."

"And the Carolina connection is?" aske Lonnie Jacobs.

"Well, me and Tommy were good mates once, cellmates in Long Kesh in fact. We ended up doing a round of the pubs for auld lang syne and then coming home with a bottle of Jameson to split between us. He asked after Mary. Now, Mary never completely lost touch with home, and I knew something of what was going on in her life, the basics only, y'understand, but I knew she was working at a place here called Cybertel. I mentioned that to Tommy, and he suddenly went all odd. I asked him what was wrong, and I guess he'd had a few too many pints followed by a few too many drams of Jameson, because he let slip that these uplink cards they wanted me to come over here and obtain were manufactured by Cybertel, and the source for them was an employee there who had access to all the research and prototype gear. Tommy wanted to know if there was any way I could get inside through Mary and bypass this source. The per-card price demanded was a wee bit high in his opinion. I turned him down flat at that point."

"David Cross works in PR & D, product research and development," said Matt in an excited voice. "Did this O'Hara give a name to this person at the company?"

"He wasn't *that* drunk," said Donovan. "It wasn't David Cross, though. He did let slip that much. It was a woman. He didn't give her name."

"Well, Matt, looks like you're right about it being a whole new ball game," said Lonnie. "We know that Mary Donovan was passionately opposed to the Provos and their terrorism, and if she had suspected anything like that going on she would have gone right to the law. It also gives us a whole new field of inquiry, in that our killer may be a woman. We don't think of a woman stabbing another woman in the woods seventy times, that naturally says sex or jealousy or homicidal maniac to us. Trouble is, that lets Cross off the hook."

"No, not at all," mused Redmond. "It means that we now have probable cause to extrapolate something we never had before…an accomplice! A normal woman wouldn't cover up for a man who killed a another woman like that unless she herself had something to gain, i.e. Mary Donovan was about to send her to prison as well as Cross. We need to take this whole thing right from the top again. I know Phil will give me the extra time now. Is that all of it, Donovan?"

"That's all of it," Donovan assured him.

"You came over here to a foreign country to dig into this without a name, without the slightest idea who or what you were looking for?" demanded Redmond. "I don't buy that!"

"Now, did I say I was selling anything?" replied Donovan calmly.

"You don't seriously think I'm going to let you walk out of here and play Lone Ranger with this investigation, do you?" snapped Matt.

"Sure, why would I do that?" asked Donovan innocently. "Besides, I haven't the hat for it." He pointed to Matt's fedora on the table. "I told you, I came here to take Mary home."

"You're going nowhere until I say you can go!" growled Redmond. "Okay, granted, I can't at the moment see that you've broken any laws. It's not a crime to pretend to be a dead woman's brother instead of her husband. But there is a little something called material witness I can use to clang you into a cell if I find it necessary."

"It won't be the first time," replied the Irishman.

"Touché," replied Matt. "But withholding vital information from the police also constitutes obstruction of justice in this country." He sighed. "Dammit, Donovan, you're not the one I'm after! I understand you don't like cops, but play ball with me here! You want Mary's killer and I want Mary's killer! If what you've told me is true and you're out of that crap in the North and you're raising the child of a man you murdered as atonement, then I've got a lot of time for you. But this is my country, my state, my law, and my case. Not yours! Detective Jacobs and I will deal with this, not you! Don't make me come down on you, Mike. Stay in town and stay handy and don't go poking into things. All other things aside, you could gum up the works. We are going to nail the bastard and maybe the bitch who killed your Mary. Stand back and let us do our jobs! I'll keep you posted and as soon as possible I'll let you know how we're doing and when you can take Mary's remains home. Until then stay out of our way. Starting now."

"Now what?" asked Lonnie after the Irishman left.

"Now let's indulge ourselves, hoss," chuckled Matt. "Let's take a ride out to Cybertel and rattle David Cross's cage."

"Aw *right!*" laughed Jacobs.

In the foyer of the Public Safety Building, Michael Donovan spotted a blond young Chapel Hill police officer coming into the building. "Excuse me, constable," he said. "Perhaps you can help me?"

"Here to protect and serve, sir," said the cop. "What kin I do fer you?"

"I'm over here on holiday, and there's something I've always wanted to do if ever I came to America, although sure you'll think it a bit odd of me," said the Irishman jovially, deliberately thickening his accent into Stage Paddy. "I've always wanted to go to a real redneck bar, loike the kind ye see in the pictures, you know, Confederate flags on the wall and sawdust floor and a hundred country oldie-goldie discs on the juke box. Not these yuppie fern bar places I've seen so far, I mean a real Southern workin' man's pub, the koind of place where the bartender keeps a gun behoind the counter to deal with rowdy customers. The koind of place where I might run into David Allen Coe and his mates."

"What we call a scufflin' joint," laughed the young officer. "Uh, sir, with respect, I don't think you want to go to a place like that, and I'm not sure I'm the guy you should be asking for a referral."

"Ah, to be sure, to be sure," said Donovan, smiling beatifically. "Let me put it this way. Where do you get the most calls from on a Saturday night?"

The kid looked around. "Not us, Orange County Sheriff. On Saturday nights they usually park a couple of cars just down from the Dew Drop Inn out at White Cross, to save time. That's just down Highway 54 towards Burlington about ten miles. The woman who runs it is a skank named Helen Lloyd, used to be real heavy into the drug trade in Robeson County. She was the sheriff's girl friend and mule. If it helps your sense of redneck ambience she's got a whole goddamned arsenal behind the bar, and sometimes she needs it to keep things cool.

Don't stay there too long after dark, sir. Funny accents don't go over too well in that honky-tonk. No offense meant."

"None taken, lad, none taken," replied Donovan.

*   *   *

The two detectives located Dave Cross's white Bronco in the parking lot of the huge, impeccably landscaped glass and steel Cybertel complex just off I-40. "There's Dave's OJ-mobile," said Jacobs.

"It's almost lunchtime," said Matt. "Let's park beside his vehicle and hope he comes out to go to Mickey D's or something. If he doesn't, we'll go in. We just want to shake the box gently and see what rattles. Let's not get too rambunctious or he'll start screaming for Mack Terry." They parked their black unmarked Dodge sedan beside the Bronco.

"Here he comes," said Jacobs after a while, scanning the main entrance with field glasses. Cross was a thickset, swarthy young man with a sullen and puffy face and shifty brown eyes. Today he wore a blue baseball cap pulled over his brow. "Just leaving the building and headed this way. Blue jeans and a t-shirt. God, they pay a kid half our age who dresses like that twice as much as you or me!"

"You and me put together. Hey, easy on the jealousy, hoss. The New World Order does have its rewards for those fortunate enough to be of the Seinfeld generation. If you can make them little cyber-thangs go beep and bleep, you get the big bucks," said Matt with a philosophical shrug. "It's a different world than we were born into, Lonnie, make no mistake about that. You and me remember when work meant sweating and hefting and toting and swinging heavy things. We import Mexicans for that nowadays and our sons and daughters work in Dilbertine cubicles and do things we would never have dreamed of. You take away any sense of right and wrong and life can get damned interesting, I'll give 'em that."

"Matt, I wish you'd jest shut the hell up, go ahead and run for office…no, wait, that's a contradiction in terms, isn't it?" said Jacobs.

"I don't believe in working within the system. I want a guillotine in Lafayette Park where Heather can sit and knit while the heads roll," said Matt. Jacobs looked at him, at first unsure that Matt was joking. Then he realized Matt wasn't joking at all, and he decided he'd better change the subject.

"You know, one of the biggest mysteries to me is why Mary Donovan could never see through this creep?" continued Jacobs as they watched David Cross trudge down the front sidewalk towards his truck. "He's a liar, he's a womanizer, now it appears he's a thief and a traitor as well. Five will get you ten that when we find this female accomplice who was helping him sell instruments of murder to international killers he will have been fucking her too, probably at the same time he was squiring Mary Donovan around the Triangle and shopping for her engagement ring. It strikes me that in all the interviews we did over here with everyone who knew them, it was always Mary who was the angel. Young Master Cross here always seemed to evoke distinctly less enthusiasm in his co-workers. The male ones, anyway."

"Oh, sure, they all knew he was scum, and only one of them even tried to warn her, Arnie in Purchasing. I've never been a misogynist," said Matt. "At least not seriously. How could I be? In the middle of my life I had this incredible stroke of luck and I met Heather. How could I hate any species that has Heather among them? But I've always been realistic about women, Lonnie, and one of the things I noticed very early on is that some of the most intelligent, level-headed and creative women I've ever known seem to have this inexplicable blind spot in that one area of their lives. They just can't seem to get that one thing right. You know the situation we scoped over here when we started interviewing. When Mary Donovan walked through that building every man's eye in the place was on her. She had them lining up to ask her out, begging to get close to her, good men, fine young men with talent and energy and great prospects ahead of them. Any one of them would have made her a strong and loving partner. Yet who does she choose? An unstable half-criminal who's plug-ugly to boot. Go figure."

"Maybe she wanted to mother him?" suggested Jacobs.

"Oh, jeez, man, don't *even* go there!" replied Matt with a shudder.

"The one I feel sorry for is old Arnie," said Jacobs.

"Yeah. The one time we know of when Mary Donovan ever turned sour on anybody. The poor old fart falls in love with her and spends months worshipping her from afar. With his big heart and his small head he actually tried to tell her, tried to talk to Mary about this terrible mistake she was making, and she got her Irish up and bit his head off. In public, no less. Well, the girl didn't listen and she paid for that mistake. Dear God, how she paid for it!"

"Paid more than she should have," agreed Jacobs grimly. "Much more. Some lessons in life shouldn't be bought at that cost." Cross stopped to talk to another man at the edge of the parking lot. "You carry a hold-out, Matt?" asked Jacobs casually. Matt looked at him.

"I've thought about it," he sighed. "I've never wound up a case like that before, Lonnie. I've never had to. But in this case?" Matt pulled up his left trouser leg and revealed an ankle holster. ".380 auto, stolen in a burglary from a pawn shop in Jacksonville a year ago. Loaded with hollow-points and totally untraceable. I've thought about it, Lonnie. I just hope I don't have to use it. Mary was a wonderful person. I'd like to end this clean, like she would have wanted it. But by God, I intend to end it! No way in hell I'm letting that girl lie in the ground, here or in Ireland, with her blood unavenged. I promised Tori."

"If it comes to that I'll back you all the way," said Jacobs. "Here he comes." Both detectives got out of their car. "Top o' the mornin' to yez, Davey me lad!" he called out in a fair imitation of Mike Donovan's accent. Cross saw them and started back against the door of his truck. They were on either side of him before he could react.

"How's it been going, Dave?" asked Matt genially.

"I'm not speaking to either of you without my attorney present!" snapped Cross in a panic.

"Oh, we didn't come to see you," said Matt. "We're here on other business. No, no, we didn't come to see you about a butchered girl in Carrboro park at all, Dave. We didn't even come to see if we could persuade you to take that polygraph test you've been avoiding like the plague."

"Polygraphs are not an exact science, they are dependent on the interpretations of the operator, they are not admissible in court and no one can be legally forced to take one," responded Cross by rote.

"Got it off by heart, I see," said Matt. "Mack has you trained real well, son. No, we're here about something else. A lot more minor. Just petty pilferage, really. Seems someone in your company has been doing a little moonlighting. Getting a five-finger discount on some electronic stuff. Some kind of satellite uplink cards for computers that send beeper signals all over the world. The problem is, some of those cards have wound up in the wrong hands across the seas and some really big guys in really big offices in Washington and London are getting really up tight about it. You know, Dave, I hate to admit this, but a lot more official attention is being paid to those missing computer whatsits from your company than is being paid to the destruction of a human life in those long minutes of horror back there in the summer. You remember the long minutes of horror, don't you, Dave? Back there under the bridge, in the dark, in the heat, with no one but God and you to hear her screams and her pleas for mercy?" Matt's voice went cold. "How can a man do something like that, Dave? She loved you with all her heart and soul. How can a man throw something like that away? Destroy an angel like that just to save his own worthless skin?"

"Get away from me!" screamed Cross, ripping open the door of his truck and leaping behind the wheel, fumbling frantically for his keys. *"Get the fuck away from me or I'll call my lawyer! I swear I'll call my lawyer!"* The Bronco's engine roared to life and Cross nearly ran over

Lonnie Jacobs' foot as he hurled the vehicle into reverse. He was out of the parking lot and roaring down the interstate before Jacobs stopped laughing.

"I'd say we scored a hit there, Matt!" he chuckled.

"If this were a movie we'd have enough manpower to have that asshole followed twenty-four seven," said Matt. "Maybe even a helicopter. Since this ain't a movie we've got zip in the way of manpower, so we'll just have to hope he goes running to his accomplice, rattles the hell out of her.."

"And doesn't kill her," put in Jacobs.

"And doesn't kill her," agreed Matt, "And in the meantime we can hopefully make an educated guess as to who she is and do some rattling ourselves. Back to the Batcave!" Matt opened his cellular phone and called his wife. "Hi, Watson. You haven't taken any Weirdness Leave for a while, so you figure your boss could give you the rest of the day? Lonnie and me could use some help on Donovan."

"Kris and I have a rule," said Heather. "I can have flexi-time to participate in my wild and exciting secret life with the Southern Sherlock Holmes, but afterwards I have to do a long lunch with her and tell her all about it. By the by, any chance you could set Lonnie up with Kris? She's only a year older than I am and her kids are at college and she needs something besides two cats and my second-hand adventures in her life."

"I'll inquire," said Matt with a chortle.

"What do you need?"

"Can you meet Lonnie and me over at the Chapel Hill cop shop ASAP? I need somebody who's good on the computer and understands accounting and inventory software. I need you to go over Mary Donovan's office and work records."

"What are you looking for?" asked Heather.

"Motive," said Matt. "The real reason why Mary Donovan died in those woods that night."

*   *   *

The Dew Drop Inn was fairly empty in the early afternoon. There were only a handful of hardened barflies and the odd off duty trucker from a nearby motel sucking on the black bottles of Budweiser and Coors or the clear Millers. The juke box was playing an Allman Brothers oldie, *I'm No Angel*. Donovan finished his Bud and beckoned the woman behind the bar. Helen Lloyd was forty-something and undeniably handsome in a country kind of way. She was wearing a denim shirt tied up around her ribs below a fine rack and tight jeans around a still slim and hard body. The face was even harder; long flower-child like brown hair threaded with gray could not disguise the cold eyes. As the woman took away the empty bottle and brought Donovan another he saw the homemade tattoo between her thumb and forefinger. He almost decided to ask her about the significance of the tattoo in the subculture of Southern womens' prisons, then he decided he didn't want to know. As she plunked down the beer bottle he slid three crisp $100 bills across the bar.

"Hey, if you'd stuck around until closing time and played your cards right, you mighta got it fer free," she said with a sultry smile.

"Now, don't take this wrong, lass, but I hear ye've something behind the bar there which interests me a wee bit more that yer undeniably lovely self," said Donovan, hamming up the accent again. "Some iron-mongery, if ye get me drift." Suspicion immediately flared in her eyes. "Lass, earlier today a fella told me he could tell that I was either one of his kind or one of t'other. That fella was a cop, and he decided that I wasn't one of his kind. I'm not, ye know."

Helen looked at him and decided quickly. "Go take a leak while I think about it." Donovan got up and eyed the bills. "Don't worry, they'll be here when you get back, or if they ain't you'll find something else."

"So long as it's not pointing at me," said Donovan with a chilly smile. As tough as she was, Helen read the signs and understood she'd best play straight with this one. Donovan went to the bathroom, relieved himself, washed his hands, and returned to the bar. When he got back the three C-notes were gone and a plastic carrier bag rested by his beer bottle.

".45-caliber Browning, extra clip and a box of APC shells," Helen said. "That's all I can spare. Get rid of it after you use it. I know it's hot and I got no guarantee it ain't killed nobody. If it has then the cops will have the ballistics on file and you might end up in even more trouble than whatever you're planning. I also got this," she said, hefting a heavy short barreled shotgun. She jacked a round into the chamber with an expert motion, single-handed. "Just in case you figured on test firing it in here. I hope not. I'd sure love to give you something beside a load of double-ought buck, sugar."

"Sure the thought never crossed me moind. You're a lady of distinction," said Donovan with a bow. He picked up the heavy bag and his beer and turned to go.

"Hey, Mick," she called. "You got time and you ain't too hot, come on back around midnight. That's closing time. I got a jacuzzi in my trailer out back."

"Heaven send the day!" he returned politely as he headed put the door.

"Now, was that a yes or a no?" she wondered aloud as she turned back to the beer cooler.

*   *   *

Matt commandeered an empty watch commander's office and a computer in the Public Safety Building, and by the time Heather arrived he had several cardboard file boxes of material on the desk. He ran down the latest for her. "Heather, I need you to go over Mary's work files and try to find anything in there that might indicate that she knew anything about these satellite uplink cards going out the back door at Cybertel into the grubby rookers of the Provos," said Matt. "We skimmed over this during the first few weeks but it was mostly Greek to us, we were concentrating on a sexual or jealousy motive and we had no idea what we might be looking for. I called the head of facility out there and after some hemming and hawing about proprietary company information I got out of him that what we're looking for is something called a PUP-12 card, which means Prototype Uplink Protocol Number Twelve card. I also told him to expect a visit from the FBI, which really made his day."

"Better than us getting a visit from the FBI," said Heather.

"One would hope, in view of the way our visits usually turn out. All of Mary's backed up computer files from her desk are on these diskettes. If you can go through the computer stuff, Lonnie and I will start wading through this second box, which is all paper."

"I'll search each diskette for PUP-12 and also for Protoype Uplink Protocol," said Heather, sliding a diskette into the computer. "Uh, Matt…I need her password. Any idea what it might be?"

"Try Brendan," said Matt. Heather typed it in.

"Bingo," she said softly as the screen came up. "God, that poor woman. I hope we can help her." Her fingers tapped away on the keys while Matt and Lonnie spread out the paper files. After a while she said, "One of Mary's jobs was to check the shipping and inventory records of various items against invoices, both received and paid. Let's say Company X in Baltimore ordered fifty or a hundred of these cards wholesale. She had to record the delivery receipt number from UPS or FedEx, the invoice number when it was received and mark it off when it was paid, with the check number. She also had to match it up with a picking ticket, i.e. the warehouse hand who pulled the fifty items off the shelves and packed them, plus a combined packing list and waybill number, plus match the stock quantities in her records with a monthly physical inventory which she herself and others on her team performed in the warehouse. Every quarter she had to balance the whole thing out and make sure everything matched down to the last item and the last penny. It's a pretty meticulous system and although it could be faked out, it would take a lot of bogus numbers, and a sharp accountant or bookkeeper could spot discrepancies if they were on the ball."

"From what we know of her, Mary was always on the ball where her work was concerned," grunted Lonnie.

"Cross wouldn't have to steal the components from the warehouse, I shouldn't think," said Matt. "He was in R & D, which should have given him some kind of access to the actual manufacturing floor for quality control or something of the kind. Heather, see if you can tell if there was any record kept of the number of cards manufactured and the ones that were approved and sent to the warehouse for sale and shipment, and if there are any gaping discrepancies."

Heather tapped and scanned for a while. Lonnie's pager beeped. "Hey, that's the front desk." Jacobs picked up a phone and punched an intercom button. "Yeah, this is Lonnie, I'm back here in Office Six. What's up?" A woman's voice spoke on the phone. "Yeah, he's here. OK, patch it through." Jacobs handed the receiver to Matt. "Your call to Belfast. Sounds like you got the R.U.C. working late tonight. It must be past eight there."

"The Special Branch never sleeps," said Matt. "Hello? Who's this? Inspector MacCrimmon? Yes, Matt Redmond here, North Carolina SBI. I appreciate the call when a fax or an e-mail would have served the turn, sir, and I appreciate your staying late to help us out," he added diplomatically. He listened for a while. "Yes, sir, I thought that's what we'd hear, but it had to be checked out. Yes, Donovan's over here now. Inspector, were you able to get anything on the whereabouts of one Tommy or Thomas O'Hara, both his present whereabouts and in August of this year?" As an afterthought Matt turned on the speakerphone.

"Ou, aye, and that's what caught me eye when I saw yer fax," came the Ulsterman's voice. "Passport control in Dublin checked Tommy onto Aer Lingus Flight 602 to New York on August the first. He re-entered the Republic at Shannon Airport on August 8th. Just in time for the

Marching Season up here. A bould Fenian like Tommy wouldn't want to miss the chance to mix it up with the Apprentice Boys."

"So O'Hara was in this country in exactly the right window for the Mary Donovan homicide. Where is he now?" asked Redmond. "Can you tell if by any chance he's back in the United States? On a shopping trip, perhaps?"

"Afraid not," replied MacCrimmon. "As a matter of fact, I know exactly where he is. He's lying in a freezer locker down at the Queen's University pathology department's morgue. What's left of him. He was found on some waste ground in the Ardoyne on August twenty-second. His great ungainly carcass is now evidence for the Crown, until we decoide to give it up as a bad job."

"August twenty-second?" snarled Jacobs. "So Donovan knew this O'Hara character was dead? He neglected to mention that little detail this morning. That Mick is still holding out on us, dammit!"

"What happened to O'Hara, Inspector?" asked Matt urgently. "Kneecapped by his own people, by any chance?"

"No, no bullet wounds. O'Hara was beaten to death," replied MacCrimmon. "Beaten to death with fists and brass knuckles. Must a taken a number of pretty big lads. Tommy was no elf, and he was a hard man himself in his own right."

"Or one equally large, equally hard, and very angry and vengeful man," said Matt.

"Mad Mike, is it?" said MacCrimmon. "I'll tell yez this, Redmond. Michael Donovan would tear the heart out of anybody he thought harmed a hair on Mary's head, and serve it up in an Irish stew. If there's anybody over there who fits that description, ye'd better find him before Mad Mike Donovan does, or ye'll be gathering him up in fragments, and they won't be from a bomb blast."

"Mad Mike," sighed Redmond after MacCrimmon hung up. "Beautiful. Just beautiful."

"Matt," said Heather. "I think I may have found something. Take a look at this." The two detectives leaned over the computer screen. "These are Mary's Lotus Notes. They're kind of cryptic, but see here. May twelfth, 'PUP-12 3 down FDT 33876'. Now on May nineteenth, one week later. 'PUP-12 down 3 FDT 33996'. May thirty-first, 'PUP-12 down 3 FDT 34298'. FDT means Floor Delivery Ticket, the document used when the finished products are handed over to the warehouse for onward shipping. At that point they have passed QCA, Quality Control Assurance, i.e. they have been tested and approved by a duly qualified engineer from Research and Development as fully functional and salable."

"Can you pull up copies of those tickets?" asked Matt eagerly. "Who was the R & D person who signed off on them?"

Heather diddled and tapped and clicked the mouse for a minute or so. "There they are. Mary copied them onto her own drive because she was going to query them, I'll bet. 33876, QCA Supervisor D. Cross. 33996 QCA Supervisor D. Cross. 34298 QCA Supervisor D. Cross. Matt, you were right. Cross signed off on all of these. He was stealing the things three at a time over a period of weeks, before they got to the warehouse."

"Donovan told us he was approached in June with the I.R.A.'s proposal that he come over here and buy the things and presumably arrange for them to be smuggled into Ireland," pointed out Jacobs. "Donovan turned him down. I believe that part of his story."

"So do I," agreed Matt. "Donovan turned them down, so they sent O'Hara instead. O'Hara arrived in August, and Mary Donovan somehow stumbled onto the deal. She probably knew O'Hara at least by sight from Belfast since he and Donovan were Provo associates and Donovan lived next door to her in the housing estate. Hell, maybe she recognized Cross and O'Hara meeting with one another and put two and two together. So the bastards killed her."

"Matt, I think you've got it!" cried Heather in excitement.

"You got it for us, Watson," he said, kissing her gently. "Keep on digging."

While Heather tapped on the keyboard Jacobs took Matt aside. "Matt, I grant you we've come a hell of a long way in the past twenty-four hours, and when Heather finishes we'll have enough for a warrant on Cross, even if it's not for the murder yet. But there's still a hell of a lot of gaps here. How exactly was the murder carried out, and by whom? Instead of one killer we now have three possibles, Cross himself, this I.R.A. goon O'Hara, or the as yet unknown female accomplice. And what an odd way to go about it! Why not simply make her disappear or just shoot her?"

"What have we spent the past three and a half months spinning our wheels on, Lonnie?" asked Matt. "We have assumed it was a sex or jealousy thing. Incorrectly, it would appear. That's what they wanted us to think. They wanted it to look like a hot-blooded crime of passion or maybe a serial killer to turn our attention completely away from the coldest of motives, profit and protection. So poor Mary didn't even get the mercy of a bullet in the head. She died the hard way to make it look good. Those swine!"

"Then why didn't Cross give himself a hell of a lot better alibi, if he had two willing accomplices?" argued Jacobs.

"What the hell do you think the long-distance phone call was for? Hell, he may even have spotted the Highway Patrol car and deliberately weaved a bit so he'd get pulled over. Why was he coming from the Burlington side of the turn-off?" ruminated Matt. "There's where the answer lies. He was coming *from* someplace on that side. But why? Where was he, and what was he doing?"

"Meeting with one of the accomplices?" suggested Jacobs. "But why? We know at least one of them was in the process of murdering Mary Donovan at about that time."

"But do we? Do we really know that?" asked Matt slowly. "The time frame we have for Mary's death from the medical examiner is roughly between midnight and two in the morning. Because the party broke up around midnight and Cross and Mary were gone significantly before that, and because it was hot and the body once dead would have cooled slowly, we have always looked at the high end of the time window. We assumed that she was somehow lured away from the cookout and killed either while the tag end of the party was still in progress or after everyone had just left. But suppose she was actually killed at the low end of the time frame, around two A.M.? That gives Cross time to finish his phone call and go back to Carrboro park."

"So in the meanwhile she hung around in the woods and the dark without even a flashlight, battling mosquitos and chiggers and risking copperheads for a good two or three hours, waiting for her killer? Why?" asked Jacobs.

"Or she left the party, either with Cross or without him, and later on, after everyone was gone, *she came back.* Or was brought back!" said Matt.

"That's almost three hours unaccounted for, Matt," warned Jacobs. "In a court of law we're going to have to account for it."

"There's another three hour period of her last day unaccounted for," said Matt. "The time from five o'clock when she left Cybertel and eight o'clock when she and Cross appeared at the cookout together. You're right, Lonnie. There's some yawning gaps here. Let's see if we can start filling them."

"How?" asked Jacobs.

"While Heather is doing her cyber-thing we need to get back to those interviews we did at Cybertel and start a major hunt for that female accomplice. I don't know how we'll spot her, but let's give it a shot. We need her to fill in some of those gaps."

"Question," spoke up Heather. "While we are sitting here, where is Mad Mike and what is he doing?"

"Most likely doing the same thing we're doing, hunting down the female accomplice," said Jacobs. "I think she can provide quite a few of our missing links for him as well as for us. If O'Hara didn't give Donovan a name during the pub crawl he quite likely did so during his final session with the brass knuckles."

"Let's get to those files and hope we can figure out who the hell she is before she turns up in fragments," said Matt grimly.

*   *   *

Brenda Hennessey got home from work to her apartment at about five thirty. It was almost dark outside now. She was a short and voluptuous woman of thirty-five, with neatly clipped brown hair and a not unattractive face. Brenda had allowed her parents and her family to convince her from childhood that she was an ugly and ungainly girl, and she had never overcome that idea. The result was that she was a sucker in every sense of the term for any man who would offer her a kind word, and David Cross had offered her more than kind words. David Cross had begun as Brenda's Apollo, and even though by now she had figured out he was only a common or garden variety satyr, and a homicidal one at that, she would no more have gone to the police and turned him in than she would have jumped off a cliff. Once a week for the last year, David spent the night in her apartment and made long, ecstatic love to her, and she would do nothing that might discontinue those sessions. Brenda alone of all Mary Donovan's acquaintances had hated the Irish girl, and in her less sane moments she considered Mary's murder to be a perverse testimony of David's love. In her saner moments, Brenda understood that being involved with a murderer was not a good life decision, and she also understood that there was a strong possibility that she would be murdered herself because she knew far too much to be good for her health. The thought both terrified her and turned her on. She knew that she was sick and could not find within herself the slightest desire to change or to save herself. Because what lay ahead? She would be forty in a few years, and what then? What if it turned out to be David or nothing? Besides, as dangerous as her involvement with this situation was, at least she wasn't ordinary.

Something extraordinary happened to Brenda this November evening; she found a strange man in her apartment. He stepped up behind her while she was at the kitchen sink, placed a hand over her mouth, and pressed the muzzle of a pistol gently into her hair and against her head right behind her right ear. His voice was low and even, and his accent was one she had heard before. "Don't move and don't scream, Brenda," the intruder said. He removed his hand from her mouth and grasped her hair with his left hand, holding her motionless against the sink with his body and keeping the pistol barrel against her head.

"Tommy?" gasped Brenda. "Tommy, you're back! Tommy, I didn't tell anyone anything! I swear it! Why are you doing this?"

"Mr. O'Hara has been unavoidably detained in Belfast," said the Irishman. "My name is Michael Donovan. A name ye'll be familiar with, so I hear. Tommy told me about you, Brenda. He also told me what happened to Mary Donovan." Brenda shivered, then surrendered. *Well, at least I won't have to worry about the big four-oh,* she said to herself with resignation.

"You're going to kill me, then," she said, a statement rather than a question.

"I don't know. I haven't decided yet. Do you have tea?"

"Yes," said Brenda. "I even have a proper teapot, a silver one. Most Americans don't. It was my grandmother's. She brought it from Clare in 1925. It was a wedding gift."

"Make tea," he ordered, releasing her and sitting down at the kitchen table. She turned around and saw a tall man with a heavy body and a grim square face, red hair slightly tinged with white at the temples. His huge hand rested over the automatic on the table. She glanced fleetingly at the doorway into the living room. "Don't," he advised her. "I meant what I said, lass. I haven't decided yet. You still have a chance if you'll do it my way. No promises, just that you still have a chance. Try to run, or come at me with a butcher knife or some such lark as that, and you've none. Now make the tea." Brenda took out the teapot and big A & P teabag, filled the kettle with water and turned on the front gas ring on the stove. She set the kettle on the flame and sat down at the table, looking at the gun.

"Damn," she said softly. "One minute you're hauling in groceries and putting your yogurt in the fridge, and then in the next second it's the end, the ultimate moment that you've been heading toward all your life, for every hour and every second since you were born. I never really understood that it can happen so *fast.*"

"It can so," said Donovan. "The Bible says that no man knows the day nor the hour. Are you afraid?"

"Yes, but not nearly as afraid as I would have expected," mused Brenda, surprised. "I think I always knew in the back of my mind that night would catch up with me. I thought it would be the police, though, and then prison."

"It won't be prison, lass. Ye've got me word on that. That's one thing I don't do, to anyone, for any reason," promised Donovan.

"Thank you. Okay, what now?" she asked.

"I ask the questions and you answer them," said Donovan.

"You know about Tommy, and you probably know there's someone else involved, an American man. I won't betray him and I won't help you find him or trap him."

"David Cross," said Donovan.

"Yes. I won't hurt him. You'll have to shoot me."

"Do you really mean that, lass?" asked Donovan.

"Somewhat to my own amazement, yes, I do mean it," said Brenda with a tight smile.

"Then he's a luckier man by far than he deserves. I just want to clear up a few things in me own mind. Did you know they were going to kill her before they did it?"

"No," said Brenda, shaking her head. "I know you'll think I'm lying to save myself, but no, I didn't."

"Would it have made any difference if you had known?" asked Donovan.

"I've thought about that," said Brenda. "I don't know. I hope it would have done. I hope I'm not quite that bad a person. I hated Mary because she had David and I didn't. Or let's say she had him in public all the time and I only had him once a week in there in the bedroom. I didn't want her dead. But I'm responsible, Mr. Donovan. I know that and I'm not going to pretend otherwise or excuse what I did. I was part of the deception."

"The deception that got her out in those woods in the dark of night, aye, that much I know. Why did you do that, Brenda? Why did you go along with them? You're telling me that the thought they might mean her harm never entered your head at all, at all?"

"Maybe I didn't want to know. From what I can recall I hoped you would persuade her to come back to you and the child and take her back to Ireland, and I'd get David on the rebound."

"I was home in Belfast. It was O'Hara she met in those woods," said Donovan woodenly.

"I know that now. I didn't then. All I can say in my defense is that I didn't follow through with the plan like I was supposed to do. I didn't tell the sheriff's detective or that SBI guy with the hat and the cigar anything about what happened that night, or earlier. I was supposed to give them your name with a story about how Mary confided in me that her ex-husband from Ireland was over here trying to break her and David up, and she was afraid of him. I just dummied up instead. At least they didn't come looking for you in Ireland."

"That a New York accent?" asked Donovan.

"Massachusetts," said Brenda "Woostuh."

"That answers my next question. Why did you agree to help Cross steal those uplink cards?" asked Donovan. "Don't tell me. Your grandfather was some bowzer named Sean or Cathal..."

"Dinney," said Brenda.

"Some ould bowzer named Dinney who told you all about the glories of Easter Week and sang ye to sleep with The Rising of the Moon over yer cradle and cursed the Black and Tans over his Guinness all his life, always prattling on about the glorious green land of saints and scholars that he himself ran away from as fast as he could jump into steerage, tradin' the green land for the green dollar. So ye grew up with the whole Boston Irish taradiddle bunged down yer gullet? Probably did Irish folk dancin' in the little embroidered green costume to the bangin' of a outta tune piana in the Knights of Columbus hall when ye was a colleen of eight..."

"Actually, my folks started me at six," giggled Brenda, trying to suppress her trembling. The mouth of the pistol barrel on the table looked as wide as the Holland Tunnel and she seemed to see the lead bullet hurtling down it to smash her head and make all dark forever. "I did it until I was sixteen and started to put on weight. I've still got my last dancing outfit somewhere in a closet."

"So that was it? The Patriot Game? Four Green Fields and all that shite?" demanded Donovan.

"That was part of it," admitted Brenda. "I was raised to believe it was always my duty as an Irishwoman to help The Lads if I ever got the chance."

"Do you understand that you're not Irish anymore? That none of yez are?" asked Donovan curiously.

"Yes, I think we all know that deep down. But getting back to your question, mostly it was because I am the kind of woman who, once she chooses a man, gives him anything and everything he wants. David can have me for a doormat for the rest of my life if he wants me, however long or short that life may be," she said, looking at the gun. "That's just the way it is. Not much of a plea for mercy to a man whose wife I helped to murder, is it?"

"More of a defense than you think," said Donovan.

"Good enough for you not to kill me?" asked Brenda.

"I've a few more questions," said the Irishman. The kettle started to whistle. She got up and poured the boiling water into the tea pot, put it on the table on a coaster, and took two mugs out of the cupboard along with a sugar bowl and a box of artificial sweetener. She took a cardboard container of milk out of the fridge and started to pour. Donovan stopped her.

"Ah, no. You Yanks never let it sit and steep long enough. You drink it weak as water. Proper tea should be as black and strong as coffee, ye should be able to taste it over the milk and sugar. Ulster tea anyways. Don't know what kind of horse piss ye drink down there in Clare."

"My grandpa and grandma used to drink it really strong like that," she said.

"I was able to get some of the details from the late Mr. O'Hara, but I want the whole story from you now," said Donovan.

"The late Mr. O'Hara?" asked Brenda, looking up in alarm. "You said he was detained in Belfast, I thought you meant he was arrested."

"He's been detained until Gabriel blows his horn on Judgement Day," said Donovan.

"I won't say I'm sorry," she said. "He scared me."

"He was a scary fella altogether, so he was," agreed Donovan. "Brenda, you're doing smashingly in the honesty department so far. I want you to tell me exactly what happened that night." He started pouring out the tea with his left hand, his right never leaving the grip of the Browning,

"Mary knew that the PUP cards were going missing. She found out in some kind of internal inventory audit she did. She actually asked David to track down what was happening to them!" said Brenda with a bitter laugh, sipping her strong tea, black. "She thought I was the one who was taking them. I work in the warehouse and I signed for them from David. He had to have my co-operation, to cover for him so no one in the warehouse would notice the missing cards when they were shelved and binned. It simply never occurred to her that David was in on it. Just like it never occurred to her that he was sleeping with me. Me and Sally Freeman and Jennifer Palmieri and a few others. After all, he was just this perfect gentleman in every way, right? This happy funny guy who was always teasing her and fooling around."

"The most poisonous snakes often have the brightest colors," said Donovan. "Why do you stay with a man like that, not only knowing he's playing ye false, but who with?"

"Because I love him, and because something in me enjoys pain and humiliation," said Brenda. "That's the best explanation I've ever been able to come up with for myself."

"I'm sorry. Go on."

"David met with Mary someplace after work that day and gave her a long song and dance. He said he had talked to me and forced the story out of me. How I was this misguided Noraid type who thought I was helping drive the hated Brits from the Fourth Green Field and so on. He was totally shocked and horrified, of course! Needless to say, so was Mary, since she actually came from the Six Counties and she'd lost her father and her boyfriend and God knows how many others to the Troubles. Yes, Tommy O'Hara gave us the whole 411 on her. Only I didn't know he was Tommy O'Hara then. He told me his name was Michael Donovan. I thought he was you."

"He and I were of an age and a size, and the same hair and eyes," agreed Donovan. "When you described him to Mary after six years she would have figured 'twas me all right. Go on."

"Mary and David slipped away from the cookout at the park that night and she followed him out here in her car. Mary came here that night on a mission of mercy," said Brenda. "She came here to talk me out of selling illegal high tech to the Provos. David bowed out and said he knew we girls had things to discuss, and he left. Now I know he left to establish his alibi. He was going to make a bunch of long distance calls from his apartment to show he was there while O'Hara was killing her. She sat here at this very kitchen table and for two hours she told me what I was involved in. What it was like to grow up with murder and hatred and violence and destruction all around her, with soldiers on the street and children being taught how to throw rocks and make Molotov cocktails at age ten. And funeral after funeral after funeral so the undertaker was the richest man in the community."

"She told you what you were involved in, and you still went on with it?" asked Donovan grimly.

"Yes. I know that's bringing me closer to a bullet, but I won't lie to you of all people about this. Especially since I was the one who betrayed her. Finally I played my trump card. I told her the name of my I. R. A. contact who was over here to buy the PUP cards. Commandant Michael Donovan. I even said something like, 'He actually has the same last name as you, Mary! Maybe he's a relative. Maybe you could talk to him for me and ask him to let me off the hook.'"

"Commandant, was I?" muttered Donovan. "How foine it was of O'Hara to give me a promotion! And how did she take it?"

"She went absolutely white," said Brenda. "She kind of stuttered that there were a lot of Donovans in Ireland, it was a very common name. And you see, that was what convinced her that I was telling the truth. She never mentioned anything at all about you or the child, to anyone. Tommy told us all about that, but she had no idea Tommy was here. Therefore in her mind David couldn't possibly have put me up to it, because she was sure he didn't know about her past. By the by, I think that's when David decided to help O'Hara kill her. When he found out she was already married to you. It hurt his pride."

"He didn't know I got a letter from her a month or so before," Donovan told her. "A letter telling me she'd found someone else and asking if I would agree to a divorce. I had already written her back and told her to send me whatever papers needed signing and I'd sign them. She was going to wait to tell him until after it was done. Go on. What happened after you told her about the bould and wicked Commandant Donovan?"

"Then the phone rang, Tommy O'Hara of course, supposedly to talk to me about handing over the cards and getting my money for them. Using your name. Impeccably timed," said Brenda.

"That was Tommy. His sense of timing was always spot on," agreed Donovan. "It was one of the things that made him the best we had in our brigade. He knew enough details about me and her to make it convincing enough for a brief conversation, and I suppose one Belfast accent sounds pretty much the same as another on the telephone, especially if you've not heard one for six years. I think I can take it from here."

"She wanted to meet him, to meet…you," said Brenda. "She gave him directions to the Carrboro park. That was her idea, and of course it played right into his hands. But she was afraid of…of you…so…."

"So she called Cross at home," said Donovan. "She asked David Cross to meet her there and be with her. To protect her. To protect her from me. She wouldn't go without him. She wanted the man she loved and who she thought loved her with her, then she'd feel safe. So instead of one murderer, she walked into those woods with two."

"Yes," said Brenda.

"And you let her leave here for this meeting with death in the darkness, and you said nothing?" he asked softly.

"I said nothing to her. I swear to you I did not know they meant to kill her, but you probably don't believe that, and in any case I was a part of it. Michael, whatever you decide to do to me, I am guilty."

"O'Hara told me one last detail," said Donovan, beginning to shake. *"She thought it was me!* When O'Hara came out of the woods in his jersey and balaclava and gloves and then it was stabbing and stabbing and stabbing she cried out to that dog Cross to save her, but he ran away, and then it was my name she cried out as she begged for it to stop, it was me she begged for mercy, to let her live for Brendan's sake. *She thought it was me!* Oh, cruel God of mortal punishment for my sins, *she thought it was me!* O'Hara told me her last words on earth. At the end he tried to buy his own wretched life from me with those words, may he burn in hell. As he was covering her up with leaves and dirt and branches, she whispered, "Michael, I forgive you, and I will ask God to have mercy on your soul.' So he stabbed her a few more times and left her there for the animals of the forest and the worms to eat. With her last breath, that angel on earth forgave me."

Brenda sat it silent horror for a while. "A forgiveness I have no right to ask from you," she whispered after a while. "Do what you have to do, Michael."

"Do you go to church?"

"Not for a long time. How could I?" she asked.

"Do you remember enough to perform the Act of Contrition?"

She began to cry then, in terror and shame and anguish. "I...I think so..." She got up from the chair and knelt on the kitchen floor, made the Stations of the Cross on herself and stuttered through the ritual. While she was stumbling through the words she heard him get up and move behind her. When she was finished she said "That stupid crack in the floor."

"What?" asked Donovan in a stupor.

"That long crack in the linoleum just in front of the sink. I keep bitching at the apartment manager to fix it but he never does. Now my last sight on earth is going to be that stupid crack in my kitchen floor. Michael, before God I am truly sorry for the pain that I have brought into your life. Go ahead. Do it." She closed her eyes, sobbing convulsively. After a long time Donovan moved back around the table and sat down. He set the pistol down on the table top with a clunk.

"When I was young I thought I could never get enough of vengeance," he said. "Vengeance was my meat, my drink, my waking, my sleeping, the air that I breathed, the song that I sang in the pub, the coal smoke that hangs in the air over Belfast, the sky above and the mud below. Every day there was more of it to be had, one of theirs for one of ours, two of theirs for two of ours, any of theirs any way we could get them. Mary saw that in me and she ran from it, until a day came when it all overwhelmed her and she couldn't think straight any more. I moved in and I took advantage of her in her weakness and her confusion. Despite what I told that cigar-chewing copper this morning I know well that it was a despicable wrong that I did to that angel, joining her purity to my loathsome corruption. But of that despicable thing something good came. That first wonderful magical night, when Mary came to me as my wife and I saw that ring, my ring on her left hand, she not only made me want to change, but she revealed to me that I *could* change. She married a cunning beast of prey that had sought her out, but the next morning she had as her husband a man who wanted more than anything to *be* a man, a real man, for her and her child. You don't have me to thank for your life, lass. Thank Mary. From her grave she gave me mercy, and now I pass it on to you"

Brenda stood up, too bewildered and overcome to think. "What now?" she asked.

"Any chance of some more tea?" asked Donovan.

*　　　　　　　*　　　　　　　*

"Brenda Hennessey," said Heather, peering into the computer monitor.

"What?" asked Matt, looking up from an interview report.

"I've found five floor delivery tickets for May and June, each short three PUP cards, for a total of fifteen cards," said his wife. "They're each signed off on by David Cross for quality control and Supervisor Six for the warehouse receiving section. Supervisor Six is a woman named Brenda Hennessey, according to the employee directory here. Female, Irish name, maybe grew up in an Irish-American house full of pictures of the Pope and Eamon de Valera side by side on the wall and a stereo full of Wolfe Tone and Clancy Brothers tapes and jumped at the chance to lend a hand to the Bold Lads of the Mountain and Glen."

"You know feminine intuition is like the polygraph, inadmissible in court," put in Lonnie.

"Bullshit. Tell you what, Lonnie, if I'm right you have to come to dinner at our house and meet someone for me."

"And if you're wrong?" asked Lonnie.

"Then I'll just tell her you're gay. Seriously, guys, this has to be the female accomplice. Someone had to make sure that the short batches got onto the shelves quickly and disappeared into the general inventory without anyone noticing the fifteen missing cards."

"We interviewed Brenda Hennessey," said Matt, pulled out her report. "Apartment 3-D, Westridge Condos. Just off Highway 54, one mile west of the bypass. Cross was coming from that direction when he was pulled over by the state trooper. Let's go, Lonnie." The two detectives stood up and began pulling on their coats.

"Matt!" said Heather urgently.

"No!" he said. "I mean it, Heather. You stay here. Mad Mike or Cross or both may well have gotten to her first, and we may find her dead, or we may find her watching Dan Rather. But if it breaks bad you can't be there."

"And what if this is your aces and eights?" she asked bleakly.

"Then give Tony a call in Italy," he replied. "That's a semi-serious request."

"Tony's an entirely serious kind of guy," said Heather.

"Yeah, ask the FBI." He leaned over and kissed her, and whispered in her ear, "You know."

"I know," she whispered back, her lip trembling. "Take care, Matt."

"What's aces and eights?" asked Lonnie as they rode through Carrboro in the early evening darkness, heading for Highway 54 West.

"Wild Bill Hickock, the greatest gunfighter in the West, or so he said of himself. It wasn't outlaws or bounty hunters or Indians that got him. It was a punk kid drifter named Jack McCall, a fumble-fingered amateur who shot him in the back during a poker game in Deadwood, South Dakota. When he was shot Wild Bill was holding a pair of aces and a pair of eights. Ever since it's been called the Dead Man's Hand. You know I've had a kind of wild and woolly past career?"

"So I heard," said Jacobs. "I was always curious about that story about a certain ear…"

"That wasn't me, actually. It was a gift from a friend. It's in a jar of formaldehye in my safety deposit box. But Heather and I both know that if I do buy it, it will most likely be from some strung-out street punk with a .25-caliber junk gun who pops me in the head while I'm tying my shoe or some such petty shit. Or some creep like Dave Cross who gets in a lucky shot."

"Cross I wouldn't worry about," said Jacobs. "Mr. Donovan is a different kettle of fish. Let's hope his lucky charms aren't magically delicious tonight."

*   *   *

They sat in Brenda's living room, he in a chair and she curled up on the sofa. "I still won't help you get David," she said. "I'm sorry. I know I owe you my life now and I should be willing to repay the debt. I'll repay it however you want, except for that one thing. I can't betray him."

"No need, lass," said Donovan. "I won't be needing your help there at all, at all. I can find him meself."

"Don't you think it's possible Mary's mercy might extend to David too?" she asked.

"It would indeed. But mine won't."

Matt Redmond and Lonnie Jacobs turned into the Westridge Condos parking lot. "That's building D. Apartment three was upstairs, if I remember correctly. We interviewed her there. Yeah, I see a light on. She's home."

"She has a visitor," said Lonnie. "White Ford Bronco at ten o'clock." The sheriff's officer pulled up behind the truck and shined his flashlight on the license plate. "Yep, that's Mr. C.'s ride all right."

Suddenly the doorbell rang. Brenda got up and looked through the peephole. She turned around. "It's David!" she whispered. "Michael, please! Please let me talk to him! Let me give him a chance to go turn himself in, or run away, or something! I know I don't have the right to ask you for anything, but please!"

Donovan sighed. "I'll be in the kitchen. Get rid of him, don't let him past the door. If we meet then I do what I came here to do, but if you can get him to go away I promise I won't go after him tonight. That's all I can give yez, lass."

"I'll try," said Brenda. Donovan stepped into the kitchen out of sight. Brenda opened her front door.

David Cross shot her.

Brenda saw the snub-nosed .38 in his hand just in time to try to slam the door, and it knocked the barrel downward sufficiently so that the bullet missed her heart and pierced her stomach. She staggered back into the living room, her face shocked and agonized, looking at the blood spurting and bubbling out from the front of her sweater. Cross stepped inside the apartment and shot her again as she raised her hands instinctively to ward him off and the bullet went through her palm, deflecting just enough to miss her head by a centimeter. "You ratted me out, you bitch!" he howled.

Donovan leaped out of the kitchen, roaring wordlessly. He didn't even think to use the .45 to shoot with, instead gripping it in his hand and smashing it into Cross's face and all over his body, pounding him like a jack hammer with the gun. Brenda was screaming *Why, David why? I love you, why did you do it?* until she passed out on the floor. For long seconds Cross himself screamed in terror as Donovan beat him bloody, then he managed to break away and flee out the door and down the iron stairs. Donovan stood in the door of the apartment. *"Bastard!"* he bellowed. Cross raised the .38 and fired twice, the bullets plowing into the doorframe beside the Irishman and sending splinters of wood popping and biting into his face. Donovan belatedly remembered that guns were meant to shoot, reversed the Browning in his hand and cocked it. The .45 roared twice, one bullet ricocheting off the iron balustrade and one whistling by Cross's ear. Cross fled down the stairs. Donovan took one step to follow, then turned and saw Brenda lying unconscious and bleeding to death on the living room floor. He cursed and ran back inside.

The two detectives heard the shots and the screams and saw the muzzle flashes in the darkness along the upper walkway. *"Shit!"* shouted Lonnie. "We're too late! The son of a bitch is killing her!" He drew his .9-millimeter automatic from his waistband holster and jacked a round into the chamber.

"Or maybe Donovan's killing the both of them! Radio for back-up!" ordered Matt as he leaped out of the unmarked car, tossed his burning cigar aside, slapped his fedora on his head at his customary rakish angle, and whipped the .357 Magnum out of his shoulder holster.

At the Chapel Hill police station Heather was sipping copshop coffee in the detectives' squadroom where she was by now accepted as a kind of unofficial guest when assisting Matt, She heard Jacobs' call for assistance and the words "we have shots fired!" She sat down in a chair and clenched her fists to her forehead, and waited.

David Cross hurtled down the stairs, loped down the dewy and cold grassy embankment and across the ornamental bridge heading for the Bronco, gibbering to himself, the .38 snub dangling loose in his hand. He looked up and screamed in hideous fear at the sight of Redmond and Jacobs standing beneath a parking lot streetlight, in front of his truck, barring his escape, their weapons leveled. *"What can we do for you, Dave?"* yelled Matt. Insane with terror, Cross blindly fired the last two bullets in his weapon in the general direction of the two officers. He hit the windshield and headlight respectively of his own vehicle. Matt's .357 thundered and spewed a column of flame as the first mercury fulminate-tipped exploding bullet burst into Cross's chest, spinning him around, while the second bullet splattered his skull like a ripe watermelon into the air and a tattoo of Lonnie's barking 9-mils slamming into his body made it look like Cross was break-dancing to the ground. Stepping over the blood-gushing carcass, Matt and Lonnie moved swiftly up the stairs, weapons at the ready. They paused outside the open door of the apartment. "Donovan? You in there? Brenda!" he shouted. "This is Agent Redmond. Are you okay, Brenda? What's going on in there?"

"That bastard Cross shot her!" came Michael Donovan's voice. "I've already called 911. The paramedics are on their way." Matt entered the apartment and found Donovan holding the unconscious woman up on one of his knees. Her bloodstained sweater was pulled up around her shoulders. Donovan had his shirt off and had wrapped it around Brenda's wounded midriff. He was using it as a tourniquet, twisting the cloth with his left hand and pressing Brenda's holed right palm down against the stomach wound, his own palm stanching some of the blood from hers. "This is clumsy as hell and it's not working very well," he said, gritting his teeth. "I don't dare apply too much pressure or she couldn't breathe and I might do some internal damage. I just hope it can slow the bleeding enough until the ambulance gets here. He shot her in the hand as well. Where the fuck did that gouger scarper off to?"

"His scarpering days are done," said Matt, holstering his weapon. "He's lying on the sidewalk in a heap of his own blood and guts and shit. I told you and Tori both, I'd take care of it."

"Who the hell are ye calling a Tory?" demanded Donovan.

*   *   *

If I had the power or the strength to arise,
I would blow the wind back here for to turn the blue skies.
I would blow the wind back here to make the salt sea to rise,
On the day that my love sailed away from Coolmore.

On a cold December morning Matt and Heather stood with Michael Donovan by Mary's grave. A flatbed tractor-trailer was pulled up on the gravel path nearby. The driver pulled down a ramp and another man in a heavy jacket and toboggan began maneuvering a yellow diesel backhoe down onto the ground. A black hearse stood a little ways off, ready to take Mary's coffin to the funeral home, clean it up and seal it prior to beginning her long trip back to the green land across the sea.

"One thing I still don't quite understand," asked Matt. "Mr. O'Hara had his little run-in with person or persons unknown back in the middle of August, only a few weeks after Mary's murder. But you don't show up here until late November. Why the time lapse?"

"O'Hara was a murderer, but he wasn't a coward or a weakling like Cross," said Donovan. "He was a hard man in his own right. It took a good three months for me broken ribs and wrist to heal and I also had to get some pretty extensive dental repair work done. I came as soon as I could."

"Ah," said Matt. "Now tell me. Are you going to be all right when you get back to Belfast?"

"Inspector MacCrimmon and I are ould acquaintances. He'll be after looking into the O'Hara matter, but he won't look too hard. Mac will figure Belfast's fair city is better off without such. He'll be right."

"I wasn't thinking about MacCrimmon," said Matt. "I was thinking about your former colleagues, of whom O'Hara was one. You know I could have a word with the INS about your visa status, and I am sure MacCrimmon would be able to arrange for young Brendan to get over here safely. As to Mary, well, I guess you know we'd be proud and honored to have her rest here among our own. A quick whip round at

Cybertel and the SBI and Orange County Sheriff's office should raise enough to get her a mighty fine, proper stone here."

"Every year their power gets a bit weaker," said Donovan. "People can get accustomed to peace, especially if they've never had much of it. I grant you, the danger's not small. But as conceited as this sounds, I think the old ground needs men like me. Men who can stand up and just say, 'I've had enough. No more. It's over.' What about Brenda?"

"Her record is spotless prior to this incident, she was almost murdered by her accomplice, she's co-operating fully with the authorities, and she's a middle class white female. She may not have to do any time at all, or if she does it will only be a couple of years and she'll be out in half that. My guess is she's going to be spending a lot of time sorting junk at Good Will Industries and reading to old people in nursing homes for community service, but no actual clanging barry cell doors. I'll do what I can for her. She'll probably have a pretty tight probation, but who knows? She might even be able to work in a trip to Ireland this summer."

"I visited her in the hospital and she told me she wants to go if she can," said Heather. "Something about looking up some guy and paying a debt. A big one, by the sound of it. Can I give her your phone number?"

"She already has it," said Donovan.

Redmond stuck out his hand. "We'll go now. I know this will be a private moment for you. May the road rise up to meet you, and all that."

"And all that," agreed Donovan. Heather kissed him on the cheek and then they left. The funeral home director came up to him.

"We're ready to start," he said, gesturing to the backhoe.

"A moment, please." The man went back to the hearse. Donovan knelt and plucked a large handful of cold grass and North Carolina earth from the grave, which he put carefully into a ziplock plastic bag. "This will go in with yez on the other side, lass," he told her. "I know yez wanted all of this land, for you and Brendan. I'm sorry this small piece of it is all·I can give you. Oh, Mary, my beloved…we have known the days." Still kneeling, he beckoned to the backhoe driver. Before the driver fired up his engine, Michael whispered softly to her for the last time. "Come, *Maire mo chridh*. It's time to go home."

The Stranger

I returned to Dublin in the summer when I was one hundred and seventy-two years old.

I'd passed through the ancient city many times before, and sometimes I'd stayed for a while. Change comes slowly to Dublin. Down in the old parts of the city, along the southern Liffey quays, there are cobbled streets which look almost the same was when first I wandered them back in 1830-something. In the warren of the Liberties, on Ship Street and Fishamble Street and the maze behind the Four Courts, in the narrow lanes around St. Patrick's Cathedral and Christ Church, I can still see trader's signs over shops and pubs that I can recall from the 1890s. "P. Flanagan, Victualler", "B. Molloy, Licensed Whiskey Vendor", premises almost unchanged and still owned by the same family since the days of gaslight and hansom cabs, can be found.

There are other cities which I have enjoyed for their unique and ineffable character, but they have been prey to alteration and evolution over the years, losing the elusive scents and sounds and feel that made them abide in my memory, so that I no longer remain certain that I am really there. Once fascinating and proud, old London has become a neon-lit cesspit of greasy tastelessness. San Francisco a putrescent pimple of perversion by the clean blue Pacific. Johannesburg is a chrome and steel gleaming machine without a soul in place of the lusty, brawling carnival of life I once knew. Even my native Charleston, although meticulously preserved south of Broad Street, is now surrounded by plantations of split-level bungalows and mammoth shopping malls. But I can always find my way about Dublin.

Perhaps it was because I knew that I would find the reassuring familiarity that I chose Dublin to hide out in. Actually, "hide out" is not the correct term. I could not hide from them in Dublin any more than I could escape them by trekking into the Kalahari or sailing up the Amazon, so why not pick a city for my battlefield, where there were people and light, sound and motion? Where there were pubs, theaters, food, art, all the things for which I had pursued the Great Work, in order that these things might not be denied to me by the cold of the grave? Why not wait for my enemies in comfort?

I settled into a spacious room with a high Georgian ceiling, on the top floor of a half empty building near St. Stephen's Green. The landlord was a sodden old fool, but he took my money and readily accepted my story that I was a graduate student doing research at the National Library in nearby Kildare Street. My story was credible, since my body and my neutral visage passed for that of a man of thirty years of age. Like all of his kind down through the ages, the landlord periodically rummaged though my room when I was out, but I fitted one of the two stand-up closets in the bedsitter with a sturdy new lock, and therein I kept the few necessary books and personal mementos and items of equipment I always carry with me. The bulk of my books and effects were new and totally innocuous, so I didn't care who saw them, but the contents of that locked closet might have been difficult to explain.

I was pleased to find that legalized gambling still existed in Ireland, for it simplified my money problem. I furbished my divining skills and so was able to make a series of highly profitable wagers on horse races, placing the bets in small amounts with different bookmakers. I also practiced psychokinesis on slot machines in amusement arcades, and so very quickly amassed a tidy fortune that I squirreled away in a number of different bank accounts. Then I whiled away the long summer days at my leisure, walking in Phoenix Park, doing the rounds of the theaters and cinemas, gormandizing in the best restaurants and quaffing the fine brown ales and black stouts of Ireland. I knew that soon I would have to begin the ascetic purgations necessary for action, cleansing my body of cholesterol, animal fats, and nerve-deadening alcohol like a plumber cleaning sludge out of pipes. In a thaumaturgical battle the operator's own brain and nervous system is the weapon through which he fires all manner of psychic "ammunition". A good soldier always cleans his weapon before going into combat.

By September I sensed they were getting closer. The clouds in the crystal I used for scrying warned me of their approach, the reactions to certain processes I performed with the equipment from my locked closet confirmed it, and the tingling of my own acute sensitivity put me on the alert. I sensed disturbances in the ether, ripples caused by the filaments of psychic energy which wove sinuously through the field, searching for me. One night one of those tentacles fleetingly touched my mind and I awoke in a cold sweat. I threw off the probe with ease, but now they knew where I was. What should I do? I had chosen Dublin to make my stand, but I could abandon the idea and flee again. And of course, they would seek me out and find me, but I could buy some more time by moving. I decided against this. I was tired of being hounded by these rank amateurs. It was time for the lion to turn at bay and crush these upstart jackals pursuing him.

Besides, by then I had met Rose, and under no circumstances would I leave Dublin without her.

I am by nature a reserved and private man, and I have no intention of going into salacious details regarding my personal life. However, a bit of general discussion is called for here. Adepts generally strive to rise above the so-called weaknesses of the flesh, or at least they try to appear as if they do. But I am not a formally initiated adept in any religion or school or discipline, and I have no followers to impress with my asceticism. In the course of my life I have encountered many cults, magical secret societies, hermetic and Goetic orders, and so on, but I have never joined any of them and I do not profess a particular religious or metaphysical point of view. The Arts I have mastered I have attained through my own research and experimentation and study, with the help of such teachers as I could find among these sects, and one in particular who became my Master in the magical sense. These individuals and sects had and still have varying attitudes towards the physical pleasures of the body, especially sex, but I have no axe to grind and so I indulge my assorted corporeal lusts as I choose. By indulgence I do not mean debauchery; I leave that to mountebanks like Anton LaVey and Aleister Crowley. The most essential attribute of anyone who aspires to the Arts is an iron self-discipline, and the so-called "Thelema—Do What Thou Wilt" philosophy of Crowley and his kind is destructive of that faculty and so precludes any high degree of magical advancement. Not that I haven't sampled just about every so-called vice, but I have done so purely to educate and inform myself as part of my esoteric training. As Voltaire allegedly once told the Marquis de Sade, "Once was legitimate curiosity; twice would be perversion."

But even as soldiers do not spend all their time on parade or in actual combat, magi need not spend their whole lives in constant meditation or spiritual concentration, and wise ones enjoy the good things of the material world and rejoice in them. Woman is the most wondrous and fascinating of all the Creator's works and the sweetest of all his earthly gifts to man, and it would be strange indeed if I had lived so long without desiring and pursuing her. Hence Rose, and all the many others.

Sometimes I play the game of seduction straightforwardly, and when I lose I try to do so with a rueful grace. A true gentleman can always take no for an answer. Sometimes I use the Arts indirectly, to acquire large sums of immediate cash to use in the chase, and this gambit seldom fails. The simple fact is that almost every woman has her price, especially if the payment is offered with subtlety and charm. I am aware that such views are considered crude, reactionary, and generally unacceptable in today's "polite society". If for some strange reason I had the slightest desire for entrée into today's establishment, I might point out that the reactionaries of my century built mighty empires and great works of civilization which the liberals of this century still have not managed totally to destroy despite three generations of effort, and in any case woman is as woman has been throughout the millennia and no amount of "liberation" can change her. The fact is that my horrid reactionary approach to women generally works. Women not only deserve to be treated like ladies, they enjoy it immensely, and they are grateful. The few times I use the Arts directly on the damsel in question, it is more question of keeping in practice than any shortcoming on my part. I show my ladies courtesy and consideration, I savor their bodies as I enjoy fine wine or great music or all other things of beauty, and when I have satisfied my desire for them I send them on their way gently, tactfully, and affectionately.

But the one pitfall I have ever striven to avoid is love. Oh, yes, sorcerers can love, for a man of the greatest attainment is still only a man after all. I myself have loved, sometimes wisely, but never well. This is all the more inexcusable because I know that I should not. A magus who has attained the final consummation of the Great Work has by definition surrendered his citizenship in the human community and all his rights therein. What he takes from his mortal neighbours he steals.

Besides, love between mortal woman and magus is inevitably a moral and emotional disaster for both parties. It is not difficult to see why. At first there is the timeless joy when two beings finally discover the half of themselves that was heretofore lost. But as the years go by the woman ages, and the man does not. She grows wrinkled, grey hairs appear and then white, her breasts sag, she grows fat or else shrinks or shrivels. In the normal human relationship the man too would age, and if their life together has been a full and loving one they go easily and tranquilly with one another into the deepening twilight. But when the man retains his youth while the wife bears the ravages of time there is first surprise, then envy, then anger and resentment, and finally fear and loathing, as the woman realizes she has been tricked, that her life's partner is not a natural being. The marriage has been a swindle. She has given her whole life, while he has given her but a small fraction of his.

And yet periodically I yield to the unbearable, chasmic loneliness, and instead of a casual mistress I take a wife in the true sense of the word. Never have I allowed my dear ones to come to fear and hate me, though. After ten or fifteen or twenty years there is a carefully staged accident, a drowning at sea with no body ever washed ashore, a false death on some foreign battlefield, never a simple disappearance but something which leads my wife to believe that I am dead and gone. My beloved is left a widow and grieves, but at least I know that her love for me will live as long as she does, and she will never know how cruelly I have tricked and cheated her. Whenever I can bear to do so, I try to vanish from their lives while they are still young enough to wed again, to find a true man who will stay with them to the end. I will not go into the agony of all those final partings I have gone through, leaving for the army or a simple business trip, with only I knowing that my wife and our children will never see me again. Know this of me: I have sinned, but I am not a wicked or uncaring man. And I have suffered.

I met Rose soon after she moved into a basement flat in the same semi-tenement I was living in. She knocked on my door one night to borrow a can opener, came back to return it, and we spoke for a while on the stairway landing. The next day she came up and asked me to help her operate the cranky, archaic gas heater in the communal bathroom. She little guessed that I could recall when the rusting piece of junk had been the most modern of technology. By then I realised it had happened again. I was going to change this girl's life, using secret weapons she would never suspect, manipulating her, removing rivals if necessary, winning her love by artificial means if I could not do otherwise. To give me my due, I would make her as happy as I could during the time we were together, but then I would disappear, breaking her heart and mine. Perhaps I was wrong to do this, but who is to say that she might not have been worse off if I had left her to her fate?

Rose was from some little town in the country, Killarney or Kilkenny. I didn't catch it the first time she told me and never bothered to inquire again, for it wasn't important. She was in Dublin for the usual reason, trying to defeat the unemployment the idiot politicians in Ireland and everywhere else periodically create through their incompetence. She had her dole money, and she had cadged some government body into paying her tuition at a local commercial college where she was learning to be a secretary. Again it didn't matter, since now that she had met me she would never have to earn her own living. I fell easily into conversation with her when we would meet in the hall, and I developed our relationship with the finesse of long practice. I allowed a decent interval of some weeks to lapse before I brought her into my bed, and I did so without recourse to the Arts.

She can only be described in clichés: raven hair, lily-white skin, eyes the blue of the Irish loughs, etc. More important, she was that rarity among men and even more among women, a truly *good* person, a soul constitutionally unable to harbor a mean or malicious thought, at true peace with herself and the world around her, and this I had to have above all. Rose was a rose indeed, and I meant to pluck her. I was so fascinated and eager for her that I was on the verge of eloping to Europe or back to America and putting off my confrontation with my enemies, when they finally caught up with me.

I had guessed that they would make their move before the Hallowmass intersolstice on October 31st, and I was not mistaken. Tenants' mail in the bedsitters came through a letter slot and was deposited on a table in the vestibule. One day in mid-October, when the fallen leaves of orange and yellow and green rattled along the sidewalks of St. Stephen's Green and sunset blazed scarlet tongues into a sky of lead, I returned home and found a blue envelope lying on the table. There was no postage stamp, so the letter had been delivered by hand, and it was addressed in a woman's writing to "the American gentleman". Inside was a note, in the same feminine hand, which read *"Some friends would like to see you tonight at eight o'clock at the Lincoln Inn, in Lincoln Place. Please come."* It seems they meant to try persuasion before resorting to force.

II.

The Lincoln Inn was a cozy pub behind Trinity College, generally crowded, and a mildly famous resort of Trinity students and theatrical people. I was intensely curious to learn precisely what individuals the Circle had sent after me, although I thought I could make a good guess. Only eight or ten people among them, or any of the allies they might conceivably call upon, had the requisite knowledge and skill to make an attempt against me. In any case, they wouldn't try anything in the crowded pub.

When I entered the Lincoln Inn at eight that night I immediately saw the ones I was there to meet, seated at a low table in the rear of the bar. Two were on my mental list of probable antagonists. There was a tall lean man with a goatee and a rotund, florid little man in horn-rimmed spectacles, fully bearded and wearing a yarmulke. The first was Anson Delafontaine, the leader of the Circle's outer echelon and a prominent man in the inner council. Delafontaine was a wealthy New Orleans businessman, an amateur scientist of some repute, and no mean adept at ceremonial magic, undoubtedly the most dangerous "hit man" they could have employed. The old Jew with the white beard was Dr.

Emmanuel Rosenberg, Ph. D., D. D., etc., noted Talmudic scholar, Kabalist, and professor emeritus of theology at Hofstra University.

But the third of the trio surprised me. She was a tall, willowy blond, flawlessly dressed in a chic and expensive tan suit, and languid bearing and smooth motion exuding a lithe sensuality that drew constant overt head-turning from every male in the place. I knew her from San Francisco, my last place of any extended residence. She called herself Zoraya Malinkova and liked to hint a descent from pre-1917 Russian nobility and a mysterious past replete with secret missions, secret sins, and jet-set names dropping at close intervals. Here real name was Zelda Muggins or something of the sort, and she was from middle-class Fresno. How she wandered into the Arts I don't know. She was a fair to middling *clairvoyante* and had read all the standard books on the subjects of witchcraft, apparitions, flying saucers, etc. and she did tarot card readings and played with ouija boards. She had some degree of natural talent for the Arts, but when I had known her she was simply a groupie, if you will, hanging around the fringes of the Circle's San Francisco chapter. She had never been initiated beyond the first few grades of the outer levels, not being considered sufficiently mature, and surely she could not have advanced in skill far enough in the short time since then so as to justify including her in a sort of thaumaturgical commando team that hoped to best an Ipsissimus such as myself in an astral battle. Her character aside, such powers take years of study, practice, and hard disciplined work to acquire.

I ordered a pint of Smithwick's Ale at the bar and while I was waiting for it I tried to puzzle it out. I glanced over and noticed that none of the three were drinking alcohol, a warning sign, but one pint wouldn't hurt me and might fool them into thinking I was unprepared for them. Then I stumbled onto the reason for Zoraya's presence: simple sexual bribery! They had no doubt heard about the incident where I had suggested, most courteously, that she and I adjourn to the bedroom. The resulting lecture on women's liberation, mostly in words of one syllable, I found offensive and tiresome, not to say completely unnecessary. I am fully aware that *women* can use language that would make a sailor blush; in my day *ladies* did not do so. Nowadays certain benighted female creatures calling themselves feminists indulge in foul language, wear men's clothing, cavort in the streets waving silly whining placards, debase themselves in the unspeakable practices of Sapphism, and proclaim thereby they are "liberating" themselves. Liberating themselves from what, I wonder? Reader, again I crave your indulgence. It is just that I, who remember the days when there was order and purpose in the world, know better than any of you or even any of your grandsires just how much mankind has lost when basic human decency and moral absolutes have been discarded. But I digress.

I sat down with my pint. For a time they stared at me in uneasy silence. Finally Zee spoke. "Hello, Charles," she said softly. "Are you still Charles? I imagine you change names fairly often."

"Charles will do," I returned shortly. I almost called her Zelda just to be sardonic, but in view of my own admitted superabundance of aliases down through the years it would have been the pot calling the kettle black.

"We wanted to speak to you in Washington, Charles, but you wouldn't come," said Manny Rosenberg, like a teacher admonishing a rowdy pupil. "Why did you run away from us?"

"I hoped to avoid tiresome arguments and still more tiresome subsequent events," I told him. "I had nothing to say to you in Washington. I've nothing to say to you here, either, that I have not said before. I don't suppose you'd consider leaving me alone? I'd take it kindly."

"You know we can't do that," grated Anson Delafontaine in a sepulchral voice, doing his best John Carradine imitation. "Do you think we intend to die simply because you don't feel like sharing with us the secret of eternal life?"

"I found the secret on my own, or rather I learned the basic principles from my old Master, and when I had learned all he could teach he turned me loose to achieve the Great Work or not, as I could. As it happened, I succeeded. You people have far more in the way of resources and intellectual capacity at your disposal than I had as an individual. There is no reason why you cannot attain the Great Work without my help, if you are worthy."

"Worthy?" snorted Delafontaine. "Can the crap, Charles. That's jargon for wealthy old women who have table-rapping sessions with gin-soaked phony mediums."

"Are you so far above that level, then?" I inquired gently.

"We are all adepts here," returned Delafontaine coldly.

"Even Miss Malinkova?" I couldn't resist asking. Zee arched her eyebrows expressively but said nothing. Obviously she had been well coached in her part, and her part was to come later.

"Zoraya is extremely talented in clairvoyance and mediumship, and she has made great advances in practice since we gave her rather a crash course, as it were," lectured Manny. "It was she who located you, so I shouldn't underestimate her if I were you, Charles. Oh, we know that you are more advanced than we are. Obviously you must be, since you have discovered the elixir of life." He leaned forward eagerly. "Is it an elixir, Charles?" I remained silent. "A solid substance? A purely chemical or biological process which science just hasn't stumbled onto yet? An alchemical procedure? A thaumaturgical one? Does it involve evocation, invocation, or necromancy? Won't you even tell us these things?"

I shook my head. "No."

"And you ask our Circle to pursue the search independently, our efforts furious in their intensity now that *we know it can be done,* and all the time you are just wandering aimlessly about the earth in full knowledge of the secret, without giving us even a hint or two? For someone who has lived for so long, Charles, you seem to have learned remarkably little about human nature." Manny paused, wiping the sweat from his brow with a handkerchief. "Who was this Master who taught you, then? Will you not even direct us to him? Let him teach us as he taught you?"

"I don't know where to locate him even if I were so inclined," I said, although this was not precisely true. "He wouldn't have you lot in any case."

"Who is he?" asked Manny breathlessly. "Was it the Count St. Germain?"

"Good heavens, no!" I laughed. "St. Germain was an absurd mountebank who dabbled in alchemy to keep up his front for assorted swindles at the court of Versailles. He died in Germany in 1784, at a normal age, I assure you."

"Did you know him yourself?" demanded Rosenberg eagerly. It struck me that these people obviously thought I was even older than I actually am. I felt some sympathy for Rosenberg. Delafontaine made little secret of his sheer personal greed for longevity and the power it would bring, but Rosenberg was a genuine seeker after knowledge, who sought the truth for its own sake. Here, he thought, was a man who could reveal the secrets of the ages to him and yet perversely refused. I could understand his frustration.

"I have no intention of discussing St. Germain or anything else with you, Manny." In point of fact I had learned about St. Germain from my Master, who *had* met the man personally, but I had no inclination to gossip. "I presume you people have come to me to beg and plead first, and the offer inducements, and then proceed to threats. Could we get on with it, please?"

"Is there any inducement which we could offer you which would tempt you?" asked Rosenberg urgently. I avoided looking at Zoraya. "Tell us, and if we must use the entire power and resources of our Circle, it will be given to you. As to threats, surely you must realize that for us to harm you or endanger you in any way would run counter to our purpose. You have something that we must have, that we *will* have!" he added, thumping his pudgy fist into him palm for emphasis. "Any operations which we undertake to secure your co-operation will be minimal and used only as a last resort."

"I won't bother to try and dissuade you, since obviously you haven't come all this way to be dissuaded," I sighed. "I should, however, point out to you that if you push this to desperate extremes you will probably force me to hurt you, and I don't want to do that."

"Even if you kill us, the Circle will send others against you," rumbled Delafontaine. "There will be no peace for you, Charles."

"There is never any peace for any magus," I replied quietly, and after knocking back the remains of my pint I rose to go.

"Charles," spoke up Zoraya finally, "Won't you even tell us *why* you refuse?"

"I told you. You are not worthy."

"What do you mean by worthy?" she persisted.

"Madam, the Great Work by its very nature is something that can only be *attained,* never *given.* It can only be attained by those who have assimilated a certain body of knowledge and a certain level of cosmic maturity into their very souls, so that these principles are a part of them. *Not once* has any Ipsissimus ever revealed to any other person the nature of the secret, for to do so would be an impossibility, something absolutely unthinkable in someone who has attained that degree of awareness. You cannot imagine how absurd it is for you to ask me to hand you this ultimate gift on a silver platter."

"I don't understand," said the girl.

"I know," I replied with a nod, "And that is why you are not worthy. The minute that you people comprehend that I cannot possibly give you the Great Work for any consideration, then you will have taken the first step towards attaining it yourselves."

"Sounds like the typical arrogant can of all independent adepts," growled Delafontaine. "You stumble on the greatest secret in human history, or very well, you discover it through your own efforts or worthiness as you call it. For that you certainly deserve credit, and I would be the last to withhold my applause, but then you get puffed up with delusions of your own grandeur and you come to believe that you are now elevated to godhood and you can deny us puny mortals what you will."

"Perhaps put a bit roughly, Anson," said Manny in an attempt to mollify us both. "But surely, Charles, you can see how all this looks to us? Why is it acceptable for *you* to live forever, but not us? It's not pure selfishness, Charles. I don't deny a strong self-centered desire to avoid death, of course, but I am also thinking of all the good our order could do if we had a more than mortal life span. You know the old idea of the Masters, the secret chiefs and teachers who live in immortal bodies and guide mankind from their hidden sanctuaries? Perhaps this ancient idea is true after all. Since learning of your existence, we've had to re-arrange some of our ideas, I can tell you! Perhaps you know of these Secret Chiefs?" He paused, his incredibly eager longing for knowledge almost panting from his bearded face, like a child begging for a sweet. I decided to grant the man a small modicum of mercy.

"Manny, this much I can tell you without compromising the Great Work in any way. Yes, there are others like myself. How many I do not know, where I do not know, who the oldest living person on earth is and how old that person is I again do not know. Some of these people may take an interest in human affairs and may even on occasion intervene in them. I choose not to do so. For all I know, there may be a secret organization of adepts with longer than normal life spans. All I can tell you is that I have never seen any evidence of it." That was true enough, but then the story of the Hidden Masters is a remarkably persistent legend. If they exist at all, humanity can use all the help it can get.

They, of course, did not take that view. "Then it is more important than ever for us to obtain the secret from you," declared Delafontaine grimly. "If all the others like yourself are dispersed, unorganized individuals, then we could spend the remainder of our lives searching and never find another one of you."

"I see it was a mistake on my part to speak with you at all," I sighed. "Very well. If you use discretion in your assaults against me, I'll try not to hurt you too badly. Good evening." I stood up and walked out of the pub.

III.

I half expected the knock on my door that night. It was Zoraya, and she was alone. She had done something to her makeup and her outfit, I couldn't tell what, but she was even more lusciously seductive than before. She slid into my room without being asked, brushing lightly against me with a sensual feline grace. I must confess that I deeply regretted the necessity of rejecting her upcoming advances. "I presume this is the inducement part?" I asked.

"Yes, but I hope you won't make it hard for me by gloating," she replied frankly. "I'm willing to give myself to you in any way you want, Charles, in exchange for the secret of immortality, which I suppose makes me the highest priced hooker in history. But it still doesn't sit quite right, ya know?"

"Well, you needn't worry, Zee. I have no intention of exchanging the secret of the Great Work for your admittedly most delectable person."

"Oh." She was quiet for a while. "I don't suppose I ever really believed you'd go for it, but the others thought it was at least worth a try. After all, with your skills you can have any woman you want. Or man."

"My dear young lady, I assure you that I have never!…well, I was brought up in a time when men like that shot themselves! But if you knew that I was not susceptible to bribery, why did you come along? How did you talk Delafontaine into letting you come, for that matter? Surely Professor Ingstrom or Chandra Lal or several others I could name would have been a better choice?"

"They constitute our second team, in case we don't come back," Zee told me. "To answer your question, I made rather a big deal out of that one pass you made at me. I told them you'd tried to put a love spell on me but I threw it back on you. That impressed them. I wanted to come more than anything. I'd have held up my end of the deal if you'd agreed, Charles, don't doubt that. You'd have something warm and cuddly in your bed as long as you wanted." She stared around curiously at my sparsely furnished chamber. "Is this the best you can manage? You had a regular mansion in 'Frisco. Surely you don't lack for money?"

"No, I don't lack for anything I want," I replied. "There are simply times when I prefer this kind of environment. Less distracting. I've had it all, of course. Mansions, servants, gilt coaches and matched teams and big automobiles, swimming pools and boxes at the opera, gourmet meals every day. Sometimes that is the way I feel like living. Other times I have gone out into the Appalachian mountains or the African bush and lived in shacks, tents, even caves. I've worn the same rags until they fell off my back, eaten whatever I could scrounge. Sometimes I've lived in slum tenements and Salvation Army hostels and done backbreaking work on docks or pushed a broom for the price of a quart of rotgut wine. It depends on my mood."

"And you can do that," she said, awe and wonder in her voice. "Live life exactly as you want it with no thought for the future, because you've got quite literally all the time in the world. Charles, will you let me make my own private pitch to you now?"

"Oh, plan on double-crossing your colleagues and trying to make a separate deal with me?" I asked skeptically.

"No. I've sworn an oath to the Circle and I'll keep it."

"I am glad to hear it, madam. Dishonesty ill becomes anyone."

"I just mean that I'd like to talk to you for a while," she said, sitting down in one of the worn chairs. "There's got to be some way to reach you. We hate being cast as the heavies here. We want only peace and progress for all of mankind, the elimination of war and poverty and hunger and disease and ignorance. If the adepts of our Order could have your kind of longevity, we could undertake the task of guiding humanity towards these goals over a long time span, using our accumulated knowledge and experience. You say you don't believe in the

Hidden Masters? Well, *we could become the Secret Chiefs!* And you could be our greatest magus!"

"Ah? Now you are offering me power instead of your lovely *corpus*, eh? Sorry, Zee. Not only do I have not the slightest ambition to empire, but nobody has the right to 'guide' humanity anywhere. Not me, and certainly not you people."

"And so those of us who care just let this foul world slide right on down the tubes without getting involved?" demanded Zee heatedly.

"Getting involved to change things for the better is one thing, madam," I said. "Laying out a master plan of what you want the world to be like and then attempting to dragoon everybody into it is another thing. See here," I went on earnestly, "I'll give you a very good example. You know all those things you want to eliminate like poverty, disease, ignorance, and despair? I once knew a man who wanted to eliminate those same things, far more passionately than you do, a man whose soul was on fire with genuine love of his fellow beings."

"Your Master who taught you the secret?" she asked quickly.

"No, no, madam, attend! You may have heard about this man or read of him in books. His name was Eugene V. Debs, and he was once of the early Socialists. Debs was one of the most humane and compassionate and genuinely caring men it has ever been my privilege to know. He spent his life fighting for his fellow men. Unfortunately, he fought too long. He lived to see the Russian Revolution and he was filled with horror and remorse at the slaughter and the mass destruction that Socialism involves in practice. He was stricken with grief that he had, however indirectly, helped to foment mass murder on a scale not seen in the world since the time of Genghis Khan. The point I'm trying to make is the old saying that all revolutions devour their children. Debs's intentions were every bit as good as yours, yet his dream of a socialist paradise led straight to the execution cellars of the KGB. After Debs came Lenin and Stalin, after Rousseau came Robespierre and then Napoleon. *Political* good intentions somehow seem always to end up on a jumble of barbed wire, bayonets, and mass graves, The problem of what to do with those who don't conform to the new paradise is soluble in only one way."

"But we're not political!" protested Zee.

"No. Not as yet. But if you were to possess the Great Work without the requisite maturity and perception that comes with its attainment? Who knows what you would do? If I were so wrong-headed as to give you what you ask, and you were to proceed with this master plan for humanity of yours, you would eventually produce your own Stalin. Only he would be far more powerful and dangerous to mankind than any Stalin who has ever gone before, Zee, more powerful than any of the aging lunatics who now sit around the world with their fingers on those little red buttons. I certainly will not help you create such a Demon King, not like my poor friend Gene Debs."

"But with such powers as we might attain through your secret, we could bring an end to it all, maybe keep the buttons from being ever pushed!"

"Possibly, possibly not. But who put those men of decayed mind in that position? Other people. Who maintains the whole fabric of present day society? *People,* Zee. The problem is not nuclear arms or the destruction of the environment or terrorism or anything else, the problem is *man,* the human animal. Man is nasty, violent, aggressive and a greedy predator. However much individuals may hate war and suffering, man as a whole enjoys it immensely. If the Americans and the Russians and the Chinese weren't at each other's throats they'd be at someone else's. And you couldn't change that, Zee. You would have to change the very nature of the human species, and you could never do that no matter how powerful your magic became. Man can never usurp the function of God."

"Is there a God, then?" she asked curiously.

"Great Jehosophat, woman, of course! You can ask a question like that and still claim to merit the Great Work?" I was exasperated. "Do you think the universe sprang into existence by sheer accident? There is an overall motive for creation, not an old gent sitting on a golden throne in a cloud city with pearly gates, no, but a primary principle of Order."

"Then is there a devil?" the girl pestered me eagerly. "A central force of evil? Oh, I know all about demons, I've helped to invoke them…"

"You shouldn't," I broke in. "Messing around with the Outer Entities is foolish and dangerous, and generally unnecessary in the bargain. They can do nothing for you that you can't accomplish on your own, more quickly and certainly more safely. That's the mark of the amateur. He conjures a demon or two, manages to survive the experience, and then he thinks he's thaumaturgical bee's knees. A true adept *never* uses Entities except in that one case in a hundred where nothing less will serve. And that, madam, is a piece of advice I will freely add to your occult education, although I doubt you'll take advice from someone you once termed a male chauvinist pig."

"Charles, when I got angry with you that time you propositioned me in San Francisco, I didn't know who you were!" she pleaded. "If I'd known how far beyond me you had advanced in the Arts I would have performed the whole Kama Sutra in exchange for your knowledge! I came here tonight still prepared to do so. It's just that a woman gets so tired of always hearing the same lines and getting treated like a piece of meat, an orifice for physical relief like a toilet. Men treat you like a thing until you just can't stand it any more."

"You're quite right, Zee," I said gently. "It is not only women who have grown coarse and vulgar over the years of this awful century. It's a pity you didn't accept, though. I would never have treated you like a thing, but like a lady."

"Then I'm glad I didn't accept, she said with a soft rueful laugh, "I might have grown to like it. But you never did tell me whether there was a devil."

"You'd know the answer if you'd quit playing games with ouija boards and tarot cards and do a long, solid course of basic occult reading and research. There is no good or evil in the form of absolutes. There are only forces that are either positive or negative with reference to human life and what we regard as material existence. For positive you may read constructive or forces of order, that is to say hierarchical or sequential, forces which *accumulate* matter and energy and order it into an organized form or sequence. The negative forces *disperse* ordered creation and activity into random, non-repetitive existence. Both of these primal forces, accumulation and dispersion, positive and negative, or good and evil if you will, contain small elements of the other, opposing force to ensure balance and ensure that neither ever triumphs permanently over the other. This is a gross oversimplification of doctrines which have been centuries in development and which are capable of almost infinite elaboration. If you want me to recommend a course of study for you, I suggest you go off on a retreat somewhere and spend about six months meditating on the ancient symbol of the yin and the yang, the ultimate schematic of existence. Once you comprehend that one symbol, you have the basis for any occult or spiritual accomplishment you care to try for. There, that's the closest you'll get to a hint on the Great Work, but it's no more than you could get from any of the hermetic philosophers."

"No devil?" asked Zee wonderingly.

"What is Chaos? Merely the absence of order. Darkness is the absence of light. Now is there anything else? I am expecting a visitor." Rose had taken to spending most nights in my room.

"Yes," said Zoraya. "We do seem to have strayed from the subject. May I ask precisely how old you are, Charles? We know you're at least two hundred."

"Close enough. I'm not going to discuss the matter."

"I assume that in those countless years you've known a lot of people. Maybe some were your friends, may some more than friends.

Remember them, Charles?" Indeed I did; a procession of faces flitted through my memory. "Remember Arabella, Charles? The woman you lived with in San Francisco when we first met you? I recall you used to have some wild parties in that pad of yours. She still doesn't know why you left, and she's very unhappy."

"You didn't tell her anything?" I asked with a scowl.

"No, we found she didn't know anything and then left it. But some-day she'll die, Charles, and you'll be alive somewhere, just as you are now. There must have been others like her."

"There have been, and I don't enjoy hurting them. It is your fault I had to leave before time, madam, your group's fault that is, so don't try to make me feel guilty on that score."

"But don't you ever get lonely?" she persisted. "Don't you ever get tired of wandering from place to place, without anyone you can really talk to, really confide in?" I am afraid I rather irritated her then by laughing loudly.

"A pointless attempt, madam. If ever I did choose to impart the Great Work to someone so that they could accompany me on my long sojourn in this world, it certainly would not be you and your friends!"

"And so I have to die, my body slowly crumbling, my mind decaying, my joints rusting with arthritis? Eventually I won't even be able to con-trol my bodily functions, and some nurse in an old folks' home will have to change my diapers. Our wonderful modern medical science has ensured that I may well live to be a hundred, but during my last thirty years or so I will be living in hell, trapped in the wreck that was once me!" Her voice was fearful and bitter.

"Is that what you truly fear, Zee?" I asked gently. "That I can well understand."

"I can't say I'm wild about the death of my mind, either," she said grimly. "I know that I have lived before and will live again. One of the basics of our Order is age regression and hypnosis, as you know, since you were with us for a time. Manny Rosenberg did a full past life reading on me. It didn't take more than a couple of sessions. I have only had two prior existences, both female, both totally pointless. In the early nineteenth century I was a factory girl in a textile mill in Manchester, England. I started work at the mill when I was six years old and I died when I was fourteen of some lung condition which was probably TB aggravated by brown lung from breathing cotton lint for twelve hours a day, six days a week. My most fascinating experience was being raped by a foreman in a shed."

"I may have something of a karmic obligation to you, then," I sighed. "My family's plantations supplied those mills. Go on."

"Well," she said, startled by my interjection, "My next life was at the turn of the century. I was a Jewish immigrant girl from the Ukraine, brought to New York when I was five. I was illiterate, grew up speaking nothing but Yiddish, and when I was fifteen I married a man three times my age. My parents arranged it through a matchmaker because he was well off by Lower East Side standards. He owned a kosher butcher shop. I was wretchedly unhappy, I spent what time I had left caring for his children by a previous marriage and having four more of my own, and ten years later I died in a tenement fire. That was in 1913. This is the first life I've lived where I have been anything more than a dumb broad!"

I could now understand the karmic origin of Zoraya's hatred of men, but I felt I had to disabuse her of at least once misconception. "Motherhood and caring for a family is not being a 'dumb broad', as you put it," I admonished. "The maternal function is the most vital in all human society, and it also has immense occult significance as well. We discard it at our peril."

"But it is a role I do not choose!" returned the girl with spirit. "If I die, what will I be the next time around? A housewife in Toronto? A hooker in Hong Kong? Maybe even a *man*, for Christ's sake? I am who I want to be and what I want to be *now*, Charles! I don't want to surrender either my body or my personality to death, to give up the knowledge and everything I have gained in this life!" Zoraya came over to me and clasped my hands tightly, her voice passionate with pleading. "Charles, you're not a bad person, I know it! If I were about to be run down by a bus or murdered by international terrorists I know you would save me if you could. Why, why won't you save me from the wheelchair and the diapers and the slow death of the slobbering idiot?"

I gently disengaged her hands. "I'd save you from murder or from the runaway bus because they are avoidable," I told her. "All violent or premature death is avoidable, unnecessary, and therefore morally wrong. Predestination is a foolish Presbyterian taradiddle. But natural death is part of the order of things. It is something that should be accepted philosophically and met with dignity when the time comes. It is in many cases the high point of an individual's development in the life he has just completed."

"A high point that you seem to have taken great care to avoid!" she cried angrily.

"Yes, and therein I was wrong, although I know you won't believe my sincerity when I say that. Listen, Zee, let me tell you something. As I mentioned earlier tonight in the pub, I am not the only magus in history to attain the Great Work. There are others who have done so. Most of their names would mean nothing to you, but you will have heard of some of them in your studies. Simon Magus, Appolonius of Tyana, Albertus Magnus, Thomas Aquinas, Arnauld Villeneuve, Roger Bacon, John Dee, Christian Rosenkreutz, Paracelsus, Nicholas Flamel, Swedenborg, Gurdjieff…they all attained and surpassed by far my own degree of development."

"But they all died!" exclaimed Zoraya.

"Precisely, madam. *They all died*. Because, far wiser than I, they knew when they had found the secret that it were better left unused. Think about it. Now go, and let us get on with our battle, since it seems nothing less will satisfy you."

"Very well," she said calmly. She took out a card and scribbled something on it, and tossed it onto the mantelpiece. "If you should decide to descend from your altruistic Olympus, or should I say when the Circle compels you to do so, I'll be at the Shelborne Hotel, room 206." I quickly spotted that the card was not from the hotel nor was it any ordinary calling card, but a small square of dried parchment, covered with symbols that I recognized. I tore off a paper towel from the roll below the sink and carefully picked up the card, making sure my fingers did not touch it. I grabbed her as she was at the door, whirled her around and stuffed the card down her blouse.

"I am sorry to be crude, but that was a crude attempt," I said in exasperation. I laid the paper towel aside with a mental note to destroy it within a ritual vessel of Art to make absolutely sure that none of the talisman's negative energies had been absorbed into the room. "Do you know how to disarm that damned thing, or must I tell you?"

"Burn it in a consecrated thurible with salt and sandalwood and the fourth versicle from the third Pnakotic fragment, in the original Aklo if you're good enough, which I am," said Zee tautly.

"That will do, yes."

"Sorry, Charles, you're right, it was crude, but I always start a chess game by trying a Fool's Mate."

"That only works when you're playing a fool. Go away, Zee." She opened the door to leave, then suddenly turned coyly and to my surprise gave me a long slow kiss on the lips. "*Mañana,* man," she said in a sultry voice, and then she was gone. Then I saw Rose standing outside the door, starting after the elegant Zoraya with unmistakable hurt and jealousy on her face. Zee had spotted her and taken a lucky shot in the dark to stir a bit of trouble. No doubt about it, she could think on her feet. I cursed the troublemaking Zelda silently. Not only was Rose upset, but if they guessed she meant anything to me my beloved would be in danger from this point on.

"That girl is American, isn't she?" demanded Rose as she entered the room, a tremor in her voice. "You said you didn't know anyone in Dublin."

"Nor did I," I assured her, kissing her forehead. "She's an acquaintance from San Francisco. I ran into her by pure accident in the Lincoln Inn tonight and she popped around."

"Obviously an intimate acquaintance," said Rose accusingly.

"Don't worry about the kiss, darling, everybody in California acts like that." It took me a long time to soothe her before we went to bed, but I was very much mistaken in assuming that all was well and Rose was satisfied.

IV.

Child-like and naïve in some respects, Rose was. Stupid she wasn't. She had long ago seen through any pretence that I was a writer or a student, but I had convinced her, or so I thought, that I was a wealthy scholar of eccentric tastes who enjoyed globetrotting and that as soon as she had made up her mind to marry me I would settle down with her in Ireland or America, wherever she wanted to live. She knew that I had a lot of money because she had seen my bank books. Most women would have been satisfied with a wealthy husband, but Rose had more than her share of feminine curiosity. With an attempted deviousness which I found amusing she had often tried to pump me for information about my family, my past, my sources of income (I told her I played the stock market), about the strange scars all over my body and especially about the fascinating mystery of my locked closet. I fended her off gently and idly and began inventing in my own mind a story for the time when she would understandably enough demand to know the full truth about me. But things came to a head before that.

I had underestimated her curiosity and her enterprise. Unknown to me, the little minx had taken an impression in soap of my key ring during one brief moment when my back was turned, and had her own key made to the garderobe.

The morning after Zee's visit, I went up to the communal bathroom on the landing above to take a shower. I got all ready to shower when I discovered that I had left behind the necessary 50-pence coin to activate the archaic gas heater on the tap. So I threw my robe back on and went down the stairs back to my room, and when I walked in Rose had the closet open and my large Victorian portmanteau was out on the floor. She was sitting at the desk with all my papers, books, and memorabilia laid out before her, staring at them in a state of near shock. Some of the objects I had retained over the decades through necessity, others through sentiment. The magical equipment and supplies would be meaningless to her, of course, and my workbooks and grimoires or spellbooks were mostly in cipher or languages she could not read. But unfortunately there were also the photographs, and it was these she was staring at in frightened amazement.

There was one take just after Sumter fell, with me in the regalia of the Palmetto Volunteers along with my old commander Captain Redmond, Lord Balbriggan, who had been an Irish nobleman oddly enough. There was another of me with Lord Balbriggan, by then Brigadier General Redmond, taken during the Wilderness campaign. There was a glass daguerrotype even older than these, dated London 1852, and a small hand-tinted mezzotint of me on my twenty-first birthday, before I had even embarked on my first European tour which would immerse me in the Arts. Rolling on down through the years, there was a photograph of me in buckskins taken in the Arizona Territory in the 1880s, another with my slouch hat and Mauser rifle in the trenches outside Mafeking in 1900 when I fought for the gallant Boers. There I was shaking hands with Teddy Roosevelt and with one of my wives and our children on the deck of the *Lusitania* when we went to Europe in 1911; the name of the great Cunarder was clearly was clearly visible on the life preserver behind us. There I was with a group of my fellow pilots in my Sopwith

Pup at an aerodrome on the Western Front in 1918, fighting for old Mother England this time. A week later I had disappeared into the clouds and thus terminated my marriage of the period. There was one of another wife, and me in another part of the world, in front of our new Model A Ford. There I was as a Marine captain in the radio shack on Guadalcanal in 1942, there I was getting my Silver Star from MacArthur, there I was with a youthful California politico named Nixon, there I was in jungle fatigues at Da Nang and camos in the Rhodesian bush. And there were others of me, in every age and every manner of garb, a formal portrait in Edwardian evening dress, a zoot suit, and 1970s polyester.

When Rose looked up and saw me standing in the doorway her face froze in a mask of horror. I shook my head sadly. "You shouldn't pry into other people's things," I told her, walking over and beginning to put the material back into the portmanteau, quickly checking to make sure she had not unwittingly disturbed or contaminated anything among the reagents or occult apparatus. "Remember the story of Bluebeard's wife and the forbidden door?"

"I…I thought you were in the shower," she stammered.

"A good thing I forgot my fifty pence," I said. "You might not have been here when I got back. Now, at least we can talk."

"What are you, Charles?" she quavered. "Dear God, what, oh what kind of thing can you be?"

"I am a man, Rose. A man like any other who is sometimes wise, sometimes foolish, sometimes good and sometimes bad. Please believe that."

"*You know what I mean!*" she shouted wildly. "*What are you?*"

"What do you think I am?" I asked her. "What do you deduce from what you have seen here?"

"You're a crazy man," she mumbled. "You're a bloody lunatic who gets fake pictures of himself made with phony dates on them, wearing old-time clothes. You carry a trunk full of phony documents and letters around with you that you've fixed so they look old. You get some sort of weird thrill out of pretending to be two hundred years old. You're mad!"

"That might be the explanation," I agreed.

"But is it *true?*" she demanded.

"Do you believe it's true?"

"*Stop it!*" she screamed, on the verge of hysteria. "Stop playing with me! Give me a straight answer!" She picked up the 1852 daguerrotype and studied it carefully, then studied my own face. "Charles," she whispered fearfully. "Who is the man in this picture? Is it you?"

"Yes, Rose," I told her gently. "It's me."

"Not your great-great-grandfather or some other ancestor?"

"No. Myself."

"Then the date can't be right!" she insisted. "It's a joke photo of some kind. It has to be!"

"The date is correct, Rose. That picture was made on the twelfth of February, 1852, in the studio of a man named Frederick Moxon in the Strand, in London. It snowed that day."

Rose started shaking and buried her face in her hands. For a while she moaned and rocked back and forth. Then she whispered to me, "Charles, you have told me you love me. If that is true, then I beg of you, don't do this to me. If this is some crack-brained hoax, then please don't torture me. In the name of God's Own Mother, Charles, tell the truth! All of it!"

"Rose, I'm sorry, but there are only two possibilities, as I believe you can understand for yourself. The first possibility is that these photographs are exactly what they appear to be. The second possibility is that I am a madman who carries these things around with him in secret because I get some kind of diseased thrill out of pretending to be much older than I really am. If you decide it's the second possibility, then you'd better get out of here fast. Your life might be in danger if you stay in the same room with a lunatic."

"And if it's the first, then my soul might be in danger if I stay in the same room with a sorcerer!" she groaned. "I saw all those books on black magic. Tell me, Charles, I have got to know, danger or no."

"I do love you, Rose, and so the truth it shall be. I wish with all my heart that you had never opened that closet. I wish I never had to discuss this with you, but you did and now I must. My original name is Charles Henry Benedict Huger." It had been a long time since I had spoken that name out loud, and a pang of nostalgia came as it rolled from my lips, my surname coming out with the old Carolina Low Country twang as "Ew-jee." A name I had never thought to hear spoken aloud ever again, by anyone.

"Go on," she commanded.

"I was born in Charleston, South Carolina on the thirtieth day of June, 1810." Rose exhaled and closed her eyes. She knew now that there would be no third alternative, no rational explanation forthcoming. "Go on," she said again in a quiet voice.

"My family were wealthy planters. Cotton, indigo, rice, cane, tobacco, we grew it all and shipped it to the North, to the West Indies, to England and the Continent. We had our own wharfage in the Cooper River estuary and our own fleet of packets and clippers. My father was the adventurous one of the clan and he became a sea captain, a sort of merchant adventurer type. He was killed privateering in the War of 1812. I grew up the rich, pampered heir to several fortunes, in a big mansion off the Battery in Charleston. The house is a historical landmark nowadays, which I'm glad of, because it's been nicely preserved at taxpayer's expense that way. I was raised by my grandfather, my widowed mother, and assorted maiden aunts, and I was a very solitary and lonely little boy. My one refuge during the long, hot summer afternoons was the cool dimness of my grandfather's library upstairs. He had over a thousand volumes, quite a collection for that day and age before cheap paperbacks and cheaper paperback writers. In those days a book was a significant acquisition. It said something. It contained knowledge, great thought or literature. But my grandfather's library was unusual by any standards. I think it's possible he dabbled in the Arts at one time, the magical Arts, I mean, because he had just about every major work on the subject published up until then in Europe and America. He had Remigius, Kramer and Sprenger, Joseph Glanvil. He had the complete works of Cotton Mather, plus the alchemical works of Paracelsus, Agrippa, Ashmole, translations from Latin and Arabic, and at least two full-fledged grimoires, magical procedure manuals if you will. I was never able to ask him how he acquired all those volumes or what use he made of them, because he was carried off in a typhoid epidemic when I was ten. But I had other sources of information about the Arts, mainly one of our household slaves…"

"Slaves?" giggled Rose in a dangerously high falsetto. I wasn't sure she was able to take it all in.

"Slaves. We had several thousand scattered all across the state on various plantations, but the one I am speaking of was my mammy, old Aunt Sukey. Aunt Sukey was from Barbados, and at night she told me stories of voodoo and demons and ghosts, of witches' sabbaths and coffins that danced in their tombs. At any rate," I went on, "I grew up and did the things young bloods did in Charleston in the 1820s and 1830s. I roistered in the taverns and coffee houses, gambled and raced horses, had orgies with octoroons in the fancy cathouses off Savannah Highway, hunted and fished, fought a duel or two. But I never lost my love of learning and scholarship. In my early twenties I attended several universities in America and then went to Europe where I studied at Cambridge, and also here at Trinity College Dublin. My mother died while I was away and so there was nothing to bring me back to Charleston. I had all the money I needed from the family coffers, and so I stayed in Europe. I traveled extensively, the Balkans, Egypt, the Holy Land. Been travelling ever since, really, although I did go back to Charleston in 1860 when it became obvious that secession was coming. I was able to reclaim part of my inheritance in the Huger fortune by posing as my own son, allegedly born in Europe. Lost everything to the Yanks and the carpbetbaggers four years later, though."

"Carpetbaggers!" cackled Rose. "You're not the lunatic, Charles, I am for sitting here listening to this drivel! But go on, go on. How did you chance to become immortal, then?"

"From about 1830 onward I devoted myself to the study of magic and alchemy," I said. "I roamed Europe looking for adepts in the Arts, I haunted libraries and museums and private collections. I sought out occult practitioners of all types, and in France I met a cult leader named Pierre Vintras. The name would mean nothing to you, and in any case Vintras was a fraud, a man who used the occult to gratify his ego and seduce neurotic women,. There are many such, always on the periphery of the truth. But through sheer good fortune, through the Vintras circle I managed to meet my first genuine magus, a man who liked me and became my Master in the occult sense, and I became his pupil. During my discipleship with him he taught me the basic principles of the arcane knowledge I needed to know in order to attain what alchemists call the Philosopher's Stone, or the Elixir Vitae, or the Grand Catholicon. In occult parlance it is known as the Great Work. He who achieves it and chooses to avail himself of it rather than continue his natural cycle of incarnation is called an Ipsissimus, and is considered to have crossed the Abyss."

"Abyss?" said Rose. "Wait a minute, I'm not with you. What exactly did you *do* to yourself to make yourself immortal? Drink a potion or something?"

"Ah, thereby hangs a tale, *mo chridh*," I chuckled. "Right now I am having some difficulty with some people who want to know precisely that. I didn't tell them, and I won't tell you. All you need to know is that in 1840 I attained the Great Work. I was thirty years old in body then. I am thirty years old in body now. In linear time I am one hundred and seventy-two years of age."

"And...and will you never die?" she asked in a trembling voice.

"Not until I so desire, no," I told her.

"But, assuming I believe this absurd story, what about all those pictures in uniform? You seem to end up in a lot of wars. I should think war would be the last thing you'd want to be part of. Or are you invulnerable to bullets as well?"

"I'm not sure, never having been hit directly in the heart or the head or any other vital spot. I seem to have very high recuperative powers, though, and I recover in days from injuries that would incapacitate ordinary men for weeks or months. My wounds are never infected, either. My Master taught me that it is somewhat harder to kill an Ipsissimus than an ordinary man, but it can be done. My own theory is that if I were hurt badly enough I'd die. My body has some souvenirs, as you have noticed. Remember all those scars you asked me about?" I slid my robe down off my shoulders. "This one in the hip here is from a Yankee long rifle at Chickamauga. This one in my collar bone is a near miss from an Apache tomahawk, I was hit here by shrapnel on Iwo Jima, and this slash on my leg was from a poisoned punji stake in Vietnam which by all rights should have killed me."

"But why do you risk it?" she persisted.

"I've often asked myself that. All I can say is that periodically I get these periods of depression and self loathing where it just doesn't seem worth it any more. I get sick of living high on the hog or any other way, sick of dragging my life on and on without any rhyme or reason, never able to acquire anything permanent in the way of possessions or a family, always having to move on after a few years before my failure to grow visibly old starts to excite comment. Besides, it helps to get me out of my various marriages."

"I saw all those marriage certificates. You're the original love 'em and leave 'em lad. And me? Were you going to marry me and then do a vanishing act after a few years?"

"Yes," I admitted. "Rose, I still want to marry you. This new knowledge you have will make it hard, of course, but we can still have some good years and children, and neither you nor they will ever want for anything."

"Do you think I could ever be bought, Charles?" she cried. "Do you think I'd marry a monster for money?"

"I'm not a monster, Rose!" I pleaded. "I'm a man who has lived a bit longer than most, that's all. I loved you before you opened that closet this morning, and I love you still. I could make you return that love, Rose." She started, and I started bleakly. "Oh, yes. I could use the Arts on you and have you licking my feet in sheer object adoration. But that's no good, and I won't do it. I want you to become my wife voluntarily, and now it appears that you must have your eyes wide open like none before you. Please say you will."

Rose got up and went to the door. "I have to do a whole lot of thinking about this, Charles. Do I have the option of refusing you, really? Do you swear you won't hurt me or punish me in any way if I do say no?"

"I swear it," I told her, and meant it.

"Very well. I'll think about all this. Don't come down to my room any more, Charles. If I decide I want to see you again, I'll come up here. If not, I'll move out."

"As you wish," I agreed. There was nothing more I could say.

V.

I had no time to worry about Rose for the rest of that day because I knew I had to prepare for a psychic assault of some kind. I spent the morning doing some calculations and figuring out the planetary hours for that day and year, the planetary aspects and so on. This gave me a rough idea of when they would strike, between nine thirty and ten thirty that night. There were certain chemicals I had to get hold of, more quick reading I had to do in order to furbish some of my defensive skills, and preparations to make. One thing I determined to do was change my residence for the time being, and so I packed a grip, put on a suit, and checked into the Shelborne Hotel on St. Stephen's Green myself. I took a room on the third floor, one floor above Zee and one below Anson Delafontaine and Manny Rosenberg. Before I left the flats I left a brief note taped to Rose's door telling her that I would be gone for a day or so while she made up her mind about our relationship. I stocked up on sandwiches and fruit juices in my hotel room so I wouldn't have to leave the room to eat. It wouldn't do for me to bump into my adversaries in the hallway. Then I waited.

I was reasonably sure I knew when they would strike and also reasonably sure what they would try first. I was correct. I felt the first twinges of the attack a little past nine thirty, and for some time I did nothing to counteract it, carefully feeling its strength and dimension. The force behind it was strangely weak and seemed to be entirely feminine in nature. Puzzled, I slipped up the stairs. There was no light under the door of Delafontaine's room or Rosenberg's. I nipped downstairs and peeked around the corner at room 206 and saw a faint light, probably candles of the Art. If Manny and Delafontaine were in Zee's room, why weren't they helping her? It felt to me as if she were attacking all on her own.

I have no intention of going into detail regarding the thaumaturgical procedures used by both sides in this quiet little war. One does not write such things down carelessly anymore than one scribbles the formula for nitroglycerine on a shopping list after the eggs and milk. But for clarity's sake, it is necessary for me to speak of some general theory and background. Attend. This planet is surrounded by a field of psychic energy that is both generated and transmitted by the minds and nervous systems of all living beings, but especially human beings. This field exists just as surely as the gravitational field, the radiation field, ultraviolet rays, and all other forms of energy which are invisible to the naked eye and yet which affect us. The human brain is a powerful battery of this psychic energy, and in point of fact the psy field may now be detected and measured through such techniques as the electroencephalogram.

Just as radio waves and other forms of energy may be radiated or broadcast, so can psychic energy. Throughout history there have been men and women who were able to direct or channel this energy outwards or else increase their receptivity to it and thereby achieve telepathy, clairvoyance, etc. Most of these people are born naturally talented in this way, the skill being something that they are born with. However, it is also possible to acquire these skills and abilities through certain processes that we call the Arts. The Arts involve manipulation of psychic energy that can be used for good or evil according to one's own lights. There is no such thing as black magic or white magic any more than there is black fire or white electricity. Mankind uses or abuses these powers as he chooses, and my enemies were now abusing it to coerce me against my will.

What Zoraya was trying to do to me was a simple binding spell, a straight jolt of psychic energy aimed at the cortex of the brain. If done unskillfully or with murderous intent, this can cause death or permanent insanity. Done with just the right light touch, it can cause a temporary shorting out of the upper level of the cortex, the part of the brain that deals with thought and free will. But Zee had to make sure not to use too much force, or else she might end up with an immortal zombie on her hands, and I am sure this would have mightily upset her colleagues in the Circle. To give her credit, she was exhibiting considerable dexterity; I felt her spell like light, tingly little fingers probing the defenses of my mind, first here, then there, looking for an opening rather than trying to batter down the walls, so to speak.

I set up some equipment and after about half an hour of quiet concentration of my own mental forces I began a counterspell. It was easily done. A psychic bolt is like a bullet from a gun in that once it leaves the barrel, it's going to strike somewhere. Psychic energy concentrated in this manner cannot simply dissipate; it must find a resting-place. Essentially, what I did was to catch one of Zee's filaments and *reverse* the flow of negative energy, suddenly and without warning sending her own psychic bolt smashing back into her brain. Suddenly the pressure on me was gone, and I could feel Zoraya's consternation and anger as her defences fell before me and she came into my power. Chuckling, I picked up the telephone and dialed her room. When she answered I told her, "Be quiet and listen. You will come up to room 310 immediately. You will tell no one where you are going, nor will you leave any notes or other clues for your friends. Come now." I didn't wait to hear the end of her burst of profanity before I hung up. A minute later she was knocking on my door.

She was wearing blue jeans and a denim blouse, and she looked mad enough to spit. "You bastard!" she hissed as she came into the room. "I'll get you for this, by all the Elder Gods!"

"Sit down and do not speak unless you are spoken to," I commanded. She obeyed, glaring at me ferociously. "Now before I deal with your own impudence, young lady, I want you to tell me a few things. I will ask the questions and you will answer me truthfully, in full, and without any attempt at evasion or deception. Do you understand?"

"I understand, damn you!" she snapped.

"You'll keep a civil tongue in your head as well. In fact, you shall address me as sir."

"Yes, *sir!*" she growled.

"Don't try to fight against the spell," I advised her. "It will probably last until morning. If you try and fight it, you'll just end up giving yourself a very bad headache. Now to begin with, where are Rosenberg and Delafontaine and why weren't they helping to try to bind me?"

"Anson and Manny are out arranging for a major operation. There are some local practitioners here in Dublin who have an adequate Temple and we want to use it. I had hoped to bind you and get the secret from you myself to show the men I am a better practitioner than they thought. They only brought me in the hope I could bring you around on my back. They're bastards too."

"What local people? I don't know of any adepts or Goetic orders in Dublin, at least not since the days of the Golden Dawn."

"They're strictly bush league, but we want the use of their premises because it's a more or less properly set up Temple. We don't want to risk an invocation in a hotel room."

"An invocation?" I demanded in exasperation. "Of what? Are these local people Right or Left Hand Path?"

"Right, I think. I told you, I don't know who they are," Zoraya replied sullenly. "The men don't tell me anything."

"That figures," I ruminated. "Self-righteous amateurs as opposed to vicious amateurs. They'd have a Right Hand Temple then. I can locate it if I have to from the vibrations. That means an invocation through the Sephiroth rather than the Klipoth. A handy thing to know. What sort of entity?"

"A demon," she said. I exhaled slowly.

"Damnation!" I swore.

"Precisely, sir," she chuckled grimly.

"It's not funny. I suppose it's to be on Hallowmass?"

"Yes," she admitted. "The second hour of Saturn."

"What is the name of the Power they're going to invoke?" I demanded of her.

"I don't know, sir. I tell you, the men don't let me in on anything."

"How on earth do they think a demonic entity can get the Great Work from me?" I asked in anger.

"I'm not sure," said Zee. "Bind you, force you to speak, read your mind maybe and then tell us. But the idea is to have it bring you to us and put you in our power."

"What are they planning on paying the entity with?" I queried. "A white goat or a black cockerel, or something worse? I haven't read about any missing infants in the newspapers."

"Good grief no, of course not!" Zee protested. "What sort of black magicians do you take us for, sir? I think they've got a goat lined up.

That's all I know about it." She was silent for a while, then spoke again. "What are you going to do with me now, sir?"

"If I liked I could tell you to go up onto the roof of this hotel and jump off, or go back to your own bathroom and slit your wrists. And you'd obey my will, Zoraya. I've killed meddlers before, for less than what you attempted to do."

"And what do you expect me to do? Beg for mercy?" she said, turning pale. "I won't. You may kill me, but I won't debase myself before you or any other man."

"The question doesn't arise, because I'm not going to kill you. Possibly I should, considering what you people are planning to do. But I won't." Then my voice grew stern "But madam, you've a comeuppance do, and you shall have it. Maybe I'll see if you really do know the whole Kama Sutra."

"Oh, then you really are randy for me, *sir?*" she laughed. "Well, Manny and Anson won't be back for hours, so lets hit the sack. I'll give you the screwing of a lifetime, no matter how long a lifetime that's been. But it's still a form of rape, you know, and when this binding spell wears off I'll get even with you, *sir!*" Confidently she arose and began to unbutton her blouse.

"Hold your horses, there, young lady," I interjected. "I won't give you the pleasure. In point of fact it would indeed be rape, and I have personal scruples about such things. No, I've got it!" I chuckled out loud at the glory and the humor of my idea.

"I don't like the sound of that," said Zee suspiciously.

"Listen to me very carefully, Zoraya, and obey my commands to the letter. You know O'Connell Street?" She nodded apprehensively. "You will go there now, taking with you this copy of the Gideons Bible, courtesy of the Shelborne Hotel." I handed her the hotel room's copy. "You will stand at the foot of the Parnell Monument at the far end of O'Connell Street, and there you will remove every stitch of clothing from your body. You will then start reading the Scriptures aloud to the passers-by. The theaters and the pubs will be letting out soon, so you should gather quite an audience. You probably won't get more than halfway through Genesis before the gardai come and arrest you. When you are arrested you will offer no resistance to the police, but in response to all questions from them or anyone else, you will only recite the nursery rhyme 'Mary Had A Little Lamb'. You will take with you no money, but only your passport and your room key for identification purposes. I want Anson Delafontaine to have to come down to the cop shop and bail you out. You may call him tomorrow after the spell wears off. Now get out and do as I have told you to do."

Zoraya threw herself on her knees in front of me, in an agony of horror and shock. "*No!*" she cried. "In the name of God, Charles, don't do this to me! I'd rather you killed me! If you must humiliate me, don't do it in front of the whole world! Don't do it in front of Anson and Manny and the Circle!"

"A little humiliation will do you a world of good, Zelda," I told her. "It might even lead to a little humility. Now you will leave here and follow my instructions to the letter, without any attempt to escape or evade them. Go!" She picked up the Bible and left, sobbing in rage and mortification.

I vacated my room at the Shelborne early next morning and went back to my own bedsitter. Zoraya's arrest was in all the morning papers. Apparently she had collected quite a crowd, including many drunks staggering home from the just-closed pubs, and these latter were especially appreciative of Zee's eccentric Scriptural lesson. They interfered with the Guards who were trying to haul Zee away and a small riot developed. That afternoon there was a photo of her on the front page of the *Evening Herald*. It showed a tearful Zee being taken into the Store Street Garda station wrapped in a cop's overcoat. That afternoon Rose knocked on my door, with the newspaper in her hand. "Isn't this your American girl friend?" she asked.

"She's not my girl friend," I said.

"'Tis unusual company you're after keeping, and make no mistake," she said, shaking her head. "Is this crazy mot two hundred years old as well?"

"No, but she'd like to be."

"I figured that. The old man told me," said Rose with a nod.

"What old man?" I demanded of her, my blood suddenly running cold.

"The old professor from New York with the funny hat," said Rose. "He came around this morning and we had a nice long cuppa and a chat. I think he's as dotty as you are. He promised me all sorts of mystical enlightenment if I'd join his cult or whatever it is and help them persuade you to reveal the secret of eternal life." She laughed out loud heartily. "You know, the devil of it all is that that I believe you. I don't see why I should, but I do. I suppose it's because all this would be so pointless as a joke. What would it all be in aid of? It's so outlandish it must be true."

"I want to talk to you about it," I said. "But right now I need to take care of something. Excuse me."

I went down to the street, found a pay telephone that worked, dialed the Shelborne Hotel and asked for Anson Delafontaine's room. When he answered he snapped at me, "That was a cruel and heartless trick you played on Zee, Charles! We don't…"

"I don't give a damn about Miss Zee's sensibilities," I hissed at him. "I will make this short and to the point. The girl who lives here, Rose, is off limits. She is not involved. If you attempt to involve her I will kill you. All of you. Heed what I say." I hung up and returned to my room.

"Rose," I said without preamble, "I may be a sorcerer and a few other things, but I love you sincerely. I need to know now what you intend to do."

"I'm not sure yet," said Rose slowly. "I'm still not sure what to make of this business. If I did marry you I would demand certain things of you, things you might not be willing to give me."

"Money? Security? Those things you will have, Rose, always."

"I don't mean anything material, Charles," she said. "I mean full measure as your wife. You may live to be thousands of years old, Charles, where I have maybe sixty years to live from today, maybe not that much. What you're offering me, Charles, is really nothing more than a one night stand in terms of your own lifetime. I won't get into what might happen when I am eighty and you're still thirty. Because that's not going to happen. I won't agree to a situation like that. If you want me, Charles, then you must give me the same centuries of life that you have yourself. You must give it to me, whatever the secret is, because if I am to be your wife I must be your life's partner. That's what marriage is, that's why it is a sacrament, a far nobler thing than mere lovemaking. If you want me to be your life's partner, then you must give me a life to match yours, and if you don't want to share your whole life with me, then you've no business asking."

I had been afraid of this. She was asking me for the same thing the Circle was asking, and unlike them she was morally justified in demanding it as her due.

"You know that there are others who seek to obtain the Great Work through me?" I answered her carefully. "Rosenberg must have told you that I refused them. Did he tell you why I refused?"

"I didn't understand it all. Please explain."

"The Great Work cannot be *given*. It must be *attained*. That is, it is a transformation that only you can make within yourself. I could sit here right now and describe to you in a few hundred words the physical procedures and rituals I underwent in order to become what I am today, and you could repeat them down to the last detail without succeeding unless you were properly prepared within yourself. The Great Work is merely the final step in a long process of inner learning, awakening, and development. You cannot write a book of great literature using an alphabet of A-B-C and then jumping directly to X-Y-Z. That's what

Rosenberg and his people are trying to do, and in your case you don't even have ABC yet."

"So you refuse?"

"No, I didn't say that. Rose, I *cannot* simply hand the secret over to you! It just doesn't work like that. But there is an alternative. I can take you on not only as my wife and my lover, but as my pupil in the Arts. I will give you your magical ABCs like my own Master gave them to me a century or so gone. I'll do better, I'll give you A through G, if you like the analogy. The rest of the occult alphabet you will have to complete yourself, and by the time you reach the letter M or so, you will know in your own heart whether you want to complete it."

"The bargain of Faust," whispered Rose in fascination. "What will it cost me, Charles? Must I lose my soul for it?"

"No, nothing like that. No pacts with the devil signed in blood. But it will cost you enough," I admitted. "It will cost you your innocence, your peace of mind, and every illusion you've got. You may decide that there are things you don't want to know at that price. Rose, a person who aspires to the Arts must be the supreme realist. He or she must possess something that virtually no one else on earth possesses, a truly open mind. Not an open mind with even a few reservations or exempted prejudices, but a mind that can question everything and take anything at face value if need be. Those aspects sound contradictory. They aren't."

"And if I decide to become a kind of sorcerer's apprentice for you? How do we proceed?"

"First we get rid of the people who are after me, and with them off my tail we can go somewhere, get properly set up, and get down to some serious work. For the moment though, I will give you the Rule of the Seeker: 'In my quest I reject and abjure both the Superstition of Ignorance and the Superstition of Science.' Think about that very carefully, and tomorrow come to me and explain what you think it means. In the meantime, I have some preparations to make, so leave me to them. If anyone you don't know tries to contact you or if anything unusual happens to you, you must let me know immediately."

I did some urgent reading to brush up on my anti-demonics, and reluctantly concluded that I had to include Rose in the defense. They might try to use her against me in some way in spite of my warning. I stocked up on several chemicals I was short of, carefully reconsecrated and recharged my equipment, and did some divining in search of any nearby sources of psychic vibrations that might indicate a Right-Hand Temple. By Temple I do not mean a building on its own, but any secure room or premises set up for the working of thaumaturgical operations. There would be a psychic residue that I should be able to detect. After some effort I centered in on the wealthy suburb of Howth in northern County Dublin and got a clear picture of a large house in my scrying plate. I took a 31 bus from Lower Abbey Street that evening and rode up to Howth to check the place out. I found the house in the darkening twilight, stood across the street in the shadow of a huge stately elm, and closed my eyes and "felt" the psychic energy field. In my mind the house appeared pale, like a photographic negative, the ten spheres of the Sephiroth glowing over it. I took the bus back into town. Later I learned that the house belong to a Fine Gael junior cabinet minister.

Much to my surprise, Rose came back with one of the best analyses of the Seeker's Dictum I had ever heard. "The superstition of ignorance is the refusal to question," she told me. "The superstition of science is the refusal to answer."

"Oh? Elucidate."

"The ignorant simply believe what they want to believe or what they've been taught to believe because it's easier to do so," she explained. "Questioning one's prejudices simply takes too much effort. The scientific bigots are the reverse. They take their prejudices and try to twist the facts to fit. They take something apart supposedly to see what makes it tick, then they put it back together the way they think it *should* be. If there are some parts left over, sweep them under the carpet, just so long as the thing works more or less. Again, it's a way of avoiding mental effort."

"Excellent!" I commended her, please. "How are your own illusions holding out? How steady a Catholic are you?"

"Not as steady as I should be, since I'm delving into black magic with you," she said wryly. "If Father Patrick knew I was doing this he'd take a stick to me and exorcise you with bell, book, and candle. Do I have to stop going to Mass now? I mean, the Host won't burn my tongue or anything?"

"No, Rose, to honor and worship God in any way whatsoever is a noble and pious act. There are many magical ceremonies which do just that, and the Mass itself is after all a ritual act of ceremonial and sacerdotal magic. But I don't recommend getting too explicit in confession, because I'm going to have to involve you early on in what is possibly the worst and certainly the most dangerous of the Arts, and do so in only three days' time."

"Halloween?" laughed Rose. "Ghoulies and ghoosties and long-legged beasties and things that go bump in the night?"

"I'm afraid so," I said grimly.

She looked at me strangely for a moment. "You're serious, aren't you?"

"I'm afraid so," I said again. "Make us a cup of tea, love? We've a long session ahead of us." She made the tea and sat down on my bed. I sipped and sat down in a chair before the glowing coal fire in the grate. Outside it was afternoon, with wan autumn sunlight filtering through the windows into the high-ceilinged Georgian chamber. "I will now instruct you about demons," I told her.

But first I told her the full story of how the present problem had come about. I told her how I had joined the Circle in San Francisco to learn about them, how much they knew, if they could teach me anything new, if they posed a possible threat to me. But the cultists had stumbled upon my secret when they acquired some original

Theosophical Society material from the 1890s, books and letters and archives including a number of photographs, several of which showed me with Madame Blavatsky and Colonel Olcott, the founders of the society. I had been associated with the San Francisco group for some time, and they respected me as an adept of great learning, but once they suspected my true nature they dug into my background using normal research procedures as well as the Arts, and they learned enough to convince them that I was the Count St. Germain or the Wandering Jew or Methuselah or some such personage. I told her of my subsequent flight and of recent events here in Dublin. "And you sent that poor lass out into the nippy autumn air in her birthday suit?" laughed Rose. "Charles, you're *awful!*"

"No," I said, shaking my head. "They are the awful ones, because they are planning on invoking a non-human Intelligence from another dimension. What may be called a demon, for want of a better term."

"You mean there really are such things?" asked Rose with a shudder.

"Yes. Basically, there are two kinds of occult intelligences, those of human origin, i.e. ghosts, and those of non-human origin. The non-human ones can in turn be divided into two categories, those that are native to this planet or dimension or universe, and those that are not. The process of contacting, suborning, and utilizing human spirits is called necromancy, and I won't get into that with you because it is a very specialized field all its own. Daemonic invocation is even more complex, and under normal circumstances I would never dream of getting you involved in it until you had studied under me for years and learned all the basics. But these wretched people leave us no choice."

"You realize you're frightening me?" said Rose in a low voice.

"Good. You need to be frightened. *I'm* frightened of these Outside Entities." I got up and put the kettle on for more tea, and kept on talking while I made two cups. "There are two basic types of demonic being, as I said. The home grown ones which are of these planet's astral plane are called elementals, of the nature of the four alchemical Elements, that is to say Fire, Water, Earth, and Air. In modern scientific terms this would be electrical energy, liquid, matter, and gas. I don't think these Americans will fool around with an elemental, because these beings are rather unsuitable for the purpose they have in mind, and also to be frank they are not very intelligent. I could easily defend myself against them and I don't see any way they could really use one, or even think they could use one, to obtain the desired result. No, it will almost certainly be a more powerful being, from outside the bounds of space and time as we know it." I sipped my tea. Rose was staring at me in horror. "I cannot overemphasize how incredibly dangerous these Outer Ones are, Rose. They are filled with rage at being dragged into this dimension and compelled to perform pointless and silly errands for beings that they regard as microbes. They do, however, enjoy feasting on avian or mammalian blood, especially human blood, from which they draw sustenance, and best of all they enjoy feeding on souls."

"*Souls?*" exclaimed Rose incredulously.

"The essential, indestructible life force. It is a form of energy, of course, and occultists knew long before scientists that energy can neither be created nor destroyed. The soul is immortal, but it can in some cases be absorbed or assimilated into that of another entity. Hence vampires and other psychophages. Hence Faust." I grinned at her. "Dummies like Faust agree to the absorption and transmutation of their individual life force into an alien pattern, obliterating all that is human in them. They do this for a century of life or the possession of a woman or a flat cash fee. Imbeciles! All of these things they could have gained through the Arts without the aid of Those Outside."

"How are these devil things summoned?" asked Rose, fascinated in spite of her revulsion.

"Through a series of rituals called invocation. By the way, you *evoke* the beings of this astral plane, elementals, earthly spirits, etcetera, while you *invoke* beings from outside it. The two processes are essentially different in a number of important respects. Evocation I won't get into now, but invocation consists of and invoking ritual performed in a particular place which has been properly laid out and prepared, at a particular time determined by the planetary hours, and by persons suitably prepared and attired. The two most important aspects of the ritual are protection for the operators and the use of what is called the *sigil,* a metal plate bearing a strange diagram or pattern. This sigil is in fact a two-dimensional representation of the route that the entity must take between this world and ours, rather like a road map or the combination to a safe. You need to ensure that you use the correct sigil to get hold of the right entity. Believe me, you don't want to get hold of the wrong one!"

"I don't want to get hold of *any* of them!" protested Rose.

"Very wise. But the most important element of all in an invocation is the sacrifice."

"The sacrifice?" cried Rose.

"Yes. These Outer Ones must have blood in order to take on form and draw enough of this world's psychic energy to stay here any length of time. Their own power is very great, but when they enter this dimension it is of the wrong wave length, AC as opposed to DC you might say. They need a shot of blood-power as a sort of transformer or adaptor, so they can bring their own power to bear. But more than that, they *like* it. You may have heard the old saying of how the blood is the life. These beings crave blood and souls like a drunkard craves wine or an addict heroin. It is possible for humans to control these entities for short periods of time and make them do human bidding, but the Power must be rewarded with a certain amount of earthly life force. Remember, these beings are intelligent, and they know their occult labor laws. Just as you can't expect a human artisan to work for nothing, you can't expect a demon to do your bidding and then just go away. The demon simply won't do it, or what's worse it will hang around looking for an opportunity to help itself to the operator's soul."

"Dear God in Heaven," breathed Rose, her face white as a sheet. "Charles, what happens if one just gets loose in our dimension without warning?"

"That, my darling, happens far more often than anyone realizes," I told her grimly. "The consequence of amateur sorcerers playing games with the Powers. Sometimes a summoning goes wrong and the demon kills and absorbs the would-be magus. Other times the foolish and wicked people who call up these things have protected themselves well enough, but lose control of the entity, like Pandora opening the box. Then the results are hellish in every sense of the word. You read stories in the paper of normal people suddenly going berserk and shooting down a dozen strangers, teenagers murdering their parents, men coming home from work and eating their dinner and then while their families are watching television they come in and chop everyone up with an axe. Most of these sudden, inexplicable outbursts of violence are the result of uncontrolled demonic influences. You may have noticed that this type of thing has become more common every year. That's because there are more silly dilettantes dabbling in the occult nowadays than ever before. Our ancestors weren't total fools when they forbade by law the practice of the occult Arts."

"But what happens to the demons afterwards?" asked Rose faintly.

"Generally they can't hang on too long in this dimension, so they gorge themselves on blood and souls in one quick massacre and then return to the Outer Darkness. However, sometimes one gets a firm hold in the mind of an individual and can stay longer, and then you've got a genuine monster. Some such possessed men become Jack the Rippers, compulsive serial killers who strike again and again, feeding on the spilled blood and the mass terror they create, with an uncanny ability to avoid getting caught which people find as frightening as the murders themselves.. Even worse, the entity might possess someone in a key position in government or someone capable of rising to political power, and then you have a Caligula or an Idi Amin or a Mao Tse-tung."

"Like Hitler, you mean?" ventured Rose.

"No, Hitler was a logoidal atavism, and don't ask me what *that* is or we'll be here all night. We've got years to instill a complete occult education into you, my dear, but right now through no fault of your own you're caught in the middle of a very nasty situation, and I have to give you a crash course in anti-demonics."

"What's so dangerous about Halloween?" she wanted to know. "Is it really the night when the powers of evil are exalted, like the legends say?"

"One of four such nights," I replied. "Hallowmass on October 31st, Candlemas on February 2nd, Beltane of Walpurgis Night on April the 30th, and Lammas Night on August the first. In occult terms, these ancient festivals are called intersolstices, a time almost precisely between each planetary solstice when the barriers between the spheres and dimensions are weakest, and so most favorable to invocation. The solstices themselves are the most favorable times for anti-demonic operations or rites of exorcism, since the barriers are the strongest then and the entities have to exert so much more power to break through and hold onto their presence here. If we're still having this trouble by December 21st, I've got an expulsion ritual that will boot out anything these clowns can call up."

"My God, I hope this doesn't last that long!" Rose sighed. "Two more months of this? I don't think I could stand it. I'd go mad. How will these people call the demon out of hell?"

"There are a number of ceremonies they might use, depending on many factors, but all of these operations are essentially divided into three parts. First, they must use the sigil to open the door between the dimensions and let in the entity they want, and *only* the one they want. Once the spirit has responded, they must *charge* it, i.e. give It their orders, and *bind* it, that is they must sacrifice earthly blood to give It power, compelling It to perform their bidding while protecting themselves from It at the same time. They will do this using a number of rituals and magically charged and significant objects to create a shield of psychic vibrations strong enough to protect themselves, quite literally to keep the demon from their throats, and block the exit, so to speak. Once they have charged and bound the Power, then It will come after us."

"*Us?*" interjected Rose.

"Me specifically, or so I believe. I'd send you away, Rose, but there's always the chance that they might try to attack you, have the demon possess you or carry you off or something to blackmail me into co-operating with them." She turned a ghastly white. "That's why you've got to be inside the defenses with me." This time I didn't bother with tea, but poured Rose a large Jameson. I wanted one myself, but couldn't afford the damage the whiskey might do to my psychic force emanating from my nervous system. "Rose, my dearest love, I am damnably sorry about getting you involved in this."

"Alice followed a white rabbit down a hole, I opened the wrong cupboard one morning," she said with a shaky laugh, downing the golden liquid. "Alice found Wonderland. I seem to have ended up in the Twilight Zone. Or Transylvania. Charles, I'm still not quite clear on this. How can these people *force* this horrible devil creature to come after you, after us, when apparently it doesn't want to?"

"That's the third part of the invocation, the dismissal. Look at it in this very oversimplified way. These people will be reaching a long lariat through space and time and lassoing this being. They will then drag it into our world. The being will enjoy certain aspects of this world, such as the menu of blood and soul-force, but otherwise this dimension is very unpleasant for It, rather as if you had to dive to the bottom of the sea for a sip of champagne. You might like champagne enough to stay down a little while, but eventually you'd want to return to land. The demon wants to go home, but It *can't* unless the people who lassoed It let go of their end of the rope. It can get at them and kill them and devour their blood and souls if their defenses are weak, and that would release It. But if their defenses are strong, and they tug on the rope, then It will perform whatever they ask in order to be dismissed."

"But how do we defend ourselves against It?" Rose wailed.

"The same way they do, by erecting around ourselves a barrier of psychic power vibrating at a pitch so powerful that the entity cannot break through. If our defensive barrier is stronger than theirs, eventually our current of psychic force will override theirs, and their barrier will collapse, thus leaving the entity an exit through which It can escape and severing the rope, the magical lasso, that holds It here."

"But if their protection collapses, will It hurt them?" asked Rose hesitantly. "The old professor was a nice enough oul' fella, and even though naturally enough I don't care for your chic American mot I don't want to sic some kind of evil monster on her."

"Just about anything could happen, Rose," I said grimly. "But we're not calling up the demon, Rose, they are. Better them than us. These people are planning to do something that goes beyond mere murder. If Zee or Manny Rosenberg were to put a pistol to your head and shoot you, all they would be doing is to kill your present body in your present incarnation. Your soul would go on in the natural way to be re-born, hopefully as someone who knows when not to go poking into locked cupboards. Messing with the Outer Ones is endangering all that is you, and I will not permit it. These fools don't know the extent of my power, but they're about to learn, and they must pay folly's price. I hope for their sake that price is not too high."

"So do I, Charles," she said. "I know we've no choice. It's them or us. Now, tell me about this defensive barrier. How is it made? How will we get inside? What will the demon do when....?" We talked on, late into the night.

VI.

On the morning of the 31st we were ready, except for one thing. I talked to Rose while carefully rolling up the carpet in my room, exposing the wooden floorboards from the eighteenth century, which together we scrubbed thoroughly clean on our hands and knees. "I've decided to use a combined carrot and stick approach," I told her. "Zee told me they are planning on sacrificing the blood and soul of a goat, quite a powerful offering. I just hope they haven't decided on something stronger since then. But still, animal blood and animal life-force is still only fish and chips by demonic culinary standards. A demon longs to feast on the steak and potatoes of a human soul and quaff the vintage wine of human blood. I don't think they'd go that far in a foreign country, although they may get that desperate later. So we may be able to outbid Delafontaine and his people, in conjunction with our stronger defenses. We'll try to bribe the demon, after we frustrate Its initial efforts."

"Eh? You mean offer It a jar full of human blood from a blood bank or something?" asked Rose, disgust in her voice.

"No, I have in mind offering It a rare delicacy, a kind of bon-bon."

"And what is that?" she asked curiously.

"Sit here," I commanded, and seating her on the floor I carefully drew a complex diagram around her. Then I drew a magic circle around the both of us and quickly sealed it with an incantation. "Tell me," I asked her casually. "Hear about what happened in the North last night? The bold lads of the I. R. A. blew up a policeman by wiring a bomb to his car. Trouble was, the officer's two children aged three and five were in the car with him."

"I just try to forget about that whole lunatic scene up there," Rose said with a shrug. "You just get hardened to it after a while, I suppose. You have to, else you'd go mad. If I thought about it I'd be crying all the time."

"But I want you to cry, Rose. I want you to weep, right now."

"I beg your pardon?" she asked incredulously.

"A little trick I was taught by my Master a long time ago. Tears, salinated water, hold a powerful psychic charge if wept in genuine emotion. Rose, I am going to sit here saying horrible, terrible things to you in order to make you weep. I thought about making you recall your own personal griefs, remember when your mother died and so on, but I can't be that cruel to you. The object of this exercise is to produce a bribe for a demon, not torture a loved one. I'd wish I could just slice an onion under your nose. That won't do, though. There has to be genuine emotion involved. So I have chosen as my theme the Ould Sod itself, Mother Ireland, and all the agony your country has gone through at the hands of assorted foreign invaders and despoilers."

"Starting with the Vikings?" she asked dryly. "I rather doubt I could get maudlin over the invasion of Strongbow or even Cromwell. That's my Uncle Shamie you want. You read such things in books, they aren't real."

"Aren't they? Yesterday a man and a five year old girl and a three year old boy were roasted alive by burning petrol in their own motor vehicle. Are they any more real than the children roasted alive by Cromwell in the church at Drogheda? Flames seared flesh just as hot three centuries ago. In 1798 the British used the O'Connell Bridge here in Dublin as a ready-made gallows and hanged Irishmen by the score over the river. They had a custom called pitch-capping back in those days, which involved jamming a sticky hat soaked in pitch down into a suspect's head and setting fire to it. Nowadays they use electric shock and sleep deprivation, and if they can't get their man any other way they pay some half-insane petty criminal to get up in a Diplock court and swear away the lives of twenty or thirty at a time. On the other hand, the Catholic lunatics take a much simpler approach. They shoot men in the back or blow them up with concealed bombs. They blow up Protestants and shoot them in the back and burn them alive in their cars along with their children, blow off arms and legs and occasionally kill the wrong man by mistake, and then they just can't for the life of them understand why the Protestant Irish don't rush into their open arms like long lost brothers and hand over the six counties."

"It's not that simple!" protested Rose. "There's a whole lot more to the problem than that!"

"Yes, yes, I know that," I said impatiently. "You're missing the point. I am not asking for a political debate, I want to get you *upset*, genuinely upset so that you will weep grief-laden tears. I wish I could convey to you some of my own memories and experiences…listen, darling. I am going to tell you about the Famine. I am going to tell you what I myself saw here in this country in the terrible third year of 1848…" I told her every sickening detail I could remember. I told her of dead mothers lying in ditches with dead babies in their arms, babies that were gnawed and chewed and half eaten by those starving mothers. I told her of corpses littering the fields with their lips stained green from trying to eat the grass, of men and women crawling along the roadsides of Kerry and Limerick on their hands and knees because they were to weak to stand and walk. I told of how England's response to the crisis was to send regiments of troops to guard the warehouses and ships that bulged with meat, milk, bacon, grain, and salted fish, because these foodstuffs were the produce and property of English landlords and were for export to put money in English bank accounts and rolls of fat around Ascendancy waistlines. I told of the munificent charity of John Bull who established workhouses and road building schemes where a man might earn the princely sum of ninepence a day, provided he worked from dark to dawn like a dray horse. I told of men hanged or transported in the hellish prison ships to Australia for stealing a rabbit or a few eggs to feed their children. I told of overcrowded emigrant ships that wallowed out of Cork and Galway and arrived in America with eight out of ten dead from starvation or disease. I told of a million people who died in agony and despair because England considered the Irish to be sub human animals and did not care whether they lived or died. Then I went through the evictions where families were turned out of their homes to wander in the woods because the English found sheep and cattle more profitable than Irish.

In the end she wept, and I siphoned the tears off her sweet face with a straw into a small vial. When the vial was full I stoppered it and carefully wrapped it in a silken cloth of the art. Then I opened the magic circle, carried her to the bed and made love to her.

"Soon it will be over, my love," I whispered to her. "Just this one very bad night to go through, and we will be free of this trouble, and I will help you come to know the world, and the worlds beyond this one, and your own self." I hoped that I told her the truth, and that it would end tonight, and that it would go the right way. Many a famous duellist has fallen to some rank amateur who has gotten lucky. A thaumaturgical duel is not the same as flintlocks at dawn, admittedly, but I found myself running over yet again in my mind everything I knew about the Order and its capabilities. I was still certain that I could defeat them. But could Rose stand the strain?

That night just before sundown I laid out the grand circle of the Arts, our outer line of defense, and within a smaller one, the Great Seal of Solomon. Within the Great Seal I placed two pentagrams, one for myself and one for Rose. Rose herself was robed in white, and I in blue, a strong defensive color. All of our circles were lined within and without with an anti-demonic of my own devising, salt and iron filings and powdered garlic along with several other less describable substances, all charged with a powerful incantation. Within each pentagram I placed lighted candles and vials of holy water, and in my own pentagram I had the equipment I would need, the athame ritual knife, the wand, the thurible, the smoking censor, the fumigants in small silver bowls. Zee had told me the enemy would begin their assault at the second Hour of Saturn, on this particular evening beginning at about ten o'clock, and so for several hours Rose and I practiced rituals I had taught her during the last few days, ceremonial exercises designed to create serenity and strength of mind in us, charge the circle and the atmosphere with positive psychic vibrations, and concentrate our powers. The lights were all on, and no doubt to an observer the whole business would have seemed absurd. But the danger was all too real, as we discovered about ten thirty.

Rose and I were sitting in our pentagrams conversing quietly, when the lights flickered. I rose to my feet and made a few last-minute preparations of the equipment, lighting the censor and sprinkling fumigants into it, and unsheathing the athame. "Be strong, be brave, be calm," I adjured Rose for the last time. "Above all, at peril of your very soul, *do not leave the circle!*"

"I love you," whispered the girl.

"And I you," I replied. The lights went very dim, although throughout the subsequent events they never went out completely. Sounds began, thumping and scraping and scratching as if some strange creature were scampering up the walls and across the high Georgian ceiling. Then came a tinny, hysterical laughter which sounded very far away, and then the sound of a high and ferocious wind, whistling and roaring across the barren plains of God alone knew what world, in what time and place. Finally, in the corner of the ceiling, a small inky black cloud formed, black and impenetrable. It pulsed.

"Up there, Charles," said Rose, pointing. Her voice was commendably calm.

"I see it," I replied. The cloud or ink spot drifted out into the room and then began to drip oily black ooze all around the boundaries of the circle. The cloud settled down into the sink, and soon the sink was gurgling and overflowing with filthy black goo containing turds, long slimy tapeworms, squamous insect life and other unidentifiable but repulsive matter. The effluence roiled and steamed and stank all over the room, but did not cross the boundaries of the grand circle. Then from the bubbling tarry sink arose a Face. It was the Face of a young man, black as ebon, of classical beauty and with finely chiseled features, and in the eyes of that Face glowed the lambent lights of hell. The mouth opened, and from it protruded not a tongue but a long and sinuous arm ending in a woman's bejeweled and dainty hand, all fish-belly white. The arm extended and extended until it was at least nine feet long, and it gently probed the circle, unable to reach in and grab either of us. The slender hand waved mockingly before me at eye level, beckoning and taunting. Then the arm dissolved into mist and disappeared. I glanced over at Rose. She stood upright in her pentagram, clutching her rosary and praying quietly, her eyes open but downcast.

I trembled within, for I knew this Power in this present manifestation, and It was a much higher level of entity than I had anticipated. "Welcome, O Prince," I greeted It courteously.

"Foolish little wizard, cozen me not," came a Voice. It was a Voice of utter loathsomeness, like the tearing of rotten meat. "I shall bear you to those who have summoned me, and you shall be humbled and obedient as a slave. Upon your wretched body I will carve a masterpiece in pain and suffering until you speak that which my summoners wish to hear. I will breathe hellfire into your fundament and roast your living guts, I will lick your living brain from your skull with a tongue of fire, I will rend you and feed your quartered flesh to the dogs of the desert. I shall make this comely maiden naked and shamed before the world, I shall plow her with a phallus of ice and lash her with white hot iron flails, and she shall hang head downward upon a gibbet while an imp bastes her body in boiling oil."

I breathed an inward sigh of relief. If the Thing was reduced to threats, then our barrier would hold. "You must appear before me in a more pleasing form, O Prince," I commanded, and lit the thurible. I plunged the wand into the depths of the flames and a shriek went up that seemed to shake the whole house. Suddenly the black ooze and the Face were gone, and over the sink crouched a huge, writhing spider, eyes glowing and mandibles slavering. It growled like a bear or lion. Again I thrust the wand into the burning vessel, and again anguished howls reverberated. Then a little old man stood before us, bent and gray and wrinkled, attired in a tattered frock coat, the lower half of a pair of red flannel long johns, a green top hat, and purple spats.

"Now, yew just hold on thar, young whippersnapper!" whined the old man pleadingly. "Ain't no call to be so dadburned cranky! Why, it ain't none o' my own choice to come aroun' here pesterin' folks! Why, iffen it was up to me, I'd…"

"Away, vision of foolishness!" I shouted, and thrust the wand for the third time into the flames. The shrieks of the demon were ear-splitting. I took another quick glance at Rose, and saw that although she was white as a sheet she was holding up. Now there stood before us a tall bearded man, handsome and calm of visage, a negro robed resplendently in jewels and fantastic plumage like some ancient African king. I recalled the ancient manuscript that had stated, "…and ye Magus shalle Commande and Adjure ye Mightie Prince, even unto ye Seventie-Two Holie Names if neede shalle be, until He shalle Appeare Before ye Magus in Comelie and Pleasaunt Forme, that is, in ye Shape and Guise of an Ethiope, Richlie Apparell'd, ande with no Stinke." Now I knew that I had forced the entity to assume the proper shape for negotiating with humans, a victory in itself.

"Oh wizard, your power is indeed great," said the Thing, in a voice of dead ashes. "But you know that in the end you must succumb. Yield now, and in my admiration and respect for your skill I shall do no scathe either to you or your handmaiden. I shall carry you to those who have charged me with this commission, you will reveal to them the secret knowledge that they seek, and then I shall depart, leaving none the worse for my coming."

"That I shall not do, O great and puissant Prince," I replied. "But I would not have you depart this plane thinking me lacking in the awe and humble respect which is due a Power such as thyself. I have here a tribute to your might and a reward for your troubles." I held up the vial and waved it at him. "Do you know what it is, O Prince?"

If it were possible for a totally motionless face to take on an appearance of greed, the face of the demon did so. "Give it me!" It ordered peremptorily.

"The tears of a woman of Ireland, wept for her slashed and savaged land, wept for her butchered and starved people, wept for the faith which foreigners tried to rip from her nation's soul with the bloody sword."

"Give it me!" rumbled the Thing.

"Sweeter than the icy frozen air of Yuggoth, O Prince!" I said temptingly. "More potent than the Black Wine of the Hundred Year sacrifice! A balm you cannot resist!"

"Give it me!" hissed the demon.

"A boon then, O Prince!" I replied.

"Give it me!" screamed the creature hoarsely.

"Then do my bidding!" I commanded.

"I cannot! I have been charged and bound by those others who brought me hither! Give me that vial!" cried the demon in torment.

"The longer you dally here, the stronger my wall of magical power presses against theirs, the closer their barrier comes to collapse! Soon they will not be able to hold you! You may flee this plane then, but unless you binds yourself here and now to do my bidding you shall leave it without this vial and the nectar it contains!"

"*Give it me!*" roared the entity. "*I must have it! I must have it!*" The being clawed at the invisible wall of the circle with talon-like fingers, trying to reach the bottle I dangled before it.

"Time grows short, O Prince!" I said sternly. "Do you agree?"

"*I will obey thee!*" shrieked the creature. "Make the charge!"

"Return now to those who have summoned you. Leave this plane however you can, deal with them in whatever way you wish, but never again come to molest myself or this maiden. You have thirty-six thousand lesser demons, imps, incubi, succubi, ghouls, vampires, and famil-iars at your command, O Prince. Never allow them, any of them, to come unto myself or this maiden for any hurtful purpose." I thought it best to take this precaution for the future while the opportunity offered. "Do you agree? Swear it by every one of the Seventy-Two Names of God!"

"I agree," said the demon. "I seal my word with my oath by Adonai, by Jehovah, by Tetragrammaton, by Elohim..." The entity quickly recited all Seventy-Two Names, and so greedy was It for the delicacy I proffered that it didn't even try to cheat by omitting one. "Now give it me," concluded the demon. I tossed it the vial of tears, and from the fig-ure's mouth the long, sickly feminine hand shot out and caught the bot-tle, then slid back into the mouth that was no mouth. With a bestial roar of pure pleasure the demon vanished in a puff of blue smoke and a crackling of ozone, like a burst of ball lightning.

Rose looked at me. "Is it over?" she asked in a calm voice.

"Yes," I replied with a nod.

"Praise be unto God!" she said, and fainted.

VI.

But it wasn't quite over. The next afternoon, while Rose was still sleeping, I slipped out for the newspapers and a front page story caught my eye under the headline *Nude Bible Girl Found Slain In Liffey.* I groaned and went back to my room where I read the story minutely, trying to figure out precisely what had happened. After a time I was sure I knew.

The story said that one Zelda Moskowitz, an America tourist from Fresno, California, had been found dead that morning, floating in the river. Miss Moskowitz had recently attracted public attention when she was arrested by gardai for indecent exposure and disorderly conduct on O'Connell Street when she publicly disrobed and etc., etc. Her body had again been nude when recovered by a police launch below Halfpenny Bridge, her throat had been cut, and the State Pathologist stated that she had been tortured extensively before her death, but would give no details. I slipped down to the pay phone and called the Shelborne Hotel. A haggard-sounding Emmanuel Rosenberg answered the telephone. "Happy now, Manny, you son of a bitch?" I snarled at him.

"You made us do it!" shrieked the old man hysterically. "You monster! Don't you see that we had no choice? You broke our barrier, it would have gotten all of us if we hadn't done it! My God, my God, poor Zee!"

Delafontaine grabbed the telephone and began cursing me in mad rage. "We'll get you, Charles!" he finished up. "We'll hound you to the ends of the earth! We'll.."

"You will do no such thing," I interrupted in a voice of steel. As impassioned as Anson was, he could still recognize the sound of death brushing his elbow, and he shut up. "This is it, Anson, it's over. If I have any trouble with any of you people ever again, by all that I hold sacred, by the Seventy-Two Names, I shall bring onto this plane once again a certain mighty Prince that we both know of, and this time I will send him after you, with very specific instructions. Do you understand me, Anson? You'd better!"

There was a commotion in the background, a knocking on the door, and muffled conversation. Delafontaine put down the receiver and Rosenberg picked it up again. "It's the police!" he whispered tremulously.

"Good. That ought to keep you out of mischief for a while." I hung up the telephone and leaned against the wall, knowing now what had happened. I desperately tried to avoid thinking about what the dead girl's last few minutes must have been like, not only the torture but knowing and understanding what was about to happen to her, as she must have done. Was Rosenberg right? Was I responsible? If I hadn't humiliated her as I did, would she have had sense enough to stay out of the invocation? At any rate, Rose and I were safe. The cultists would leave Ireland as soon as the law would let them, and they wouldn't dare to try anything else now that the police were breathing down their necks and asking questions about Zee. Those two were in for an unpleasant time in the next few days.

When Rose awoke I handed her the paper wordlessly. While she read it I nerved herself to say what I had to say to her. She put down the paper and crossed herself. "Oh, dear God, that poor girl! I must go to church and pray for her."

"You needn't bother, Rose," I told her gently. "It wouldn't do any good."

"What do you mean, Charles?" she quavered, knowing full well what I meant.

"Can't you guess what happened? Last night our magic was stronger, we broke their defenses, and the demon could then escape out that end of the interdimensional tunnel. In Its path stood only a few petty and insignificant beings, totally unprotected. I had hoped that in Its eagerness to return to its own universe, the demon would ignore those people. Instead It punished them. It demanded an act of submission from them, an offering of human blood and life force. Why It did not simply devour all of them we will never know, although the sages of the past do give us some hints. These entities occasionally enjoy playing with humans rather than simply destroying them, for sport or pleasure. At any rate, It offered those wretched men a bargain to save their own skins and their own souls, and they took it. They quite literally sacrificed Zee."

"Her…her soul as well?"

"I'm afraid so. The girl is dead now, dead in every sense of the word. Her life force still exists, because it is energy and cannot be destroyed, but it is broken down, scrambled up, and absorbed into the life force of a totally alien organism that exists somewhere outside the bounds of space and time and reality as we know it, all vestige of her human consciousness destroyed. There is nothing left for God to have mercy on. You read in the Bible about damnation. Well, that's it."

Rose sobbed for a long time while I held her close. When she finally spoke, she spoke words which saved me from having to tell her what I intended. "Charles, I can't marry you now, not after this."

"I know, my darling. I was going to tell you the same thing. I simply couldn't go through with my part of the bargain. You don't belong in the Arts, you don't belong in the kind of life you would have with me, and if I cannot bring back that girl who was destroyed, I can at least make sure that this foulness never soils you again. But do you believe that I love you?"

"Yes," she wept. "And so do I love you. But I just can't be part of all this. I'd never have any peace of mind even if I lived for a thousand years. I thought you were cruel, at first, to deceive all your other wives all those years ago, never telling them the truth and making them think you were dead after you deserted them. Now I know it was a mercy. I wish I could have had those years with you, Charles, before you created some fake accident and left me sad but with wonderful memories. I would have accepted it as God's will and been grateful for the life we had together. I'm sorry that can never be now."

"When I first met those folly-bent people in the Lincoln Inn I tried to make them understand," I said. "Later I told Zee of the ancient magi who attained the Great Work like me and yet had chosen to end their incarnations in the normal way, voluntarily resigning immortality of body for the benefit and advancement of the spirit. I wish I myself had their courage and wisdom. And yours. I have prolonged my life to no end, Rose. I haven't gotten a damned thing worth having out of this last stolen, unnatural century of life," I went on, rising and walking over to the window. "You see this street? When first I strolled down this side-walk from Stephen's Green it was new and wondrous to me, the street lamps newly blacked and burning with gas, all these priceless Georgian doorways freshly painted and the steps swept, the beauty of it beyond telling. Now there is garbage and empty cider bottles in the doorways, the paint is flaking and the street lamps are rusted out. In place of the soft sound of horses' hooves and the creak of hansom cabs every morning I hear these god-awful automobiles and lorries, and smell the stink of them. And it tears at my heart because *I remember.* It is the same everywhere I go. I remember what was and can never be again. I conceal my ancient age well, Rose, but despite all the twentieth century language and mannerisms I have acquired I am still a man whose day was in 1840, when Charles Dickens first started to scribble with a quill pen. And were you to choose this path I have taken, Rose, then some day you would find yourself a girl of this time and place in the horrible world of 2150 or so, with a husband even more wretchedly out of time and place than you. I am a stranger in a time and a place wherein I was never meant to dwell. I will never make you that kind of a stranger, Rose. I love you too well."

*　　　　*　　　　*

We parted for the last time on a bleak winter morning several months later, on St. Stephen's Green. She was wearing a natty little two-piece tweed suit and a fur hat, and she was very beautiful. She was on her way to the train station and I was on my way to the airport. She had decided to return home for a while. "My da's sick and he can use some company," she explained. "And I need some time to reflect."

"I understand. Still thinking of becoming a nun?"

"I don't think so. I want a husband and a family of my own." She looked at me for a while. "Where will you go?"

"Back to Charleston for a time, I think. Last time I was there they were digging up King Street from the old Citadel grounds all the way up to Rivers Avenue, redeveloping or whatever they call it, building huge shopping malls and office complexes. I want to catch what's left before it goes on forever. Then maybe I'll find another war somewhere. The

Balkans looks interesting. Then again, I have some descendants I'd like to check up on in South Africa."

"You really want to end it all, don't you?" she asked. "That's why you keep dicing with death in combat. You keep hoping you'll lose."

"Perhaps. I could always shoot myself or step in front of a speeding lorry or something, but it wouldn't be playing the game. When I lose, I want to lose honestly."

"Will those people bother you any more?" she wondered.

"Possibly. If so, it will add some spice to my life. A long one like mine needs a lot of spice."

"Well, I suppose this is it," she said after an awkward silence. She leaned over and kissed me. "Goodbye, my beloved stranger."

"Goodbye, my Rose of Ireland." The pain was strong, but it was one I had felt often enough before, and at least this time she knew that our parting was final. Rose turned and walked across the barren park, and I watched her until she was out of sight. Then I picked up my old Victorian portmanteau and walked towards the taxi ranks, looking for a cab to take me to the airport.

The Madman And Marina

I. The Madman, The Lump, and The Dwarf

"This inhuman place makes human monsters."
-Stephen King, The Shining

*I*van Vasilievitch Yesenin lived and worked in the largest circus in the world. Every day millions of people walked the high wire, and sometimes tumbled off to death and destruction. Others twirled high above the rock-hard earth in intricate trapeze aerobatics, without the benefit of a net. Often they fell down into the merciless dirt and perished horribly. Men and women in cages fought to tame wild beasts. Sometimes they failed and were devoured, screaming. Trained bears in ballet costumes danced foolishly to the music of victrolas and wobbled around in

217

long circles on unicycles, drunk on peppered vodka. Sometimes the bears went berserk and rampaged among the spectators, killing and maiming.

Above all there were the clowns, thousands and thousands of clowns with baggy pants, big huge boots, red rubber noses, blue shoulder-boards on their epaulettes and blue bands around their visored caps. Clowns who grinned and capered and blew toy horns as they smashed human flesh with truncheons, burned human bodies with cigarettes, and fired nine grams of lead into human brains in porcelain tiled cellars with specially fitted drains and hoses to wash away the blood and the bone fragments.

The name of this great unearthly circus was the Union of Soviet Socialist Republics. The yellow-eyed, rat-muzzled ringmaster was the Father Of The Peoples himself, Comrade General Secretary Stalin. Colonel Ivan Vasilievitch Yesenin of the People's Commissariat of Internal Affairs, the NKVD, was one of the ghastly ringmaster's most terrible and dangerous clowns. Yesenin was called The Madman by those who knew and feared him, because he said things that made terrible sense, and in the Soviet Union making sense was a mad thing to do.

It was 1938, the most terrible of the purge years. 1936 and 1937 had been bad enough, as political differences were settled and the Communist Party literally sweated blood in order to purify itself of Right Wing Opportunism, Trotskyite Deviationism, Riutinism, Secret Oppositional Centers, bourgeois intellectualism and other such deadly threats to the wise and benevolent rule of the Father Of The Peoples. The Party and the military had been burned clean by the cleansing fire of the purge, and now it was the turn of the country as a whole. The academic Trotskyite intellectual, the bureaucratic wrecker and the field marshall of dubious loyalty had been dealt with. Now the time had come to mop up the small fry.

The army of NKVD informers worked overtime. Black Marias rolled through the streets in the dead of night hauling in the little people with little imperfections. There went the worker who complained about the incompetent management at his factory; the office clerk who told a disrespectful joke; the old woman who absent-mindedly wrapped fish in a newspaper containing a picture of Comrade Stalin; the engineer who made the mistake of praising Western technology; the drunk who forgot himself and said too much at a party; the pretty girl who didn't know when to say yes to a man in uniform; the apparently loyal Party member whose parents were discovered to have been bourgeois shop owners; and of course the countless thousands of people who had in the past served the Tsar's régime in any capacity however minor, or who had once shaken Leon Trotsky's hand at a reception in 1921. Now these dangerous and anti-social elements were stood up in line to receive their nine grams or their "ten ruble notes" in the frozen hell of the GULAG archipelago.

Finally, it was in 1938 that the clowns with the blue shoulderboards began to rend their own entrails as the very apparatus of terror purged itself. The flabby, bespectacled horror Genrikh Yagoda fell and took his place at his own show trial, gabbling hysterical denunciations of himself and praise for Stalin before he descended into the cellar room with the tiled floor, the hose and the drain. He was replaced by Nikolai Ivanovitch Yezhov, who liked to call himself "the Iron Commissar" but who was known to the people he butchered as "The Malignant Dwarf". Behind The Dwarf stood the beady-eyed Lavrenti Pavlovich Beria, his fingers creeping forward slowly to grab The Dwarf's throat and twist his neck that he, Beria, might sit at the Right Hand of Stalin the Father Almighty in Yezhov's stead. During the time that became known as the *Yezhovschina*, Russia lived in a nightmare world of fear and paranoia and madness that has no parallel anywhere in the annals of human civilization.

In the summer of 1938, at the height of his power, N. I. Yezhov the Dwarf summoned I. V. Yesenin the Madman to a meeting in the Kremlin. Yesenin brought with him his driver and assistant, a squat and stupid muscleman with a Neanderthal brow named Brodsky. Zoltan Bogdanovitch Brodsky did not seem to walk, but ambled low to the earth, his knuckles almost dragging the ground like a monkey. He drove Yesenin's private Daimler touring car, with the three hundred and twenty horsepower engine and the heavy armor plating against bombs and bullets, the only such vehicle in the entire NKVD. The fact that Yesenin was allowed to own a foreign vehicle spoke volumes of his prestige and power. Zoltan Bogdanovitch did errands for Colonel Yesenin such as delivering and picking up his laundry, shining his boots, carrying messages and buying the colonel's groceries and liquor at the special Gastronom for senior Party officials, the one that actually had food in it for sale, and cooking his breakfast. Zoltan Bogdanovitch also helped out during arrests and interrogations, using his strong hands to pry away the fingers of desperate men and women clinging to furniture or one another as they were dragged away, and smashing mens' bones and testicles with a hammer when it was required to make them confess to their crimes against society. Brodsky was called The Lump.

When he came to see The Dwarf, Ivan Vasilievitch also brought Marina with him. The simian Lump Yesenin left cooling his heels in the outer vestibule, but Marina he could not leave behind. Marina came with him wherever he went.

*　　　　　　　*　　　　　　　*

The Dwarf occupied a luxurious suite of Kremlin offices one floor below the inner sanctum of the General Secretary himself. The parquet floor was soft with Bokhara rugs, the Dwarf's desk was pure black mahogany, and the paneled walls were covered with photographs of himself with Comrade Stalin. The office was meant to be impressive, but Yesenin was not impressed. It was the den of a toad. Stalin's own offices a floor above were simple and functional and unadorned, a Spartan working environment for a working tyrant. A sideboard in

Yezhov's rooms groaned with a huge silver samovar, bottles of wine and peppered vodka, and a priceless bone china buffet of iced salmon, cold cuts, caviar, slices of white bread, pickled mushrooms, fruit and vegetables. The buffet contained more protein and calories than a Soviet worker consumed in a month. Colonel Yesenin stomped into the office, his boots thudding in the soft carpet. He grunted to Yezhov behind the desk, walked over to the samovar and drew himself a glass of hot tea in a wooden holder, into which he squeezed a large slice of lemon. He spread caviar on a slice of bread and folded it, walked over to a straight-backed upholstered chair in front of the desk and sat down, crossed his legs and began to eat.

Yesenin didn't look like a Russian, or rather he was of a certain less common Russian racial type than the usual square, muscular bodies one saw in the Metro. In his youth he had been tall and blond, a throwback to the days when the Norse settlers along the rivers of the interior who called themselves Rus had ruled the land. Now he was still a tall and straight-backed man of military bearing, with a seamed and weather-beaten face, a mop of graying hair slightly too long beneath his blue-banded visored cap, and gleaming gray eyes. His lip twisted as he spoke. He said to Yezhov between munches, "What do you want, Nikolai Ivanovitch?" No other person on the face of the earth besides Stalin himself would have dared to behave in such a manner. Men stood to attention in Yezhov's presence, desperately listening to every nuance of every word he said, praying to the God who wasn't supposed to exist that those words did not mean death in agony or life in the Kolyma gold mines, while at the same time they listened they fought not to foul their breeches in sheer terror. Yesenin was not afraid of anyone, not even Stalin. It wasn't a pose. He really wasn't afraid of anyone, and in the Soviet Union that was insanity. This was one reason why Yesenin was called The Madman. Marina was the second reason.

Marina spoke to him now. "He really is a dwarf!" she exclaimed in mild surprise. "I suppose that's why he hates people and hurts them. He is afraid people will laugh at him and ignore him because of his height if they're not afraid of him. That's probably true," she mused. "Poor little man." Her voice was soft, as it had always been in life, not quite a whisper but soft enough so that Yesenin had to strain a bit to hear what she was saying. She seemed to be standing behind him just to his right, as she always seemed to be when he heard her voice. Yesenin ignored her. He was getting practiced at ignoring Marina when he was in the company of others, although it had been very hard to do so at first. Word shot through the corridors of the Kremlin and the Lubyanka that the dreaded Colonel Yesenin was hearing voices and expostulating to thin air, and that also contributed to his nickname of The Madman.

"So what do you want?" he asked again of the tiny man behind the desk. "Not the usual enemies of the people rubbish, I suppose? Got somebody special you want to pull into the mincing machine? Or is it a bit of a mystery? I am the man the Central Committee always calls when you really do want something solved, as opposed to simply having someone destroyed. So what is it?"

Yezhov smiled, showing his black and decaying teeth. With Stalin one always remembered the yellow eyes. With Yezhov it was the rotten teeth, and the smell of his breath if one were unfortunate enough to get that close. "You were listening to something just now," he hissed like an accusing snake. "I suppose in a minute you'll say something to one of your invisible playmates. You can't fool me, Ivan Vasilievitch. I know perfectly well that it's all an act. It won't save you when your name pops up on one of our little lists."

"And what do you think will save *you*, Nikolai Ivanovitch?" demanded Yesenin, taking another big bit of the bread and caviar. "Who will save you from that Mingrelian snake down the hall, eh, wee fellow? Lavrenti Pavlovitch wants your job so bad he can taste it, and I'd be willing to wager he gets it. Who will save you, eh, Dwarf? The Boss upstairs? Do you know we've a betting pool down at the Lubyanka on whether the Boss or Beria will be the one who defunctionalizes your wee carcass?

Now what do you want?" Yezhov looked at him with loathing, and drew a file folder from his desk. He pulled out a photograph and put it on top of the folder, and threw it down in front of Yesenin on the desk. Yesenin took one look and almost choked on his caviar. It was a photograph of Marina. Yezhov spoke. "You may be surprised to learn, Ivan Vasilievitch, that even in our wonderful proletarian society, people sometimes disappear."

"You amaze me, Nikolai Ivanovitch," replied Yesenin dryly. "Imagine such a thing! People disappearing, here in the Soviet Motherland?"

"No, I mean really disappear," said Yezhov. "This citizeness, for example. Marina Antonovna Galinskaya. I am told you know her. Or should I say knew her?"

"If she has disappeared, what makes you think she is dead?" asked Yesenin casually. He picked up the photograph. It was a studio portrait. Marina looked into the camera, the faint Mona Lisa smile that had driven so many men to the point of distraction playing about her lips. Her chin rested pensively on her hand, her dark hair was brushed forward and framed her face. She had a fine enough face, but it was always her eyes or her smile that one remembered. The huge dark eyes so deep and fathomless that one could sink into them like a well. The smile that lit up the room and suddenly made life seem worth living.

"Not one of my better photographs," said Marina with rueful humor. "I always thought it was too stylized and pretentious. I was a bit of a *poseuse*. Sobransky the photographer got down on his knees and asked me to marry him after he took it."

"She hasn't turned up abroad, and she hasn't turned up anywhere in Russia," said Yezhov. "Do you think a face like that could stay hidden? From us?"

"Very well. What about her?" asked Yesenin.

"This comes from the very top." Yezhov elevated his eyes towards the next floor up. "We want you to find Citizeness Galinskaya, or else discover what became of her, and arrest and punish the guilty parties if as we suspect she has met with foul play."

"How is your appetite for irony, Ivan Vasilievitch?" said Marina. She never laughed, but her voice sounded amused.

Yezhov continued, "Citizeness Galinskaya was officially employed as a special assignment translator and administrative assistant by the Ministry of Arts and Culture."

"She always refused to spy on her employers of the moment for the NKVD," pointed out Yesenin. "I know. I asked her often enough."

"That is in the file, yes. As you are doubtless aware in view of your personal acquaintance with the lady, since she was seventeen years of age Marina Antonovna has at one time or another managed to acquire as lovers most of the top creative men in the Soviet Union, as well as one of our most brilliant scientists and a Spanish Republican general. She is a heroine of the anti-Fascist struggle in Spain in her own right, and she is justly considered to be one of our most famous Russian beauties. Her continued absence is not only mysterious, it is becoming somewhat embarrassing. The Boss has taken a personal interest in her fate."

"I see," said Yesenin.

"It was an unsuccessful interest, Vanya," said Marina gently.

"I don't care!" Yesenin snapped back at her.

"You'd better care," said Yezhov warningly. "He's serious about this. You're supposed to be such a hotshot detective. Now we'll see how good you really are."

"What are the known facts surrounding Citizeness Galinskaya's disappearance?" asked Yesenin, picking up the folder.

"She was last seen on New Year's Eve. She was at a party with her then current employer and lover, with whom she was living at the time, the renowned international chess master Boris Podichevsky. That evening some of our glorious Chekists raided an illegal night club in the Arbat, a gathering place of black marketeers and anti-socialist elements known to cater to foreigners and indulging in the cacophanous form of

Western degeneracy known as jazz. Several members of the band and a number of patrons were arrested and found to be in possession of drugs and contraband foreign newspapers. The ringleaders were determined to be a saxophone player called Sergei Abramovitch Rosengolts and his mistress, a certain Kaminskaya. Under detailed questioning by the Organs they both subsequently confessed to espionage and Trotskyist cultural wrecking and they each received sentences of twenty-five years, but that came later. Someone who escaped the raid knew where Citizeness Galinskaya was that night, telephoned her, and told her what happened."

"Where exactly was she?" asked Yesenin. "Where was this New Year's party?"

"At the apartment of the novelist, A. F. Kolchin."

"I know Kolchin," said Ivan Vasilievitch. "I served with him in the Partisan Brigades in the Urals. I haven't seen him for a while."

"Marina Antonovna was wearing a simple but well cut evening gown of green silk, with diamond earrings and a gold chain around her neck. Over this she put on her coat, a very fine heavy raglan of astrakhan, and a sable fur hat of high quality. Her gloves were of black chamois, and she wore fur-lined *valenki* knee-boots of felt. These were the clothes she was wearing when she was last seen. They all had makers' marks and should be possible to identify if found. That information is in the file," Yezhov told him. "They have not turned up in any of the usual outlets for stolen goods. Marina Antonovna told a female friend of hers what had occurred and said she was going to see someone in authority whom she thought might be willing and able to intervene on behalf of these degenerate anti-socials. She then slipped out without the knowledge of Boris Mikhailovitch or Arkady Fyodorovitch or any of the other guests."

"Did she mention the name of the person she was going to see?" asked Yesenin, thumbing through the folder. "Did she give any details to this, ah, Nadezhda Morozova, it says here?"

"She did not. That is the last time anyone saw her. When she did not return to Master Podichevsky's apartment by noon the next day he instituted inquiries, first with the militia and then through the NKVD, but the woman has disappeared completely. Not one trace of her in the past seven months. I do not have to tell you how difficult that is to do in the Soviet Union, Ivan Vasilievitch. Virtually impossible. You have in that file all that is known, which is precious little. The Central Committee has become concerned, Yesenin. We can't have this type of thing. Soviet citizens must not be allowed disappear without going through the proper channels. It smacks of anarchy."

"But I *did* disappear through proper channels!" protested Marina. Yesenin rose abruptly. He needed to terminate the interview before he started screaming and cursing at the top of his lungs. A slight reputation for madness was a shield in an insane world, but he knew he couldn't afford ever to seem totally out of control. He might escape the GULAG, but a mental institution was not an especially attractive alternative.

"It's been seven months," he told Yezhov. "You should have called me in on January the first, but there's no help for it. I will do what I can."

"You will succeed," said Yezhov flatly.

"I see," said Yesenin. "Very well, I will succeed. Anyone in particular you want me to succeed with? Alternatively, is there anyone in this file who is considered non-expendable for the moment?"

"Everyone is expendable, Comrade Colonel," said Yezhov. "Even you."

"I will mention you said that to the Comrade General Secretary next time I see him," said Yesenin. Yezhov turned white, suddenly realizing the potentially fatal slip he had made.

"You know perfectly well that I meant everyone except...!" Yezhov shouted.

"Of course, Nikolai Ivanovitch," said Yesenin with a wintry smile. "How could the Father Of The Peoples ever be expendable?"

"Go away now, Yesenin," spat Yezhov. "Don't come back empty-handed."

Yesenin left the room. Outside he passed the blue-capped, white-gloved sentries from the NKVD Interior troops standing on guard. They saluted him and he returned their salute, then he strode back down the high ceilinged corridor towards the lobby where he had left The Lump. He stopped at a tall window and stared down into the sun-dappled, cobbled courtyard below. "Vanya?" came her voice. He knew what he was going to ask, and she did. "Why did you kill me, Vanya?" came Marina's sad voice.

*   *   *

"Why did you kill me, Vanya?"

How many times had she asked him that? He had lost count. The first time he heard her voice had been as he leaned at the window in his apartment, just back from digging her grave. He was standing exhausted and wracked with torture in his soul. The cold sun rose in the clear blue light of morning on January the first, as he stared down at the chunks of ice bobbing in the Moskva river below. Then from behind him, to his right, he heard her ask *"Why did you kill me, Vanya?"*

For a week after that he had been truly mad. He had not left his apartment, but had wept and shouted and cursed and screamed and pleaded for mercy, for forgiveness, anything to make her go away. A dozen times he had put the muzzle of his heavy, old-fashioned Nagant revolver to his head, offering to expiate his sin by taking his own life if that was what she wanted of him, but gently and firmly she had dissuaded him, like someone speaking to an upset and frightened child. At intervals he had paused to drink himself into a stupor and collapse for twelve hours on his settee or on the floor. During these times The Lump had entered the apartment silently, put him to bed, cleaned up his vomit, and occasionally forced bread and broth between his lips.

The Lump simply assumed that his boss was on a bender, a form of stress relief by no means unknown in the senior ranks of the NKVD. It was an explanation accepted by Yesenin's superiors so long as he didn't go completely to pieces and came back to work within a reasonable length of time. Rank hath its privileges.

During that time the one thing he discovered for certain was that his punishment, whatever it meant, involved his staying alive. They had reached an agreement, which was that she would speak only, for he swore to her that if he ever actually saw her, he would blow his brains out on the spot. Beyond that he had been unable to get her to tell him anything of why she haunted him, only that it was "for his own good." She almost never answered any question directly. But there was one she asked time and again.

"*Why did you kill me, Vanya?*" It was the infinite sadness combined with forgiveness and acceptance in her voice that drove Yesenin mad. If only she would curse him, reproach him, revile him, vow vengeance against him, mock him! But she never did. In life she had been the very essence of love and compassion and kindness, and now her gentleness and forgiveness with her murderer was like a branding iron searing his soul.

"*Why did you kill me, Vanya?*"

He had tried every answer he could think of to appease her. "I killed you because you were an enemy of the people. You were trying to help anti-socials."

"I was trying to help my friends, who were being destroyed for nothing, yes. But that's not why you killed me, Ivan Vasilievitch," she replied, always gently but firmly.

"Isn't obvious?" growled Yesenin. "I killed you because I hated you. You rejected me. You wouldn't go to bed with me."

"That's not why you killed me, Vanya. You know perfectly well that you loved me. I have never doubted that, before or since."

"Yes, I loved you, so I had to kill you so that no one else could have you!" responded Yesenin desperately. "I could not bear the thought of you in another man's arms!"

"That's not why, Vanya. I spent many years in other mens' arms before you took my life. Why on that one night?"

"I killed you because I was drunk that night," he argued wildly. "I didn't know what I was doing."

"You were drinking nothing but tea, Ivan Vasilievitch. That's not why."

"I killed you because I am an evil man and I enjoy killing and hurting people!" he shouted. "There, does that satisfy you?"

"You are not an evil man, Vanya. That's not why."

It went on and on and on. Some thread of strength and resilience and reality had kept Yesenin from going completely insane, and after a week he went back to work. Sometimes she went several days without speaking to him, although every night as he got into bed and lay back staring at the black ceiling above him she would always say "Goodnight, Ivan Vasilievitch. Sleep well," just to let him know that she was still there. She always let him sleep, and he was grateful to her for that. But there was one thing. During the past seven months, he had managed to avoid doing any actual secret police-type work. No arrests, no interrogations, no investigations. It wasn't hard. In an outfit like the NKVD there was always plenty of bureaucracy and meetings and paperwork and petty intrigue to occupy his time. But now he had to conduct an investigation again, an investigation into the death of a woman he himself had murdered. Staring out of the Kremlin window, he asked, "Did you really turn down Stalin?"

"I told Joseph Vissarionovitch that he could of course command me at any time, but I could not find it in my heart to be with him willingly," she replied from behind him. "He understood that and respected it. He knew that there would no point in doing with me what he could do with any woman in Russia. I was supposed to be something special, although I never understood why. He laughed and bowed to me and kissed my hand, and he told me that he wasn't quite a Tsar in all things, and that was that."

"You asked me how my appetite for irony is, Marina Antonovna. How is yours?"

"What do you mean?" she asked behind him.

"You heard The Dwarf. I have *carte blanche* on this one. I can blame anyone I want for your death. I can fabricate any kind of case I want against anyone. One hour in a Lubyanka interrogation room and I can get a confession from anyone I want, and as proof I can clinch it by recovering your body. It's perfect. So I will offer you a bargain, Marina Antonovna. Despite the damage to my reputation, I will give you my word that this case will be my one failure. I will be able to find neither hide nor hair of the foul Fascist Trotskyite assassins who deprived the Soviet Union of your beauteous presence. No one will suffer in my place for my crime. But in return, you will go away. You will never speak to me or haunt me again."

"You won't do that, Ivan Vasilievitch," replied Marina quietly.

"Oh, won't I?" he growled.

"No. You won't." She was calm and completely confident.

"Watch me!" he told her viciously. "You remember once that I asked you why you didn't stay with one man, with any of the fine and brilliant men who wanted you so badly with all their hearts and souls? Do you remember what you answered?"

"I told you that I could not bear to choose, because in making one man happy I would cause terrible pain to others whom I knew loved me deeply and truly," Marina replied.

"*Pravilno.* Well, you can't get away with that any more, Marina Antonovna. One cannot avoid making choices forever. Either you go away, or else I will make you choose. I will make you choose one of the men who loved you to stand condemned before the world as your murderer. If you persist in dogging me like my shadow then I will make you watch as I personally take your chosen victim down into the cellar and I fire a bullet into his brain. I don't know exactly how this ghost business works, but maybe just after I shoot him you will get to explain to him why you chose him to die when no one had to die at all. Do you think I won't do that to you? I loved you then and I love you still, Marina, but yes, I'll do it to you if I have to, if you won't stop torturing me. I swear it. You'd best believe me."

"I don't think you will," she replied. "Of course, I could be wrong. I'm not all-knowing, Ivan Vasilievitch. I have made mistakes, many of them. I made one the night I came to you for help. Will you really do as you have said? We must see what we shall see."

"If you will allow me to do such a thing, then you are just as cruel as I am and just as guilty," he told her.

"Ivan Vasilievitch, it is you who must decide whether or not you are going to commit a crime. Not me," Marina replied firmly. "Surely you don't think you can threaten me with anything? I'm already dead, remember?"

"Are you real, Marina Antonovna?" he asked her for the hundredth time. "Are you a true ghost or are you something in my own demented brain? I have never denied the terrible guilt I feel at what I did to you, and I understand that guilt may be producing your voice that I hear. I know that the end result is the same. I still hear you. But I have to confess that I have become genuinely curious."

"Do you think I'm real?" she asked.

"You always do that," he complained. "You never give me a straight answer."

"There are very few straight answers in this world, Ivan Vasilievitch," she said, the amusement in her voice again.

"There you go again." He shook his head. "It really is ironic. Of all the many men who wanted you to be with them forever, I am the one who has you now."

"The Chinese have a saying..." Marina responded.

"Yes, I know. Be careful what you wish for, or you may get it." Yesenin sighed. "Well? I've told you my offer. Will you go away if I agree not to punish anyone else for what I did?"

"Ivan Vasilievitch, I will be with you so long as you need me. You have my promise," she said.

"You bitch!" he snapped.

"Oh, yes, I did have a bitchy side," she replied merrily, again almost laughing but not quite. "Still do."

"Very well, let's go." Yesenin looked down the long corridor. The two NKVD guards outside Yezhov's office were standing ramrod straight, staring ahead into space, but no doubt word would soon be out in the canteens that The Madman had been talking to himself in the halls again.

He picked up The Lump and they returned to Yesenin's limousine. Yesenin got into the back and Brodsky got behind the wheel. "Where to, boss?" asked The Lump. Every time The Lump called Yesenin "boss" he always used the criminal term *khozyain* instead of the more respectful *vozhd*, but Yesenin had stopped trying to correct him. It was rather an appropriate term for an NKVD officer, in any case.

"Kuntsevo. I am going to speak to Boris Podichevsky, the chess master. He will be at his summer dacha. I also need to question a woman named Nadezhda Morozova. She was the last person to speak to Marina Antonovna Galinskaya before her disappearance. According to this case file she has since taken over Citizeness Galinskaya's place as Podichevsky's secretary and translator for his correspondence. She has also taken over Galinskaya's place in the Master's bed," he added brutally, studying the file. "Unlike her predecessor, Citizeness Morozova is of a sufficiently patriotic fiber so that she willingly offers her co-operation to the Organs of state security."

"I already knew that she would come after me," Marina told him.

"I didn't know you went in for puns," replied Yesenin sarcastically.

"I don't. Nor do I go in for coarse jests," Marina said primly.

"Say what, boss? Puns?" asked The Lump. A thought struck him. "Wait a minute. We already know what happened to that citizeness. Hey, you copped her case? That's brilliant, boss!" he said admiringly. Brodsky knew that Marina was dead, since he had helped bury her. The ground in December had been frozen hard as rock, time was a factor, and Yesenin knew he had to have help if he was to dispose of her before dawn. The one thing he remembered about that night most clearly of all was himself and Brodsky slamming their picks into the ground, hacking away at the frozen earth, sending icy splinters of dirt flying beneath the baleful light of the setting moon. Brodsky had never made any comment about that night's work. His boss killed people; how and where and why wasn't his department. The Lump did not know that Marina spoke to Yesenin. To him Ivan Vasilievitch's recent habit of talking to himself was a mild eccentricity more than compensated for by the big car and the good food and the warm bed in the upstairs servant's quarters at Government Mansions.

II. The Master

The community of dachas at Kuntsevo was situated about thirty miles outside Moscow, at the end of a long paved access highway that was one of the best-maintained in Russia. These dachas were the ultimate prizes in Soviet life, awarded only to the cream of the *nomenklatura* and to such ornaments of the Soviet state as Podichevsky, the greatest master of Russia's national game in his century. The word dacha implied a small cottage or hunting lodge, but many of these homes had ten or more rooms and came with the most luxurious furniture, appliances, and modern conveniences imported from the West, as well as a Volga or Zhiguli sedan and often a chauffeur as well. They were surrounded by huge landscaped gardens and forests, white petaled fruit orchards and leafy grape arbors, exquisite man-made lakes full of fish and ducks and swans, threaded with well swept sandy paths or brick walkways. The whole village was like a great nobleman's estate from the Tsar's time. It was maintained by a discreet and efficient army of caretakers, gardeners, laborers, and of course the ubiquitous NKVD Interior troops with machine guns who were necessary to safeguard the repose of the Soviet ruling élite.

Yesenin left The Lump smoking *papirosi* by the car and knocked on the oak-paneled door. It was opened by a lovely young woman, short and slim but with a finely curved figure beneath a simple patterned cotton summer dress. She was wearing leather-thonged sandals on her small feet, an exotic affectation that Ivan Vasilievitch found attractive and intriguing. Her yellow hair hung down her back in a single braid. Her slanting blue eyes widened as she saw the blue shoulderboards and cap band. She flinched back in fear. "Citizeness Morozova?" said Yesenin in a flat, official voice.

"Yes," she stammered, looking over her shoulder. "I....I usually deal with Major Korchagin. Where is he? Who are you?"

"I am Colonel Ivan Vasilievitch Yesenin," replied Yesenin in his flat official voice. The girl turned as white as a sheet.

"The Madman?" she blurted. Then she realized what she said and to whom she had said it, and she turned even whiter. "Oh God! I mean no, not God, of course there is none! Comrade Colonel, please forgive me, I am an idiot. I was wrong, I wasn't thinking, I should not have said...Major Korchagin, has he...I, I didn't really know him...he never told me anything. I just did what I was told!" she babbled in panic.

"Yes. The Madman. You think Korchagin has fallen?" asked Yesenin. "Why would you think that, Citizeness Morozova? Have you ever heard Major Korchagin say anything which might appear to have criminal tendencies?"

"Please, Comrade Colonel," she whispered miserably. "I'm just a little person. Very ordinary, very small. I'm not worth it. Really I'm not. Just tell me what you want of me. Please. Just tell me what you want me to do."

"I want you to take me to Master Podichevsky, Nadezhda Pavlovna. You will then find something to do elsewhere while I speak with him. But first, I want to speak with you. You will tell me everything you know about the disappearance of Marina Antonovna Galinskaya. You will tell me everything you even *think* about the disappearance of Marina Antonovna Galinskaya. You will not allow the notion of deceiving me to enter your mind for a single moment. I will think about what you have to say for a while, and then I will decide what shall become of you." She hung her head and turned back inside the house, motioning for him to follow.

"Why are you frightening her?" asked Marina. "That's cruel and not very manly, Ivan Vasilievitch. She never harmed you. Why do you want to hurt her?"

"Be quiet!" ordered Yesenin, although he knew that ordering Marina to silence never worked.

"I said nothing, Comrade Colonel," protested Nadia faintly.

"Will you do something for me, Vanya?" asked Marina gently. "Please? She's terribly afraid of you. Will you give her some word of comfort and encouragement so she won't be so worried while you speak with Boris Mikhailovitch?"

"Why should I do anything for you?" muttered Yesenin. Nadia heard him and said nothing, but bit her hand to stifle a cry.

She stepped into a long room with high wooden rafter beams and lush rugs covering the parquet floor. There were comfortable armchairs and settees, a huge fireplace in one corner and a more functional wood burning stove in another. The solid oak-paneled walls were decorated with fine original landscapes and hunting trophies. Along one whole wall of the room stood a series of tables on which rested heavy varnished chessboards of teak and mahogany. The chessmen were carved antique ivory, whalebone, or lacquered and polished plumwood. Each board held a game in various stages of play, captured pieces both white and black neatly lined up beside the board. Behind each game board was a folded cardboard label bearing a name and the date the game had begun: Vishevsky, 4-10-36; Manuel 6-6-37; Lightbourne 6-30-37; Johanssen 11-15-35; and one game with the famous Cuban master Gonsalvo Moncada which dated from August of 1932. "At any given time, Podichevsky is playing a number of games by mail," explained Nadia. "The Master speaks German and several Scandinavian dialects, while I speak English, French, Spanish, Italian, and Portuguese. I handle his correspondence in those languages."

"How many languages did Marina Galinskaya speak?" asked Yesenin.

"All of those, plus Turkish and Japanese," replied Nadia. "She spoke all of them like a native. She had a natural talent for languages. She was brilliant."

"You say she *was* brilliant?" asked Yesenin. "Why do you speak of her in the past tense? Where do you think Marina Antonovna is now?"

"In hell, I hope," whispered Nadia. "I hated her."

"Why?" asked Yesenin.

"What do you care?" demanded Nadia sullenly.

"It is my job to care. I am here to investigate her fate," said Yesenin. "Why did you hate Marina?"

"I love the Master. She didn't," said the girl. "I spent a year just trying to get his attention away from a chessboard long enough to notice me. I almost had him, and then she breezed in one day from the Ministry to translate a challenge and the first move from the Turkish master Feyd-Gecevit. A game Boris Mikhailovitch eventually won, of course. He has never been defeated."

"I know," said Yesenin.

"She was in his bed that very night, and I was forgotten until she went away. Then he finally turned to me, but only to use my body so he can forget her when chess and vodka don't suffice. I hate her!"

"She doesn't hate me," said Marina compassionately.

"You don't hate her," said Yesenin.

"No," whispered Nadia. "How did you know?"

"Because I know that everyone loved her," said Yesenin.

"She was wonderful," whispered Nadia. "I didn't hate her, not really. I wanted to be her. I would have given anything in the world to be her." She looked up. "Is she dead?"

"How would you feel if she was dead?" asked Yesenin.

"Now who's being evasive?" demanded Marina.

"If she would only walk in that door alive, even if I knew she was coming to take him from me forever, I would embrace her," said Nadia. "The Master is out in the garden, Colonel."

Yesenin ignored Nadia's attempt to evade his questioning. "When Marina Antonovna left the New Year's party at the apartment of A. F. Kolchin, what exactly did she tell you about where she was going and why?"

"Marina loved American jazz. We both did. Sergei Rosengolts was a brilliant musician and artiste, and Marina and Elena Kaminskaya were close friends. She said they brought out her wild and Bohemian impulses."

"They also sold cocaine and heroin," said Yesenin.

"That's because the Moscow State Symphony only pays fifty-five rubles a month to second chair saxophonists. They never sold any of that stuff to Marina. Or to me. But they paid for their little NEP, did they not? You *gaybisty* got them that New Year's eve at the Black Cat club. Are they dead yet?"

"They may be," replied Yesenin with a shrug. "He went to Kolyma and she to Karaganda. A jazz musician won't last too long in the gold mines. If the girl's smart and even halfway pretty, she'll get by."

"Poor Sergei. Poor Elena," whispered Marina dismally. "Vanya, I came to you begging for your help, and instead you murdered me. Please, please tell me why?" It was all Yesenin could do to keep from whirling around and screaming curses and abuse at thin air. Instead he resolutely held his attention on Nadezhda.

"You stated to the first militia investigator and later to Major Korchagin that Marina Antonovna told you she was going to see someone whom she believed might intervene in the case of these anti-social elements. Do you still insist that she did not tell you who this person was?"

"Who do you want it to be?" asked Nadia. "I'll denounce whoever you tell me to. Major Korchagin said he'd get back to me on that."

"Mmmm, yes, I imagine so. It's always good practice to have a few ready-made denunciations handy if you don't have time to fit one up. But right now I want the truth. She really didn't say who she was going to see?"

"No. She said she didn't want to compromise him or compromise me by telling me. She was also afraid I would betray her secret, since she knew I love the Master, but that's understandable enough and I didn't hold it against her. It was cold and I offered to call the Master's chauffeur or find her a taxi, but she said she would take the Metro so she couldn't be traced. She left the apartment while everyone was listening to the pianist Nazarian. He was playing a Rachmaninoff concerto. Nazarian was probably in line to be her next lover. I was doing everything I could to encourage them so she would leave the Master and he would turn to me. He did, but now he hates me and suspects me of betraying Marina. He also suspects I am spying on him for the Organs, which is true." The girl looked up at him in weary despair. "I didn't betray Marina, Comrade Colonel. I don't know what happened to her."

"Did anyone leave the apartment after that, in a manner possibly furtive?" asked Yesenin.

"No, Comrade Colonel, no one followed her. The party broke up at dawn, everyone was drunk, they all piled into their various cars and the chauffeurs took them home. I was living in a hostel for Culture Ministry workers at the time so I took the Metro. The Master thought he would find Marina waiting for him at his apartment, since she didn't like drunkenness and often left early when the vodka and the cognac started to really flow. But she wasn't there. It took him about a week to accept that she was gone, and a week after that to accept that she is dead. She is dead, isn't she?"

"What does the Master think happened to her?" asked Yesenin.

"He thinks someone, most likely me, denounced her to the NKVD and that for some reason she has been executed secretly. Maybe Beria wanted her and killed her when she wouldn't give in to him. He has a reputation for that kind of thing."

"I know," replied Yesenin.

"I think Boris Mikhailovitch's reasoning is sound, even though it wasn't me who betrayed her. If she were sent to a camp there's usually some kind of formal notification, the Master's apartment would have been searched and all her things confiscated, and so on. Also, if she was being purged in the usual way she would have been put through the standard interrogation procedure and she would have denounced at least a few of her friends, but no one in our circle has been arrested recently and her name hasn't appeared on any transcripts or accusation affidavits."

"She's right," said Marina with a sigh. "I wasn't strong enough or brave enough to resist. I would have denounced someone eventually. Thank you for not putting me through that at least, Ivan Vasilievitch. I couldn't have lived with myself."

"So you no longer live at the worker's hostel, Nadezhda Pavlovna?" asked Yesenin.

"No. In February the Master asked me to move in with him. He told me I had earned it. He has always been very polite and considerate with me since then, but he thinks I betrayed Marina and he knows I report to the NKVD on him. In view of that fact I can hardly protest my innocence to him."

"If you love Master Podichevsky, how is it that you betray him on a regular basis by informing on him to Major Korchagin?" demanded Yesenin.

"Because I am a coward," Nadezhda told him, looking him in the eye for the first time. "My father was a drunkard and he beat all his children until my brother Pavlik fought back one day, but by then the damage was done in my case. With me it's very simple, Colonel. I am terrified of being beaten. Not of being shot, not of the camps, not of blades or needles or spiders or snakes or rats like so many women. I'll play with a snake all day. Come at me with a knife and I'll kick you in the balls. Point a pistol at me and I'll laugh. Sentence me to ten years and I'll tell my judges how I love snow and outdoor exercise. Raise your hand to hit me and I will fall at your feet and scream for mercy. That's how Korchagin turned me against the man I love more than life. He had a hairy monkey like that thing out there driving your car hold me down in a chair. Then he slapped me. Again and again and again and again..." The woman pulled a long Armenian cigarette from her pocket and fished absently for matches, her mind still in Korchagin's chair. Yesenin lit the cigarette for her with him American Zippo lighter. He also took out his pack of American Lucky Strikes and lit one for himself. "I love Boris Mikhailovitch, but apparently not enough to take a few clouts for him. So I betrayed him. Marina would never have betrayed him. She didn't love him, but she would have died rather than betray him. What the hell am I supposed to do in the face of an example like that? She shamed me. Her memory shames me still. She was so much better than I am, than ever I could be. It's very simple. I'm a whore and a coward and a traitress. Marina was an angel."

"*No, Nadia, no!*" protested Marina, genuinely upset in a way Yesenin had never heard from her since she died. "Vanya! Please, in the name of mercy, say something to comfort her! You can't just walk away and leave her hating herself like this, because of me!"

Yesenin lifted the wretched woman's chin. "I will make you a bargain, Nadezhda Pavlovna," he said. "If you ever lie to me or play me false, I'll kill you without a second's hesitation. But I will never, ever hit you. Not for any reason. I will take your life if I find it necessary, but I will not humiliate and degrade you. Do you agree?"

"Agreed, Comrade Colonel," she said, looking him in the eye.

"Take me to the Master now."

Boris Mikhailovitch Podichevsky sat in a wicker armchair in a shady, grassy dell. A small stream bubbled merrily over rocks behind him, and the bank of the stream was lined with small weeping willows. A wooden plank bridge rose over the stream and led onto a gravel path into a fragrant forest of pine. A trellised arbor of grapevines stood a few feet to one side. On a glass-topped table was a fine copper samovar warmed by a small alcohol lamp. Podichevsky was a slim and ascetic looking man of middle years, with a receding dark hairline and aquiline nose. He wore canvas shoes and a casual wool jacket. He was studying the chessboard on a second glass-topped, wrought iron white table in front of him. He did not look up as Ivan Vasilievitch approached, but gestured vaguely in the direction of the samovar, so he knew that someone was there. Ivan Vasilievitch drew himself a glass of steaming black tea and squeezed a generous hunk of sliced lemon into it. He sat down in a wicker chair opposite. He looked over the board. "I am a rank amateur, of course, but it looks to me like White has got you," said Ivan Vasilievitch after a while. "I'm damned if I can see any way out of it. Checkmate in three moves no matter which way you turn."

"Two," said Podichevsky. "I agree. Black is done for. I just wanted to make sure." He reversed the board. "I am White." The Master picked up a tablet with printed chessboards on each page, marked several notations on it, and put it aside. "That ought to do for Sir Angus quite nicely."

"Sir Angus Robertson, the British champion?" asked Yesenin.

"Yes," said Podichevsky. "I have been studying his past matches and anticipating every variation he might use, planning my counters against them. He has been aching for a rematch. So have the other four. They will get it in Vienna on August twenty-second."

"Will you take on all five of them at once like you did in Moscow last year?" queried Yesenin with a smile. "You won the admiration of the whole Soviet Union and every chess player in the world."

"And so I should have," chuckled Boris Mikhailovitch, sipping his own glass of tea, now cold. "Walked right onto the floor of the Hall of Columns, strode up to the tournament judges, and told them to forget the scheduled matches. I would take on all five of the foreign masters at once, simultaneously, their choice of colors. Robertson from Britain, Kreisler from Switzerland, Lightbourne the American, Avigdor from Argentina and Gomez from Cuba. Moncada's too old to travel now, but Velasco Gomez is his star pupil and protegé. Robertson and Gomez played it canny and took Black, the other three chose White. I beat all five of them inside of an hour. I even caught poor Lightbourne in an extended Fool's Mate! Avigdor lost his queen on the seventh move, tried the Sicilian Defense, and I stripped every piece of his off the board and checkmated him in fourteen minutes. Robertson lasted the longest, fifty-seven minutes before he conceded. Gomez came close at fifty-three minutes. My longest move on the timer was one against Gomez, forty-three seconds. My longest move against Robertson was twenty-eight seconds."

"An incredible feat, Master," said Yesenin with a bow. "Also very courageous. Will you try to repeat it in Vienna?"

"Courageous in the sense of what would have happened to me had I failed?" responded Boris Mikhailovitch. "I wasn't afraid of anything that morning, Yesenin. Oh, yes, I know who you are. I didn't get one of your famous telegrams, but yes, my will is made. Am I going to be arrested? If so, can you give me a few minutes to dash off one last letter to Moncada in Cuba? I haven't quite got the old fox yet, but I've come up with a move that will at least make him break a sweat."

"Why should I arrest you?" asked Ivan Vasilievitch.

"The Father Of The Peoples sometimes gets nervous when one of his prize specimens of the New Soviet Man is about to go abroad. Very well, if I am not going to be arrested, to what do I owe a visit from Moscow's most infamous *gaybist?* Not coming to ask me for Nadia's hand in marriage, are you?"

"I am here investigating the disappearance of Marina Antonovna Galinskaya," Yesenin told him.

"Why are you doing that?" asked Podichevsky in surprise. "I thought you killed her?"

"I beg your pardon? What did you say?" replied Yesenin, fighting to keep his voice casual.

"Not you specifically, of course. I mean the NKVD. I always assumed that you people...that you...oh *damnation!*" the Master muttered, suddenly putting his head in his hands with a sob of agony. "I thought I was prepared for this. Like I prepare for my matches. Every variation you might try would meet a scripted and practiced response," he whispered. He looked up at the colonel, his face haggard. "Now I can't do it. All I can do is implore you, in the name of any human compassion you might have left in that murderous Bolshevik soul of yours to tell me the truth. Is she dead, Yesenin? I beg of you to tell me. Let me know so I can mourn."

"Boris Mikhailovitch, it would be very wrong of me to encourage false hope," replied Yesenin carefully.

The man's shoulders sagged. After seven months, he finally surrendered. "Thank you, Ivan Vasilievitch. Can you tell me anything further at all?"

"No, Boris Mikhailovitch. Not at this time. I am sorry."

"Why exactly are you here? Surely you know more than I could ever tell you."

"I have to put down in my report that I spoke with you," Yesenin told him honestly.

"I understand. Can you at least tell me if there is...someplace I can go? Someplace I can lay some flowers, maybe sit and talk to her for a while?" His voice was devastated. He stared at the White knight on the board.

"You don't want to talk to her, Boris Mikhailovitch," said Yesenin with a shudder. "Believe me, you don't!"

"Why not tell him, Vanya?" asked Marina. "It's a lovely spot this time of year. The sun falls in columns through the larches, you can hear the river, and there's a meadow nearby with beautiful grass and cornflowers. What would be the harm in telling him? It would be nice if I had a stone, or at least a little marker with my name, but I'm content there."

"You're right, Ivan Vasilievitch," said Podichevsky. "I fear she might answer me back, and I fear what I might hear. Did...did she suffer much? Can you tell me that?"

"Well, it certainly wasn't one of my more pleasant experiences in recent memory!" put in Marina. Yesenin ignored her.

"Boris Mikhailovitch," he responded, "Let me phrase this very carefully. There is much in this matter that is still obscure. I can assure you that I am in fact conducting a bona fide investigation which may well result in a few surprises." *Such as me arresting you for her murder,* he added to himself.

Podichevsky spoke in a monotone. "That morning I charged into the Hall of Columns and challenged all five of the foreigners at once, and defeated them all. Do you know why I did that, Ivan Vasilievitch? Do you know why I *could* do it? It was because that night had been our first together. I only met her the day before. Twenty-four hours in her presence and I reached a height of power and concentration and analytical thinking which has been achieved by how many men down through the ages? A dozen? Two dozen? Alexander at Arbela, Archimedes in his bath, Newton and the apple, Franklin and his kite, myself and Marina. With me it has always been chess, the ultimate expression of the rationality of the human mind. The ultimate proof that man is something more than an economic unit of production and consumption. Not a very popular idea in Russia these days, eh? Do you know that there are idiots who write learned textbooks entitled *The Marxist Dialectic of Chess* and give speeches entitled 'Victory On The International Chess Front Through the Correct Line of Lenin and Stalin?'"

"I am an officer of the NKVD, Boris Mikhailovitch," Yesenin reminded him. "Do you think it wise to speak so indiscreetly in my hearing?"

"You are one of the most powerful men in the nation, Ivan Vasilievitch," said the Master. "You are Stalin's hatchet and if you decide that you are going to arrest me and torture me and blow my brains all over the wall of some cellar in the Lubyanka, you will do it, and there is nothing I can do to stop you. What I say to you doesn't matter. Marina burned all of that Marxist claptrap out of my mind and all the fear out of my soul. On that morning I walked into that hall as pure intellect wrapped in a body of flesh. I knew full well that Stalin would destroy me if I failed, but the very idea of failure never crossed my mind. Why should it? Marina was with me, and I was invincible. When I came home that night and found she was still there, waiting for me, I knelt before her and kissed her hand as if she were a queen. She gave to me the gift that I had always striven for all my life. Dear God, how I loved her!"

"Would you have loved her after she went with Nazarian the pianist?" asked Yesenin.

"I see where you lead, Ivan Vasilievitch," replied Podichevsky grimly. "I'll save you some time. I would never have harmed a single hair on Marina Antonovna's head."

"You didn't answer my question," pointed out Yesenin.

"I did," replied Boris Mikhailovitch. "It works like this. You meet Marina. You love her. You never stop loving her. Not ever. Do you think I didn't know when we began that my time with her would be short? Do you know why none of her former lovers has ever made a scene or challenged their successor to a duel or denounced them to the NKVD? Because none of us could bear the thought that we would cause her pain or embarrassment or guilt. Yes, she would have gone with Nazarian. And then she would have left Nazarian for someone else. After which both he and I would have loved her for the rest of our lives. Every now and then down through the years Nazarian and I would get together and bring one another up to date on her latest doings, toast her in the finest cognac, and get stinking sloppy maudlin drunk while telling one another how much we loved her. And we'd still be doing that in our seventies, if Yezhov lets any of us live that long. No man who loved her could ever have killed her, Ivan Vasilievitch."

"I think only a man who loved her could have killed her, Boris Mikhailovitch," returned Yesenin.

Podichevsky looked at him oddly. "I wonder what you mean by that....? Never mind. Look, Yesenin, I'm going to ask you something. Was Marina betrayed to her killers by that slut Nadezhda?"

"No, absolutely not," answered Ivan Vasilievitch immediately.

"Too quick and too firm," said Podichevsky with a grim smile. "Very well, I certainly don't expect you to reveal an NKVD informant. But I'm no fool and I can see a church by daylight, if you will forgive me quoting from the bourgeois apologist lackey Shakespeare. Well, little Nadia has a surprise coming," he chuckled gloatingly. "If she hasn't been very nice to you lads in the blue shoulderboards, don't worry, she will be."

"What do you mean?" asked Yesenin casually. "You're going to denounce her, I suppose? Don't bother. She's not my informant, as you seem to think, but I will make sure that any such denunciation on your part goes into the circular file. That poor little girl wouldn't know a Trotskyite from a trombone. A man of your stature shouldn't stoop to abusing the Organs, Boris Mikhailovitch."

"I don't abuse the organs, that's why I have Nadia here," said the Master with a lewd laugh. "No, I don't have to denounce her at all. I needn't ever utter a single word against her. She thinks she's going to Vienna with me in August. I believe she already has a shopping list ready for the big department stores in the Ringstrasse. Well, I'm not totally without friends, you know, and what little Nadia doesn't realize is that at the last minute there will arise a problem with her exit visa. She will have to stay behind here in Mother Russia. How very disappointed she will be! I am saddened at the prospect."

Understanding hit Yesenin like a dash of cold water. He leaped over and grabbed Podichevsky by the lapels of his coat, lifted him from the chair and shook him. *"You son of a bitch!"* he hissed. "You're not coming back! You're going to defect, aren't you? No doubt you'll ask your good friend and quondam opponent Sir Angus Robertson for a favor. Do you think we don't know Robertson has been MI6 for years? You're going to leave that girl here, you bastard? Knowing full well what will happen to her? You know what kind of rage Stalin will go into after you defect? She's on paper as our official observer on you, she's supposed to tip us off to that sort of thing, and then she fails and causes The Father Of The Peoples embarrassment in public? It won't be just the camps, it will be nine bloody grams of lead behind her ear! Plus what Beria and his cronies will do to her beforehand! How can you do such a thing?"

"This from a monster like you, who once said 'I believe you are innocent, but you have the look of a man who may be guilty one day?'" said Podichevsky with a bitter laugh. "You hypocrite!"

"The man I said that to was a fanatic who in his time had himself sent thousands of people to their death," replied Yesenin. "Not a poor frightened girl who never harmed a soul! Holy Peter, man, do you really hate her so badly you want to kill her?"

"She killed Marina," said Podichevsky. "Or she made a phone call to those who did. Maybe it was you bluecaps, maybe it was Fascists, maybe it was a jealous man, hell, you imply you know all about it." Yesenin caught a slight movement out of the corner of his eye and saw a small white foot in a sandal protruding just beyond the edge of the grape arbor. She was listening like a good spy.

Yesenin threw the Master back into the chair. "I'm working on a scenario now, Boris Mikhailovitch. I can still write you into the script, and we've more than a month to go before you leave for Vienna. Think about what you're doing. Think very carefully." He turned and stalked back up the gravel path and through the house. As he exited by the front door to the waiting Daimler, Nadia Morozova ran around the corner of the house. She grabbed his arm, her eyes staring and her lips trembling in horror as tears coursed down his face.

"What must I do?" she begged him. "What can I do? Oh, dear God, he hates me, he wants me dead! But I am innocent! I didn't betray Marina! Please Comrade Colonel, you must find some way to convince him that I am innocent!"

Yesenin took both her hands in his. "There is only one thing you can do to save yourself, Nadia," he told her urgently. "You must denounce him! You must accuse him now, to me. It won't be a false denunciation like so many are, Nadia. It's true, he really means to join the capitalist reactionary Fascist wreckers. I sense it. You heard him more or less admit that he was planning to defect, or at least he didn't deny it. He is corresponding with a known foreign intelligence agent. Chess moves are a good cover for secret code. Brodsky and I will go back there and arrest him right now! Denounce him! Accuse him!"

"No," she whispered, closing her eyes. "No. I will not. Not even if I die for it."

"Why not?" demanded Yesenin, incredulous. "Because you love him? The man you love wants you to die in fear and pain and suffering, Nadia! He gloats at the thought! If you don't move now to protect your-self he's going to kill you as certainly as if he pulled the trigger himself! One night a few months from now, Zoltan Bogdanovitch over there will be standing in his galoshes washing bits of your brain and fragments of your skull down the drain with a hose! It's him or you! In God's name, girl, *do it!*"

"No," she moaned softly.

"Why not?" shouted Yesenin again, enraged.

"Because Marina wouldn't!" she cried. "Don't you understand! This is the only way I can prove to him that I am as good a person as she was! It is the only way I can prove it to myself!"

III. The General

Senior Comintern representatives visiting the Soviet Motherland were housed in the grandiose but run-down premises of the old Grand Hotel, now called Hotel Metropole on Revolution Square, which before the Revolution had been known as Resurrection Square. Yesenin inquired at the desk for the renowned and heroic anti-Fascist General Rodrigo Diaz, known to the world press and a global legion of swooning and adoring left-wing dilettantes as El Campesino.

He found the mighty fighter for proletarian freedom sitting slumped over a table at the rear of the hotel bar, wearing a cheap Russian suit of the latest Soviet synthetic fibre, a compound that in the West was known as cardboard. General Diaz was a squat man with dark hair and deep sunken bloodshot eyes, a surprising green. He had a sullen, pale square pasty face on which grew a thick reddish stubble, a nose like a ball of dough and a very pale coloring from the long Russian winter. His waistline was spreading and his body was going rapidly to seed, but Yesenin could see that it had recently been hard and strong. Diaz had a bottle of cheap vodka and a glass in front of him, and he was just on the dangerous edge of drunk. He scowled up at his visitor. "What the hell do you want, *gaybist?*" the Spaniard demanded. His Russian was quite good, although accented. Yesenin seated himself without being asked.

"I am Colonel Ivan Vasilievitch Yesenin," he said.

"Really? I didn't get a telegram asking me to make my will. Not that I have anything to leave anyone other than this lousy suit. Do I have the appearance of a man who may someday be guilty? You see, Comrade Colonel, your reputation precedes you. Have you motherfuckers decided to shoot me instead of letting me go home to Spain? I'm not surprised." He poured himself a glass of vodka and shoved the bottle to Yesenin, who lifted it to his lips and took a long slug.

"I am here regarding the disappearance last December of Marina Antonovna Galinskaya," said Ivan Vasilievitch.

"I thought you blue-capped bastards killed her," growled the Spaniard.

"Believe it or not, Comrade General, we don't kill everyone who dies or disappears in Russia."

"I don't believe it, Comrade Colonel. So what can I tell you? I haven't seen her for months, not since she took up with that chess player. What the hell kind of a way is that for a man to make a living? Playing a damned game? Why does this great proletarian paradise of yours pay a character like that a fortune to sit around and do nothing but move little men around a checkered board? This is supposed to be a workers' state. So why the hell don't you make that leech Podichevsky do some work?"

"A bit jealous, are we?" remarked Yesenin.

"*Cristo*, yes! My God, to lose a woman like that! And to lose her to a parasite like Podichevsky! I'm damned near insane with jealousy and I don't care who knows it."

"Jealous enough to kill her?" asked Yesenin.

"Don't be bloody stupid," growled the Spaniard.

"Where were you on the night of December 31st, 1937?" asked Yesenin.

"I was attending a Comintern meeting and reception at the Kremlin, where I sat around listening to the most incredibly dull speeches that you can possibly imagine until ten o'clock, after which we adjourned to the ballroom for an evening of convivial and edifying socialist entertainment. At midnight we saw the New Year in, boiled as owls. By one o'clock I was fucking some commissar's wife in a broom closet and by two o'clock I was so drunk that when I tried the same thing with one of the banquet hostesses I couldn't get it up. I passed out about three and was carried back here and dumped onto my bed by someone, I can't remember who. You want a witness? Ask Comrade Stalin. He was there presiding over it all like the Masque of the Red Death. He made Pauker dance with his wife, which is probably forbidden by the Hague Convention. He made Anastas Mikoyan bob for apples in the punchbowl wearing his tux, and he made young Khruschev, the Ukrainian Party Secretary, sing "Me and Annushka By The Samovar" while wearing Madame Molotov's hat. It is possible that I found time during all of this rough-and-ready proletarian camaraderie to sneak out and murder the only woman whom I have ever truly loved in my life and hide her body so successfully no one has ever found it, but if so I was so drunk I don't remember the dirty deed. Satisfied?" concluded the Spaniard, lifting another glass of vodka to his lips.

"You speak Russian very well, Comrade General," said Yesenin.

"I had a good teacher," Diaz replied morosely.

"Marina Antonovna?"

"Yes." He looked up at him. "Is she really dead?"

Yesenin couldn't find the strength to lie or equivocate. He simply nodded. The Spaniard laid aside his vodka glass and lowered his face onto his fists. As if from a mortally wounded animal came a scream that ran over the bar out into the street, the cry of a man in mortal agony. "*Marishka!*" he screamed once, and then for long minutes Diaz sobbed piteously like a child, uncontrolled, unashamed. People looked over at the table and stared, but they saw the blue shoulder boards and blue cap band and looked away again. They began to drink up quickly and drift out of the bar, trying to remain casual. Diaz pulled himself together, wiped his face and eyes with a soiled napkin and looked up at him. "In God's name, Yesenin, I didn't kill her! You can't think that!"

"He cared more than I thought he did," said Marina softly. "Once more I have hurt someone almost beyond repair. Sometimes I think you did me a great kindness and a favor, Ivan Vasilievitch. Maybe you did a great kindness and favor to the world. You put a stop to the havoc and pain I brought into the lives of others."

"Never say that!" replied Yesenin despairingly.

"So you don't think I killed her?" asked Diaz.

"I don't think you killed her, Comrade General," said Yesenin.

"Then why are you here?"

"I have to put in my report that I interviewed you."

"Ah, I see. You know who killed her and it's someone beyond reach."

"Yes," said Yesenin.

"And you're just going through the motions?" asked Diaz in a dull tone. "Why bother? This is Russia. No one expects you to bother."

"Sometimes the motions can produce results in spite of all, Comrade General."

"If you can't touch him, I can," replied Diaz. "I don't care any more. I embarrassed the General Secretary by winning too many battles while my lips were pressed with insufficient firmness to his ass. They got me here under false pretenses in the guise of a diplomatic mission to increase the level of military assistance to the Spanish Republic. We need more of everything, more airplanes, more guns, more ammunition, more uniforms, more medicine and bandages, more money, more newsprint, more vehicles and machinery and replacement parts. I got here and they took my passport and now they won't let me leave. They'd probably shoot me if it weren't for the bad publicity. I've got your people following me everywhere, but I can shake them off if I have to do something important. Like cutting the throat of Marina's murderer. Just give me a name, Comrade Colonel. It wasn't that chess pansy, was it?" The thought crossed Yesenin's mind that here was an opportunity to kill two birds with one stone. *I sick this durok onto Podichevsky. If he cuts Podichevsky's throat then Podichevsky is the killer of Marina, and if Podichevsky gets to his state-issued Makarov first and blows this beaner away, then the beaner's our boy for the Galinskaya job.*

"You can't do that, Ivan Vasilievitch," said Marina firmly. "It's wrong." By now he was used to her ability to read his thoughts. It was one of the things that made him think perhaps she was a construction of his own guilt-ridden mind and conscience. He ignored her and changed the subject.

"How did you and she get together?" asked Yesenin. "It's all in the files, of course, but I'd like to hear your version of events."

"Marina came out to Spain with the first wave of international volunteers, back in '36," said Diaz. "It wasn't that she was interested in politics or saving the bloody Republic or anything like that. She couldn't have cared less about anything political. She was following her lover of the time, that journalist and poet fellow Ilya Vyacheslavsky. Marina read me some of his poetry once. Didn't make any sense to me. I think he must have been pissed when he wrote it. Vyacheslavsky later became disillusioned when he saw what the Communists were doing to the Republican war effort. He talked too much to some of the other foreign correspondents and he was too damned naive to understand how many of them were Comintern agents. Your little poet died mysteriously when someone wired a bomb to his car in Barcelona. Wonder who that could have been, eh, Yesenin? Well, whoever it was, you got another martyr for the struggle against Fascism, didn't you? Dead martyrs are a lot more useful than live journalists."

"I wept for Ilya Romanovitch all the more because he went to Spain for me," said Marina sadly. "He felt he had to prove himself to me, to show himself brave. He was a romantic and he thought there was something dashing and adventurous about war. He wanted to be a soldier but I dissuaded him. I went along to make sure he kept his word and didn't get involved in the fighting. I failed him. I guess I'm just bad luck."

"Vyacheslavsky and Marina arrived in late July of '36," Diaz continued. "The Fascists got close enough to bomb Madrid during the first couple of months of the revolt, and although she was totally untrained

Marina became a hospital nurse in one of the children's wards. Vyacheslavsky wrote her up a smashing article with some really dishy photos of Marishka in her nurse's uniform playing with bandaged babies, and all of a sudden she was a world-wide celebrity. 'The Russian Angel of War-Torn Madrid', that kind of thing. The lefty press in Europe and America ate it up. She was great propaganda. For the rest of that year she did all kinds of first-rate agitprop photo shoots, more baby pictures of all kinds with teddy bears and toys, ladling out soup in the bomb shelters, working in a makeshift greenhouse to grow vegetables for food during the siege, sitting behind a sewing machine making uniforms for the troops and baby clothes for the little victims of Fascism, you get the idea. She was the poster girl for kindly Uncle Joe and his loving concern and solidarity with the struggle of the Spanish proletariat. They wanted her to do *La Pasionaria*-type material, pose in a beret with a rifle on her hip, looking strong and proud with the top three buttons of her blouse undone, or a good profile shot in something tight-fitting behind an anti-aircraft gun looking with grim determination at the sky, that kind of thing, but she wouldn't do it."

"No," said Ivan Vasilievitch with a nod. "She wouldn't. She hated guns and violence."

"I know," agreed Diaz. "That was one of the reasons I loved her so. I was just a dog who went around biting everybody. She was an angel."

"Yes. Go on," urged Yesenin.

"I was pretty hot copy myself that autumn of '36, since I led the Asturian miners who sapped under the Alcazar of Toledo and blew the walls down. They call me El Campesino, The Peasant, but I'm not a clodhopper, I'm a miner." Diaz held up his hands, scarred and burned from steel and cinders and metal fragments. "Coal, tin, copper, I've dug it all."

"But you never captured the Alcazar," pointed out Yesenin.

"No," agreed Diaz with a frown. "No, we never did. Moscardo had less than two hundred men, half of them sick and wounded, plus a few teenaged boy cadets and a few civilians. We called Moscardo up before we cut the telephone lines to the Alcazar, and we told him we'd shoot his seventeen year-old son if he didn't surrender. We put Junior on the phone to convince him. You know what the kid said? 'Father, if you surrender your command to the enemies of Spain in order to save me, I will disown you, and will no longer consider myself your son.' The old man replied, 'Die like a Spaniard, my son!'"

"You shot the boy?"

"Of course." Diaz scowled in drunken profundity. "I'll let you in on a secret, Yesenin. Fascists may be bastards, but they're tough and they're brave and they fight like devils. They're just as passionate and patriotic about their beliefs as we are, and they are just as convinced as we are that they're right. They know why they fight and love what they know. Time and time again we attacked the Alcazar and Moscardo's handful beat us back, singing *Cara al Sol* with their dying breath. I have never been so proud to be a Spaniard as when I saw those men stand up to us in all our thousands. "

"I remember, Comrade General," said Yesenin. "I fought against the Whites during our own Civil War. No finer soldiers or braver men ever called themselves Russians. Marina Antonovna?" he prodded gently.

"Oh, yes. Wandering into war stories, was I? Well, I'm a soldier now so I have stories to tell. Better than miners' stories. Where was I? After the Alcazar was relieved we fought our way back to Madrid. That's when we in turn showed the world what we were made of. They were waiting for us behind every wall and in every olive orchard, snipers and grenade-throwers and peasants who attacked us with nothing but shotguns and reaping hooks. We left our dead and theirs at every village and crossroads, but we made it. That was in late September. I had a lot of friends in the POUM division and they elected me their general a few days before the Fascist General Molina made his push against the city."

"POUM? You're not a Bolshevik, then?" inquired Yesenin.

"*Dios*, no," laughed Diaz. "Do I look like I have a board up my ass? *Viva l'Anarchia!* Long live Anarchy!" he shouted, downing another vodka. The last remaining bar patrons fled in terror from this insane man who dared to say such a thing, in front of a *gaybist*, no less. Surely, this crazy foreigner was suicidal. "Anyway, our press people wanted some agitprop, so I did a tour of the hospitals wearing my new general's uniform. Of course I had to get my photograph taken with the Russian Angel of Madrid, both of us holding bandaged babies. The little bastard they handed me pissed all over my shirtfront, but I didn't care. I had eyes only for Marina. And oh Blessed Virgin of Guadaloupe!" he went on in awe, "Through some inconceivable miracle, she only had eyes for me! Those dark eyes with all the wisdom and wile of woman within them. Me, a man who did nothing all his life but dig holes in the ground. I still can't believe it."

"Please don't take this wrongly, Comrade General," asked Yesenin carefully, "But I am curious about something. Marina Antonovna was famous for her many tempestuous relationships with a number of very creative, very intellectual, cultured and educated men. I must confess that I am puzzled. I can think of no other way to say this but to ask you bluntly: what the hell did she ever see in you?"

"You wouldn't believe me if I told you, Ivan Vasilievitch," said Marina behind him in an amused voice.

"You wouldn't believe me if I told you, Ivan Vasilievitch," said El Campesino with a grin.

"Try me," said Yesenin dryly to both of them.

"It was his charm," said Marina.

"It was my charm," said Diaz.

"Charm?" asked Yesenin, uncertain he had heard correctly.

"I am a Spaniard, Comrade Colonel," said Diaz with an ironic smile. "We have a reputation as a grimly formal people, which I won't say is undeserved, but yes, we can be charming. When we want to do so, we can display Latin gallantry better than any Frenchman or Italian. You see me now sitting here half paralytic on this god-awful grain spirit, which I drink because I can't get a decent glass of wine in this godforsaken country, and don't even talk to me about that horse piss from Georgia." Yesenin smiled and snapped his fingers to the barkeep, a stocky man who hurried over, perspiring in fear. Yesenin whispered something into his ear and the bartender fled. Diaz ignored the interruption and went on. "The minute I saw those dark eyes turned on me I immediately overflowed with boyish charm. I was light, I was gay, I was debonair, I was as gallant as any knight of old, and to be fair I also was a lot more handsome two years ago before I spent a Russian winter cooling my heels in every sense of the word and swilling this damnable hellbroth."

"Yes," agreed Marina. "He was handsome in his uniform, his skin burned brown by the sun, his beard full and hand grenades dangling from his chest like jewelry. I always tried never to be swayed by a merely handsome man, but a girl sometimes slips in spite of herself."

"Above all," concluded Diaz, "I made her laugh. In the midst of all that blood, death, and fire, as the shells and the bombs rained down on Madrid, I made her laugh."

"So he did," sighed Marina reminiscently. "He gave me laughter in a place and time when laughter was an incredibly precious commodity. He was a different man from the one you see today, Ivan Vasilievitch."

The barkeep returned with a tray on which stood two dark green glass bottles and two capacious brandy snifters, in a state almost approaching clean. He put the tray down on the table and bowed and scraped away. Diaz eyed the bottles with interest. Yesenin uncorked one. "Bull's Blood, from our country cousins in Bulgaria," he said. "Try it, Comrade General." He poured two large snifters of the dark red wine and handed one to Diaz. Yesenin raised his glass. "To the dark eyes!"

"To the dark eyes!" Diaz replied in a low tone. He took a long sip. "Not half bad," he had to admit. "Where was I? Vyacheslavsky vanished from the scene, which I always thought was gentlemanly of him, and for the rest of that year Marina and I were one. Together we saved Madrid. I couldn't have done a quarter of the things I did without the memory of her voice, the memory of her smile, the memory of her in my arms. Sometimes I couldn't get to her, couldn't see her for days at a time, but every messenger from within the city brought me a little note, a few words of encouragement. I knew she was mine, and when she was mine I was invincible. Every time I heard a shell or a bomb land in our rear my heart froze and I fought like a madman to get them out of artillery range of her, to capture and destroy their forward airfields that sent the planes, to destroy those who would harm her. I wasn't fighting for my country, Yesenin. I wasn't fighting for the proletariat or for the stinking Party. I was fighting for my beloved."

"One of the best motivations of all for a soldier," agreed Yesenin.

"We drove them back, the threat to the capital was over, and then I fucked it up. I lost her," moaned Diaz. "I was a bloody hero to literally hundreds of hot lefty bitches in the rear echelons, some Spanish senoritas but mostly these half-crazed foreign girls from middle class families in England and America and Germany who were in Spain as nurses or reporters or clerk-typists or general hangers-on. They were all convinced they were Rosa Luxemburg or Louise Bryant, raving Bolshevik nymphomaniacs who wanted to make their contribution to the great Anti-Fascist Struggle on their backs with a real live, hard-handed proletarian son of the soil, or in my case son of the slag heaps. I'm a tin miner, *por Dios!* Who could possibly have expected me to resist such a feast set before me?"

"Obviously Marina Antonovna did. Caught you *in flagrante delicto*, I presume?" suggested Yesenin.

"Me and a red-headed Jewish girl from the CPUSA in New York. One of the type who liked to swagger about the cafés wearing a pistol and jodhpurs, and a beret and a khaki uniform shirt she could barely button over those two *magnificos* on her chest. Her ass never hit twice in the same place, but unfortunately Marina walked in on us while her ass wasn't hitting twice in the same place. *Carramba,* what was I thinking?" Diaz smashed his fist down on the table.

"It was a shock," admitted Marina. "The only time to my knowledge I was ever so deceived. Well, not the only time."

"Not the only time," agreed Yesenin. "Comrade General, you may not realize it, but you are somewhat unique in the history of Marina Antonovna's liasions. So far as I can determine, you are the only one who ever got a second chance. Our records at the NKVD indicate that when you arrived here in August of 1937, Marina Antonovna agreed to resume your relationship and did so for a brief period until she broke it off again due to your simultaneous involvement with an English milady of Bolshevik sympathies, specifically Lady Dianne..."

"I know her name," snapped Diaz.

"He swore to me that he could change," said Marina tiredly. "I was a woman, and women are always suckers for that line."

"You also evinced an interest in one of our own *Russkaya krasivas,* to the point of bringing her up to your room in this hotel on a number of occasions, the last of which was four nights ago. I refer to Citizeness Sonia..."

"I know her name too, Yesenin. A gentleman does not discuss ladies in a cantina."

"But the main difficulty appears to have arisen regarding a woman whom Marina Antonovna genuinely regarded as her friend and confidante. You understand to whom I refer?"

"Yes. The electronics technician. When Marina found out, it was over. I had finally destroyed the best thing in my life. Don't ask me why, Yesenin. I just can't seem to get that kind of thing right. Sonia is beautiful and sweet and too naive to understand what she risks in seeing me, but she can never be Marina." Diaz sighed and slumped in the chair and drained off his glass of wine. He appeared about ready to pass out.

"It was a revelation," said Marina. "In a way a necessary one, maybe even a good one. I learned that I could be made a fool of, that I could be betrayed. I learned that everyone around me knew of this affair between them and no one had done me the courtesy of telling me what was going on. All of a sudden I was no longer Russia's official goddess of love, I was a common or garden variety female fool whose best friend was sleeping with her man, the kind of female fool who can be found in any tea shop or on any factory floor. It was a humbling and painful experience, but I am glad I experienced it before I died. It gave me a much-needed lesson in humility. I made up my mind I was going to try to build something permanent with Anastas Nazarian. I like to think I could have done so. Oh, Vanya! Why did you kill me? Now I'll never know if I myself could have changed, if I could have done what I demanded of Rodrigo. By the by, why didn't you ever tell me about Rodrigo and…and her?"

"I loved you," Yesenin muttered. "You knew that I loved you. Suppose I had come to you and told you? What would you have thought? You would have believed I was just trying to cause trouble, trying to get your attention, lying to you out of jealousy."

Diaz looked at him strangely. "Is it the wine or is this why they call you The Madman?" he asked.

"This is why they call me The Madman," returned Yesenin brusquely. "Answer me this, Comrade General. You clearly understand the gift that destiny offered you in Marina Antonovna. Why did you seemingly go out of your way to destroy it? I knew her, as I am sure you have gathered. I was never her lover, but I have spoken to others who were granted that privilege. In every case these men have told me that their relationship with Marina Antonovna approached the level of a religious experience."

"They do not exaggerate, Comrade Colonel," said Diaz, staring into space. "She was fire. She was ice. She was the wind. She was the spirit of the night. Imagine all that woman can be, and she was that."

"I seem to be turning into rather a caricature!" remarked Marina acerbically. "Come now! I was never *that* good!"

"Well, I wouldn't know, would I?" Yesenin reminded her.

"Now who's jealous?" asked Diaz with a chuckle.

"Jealous as hell, Comrade General," admitted Yesenin. "Yet you alone seem to have found that experience inadequate. You alone sought diversity. As you yourself put it, you quite deliberately destroyed the best thing in your life. I have reason to believe that her murderer did the same thing, only in his case, he destroyed Marina Antonovna. It is of some importance that I understand this man's motives. May I ask why you committed romantic hara-kari, so to speak?"

"No, Vanya. You can't cheat," said Marina warningly. "You have to answer me yourself, for yourself." Yesenin succeeded in ignoring her this time.

"I have asked myself that same question a number of times. It is due to a defect in my character, Comrade Colonel," said Diaz glumly.

"Defects in character are the NKVD's speciality, Comrade General. Please be more specific."

"My defect is a simple and common one. I am an asshole." He held up his hand. "No, no, I'm not being facetious. That is the best way I can possibly put it. I am one of those people who is utterly selfish and yet at the same time incapable of understanding his own true self-interest, and who as a result does all manner of stupid things in his personal life, however successful or not he may be in his public life or his trade. I think Marina came to understand that, however fond of me she might be, I am an asshole. I will always be an asshole, and she did not belong with me. Now, is there anything else? I'm not unconscious yet, and this talk with you has put me behind schedule. By the by, thank you for introducing me to Bull's Blood. Yesenin!" said Diaz as Ivan Vasilievitch rose to go. "Any chance you can pull some strings with the Comintern and the Foreign Ministry or even the Boss himself, so they will let me go back to Spain? Franco will have won in another few months and I don't want to have to spend the rest of my life in this freezing hellhole. I want to die in the mountains with a bullet in the front, fired by one of those real *hombres* like the ones who fought us off at the Alcazar, not shot from behind in your filthy cellar."

"I will see what I can do," said Ivan Vasilievitch.

Yesenin stood outside the hotel, luxuriating in the warm afternoon sun. He saw people crossing the square to avoid him and a few older women making the sign against the evil eye as they saw his blue shoulderboards, but he didn't care. "Well, do you think he should get his wish, Marina Antonovna?" he asked. "Get his bullet from the front like an *hombre* or in the back of the head from my trusty Nagant here, in our little room downstairs? I don't think the Boss would be too displeased if I were to rid him of a potential propaganda embarrassment, and it would be a black mark against the Anarchists in Spain."

"You're not getting me involved in something that is your decision to make, Ivan Vasilievitch," she said firmly. "If you are going to murder someone, though, please tell them why before you kill them. It makes the dead rest much easier, as I believe you have already deduced. Now you're going to see your old friend Arkady Fyodorovitch.. Will you kill him if you find it convenient?"

"He might thank me for it," replied Yesenin. "The last time I saw Kolchin, he spoke to me about you. He told me that of all the men who ever fell under your spell, it was he who loved you the most. The scary thing was, he was stone cold sober when he said it."

IV. The Writer

"You don't have to tell me that she is dead, Ivan Vasilievitch," said Arkady Kolchin in a sad voice. "I already know. I had a dream, you see…"

The famous novelist sat in a comfortable leather armchair, his slippered heels resting on an upholstered footstool. He was a large, heavy man of middle age with a once powerful weight-lifter's physique that was collapsing into flab through long neglect, poor diet, and far too much alcohol. His dress was sloppy and seedy, his jacket was burned with small holes from stray pipe and cigarette ash, his shirtfront was soup-stained, and his shoes were scuffed. Kolchin was smoking one of his filthy pipes, but he gestured towards a large silver cigarette casket. "Egyptian. You're not the only big knob who can get away with foreign cigarettes, you know. I have them made up specially in case lots of ten thousand by Ionides of Alexandria. Take a handful of them when you go, or if you're going to arrest me you can take them all."

The two men were sitting in the study of Kolchin's apartment on Petrovka Street, in a comfortable haze of tobacco and caffeine. It was what one might expect the study of a man of letters to look like, albeit a sloppy and disorderly man of letters. Books, magazines, manuscripts, and mail were piled up in promiscuous stacks on the shelves. The room was littered with half-empty liquor bottles, bits and pieces of tobacco products and ashtrays, and one or two plates containing the desiccated remains of sandwiches, fruit pits, and meat bones. A high fidelity phonograph made in Germany stood against one wall, and beside it was a long rack containing 78-RPM discs of the great classical composers, Tchaikovsky and Wagner and Beethoven, Mozart and even the strictly banned work of Igor Stravinsky. Two Underwood typewriters stood on his cluttered worktable, one with Cyrillic keys and one with English, but the actual work of creation was done over in the corner.

There the author had created a kind of alcove or cubbyhole, almost like a child building a play fort with furniture and cushions. "I can't create a fantasy world until I barricade myself against the real world," remarked Kolchin. "I'm lucky Stalin likes the crap I write. Because of that I get this apartment, great buffets at the Moslit restaurant for three rubles fifty kopecks so I don't need a wife or a cook, and above all I am one of the few Soviet citizens allowed to shut out the Brave New World." A long single curtain hung from a rod set into the wall which shielded most of the alcove from view, and behind it was a small but well made wooden desk, with drawers and a green shaded bankers' lamp. To one side stood a large candelabrum with nine candlesticks. "You see the small hot plate to one side of the desk?" Kolchin pointed out. "I'm like Balzac. When I'm actually working, I write at night and subsist on black coffee."

"Speaking of which, this is quite good," Yesenin, sipping his own brew from a tin mug, an affectation from Kolchin's army days which as an old soldier himself he appreciated. "No vodka this time?"

"I'm cutting down on the sauce. She did that for me. You see I also keep my pipe rack and a good full humidor of tobacco on the desk, so when I finally get my ass in gear and sit down to work, I'm all tooled up. In the hours of darkness I sit there in a dressing gown, sometimes wrapping myself in a blanket and warming my hands over the hot plate in winter. On these nights I write out in longhand, with many corrections, whatever latest variation on my formula my instincts tell me will best entertain the cruel humor of a slippery Georgian gangster."

"I like your books, Arkady Fyodorovitch!" protested Yesenin.

"They're all pretty much the same," said Kolchin with a shrug. "Strong-jawed Russian heroes in various historical epochs defeat the evil machinations of assorted foreign conspirators, chop and stab and shoot and otherwise bring about the sticky and gory demise of said foreign conspirators, save Russia and get the *devotchka*."

"You're a good storyteller, Arkasha. Don't belittle your talent," said Yesenin.

"Oh, I'm a good enough storyteller, agreed," replied Kolchin with a smile. "I have a certain way with words, and above all I am a practised expert at conveying sexual situations and implying the sexual act without running afoul of these blue-nosed Communist censors. By Soviet standards my books are pretty racy, and they sell without too much help from the Ministry. Stalin is reported to have once said that his favorite bedtime reading is a Kolchin novel, and from then on my reputation and fortune were made. If I were an American I'd write cowboy stories, but I really long to write in the vein of Edgar Allan Poe, or M. R. James, or the Englishman Russell Wakefield, or my late American correspondent H. P. Lovecraft."

"Lovecraft?" asked Yesenin. "Never heard of him,"

"Howard died last year in Providence, Rhode Island. Died in poverty in the charity ward of his local hospital. Well, I don't have to worry about that, thanks to The Father Of The Peoples. I'll either die down there in your cellar from nine grams if I write something politically incorrect, or else in a nice private clinic by the Black Sea when my liver gives out. The world will hear of Howard Lovecraft one day, though, long after I'm forgotten. Best writer of supernatural fiction since Poe, best *fantaisist* since Lord Dunsany. The candelabrum over there I use to light my cubbyhole for mood creation, when I have finished my latest historical swashbuckler from the time of Peter the Great or whenever. Then I can then return to my first love and write violent and fearful ghost stories, tales of bizarre murder and supernatural revenge."

"Why would anyone want to read of supernatural revenge?" wondered Yesenin with a shudder. Marina was keeping unusually quiet. *Surely she couldn't resist an opening like that?* he thought curiously.

"I don't even bother to submit my murder mysteries or my ghost stories for publication," said Kolchin. "Murder is no mystery to The Father Of The Peoples, and he doesn't believe in ghosts. He can't afford to, with all the people he's killed. Nobody believes in ghosts any more."

"Oh, I wouldn't say that, Arkady Fyodorovitch," said Yesenin. "You mentioned a dream, Arkady?"

"I'm coming to that," replied Kolchin. "First let me tell you about Marina Antonovna Galinskaya and me, insofar as there ever was a Marina and me, which wasn't very far. I first met Marina Antonovna in the Moslit Library. Stalin has sense enough to understand that we sometimes need actually to do a little bit of research to produce a plausible piece of shit, and he lets us have a pretty well stocked archive, better than any of the public biblios. There's a nice little pub and café on the ground floor. It used to be called Pero until someone remembered that was Trotsky's pen name before the Revolution, so now it is called the Chestnut Tree for some reason. The bartender is an NKVD spy of course, but other than that the library is a great place to while away a snowy afternoon reading books you can't get elsewhere. I always have dibs on the latest Agatha Christies and John Dickson Carrs as soon as they arrive.

"The Moslit Library is one of the few places in Moscow legally allowed to receive foreign newspapers and periodicals, and of course it's strictly off limits to the public, but Marina was able to get an admittance ticket through one of her lovers who was a member of the Soviet Writers' Union. Vyacheslavsky, I think, or perhaps Sergei Eisenstein the film director. I understand he made a play for Marishka, offered her the female lead in *Alexander Nevsky* if she'd go to bed with him, but she declined. At any rate, Marina Antonovna would come in and get a whole armful of books on linguistics, Turkish grammars and Portuguese dictionaries and whatnot, and she'd pile them up in her study carrel. She always picked the one in the back where she couldn't be seen too well, and she would reserve it by placing a cardboard tag with her name on it along the top of the partition, as is the custom. As it turned out, this backed onto the one I generally use. I noticed that what she was really doing was sneaking foreign newspapers and magazines from the rack, going back into her carrel, and then reading them behind these big piles of language books. I couldn't see anything but the top of her head, but I could hear her furtively turning the pages of the *Times* of London and the *Frankfurter Zeitung*. The third afternoon when she was in the library doing this, I quietly slid the latest copy of the *Saturday Evening Post* over the top of the carrel and held it there. After a moment I saw this beautiful hand with slim fingers come up and take it. It was like feeding a fawn or a gazelle or some other shy woodland creature, trying to coax her to eat out of my hand. Over the next several hours I slipped her the Rand *Daily Mail*, Paris Match, Oscar Wilde's *The Importance of Being Earnest*, and the latest number of *Weird Tales*, all of which she accepted in silence. Finally I stood up to go. I saw her look up at me, with those fathomless dark eyes, I bowed to her formally and when I straightened up she smiled at me."

"And you were lost," stated Yesenin.

"For the rest of my days, yes," confirmed Kolchin in a sad, soft voice. "What there was of it proceeded from there, all very intellectual and platonic. We'd get together for coffee in the little pub downstairs or at some café in the Arbat and talk about literature, world events, we'd talk about everything but what was important."

"You spoke of the war?" asked Yesenin. "I am curious as to how Marina Antonovna dealt with that part of your past."

"Yes, I know. I was terrified she would find out some of the things we did, against the Germans in the first war and then later when we went up against Wrangel and Kolchak. Here I was with this gentle and wonderful creature who was actually acknowledging my existence and speaking to me as if I were a human being, a friend. I'm sure that to her I was a mildly amusing figure of fun, kind of a combination between Falstaff and her old dedushka, and perfectly harmless. But what if she found out what I once was before I became so old and fat and amusing? What if she learned of the time when I was most definitely *not* harmless? I could not bear the thought that she would come to hate and fear me."

"Did she find out?" asked Yesenin. "Our Red Partisan Brigade is not unknown to the history books and the writers of memoirs, Arkasha. You tried to put it behind you, possibly because of us two you were always the true believer, and of course there came a time when you could believe no longer. I never had a problem with belief. Life is the exercise of power. There are two kinds of people, those who are beat and those who are beaten. I was always the first kind. I tread on my wartime reputation in my work. I was tapped for the OGPU by Dzherzhinsky himself, he was so impressed with my work in the field. You were too, but you didn't accept."

"I'd had enough wet work, Ivan Vasilievitch. You know that you are me, Vanya? That you are what I would have become had I not been so lazy and decided it was all too much effort?"

"I believe we have both drawn that parallel before, Arkasha, usually well into the second bottle of vodka. Did Marina Antonovna ever find out any of the details from the war?" asked Yesenin. *Why doesn't she speak?* he thought.

"I was determined that if she had to learn, she would at least hear it from me," said Kolchin. "I tried to tell her a few times, tried to discuss it, and she cut me off. She told me plainly that she didn't want to know. I think she did it to save my feelings, because she did know, and she understood that I really didn't want to talk about it, that it would almost kill me to confess to her, who was all that is good, of the evil that I have done. Oh, that angel! That wonderful merciful angel! I never drank when I was with her. It would have seemed like blasphemy. I couldn't stand the thought of her seeing me drunk, or even a little under the influence. Her effect on my work was galvanic. I don't know if you've bothered to read my latest novel, *Fire and Sword Along the Don?* That albatross hung around my neck in bits and pieces of manuscript that lay around here for almost five years, less than a third done, and I had totally lost interest in it. After that first smile and that first casual coffee I came back here and attacked it like my Cossack hero charging into the Tartars. I wrote 70,000 words in two weeks, and it wasn't just hackwork any more, it became a titanic struggle between the forces of good and evil. It's become my best seller yet and is most likely the best book I've ever done, one of the few things I've written which rises above adequate mediocrity. I wish I could say that I stopped drinking altogether, but I did cut way back and I started eating better and actually taking a little care of myself. Not before time. The old carcass was starting to send me signals that I'd damned well better mend my ways."

"That always tends to happen with older men who fall in love with younger women," pointed out Yesenin practically.

"No doubt. It's ironic. When I turned forty I swore to myself that one of the common pitfalls of middle age I intended to avoid at all costs was to make a fool of myself over some girl young enough to be my daughter. Needless to say, I immediately went out and made a fool of myself over a woman my own age, but we won't get into that."

"So what happened then, Arkady Fyodorovitch?" asked Yesenin.

"Nothing, of course," replied Kolchin. "What *could* happen? I was always realistic, Ivan Vasilievitch. I never had any expectations. I was twenty-two years older than she was, ugly as homemade sin and a fat slob to boot. I hadn't made love to a woman, in any sense of the word, for so long that I had forgotten what little social grace I ever had. Whenever I was with her it was all I could do to keep from tripping over my own shoelaces and chattering like a parrot. I gratefully accepted the small occasions of friendship and companionship she provided and did my best not to think of where she was, what she was doing, and who she was with when she wasn't around me."

"Bukharin married the beautiful Anna Larina, who was even younger than Marina," pointed out Yesenin.

"Yes, and look what happened to Bukharin!"

"You never tried to deepen the relationship?" queried Yesenin.

"No. What would be the point? She didn't love me. I always understood and accepted that. If I had ever thought for a single second that there was any chance she would say yes, I would have asked her to marry me without hesitation. Damn the consequences, never mind what anyone else thought, never mind how foolish I would have looked. But I knew it would only have embarrassed her and upset her. She would of course have been very, very kind with me, and that would have added to my humiliation."

"You were afraid of making a fool of yourself?" suggested Ivan Vasilievitch.

"I was terrified of making myself look foolish to *her*, which is not quite the same thing," said Kolchin with a sigh. "Needless to say, I eventually managed to accomplish that very feat."

"Ah," said Yesenin. "You told her that you loved her."

"Yes. It reached the point where my heart was bursting. I walked around in a daze all day not able to think of anything but her. I knew that by then she must surely at least suspect how I felt about her, but I couldn't bear the idea that she might never *know*. So yes, I told her, in about the most idiotic and stumblebum manner possible. I write stories wherein my two-fisted heroes are never at a loss as to how to deal with women, good women or bad, but in real life I am a brainless clown where women are concerned. You remember my two marriages and what disasters they were?"

"So what happened when you told her?" asked Yesenin.

"I'd rather spare both of us the details, if you don't mind," said Kolchin wryly. "It was not one of my better moments. I not only managed to make myself look like an idiot, I scared the hell out of her. For days she wouldn't meet me or speak to me. I finally sat down and wrote her a letter. I told her that if she never wanted to have anything to do with me again I would honor wishes in that as I would always honor her in all things, but that I had meant every word I said, I was glad she knew and I would never regret telling her. She at least spoke to me after that, and I counted myself lucky that I did not frighten her away completely."

"Surely she must have said *something?*" prodded Yesenin, wondering again why Marina was saying nothing now.

"She told me she was sorry that she had come into my life and could give nothing back. Dear Christ, she gave me back everything! She gave me back my art and my purpose in living. I had been dead inside for so long, and all of a sudden I *felt* again. Even the pain was welcome. You can't feel pain if you're dead. She did that for me, and she apologized!"

"You mentioned a dream, Arkady Fyodorovitch?" prompted Yesenin. *Why isn't she saying anything?* he wondered curiously.

"Yes, all of this bears on my dream, by which I know she is dead. Do you believe in the paranormal at all, Ivan Vasilievitch?" asked Kolchin.

"Let's just say that I have an open mind on the subject," replied Yesenin guardedly, lighting another Egyptian cigarette.

Slowly, Arkady Fyodorovitch began to speak. "I may have mentioned to you in the past, Ivan Vasilievitch, that ever since I was a child I have sometimes had certain special dreams of a psychic nature, what might be called perceptive or precognitive dreams. I can recognize these dreams when I have them. These dreams are always episodic and repetitive, and they are *specific,* never symbolic or allegorical. By that I mean that I may not understand what I see, but I see specific things and people. One winter night earlier this year, shortly after Marina Antonovna disappeared, I had a dream that was unlike any I have ever experienced before. I cannot overemphasize this unique aspect. I am 47 years old and I have never, *ever* had a dream remotely resembling this one. It was complete, of full clarity and it was not until the very end that I realized I was dreaming.

"It began about dawn, I think. The dream was as follows: I come into the Moslit Library. The building is completely empty and silent. I go to my normal reading cubicle and sit down. I look across and I see that someone is removing Marina Antonovna's name tag from the top of her carrel and putting all her books and newspapers into a box. I cannot tell you who this person is or even if it is a man or a woman, it's just a gray, shadowy figure. A man comes up to my side, an old friend whom I know. He is the only person throughout the whole dream whom I recognize or see clearly. He is very solemn and sad. He puts his hand on my shoulder and tells me in a kindly voice, "Arkady, I'm sorry. Marina's gone." I seem to know what he means, but I refuse to believe it. "They arrested her?" I ask. The man shakes his head and says, "Arkady Fyodorovitch, she's dead." Then he walks off.

"I turn and I look at the bare top of her study carrel, and behind me I hear two women weeping, not very loud but bitterly and desolately. I don't turn to see who they are. For some reason I'm not interested. Here is where it gets bad. The whole atmosphere becomes heavy with a sense of foreboding, depression and gloom. Not fear or normal grief over a death, but an utterly hideous kind of black poison which I can't possibly convey to you, pure cosmic despair and horror. It just goes on and on and on and on and on. I sit and stare in silence at an empty space over the cubicle and these women weep behind me out of sight and this terrible black suffering holds sway over all. Then the light starts to fade, like the sun is setting outside and no one is turning on any lights in the building. The silence except for the weeping women and the depression and despair get worse and worse until I can't breathe. It gets darker and darker and I finally realize I am dreaming and if I let it get completely dark before I wake up I am going to be in very bad trouble. As I have never done before in my life, I literally convulsed and jerked myself awake and fell out of bed onto my hands and knees. My chest was in pain almost like I was having a heart attack and I was babbling nonsense to myself. I can still see it all right now, hours later, as clearly as when I woke up. She's dead, isn't she?"

Kolchin was a master storyteller, and he had told the story well. Ivan Vasilievitch was shaken to his core. "Yes," he said. "We…we know that much."

"I knew it." Unlike the Spaniard, Kolchin did not weep. He simply sat and started into the deal coals and ashes in the cold fireplace for a time. "She was my Lara. She always will be."

"Who?" asked Yesenin.

"Pasternak has some woman he calls Lara whom he says drives his creative energies, who inspires him and makes it possible for him to keep going. Bulgakov has the same kind of thing with that army officer's wife he ran off with, I think her name is Elena or Yevgenia or something, but he calls her Margarita. Shakespeare had his unknown Dark Lady. Shelley had Mary Wollestonecraft. Marina is my Lara, even now that she is gone. She always will be, until the hour of my death. I only wish I could be a Pasternak or a Bulgakov for her. I am not, but I will try to be, for her sake. I have to immortalize her, you see. Her memory must never be allowed to die. She must live forever in the minds and the hearts of anyone who can read. I am going to give that to her. I don't know how as yet, but one day I am going to sit down at that desk over there and turn on that lamp, with my coffee pot and my tobacco tin full, and I am going to write a novel. A real novel, not the garbage I write in exchange for this apartment and for being allowed to stuff my face at the Moslit restaurant buffet. I will let the world know that she lived, and that she was all that is good and kind and beautiful and noble in woman."

"And let the world know that you loved her?" suggested Yesenin.

"Oh, yes, I am not without the true egotism of the writer," agreed Kolchin. "It's an egotistical act to write anything, you know, because you're assuming that somewhere out there are at least a few people who give a damn what you have to say. Curiosity question, Ivan Vasilievitch. Why, exactly are you here this evening?"

"I have to put in my report that I spoke with you," said Yesenin wearily. "Can you remember anything about the New Year's eve party, the night she disappeared?"

"I remember my last sight of her, crossing the drawing room in there, moving between the guests and around the piano in her green gown," said Kolchin dully. "I know now that she was going to the vestibule where she would get her hat and her coat and her gloves and walk out into the night, and then she would be gone forever. I always understood and accepted that it would come, that one day I would see her and it would be for the last time. On the street, or in the library, a casual passing, maybe a word or two, and then she would be gone forever, and all I would ever have is a memory. She would never give me a photograph of herself, you know. She wouldn't do it because she knew that I would keep it with me for the rest of my life, be buried with it over my heart in my coffin. She didn't want me hurting myself like that. Then the time came, and of course I didn't know it was the last time I would ever see her face. She smiled at me one last time," he said, his voice sinking to a whisper. "I'm glad she smiled at me. I can remember that much, at least."

"I...have some photographs of her in the case file," said Yesenin. "Do you want me to send you a couple? I can have more made."

"It wouldn't be the same. Anyway, she didn't want me to have one, and I will honor her wish. You loved her too, didn't you, Vanya?"

"Yes," admitted Ivan Vasilievitch.

"Then why did you kill her?" asked Kolchin, looking at him.

"*What?*" cried Yesenin, stunned. *Has she been speaking to him instead of me?* his mind shouted in horror. "Why did you say that? Has someone been...talking to you?" demanded Yesenin, his face suddenly a ghastly white, his body trembling.

"I told you that in my dream, I recognized the man who came to me in the library, who put his hand on my shoulder and told me that Marina is dead. That man was you, Ivan Vasilievitch. In God's name, man, *why?*"

Yesenin rose slowly from his chair. He unbuttoned the flap on his holster, drew out his Nagant revolver, and placed the pistol on the side table at Arkady Fyodorovitch's right hand. Then he collapsed back into the chair. "I can't tell you, Arkasha," he told his friend.

"Someone ordered you to kill her? Who? Yezhov? That lizard Beria when she spurned his advances? Stalin himself?" asked Kolchin, suddenly assuming the role of interrogator.

"No. It was only me. I mean that I literally can't tell you. I cannot express it in words. Maybe some day I will be able to, if you decide not to blow my brains out. I owe you that chance, you of all men. You were my blood brother in the war and you have been the closest thing I ever had to a relative ever since. You are the only real friend I ever had, and now I have done this terrible thing to you. There is nothing I can think of which would be more ridiculously inappropriate and inadequate than to say that I am sorry. I assume you still remember how to use one of those?" he said, pointing at the pistol on the table.

"It's like riding a bicycle. Once you learn, you never forget," replied Kolchin dryly.

"Then do what you have to do, Arkady Fyodorevitch. I've got it coming. But I can't discuss anything about that night with you. I just physically can't. The words won't come."

"You were the high official she was going to see to try and get that saxophone scum and his squeeze off the hook," stated Kolchin.

"Yes."

"She came to you for help and you killed her instead? I know you well enough to understand that it wasn't out of fear she would expose you and risk your position. You haven't cared about any of that for a long time."

"No," agreed Yesenin. "That's how I have survived in this deranged zoo we call a country. Their goal is to hurt. If you don't care about something, they know they can't hurt you by taking it from you, so they don't bother."

"She came to you in an act of altruism, to save someone else from this terrible psychopathic machine that you and I created all those years ago, and the machine ate her," mused Kolchin. "My God, what a story! See here, pardon me for being indelicate, Vanya, but you've got my curiosity raging now. She chose right, you could have gotten her two jazz babies off the hook, maybe even out of the country. But she only had one thing to trade, which I presume she offered. How did that end up in you murdering her?"

"What the hell is the matter with you?" demanded Yesenin incredulously. "You ought to be bellowing with rage and either pumping me full of bullets or beating me to a bloody pulp with that fireplace poker! I confess to you the most terrible deed of my terrible life and you look at the literary angle?" *What's the matter with her? Why doesn't she speak?*

"I told you. I knew she was dead seven months ago and I've dealt with it," explained Kolchin. "After the dream I was also pretty sure that you were responsible for her death. It's your job, after all, although I thought it would have been some kind of purge thing and not personal. I have wept for her in the privacy of my own heart, and I will again, but always I knew that someday she would go out of my life. Gone is gone. If she had any future in this unspeakable charnel house we call the Soviet Union I would be angry, yes, but what did you rob her of? A life in this country is no life at all, not for someone like her. I heard she turned down Stalin himself once. How long before *Atyets Naroda* remembered that little act of ideological deviationism? There is every likelihood that you spared my beloved angel from the living hell of Karaganda."

"Are you saying I did her a favor?" asked Yesenin in disgust.

"No," replied Kolchin, quietly but forcefully. "I am saying that however it happened, it's over, she's gone, and we don't have to be afraid any more of *that* happening to that wonderful, gentle soul. We know for certain now that she will never have to tear her frozen fingers off clawing a rock face in a gold mine, or pull the caviar out of stinking dead sturgeons for eighteen hours straight, or get thrown into a barracks at night with seventy-five men who have been debased to the level of animals by what you and I have done to them with our Brave New World. I'm not God and I have no real gift of prophecy, but that's what *might* have happened to her, and if that was destined to be her fate and you spared her from it, then that's a mitigating circumstance. Consider it before you judge yourself. You may remember that poem by Oscar Wilde about how each man kills the thing he loves, but what makes men do such a thing? I helped create this berserk machine just as much as you did, Ivan Vasilievitch. I am in a sense more guilty than you are, because as you said a while ago, I actually *believed* in all this Bolshevik horse shit once. I was once a real revolutionary, and if I had any guts or manhood left in me I'd load up a rifle and pull this crumbling carcass of mine, bulging belly and all, onto a horse and be a revolutionary fighter again. But I don't. I'm tired and I'm lazy and I'm sick at heart. So I will sit here and wallow in this filthy more or less luxury that the machine gives me for my servility, until one day I wake up in the darkness at four in the morning with my chest on fire and crushing inside me as my long-abused heart finally explodes, or else I slip on an icy sidewalk while drunk and crack my stupid head open, or whatever. I am going to die alone, without her, and for that I have only myself to blame for not being the kind of man she could have given herself to. I don't deserve Marina and I never did. I have no right to judge you or punish you, Ivan Vasilievitch. Only myself, and I judge myself guilty." He tossed the pistol back to Yesenin, who caught it in the air. "Take your gun back, Comrade Colonel. If you want expiation, then try using it where it will do some good. And I don't mean on yourself."

Yesenin rose and shambled to the doorway, to ashamed to look back at his friend. "Be sure you do write that novel, Arkady Fyodorovitch," he said. "I have indeed killed the thing I love. I beg of you, make her live again! Make her live forever. She deserves immortality."

"I will," replied Kolchin. "And when that day comes, I will say to all the world everything I could never say to her."

*   *   *

Later that night, as he sat in his apartment smoking Lucky Strikes and twirling a snifter of French cognac in his hand, Yesenin broke the silence. "Are you still here, Marishka?" he asked, staring at the wall.

"I will be with you as long as you need me, Ivan Vasilievitch," said Marina.

"I have given up all hope that you will ever explain to me just what the hell you mean by that. Why did you say nothing in Arkady Fyodorovitch's apartment, Marishka?" he asked.

"There I times when I choose to say nothing. That was one of them," answered Marina.

"A man pours out his soul in your hearing like that, and you say nothing?" riposted Yesenin.

"Sometimes there is nothing to say," answered the ghost.

V. Nadia

Suddenly the door buzzer rang. Usually when Yesenin was home, The Lump would be somewhere in the apartment and would open the door, but The Lump was upstairs lying on his cot in his room. Yesenin had a buzzer he could use to summon Brodsky, but the only reason he could think of for anyone to be coming to his door at night would be an NKVD team coming to arrest him. There was no point in disturbing Brodsky's rest for that.

Yesenin had decided long ago that when they came for him he would resist and make them kill him. He had committed far too many real crimes in his life to go through the grotesque mockery of ending it by confessing to false ones. He had made it a point, on several occasions, to tell various of his NKVD colleagues that in the event he intended to kill the senior officer commanding the arresting squad before he died. Yesenin had asked most earnestly that in view of that fact, he hoped his dear friend Alexei Stepanovitch or Igor Mironych or whoever would decline to lead any such expedition, as it would pain Yesenin greatly to have to blow his brains down the stately corridor of Government Mansions. This convinced his fellow officers that Yesenin was not only mad but dangerously mad, which was the impression he intended to inculcate. No NKVD officer wished to become involved in a situation where a victim actually resisted. Such a thing would set a very bad precedent. The buzzer rang again. Yesenin went to a cupboard and pulled out a short, wooden-stocked German Erma machine pistol, not trusting any Soviet weapon to function adequately in such a supreme emergency. He had the lighter 7.65-millimetre police version. He slapped in a drum of fifty cartridges, chambered a round, clicked the safety off, lit another Lucky Strike with his Zippo, and went to answer his doorbell.

Instead of an armed party of bluecaps, he found Nadezhda Morozova waiting for him. She was wearing a different outfit from the summer dress she had worn that morning, a long dark skirt and a white cotton blouse with a low collar in the front, a light raincoat and a felt beret. Her sandals had been replaced by high-topped shoes. Her blond hair was unbound now and fell over her shoulders in golden sheaves. She looked calmly at the machine gun barrel pointed at her navel and said, "I thought I got some kind of trial first, even if it's in secret?"

Yesenin lowered the gun barrel and said, "Come in, citizeness." She followed him into the flat. "Please, have a seat," he said, gesturing towards the chairs before the fireplace. He put the machine gun back into the cupboard. "How did you get past the porter downstairs?"

"I gave him five rubles and told him I was a prostitute. He was pleased at that. He said 'Ivan Vasilievitch hasn't had a woman up for a long time, and he's been very tense lately. Talking to himself. Working too hard.' He gave me a pat on the bottom and told me to see if I could get you to unwind. He likes you."

Without being asked Yesenin walked over and poured her a glass of cognac. "Are you hungry? I can make you a sandwich."

"No, thank you, Comrade Colonel," she said, but she accepted the brandy. He refreshed his own and sat down in the other chair.

"Why have you come here, citizeness?"

"She's come because she has sunk past terror into pure despair," said Marina.

Yesenin ignored her. "Are you now prepared to denounce the spy and traitor Boris Podichevsky?"

"No," Nadia said quietly. "I spoke with the Master today. I wept, I bared my soul to him, I pleaded on my knees for him to believe that I loved him and that I did not betray Marina Antonovna or cause her death in any way. He was very kind, very gentle with me. He knows how afraid I am of angry men, of being beaten by them, and he was careful not to frighten me like that. He swore to me faithfully that he did not blame me, that he would never defect to the West and in any case I would surely be going with him to Vienna, that my fears were groundless. Then he made love to me. He gave me the kiss of Judas. All the time I knew that he lied. Somehow he has become convinced in his mind that I did this terrible thing. He is going to kill me. At the last minute he is going to tell me some made up story about why I can't go with him, and promise me I have nothing to worry about. Then he is going to walk out of that house after giving me a final Judas kiss, and he will never come back. He is going to leave me there to wait for you or someone like you to come and take me away to my death."

"You have but to say the word, and it will be him we come for," Yesenin told her again. "Will you not say that word?"

"No."

"You still love him?" he asked her gently.

"Yes. I can't help it," she said miserably.

"No. One can't help it," agreed Yesenin with a sight. "Why have you come, then?"

"In a few weeks he will be gone forever. I thought for a while that maybe I'd be better off dead after that, that I wanted to die, but I have decided to try to survive. There is only one way I can do that. I have come to you to ask you to protect me, Colonel. To take me in." She looked at him calmly. Yesenin was impressed. There was no shabby, frightened attempt at seduction, no tears or false gaiety or brittle cynicism about it. She knew that she had only one thing to offer to save her life, and she was offering it without hope or supplication or regret now that her decision was made. "When you tire of me yourself, I will do whatever you want, spy on whoever you want, seduce whoever you want, denounce whoever you want. The Master is the only one I have ever loved or ever will love, so you don't have to worry about my refusing you anything again. I am already marked in the eyes of the world as the woman who betrayed Marina Galinskaya to her death. I am now willing to be what the world believes me to be. I can be of use to you, Ivan Vasilievitch."

"Why have you come to me with this offer and not to Major Korchagin?" asked Yesenin. "After all, he is officially your case officer."

"Korchagin hits me," replied Nadia with a shudder. "Every time I go to report to him in his office he listens and takes down notes and then he slaps me or punches me a couple of times and tells me to make sure I maintain a high level of socialist vigilance against the class enemy. Sometimes the Master notices the bruises and he makes a joke out of it. He says 'Aha! You have been to see your fancy man in town today, eh, Nadi? I see Trofim Petrovich is as passionate a lover as ever!' I have come to you because you promised you wouldn't hit me. Please, Ivan Vasilievitch. Protect me."

"*Oh, Nadia...* " It was as close as he had ever heard Marina come to weeping. Yesenin was reminded of the two weeping women in the background of Kolchin's prophetic dream. "Ivan Vasilievitch, can you not understand how sad and alone she is now? How humiliated she is, how she hates herself? The only person in the world she loves hates her and wants her dead, and she has no one else. Help her! Make love to her if it's what she needs now to make her feel some sense of self-worth again. I promise I'll leave you two alone, I won't listen or watch." Yesenin could barely resist asking her where she would go while he was having it off with Nadezhda and how she would know when they were finished, but he decided it probably wasn't best to live up to his name of The Madman in front of the fragile woman before him.

"Nadezhda Pavlovna," he told her, "I think I may have some idea how painful and humiliating it is for you to come here and say these things to me. You may believe that I despise you or hold you in contempt for it. Please don't think that. I am very saddened for you."

"Thank you, Comrade Colonel," she said, hanging her head.

"As to protecting you, well, the fact is that I am uncertain from day to day whether I can even protect myself. None of us are. If it comes to that, I will do what I can. But I'd like to try something first. How did you get into the city and what did you tell Boris Mikhailovitch about where you were going?"

"I took the servants' and workers' bus. I asked to visit my sister in the city. I have no sister, and he knows it. He assumes I am coming to report to the NKVD, which in a way I am," she replied. "He gave me money for a taxi back to Kuntsevo. He is going out of his way to be kind to me before he kills me."

"Nadia, tell me the truth. If I can change his mind, do you want to go to Vienna with him? Knowing as you do that he has plotted your death?" asked Yesenin.

"Yes," she said.

"Very well. I have an idea that might work, that might convince him you are innocent. But it is going to require your co-operation as well as great trust and courage on your part."

"What do you want me to do?" she asked.

"Right now I want you to get some sleep. I have some blankets and pillows. You will spend the night on my couch in there. It is quite capacious and comfortable."

"Not in the...?" she asked in surprise.

"Not tonight. I don't take payment without providing something in return. If and when it comes to that I'll at least have you move in officially and get you registered with the housing committee as an official co-habitant or domestic partner or whatever the bloody Bolshevik term is supposed to be for one's mistress. We can't have old Volodya the porter downstairs keep thinking you're a common prostitute, can we? But with any luck that won't be necessary. You and the Master will be off to Vienna in a month and from there your life is your own." *I also don't fancy taking you to bed with a ghostly chaperone, despite her promise to modestly avert her ectoplasmic eyes,* he thought as he rooted around in his storage closet for blankets and pillows.

"Do you think I'd grade you or make helpful suggestions at critical moments?" asked Marina mischievously. Nadia in the lounge was far enough away so he could mutter back,

"In point of fact that's another reason I wish you'd go away. How am I supposed to have any kind of intimate relationship with a woman from now on? Is that part of my punishment?"

"This isn't your punishment, Ivan Vasilievitch," said Marina. "Are you really going to help her?"

"I'm going to try," he said. "Don't know how successful I'll be."

"You're not going to kill her like you killed me when I came to you for help? I'm glad, but please explain, what is the difference between my situation and hers?" asked Marina.

"Are you real?" he asked. There was silence. "I'm going to answer all your questions from now on with other questions, just like you do."

"Will you?" Marina replied. She didn't speak again until after he had tucked Nadia in on the sofa, put on his own pajamas and climbed into his own bed. "Sleep well, Ivan Vasilievitch," she said.

*   *   *

The Lump was pleasantly surprised to find Nadia in the flat in the morning when he came in to make breakfast. He thought it was about time the boss started taking an interest in life again, and Nadia was very pretty, and so he made up one of his specialities, a full English-style breakfast with poached eggs and kippers and sausages and toast and a huge samovar of black tea. "Go down and bring the car around, Zoltan Bogdanovitch. We're going to Kuntsevo. I'll be about half an hour up here," Yesenin ordered him. "Nadezhda Pavlovna, now comes the time for you to show that courage and trust I mentioned to you last night."

"I will do whatever you want me to do, Ivan Vasilievitch. I...I was somewhat surprised when you didn't change your mind and wake me up last night. You seem to be a man of your word."

"Take off your blouse," Yesenin ordered her.

"Oh, not a man of your word but a morning man?" she said with a shy smile. She started to undo the buttons.

"No, it's not what you think. This is a land of lies, Nadezhda Pavlovna, and I must try to save you by a lie." Yesenin went into the bathroom and took out gauze, surgical tape, alcohol, and iodine as well as a needle and cat-gut thread. Then he went into the kitchen and came back with a large white napkin and a long, sharp butcher knife. "Did you mean what you said yesterday, that you aren't afraid of blades?"

"Just fists and belts," she said with a nod.

"I asked you to take off your blouse so I wouldn't get blood on it. Nadia, the price you must pay for life and freedom, if this works, is that you must be scarred for life. I must convince Podichevsky that you attempted to commit suicide, and to do that I must cut you in the neck. Not deep enough to do serious harm, but it has to be believable. Will you trust me?" She laid her blouse on the settee and stood up, wearing her skirt and her slip top.

"Go ahead," she said calmly.

"Over here in front of the mirror." Yesenin stood her in front of the mirror and gave her the napkin, which he soaked in alcohol. He took up a position behind her and asked, "Are you right handed or left handed?"

"Right handed," she answered.

"Very well. Hold your hair back out of the way with your right hand, now lift your chin high and turn to the right. I'm going to make an incision just below your left jaw, so it will look as if you tried to cut your own throat. It's got to look real, Nadia. The cut will be shallow but it has to be at least three inches long to look convincing."

"Vanya!" said Marina urgently behind him, "If you mean her harm, on my knees I beg of you, don't do this! Don't make her go through what I went through, that terrible final knowledge that someone I trusted had betrayed me and destroyed me!"

"I know the thought that must be occurring to you," Yesenin said to both of them. "Yes, I am a killer. But I will not kill you. Do you trust me, Nadia? If there is the slightest doubt in your mind, I won't do anything."

"It's not a matter of trust, Ivan Vasilievitch," said Nadia. "I am totally in your hands. Do with me as you will."

"Very well. When you feel the blade cut into your neck it is going to hurt like hell and your natural reaction will be to try and jerk away. You must try to stay still. I want a good clean scar with a minimum of actual damage. When I tell you to, slap that alcohol-soaked napkin over the wound. That's going to hurt even worse, but the wound has to be sterilized quickly. Are you ready?"

"Go ahead," she said, closing her eyes. Yesenin quickly and firmly slid the blade downward. She flinched but stood still and did not cry out.

"Now! Napkin!" She shoved the wet cloth against her bleeding neck and groaned in agony. He helped her into the kitchen and sat her down at the table. "Lean back in the chair and grip the arms of it. Keep the napkin on the wound for a minute or two. Then I am going to have to sew it up. It should only take four or five stitches. It's going to hurt," he warned.

"This kind of pain I can take," groaned Nadia. "The pain of looking into his eyes and seeing my death there I cannot."

"All right, the bleeding's stopped. I didn't cut that deep. Now listen to me while I sew you up," said Yesenin, putting the gut-threaded needle to her neck. "When we get there, you just sit by in your bandaged neck looking forlorn and demure and let me do the talking. Our official story will be that I tried to rape you and you ran into the kitchen, grabbed the knife and tried to commit suicide rather than give yourself to anyone but the Master. I was able to wrestle the knife away from you, and then your beauty and your passion and your courage so shamed me that I desisted in my lecherous attempts against your virtue. I don't care how angry he is with you, any man would be impressed by a story like that. The thing is, we've got to make him believe it. Hold still, I'm almost done. These big ugly cat-gut stitches will add credibility to our little vignette of life and love in the Socialist Motherland. They look like the work of a Soviet doctor."

"Can we say something other than rape, Ivan Vasilievitch?" asked Nadia, grimacing. "You are being very kind to me and trying to help me, and I don't feel right in slandering you. What if some of your colleagues in the NKVD were to hear of this false accusation? How about we tell Boris Mikhailovitch that you threatened to take me to the Lubyanka and torture me, and I tried to kill myself rather than betray him politically? That makes more sense, and that way you're not committing a crime, you're only doing your job."

"All right," agreed Yesenin. "It's true, I'd rather not get the kind of lousy reputation with women that Beria has. Thank you for being so considerate, Nadezhda Pavlovna."

*　　　　　　*　　　　　　*

They found the Master Podichevsky in the garden behind his dacha again, studying another chessboard and making notes on his board-patterned pad. Yesenin walked up and kicked over the table with his boot, sending the pieces flying. "Do you think I can't reconstruct that board from memory?" asked Boris Mikhailovitch. He looked up and flinched at what he saw in Yesenin's face. He glanced over and saw Nadezhda standing with her head lowered, the bandages soft and lumpy on her neck with enough brown blood and iodine stain for effect. He looked at Yesenin again and there was fear in his eyes. "She has denounced me? You have come to arrest me? What idiotic crime has she made up?"

"No, I haven't come for you, worse luck," said Yesenin in a cold voice. "Even though you are one of the rare ones who actually deserves it.

What the hell did Marina ever see in you? No, your secretary unaccountably declines to co-operate with the Organs for state security. Citizeness Morozova, I ask you once again, during your employment here have you ever witnessed any indications that Boris Mikhailovitch Podichevsky has engaged in espionage? Specifically with reference to Podichevsky's correspondence with the foreign intelligence agent and nobleman Sir Angus Robertson?"

"No, Comrade Colonel. I have seen nothing like that. Boris Mikhailovitch is imbued with Marxist-Leninist principles and he is a loyal Soviet citizen," said Nadezhda without looking up.

"You have never heard him speak of plans to defect to the forces of world imperialism? Specifically, you have never heard him speak of his plans not to return from the international masters' tournament in Vienna in August?"

"I have never heard Boris Mikhailovitch say any such thing, Comrade Colonel."

"What happened to your neck, Nadia?" asked Podichevsky.

"I will show you," said Yesenin. "Come here, citizeness." Nadia shuffled forward, Yesenin grabbed her and forced her to her knees in front of Podichevsky, lifted her chin and ripped off the bloodstained bandages. The ugly puckered slash sewn together by black catgut started to bleed again under its black coating of iodine and crusted blood. "You know that this girl is terrified of being beaten by men, with reason. Last night she came to me in my apartment, and she offered me her body in exchange for letting you leave for Vienna unhindered. My name isn't Beria, so I declined, and I demanded that she remember her duty to the Motherland and denounce you for the traitor and capitalist lackey you are. I have a cut-off table leg that I keep in my apartment for occasions when I bring my work home with me. I summoned my driver to hold her down and told her that if she didn't denounce you I would give her a good working over with the club and break a few bones she doesn't really need. She broke away from Brodsky, ran into my kitchen and grabbed down a knife. She screamed that she would never betray you and then she cut her own throat. I was able to get the knife away from her in time." He stood Nadia up and handed her the bandages that she held against the bleeding wound. She was quietly weeping. "Please go inside the house now, citizeness." She turned and walked back up the pathway.

Podichevsky sat back. "Is the performance ended now, Ivan Vasilievitch?" he asked.

"It was a bit of a performance, yes, but it was a performance with a point. I am going to sit here and talk to you, Boris Mikhailovitch," said Yesenin. "I can well understand that you do not expect the truth from anyone who wears these blue boards and bands. I can't make you believe the truth, but I can damned well make you listen to it. It will be very embarrassing if you appear in Vienna with bruises on your face from being beaten by the Soviet secret police, but you are going to sit there, you are going to listen very carefully to what I have to say, and you will not interrupt me or argue with me while I am speaking, or I will come over there and bang you on your snout. I am going to tell you the truth, Boris Mikhailovitch. What you do with that truth is up to you.

"That performance, as you call it, was for the record. But it's more or less true," Yesenin went on, as Boris Mikhailovitch fingered several fallen chess pieces in his hand. "She came to me last night and offered to sleep with me if I didn't interfere in your Vienna trip. I was tempted, she's quite lovely, but I am not totally inhuman and I couldn't forget what was coming for her. I didn't want to make love to a woman I might be required to shoot dead in the near future. I told her that you were a traitor and a possible defector and it was her duty to denounce you as well as the only way that she could save herself from you. She refused. I offered to protect her as best I could from Stalin's wrath once you defect, but I had to be honest with her. I told her I probably couldn't do it and she would very likely be executed or serve a very long prison term for failing to inform against you in time to stop you from embarrassing the *Vozhd*. Do you know what she said to me? She said, 'I no longer have any thought for myself. I am innocent of the crime he thinks I committed against Marina, but if this is what he wants and it will ease the pain of his loss, then let it be so.'"

"How did she really get that cut on her neck?" asked Podichevsky.

"I told you. I decided I would try to save her from herself. I threatened her with the table leg, although I did it for her own good. I figured if the little ninny wouldn't denounce you on her own I'd make her denounce you and save her in spite of herself. I didn't mean to beat her as badly as I had threatened, just a couple of light taps to intimidate her into accusing you so I could put down on the official record that the citizeness had done her duty. That was a mistake. Brodsky's as strong as an ape, but she tore herself away from him and got to the knife. It actually took the two of us to keep her from killing herself rather than letting herself harm you through her inability to resist torture. That's the first thing I want you tell you, you arrogant and cowardly son of a bitch. That woman in there loves you so much that she is willing to die for you. Last night she damned near did. By heaven, you ought to be ashamed of yourself! Think what you have put her through! Besides, torturing Soviet citizens is the job of the Organs and we don't appreciate you amateurs butting in!

"The second thing I have come here to tell you, Boris Mikhailovitch, is this." Yesenin leaned forward. "Look at me when I tell you this, because I am only going to say it once. Nadezhda Morozova *did not betray Marina Galinskaya* to us or to anyone else. She had no hand at all in Marina's death, she was just unlucky enough to be the recipient of Marina's last confidence on New Year's Eve."

"I should have said nothing at all to anyone," remarked Marina. "Confidences are dangerous in Russia. Sometimes you do more harm with a confidence than you can with a pistol."

Yesenin ignored her and went on. "The facts in Marina's death are known. There are reasons why I cannot tell you these facts, but

Nadezhda Pavlovna was in no way involved. That's the truth, and if you don't believe it may you be damned for a fool as well as a bastard."

"Was it Beria?" asked Podichevsky tonelessly. "I was always afraid Marishka would somehow come to his notice."

"I will neither confirm nor deny that. It was someone in my own service, and it was a personal matter, not a political one. That's all I can tell you," said Yesenin.

"You're telling him more about it than you will tell me!" complained Marina.

"Beria," whispered Podichevsky. "Nadezhda was one of your inform- ers. How do I know she was not working for Beria?"

"Yes, she was, and still is, an NKVD informer, a spy. This is the U.S.S.R. and everyone spies on everyone else. That is now our way of life and you know it perfectly well, and you are wrong to hold it against her. But Nadezhda Pavlovna did not in any way inform against or compro- mise Marina Galinskaya. She has reported to Major Trofim Petrovich Korchagin for some months now, and she has reported nothing of any importance. Every time she reports nothing of importance, Major Korchagin beats her with his fists. Yet she has never tried to stop the beatings by making up false gossip or accusations. You know this. Why did you let that happen? You're not totally without influence, Boris Mikhailovitch. You could have had a word with me, or Molotov, or Poskrebyshev, and at least no one have hit her any more. That was dis- graceful on your part."

"Yes," sighed Podichevsky. "It was disgraceful. I should have stopped the hitting, no matter how I felt about her. How can I tell if you are lying to me? You are a *gaybist*. Lies are your stock in trade."

"You saw that wound on Nadia's neck," said Yesenin. "That is real enough. Do you think I did it? I would have finished what I started, I promise you. You saw the bruises on Nadia's face and body when she came back from town after her sessions with Korchagin, every one of them proof of her love for you. Boris Mikhailovitch, I tell you again that

I understand what great obstacles present themselves to your believing any man who wears this uniform. But by God, if you cannot see the incandescent flame of that girl's love for you, if you are so blind that you can see nothing at all except chess pieces on a board, then you are the biggest fool I have ever met. Suppose I am telling the truth. What then, eh, Podichevsky? Suppose every word I have said is true. Think about what you have done to Nadia! Think about what you were going to do to her!"

Boris Mikhailovitch's face went absolutely white, and Yesenin knew that he believed. "Is it possible that I could have been so deceived?" he moaned. "What do you want me to do?"

"Take her to Vienna with you, and set her free," said Yesenin. "I have noticed that sometimes very stupid men can also be very lucky. If you are one of the stupid but lucky ones, she might agree to stay with you."

They rose together and walked into the dacha. Nadezhda Pavlovna was sitting on the settee, still holding the bandages to her neck. Podichevsky went to her and got down upon his knees before her, and took her free hand. "Nadezhna Pavlovna, it seems that I have done you a terrible wrong," he said quietly. "I hope that you will give me the chance to correct that wrong as best I can. To begin with, I hope you will do me the honor of accompanying me to the tournament in Vienna."

His head was bowed. Nadia looked up at Yesenin, her eyes brimming with tears, and silently mouthed the words "Thank you, Vanya!"

"Thank you, Vanya," said Marina Antonovna from behind him.

*　　　　　*　　　　　*

Outside, Yesenin paused to light a Lucky Strike. The sun was rising and it promised to be a warm, beautiful day. The pine forest sloped downward off to his right, the quiet carpet of needles on the shady ground soft and inviting. "I'm going to stretch my legs a bit, Zoltan Bogdanovitch," called Yesenin over to where Brodsky sat in the Daimler.

"Okay, boss," answered The Lump, who would quite willingly sit there all day if required. Yesenin wandered through the woods, the sunlight dappling through the fragrant pines, until he came to the small stream that ran behind Podichevsky's dacha. There was another small wooden bridge across the stream. Yesenin stood on the bridge looking down at the running water below and lit another Lucky.

"What will you do now?" asked Marina.

"I'm tired of this stupid bogus investigation. It seems that you ran away from us, Marina Antonovna. You defected to become the lover of some aspiring Broadway actor whom no one has ever heard of. I am going to fabricate a false cablegram from New York wherein it will be reported that you have been killed in a subway accident or something of the kind. That way we can announce your death and those who loved you may mourn you officially. Including me. I know the NKVD resident in New York. He owes me a few favors and he will help with the paperwork."

"And you won't kill anyone else over me?" asked Marina.

"No. You always knew that I wouldn't," replied Yesenin.

"Yes, Vanya. I always knew. But I'm afraid your ploy won't work," she said gently.

"Why not?" he asked.

"They're digging me up now."

"*What?*" exclaimed Yesenin in amazement. "What do you mean?"

"They're at my grave and they're digging me up, right now," Marina informed him. "Some militiamen are digging and an NKVD officer is supervising. I think it's your friend Korchagin. There is an ambulance there with a bag to take away my body. There's enough of my teeth and my clothes left so that they will be able positively to identify me."

Yesenin buried his head in his hands for a while. "Brodsky, I suppose?" he asked after a time.

"Yes," answered Marina. "Please don't be angry with him, Ivan Vasilievitch. He had no choice. No one ever does."

"You chose not to dirty your hands with this filth. I know, remember? I was the one you refused, time and again. You wouldn't report on Vyacheslavsky, you wouldn't report on Diaz, you wouldn't report on Subotnikov or Podichevsky or Nazarian."

"You I refused, yes," said Marina. "I knew I could refuse you because you loved me. Suppose I'd been assigned to Major Korchagin? I might have been able to take a few more blows than Nadia before I agreed to do my duty to socialism, but not many. Everyone keeps calling me an angel, and that's embarrassing. I wasn't. I was just as weak and terrified as everyone else."

"But you came to me in the cold of night to save a couple of Arbat parasites," said Yesenin.

"I came to you to try and save two human beings, Vanya. And when I did, that you took from me my life. Are you ready to tell me why now?"

Yesenin wanted to weep, but he could not. It had been too long. "Do you remember exactly what you did that night in my apartment, Marishka? What you offered me?"

"I remember."

"And I told you that I would save your friends and get them out of the country on false passports, but the price would be far higher than that?" continued Yesenin.

"Yes, I remember," said Marina softly.

"And what was that price?"

"You demanded that I marry you. I said yes," recounted Marina. "Imagine my surprise when you then proceeded to strangle me to death! That is *not* the response a girl expects when she agrees to marry a fellow, I assure you! A tender kiss and a vow of eternal love is generally considered more *de rigeur*."

Yesenin stared into the pines, his voice heavy and slow. "Do you remember all those times down through the years, since you were what? Fifteen years old and still wearing your schoolgirl's uniform? All those times that I begged of you to accept my love, my worship, my life and my soul? Then I heard you were with this long-haired narcissistic so-called poet or that crapulous theatrical impresario or the other pompous composer. Time after time, every six months I heard how you were giving to some other man what I would have cut out my own heart to possess for even a moment? Do you know why I didn't arrange for every one of those men to be dragged down into the Lubyanka cellars or put onto a cattle car bound for someplace many time zones away where they could watch their piss freeze in mid-air? Even though I could have done it with the snap of my fingers? I didn't touch one of them, although the thought of you in their arms drove me almost insane with rage every night as I lay staring at the ceiling. I didn't touch them because I understood something. I understood that you were a human being and a human soul, of free will, and that anything I ever got from you, however little, had to be given freely. That anything I took from you by force or guile would have been worse than nothing.

"Most men my age have fantasies about younger women, usually carnal ones, seeing her naked or in bed, making love to her. It was never like that with you in my mind, Marishka. You know what my fantasy was with you, the one that got me through all the dark nights? It was a house of our own by the Black Sea or maybe by Lake Baikal, a warm fire and children and books and simply sitting and talking to you, about great things, about little things. And above all, on your left hand that golden ring that we Communists no longer wear because it supposedly symbolizes men's subjection of women. No, Marishka. That ring would have symbolized my utter subjection to you, because to get that ring on your finger and keep it there I would have built my whole life around you. I know it was a fantasy. I always recognized that. Kolchin and I have the same problem. Neither of us deserved you and neither of us had the right to ask for you. But that fantasy kept me alive, Marishka. Kolchin was able to kill his heart and his soul, build his own fantasy world at that desk behind that blanket in the night. I had only one imaginary world into which I could escape. Without that fantasy of that house, and those children, and you, and that band on your finger, and your smile in some place of tranquility that was ours alone, I would have eaten my pistol barrel a long time ago. Always, always in the back of my mind there was this hope that someday you would turn to me. I knew it was a false hope, but hope in the human heart is a stubborn thing. No matter how you try to stamp it out, you can never quite kill it."

"And then I finally agreed to marry you, and you killed me," said Marina.

"That night I asked you the question that I have asked you at least fifty times before, on my knees, in Comrade Procurator Galinsky's garden, on a train, in a restaurant, by the sea, while I was drunk, while I was sober, in my office, in Podichevsky's arbor where we were this morning. Always the answer was no. Then that night in my apartment, I asked you again, and at long last I heard the word, that *da* I had wanted to hear all my adult life. And you didn't say it for me, you said it for *them!* So quickly you answered, immediately doing for a couple of drug dealing degenerates what you would never do for a man who loved you with all his being! Why did you do that do me, Marishka? Why did you hurt me like that?"

"In case you haven't noticed, Vanya, I hurt everyone who loved me," she replied softly. "In your case it was sheer carelessness. I didn't think. I should have thought. I didn't mean to do that to you, Vanya. It's going to take a while, but I hope some day you can forgive me. I told you last night that this last seven months has not been your punishment, Vanya. I spoke the truth. It has been *my* punishment. I have at long last been forced to confront what I have done to the lives of others with my weakness and my indecision and my egotism. I should have said yes, Vanya, yes to someone. To you, to Arkady Fyodorovitch, to the noble Vyacheslavsky, to proud and brave Rodrigo...I should have said yes to someone and given him everything I could give, that he might be everything he could be. I was granted something at birth, Vanya, the power of true womanhood. This power to inspire that every man who has ever known me, to give him what he has longed for and begged me for. But I was afraid and confused and not a little selfish, and so every man I ever knew ended up the worse off for knowing me. I ask all of you to forgive me, yet I cannot forgive myself. I understand why you killed me now. You couldn't bear what I had done to you, the terrible insult to your pride I had offered you."

"No," replied Yesenin dully, light up another Lucky Strike. "That wasn't why I killed you."

"Then why?" she asked.

"Because beyond the blinding pain I understood with clarity what was happening," replied Ivan Vasilievitch. "I had finally done what I swore I would never do. I had used my power and my violence to coerce you into surrendering to me. It didn't matter that it was you who initiated the transaction on behalf of that saxophone-blowing lounge lizard. I remember that you told me once you could never marry a man with blood on his hands. In the daylight of the real world I always understood perfectly that my love was never reciprocated, and that you hated me and feared me."

"Never hated!" cried Marina passionately. "Yes, Vanya, I was afraid of you! Dear God, who wouldn't be afraid? But I never hated you, I swear it!"

"And yet, in order to save two other people from destruction, you immediately and without hesitation agreed to give your whole life, you whole future, into the bloody hands of a man you feared. You instantly agreed to what I think we both know would have been a life of misery for you, like a prison. You also knew full well that if I fell you might well fall with me, and that in order to survive you would have to degrade yourself still further in ways we can both well imagine. Without hesitation, you agreed to destroy yourself that two others might survive and be free. The people who call you an angel are not wrong, Marishka. You are the essence of goodness and mercy, and I could not stand to be the altar upon which you made your sacrifice. I knew that marriage to me would be torture for you worse than anything we inflict in the interrogation rooms, worse than anything that might await you in Karaganda when I fell. The little house by the sea was a fantasy. I live in Government Mansions in Moscow, and when I came home to you in that apartment every night we would both smell that day's blood upon my hands. I also knew myself well enough to understand that I was not strong enough, not man enough, to release you from your promise once I had heard it fall from your lips. I should have been satisfied with hearing that *da* once, and then let you go. I could not. I had you now and I could never let you go, never let you enter another man's arms. I was a weak and selfish bastard and once I had you I had to have all of you. I loved you, Marishka, you were in danger, and I had to save you. I had to save you from *me*. I did so."

There was silence, for a long time, as the birds sang and the dust floated in the columns of sunlight, and the water gurgled over the rocks below the bridge. Yesenin lit and smoked another Lucky, down to the point where the fire burned his lips, then tossed the butt into the water. "Is that enough, Marina Antonovna?" he asked quietly. "Is that what you have sought all these months, and have you left me now? Are you still there, Marishka?"

"I am still here," she replied.

"Why do you remain?" he asked. "You have what you want, the best answer I will ever be able to give you."

"I told you, Ivan Vasilievitch. I will stay with you as long as you need me." She was quiet for a time. "Do you want me to go?"

"Would...would you mind staying with me a while longer?" he asked. "If Brodsky has told them what I did, and they have found your body, it won't be for long." Finally he broke down and wept. *"Stay with me, Marishka! Please stay with me!"*

"As long as you need me," she repeated.

*   *   *

When Yesenin got back to the Daimler and got in, The Lump said, "Lubyanka, boss?"

"Later yes, but I want to stop by my apartment first." They drove back into the city in silence. "Put the car away and come upstairs," Yesenin told his driver. When Brodsky entered the apartment he saw Yesenin burning a pile of papers in the hearth. Ivan Vasilievitch looked up. "They've dug up her body. I presume they've taken her to the police morgue for a formal autopsy on what's left. Who did you report to? Korchagin?"

Brodsky collapsed on a chair, his head in his hands, and began to sob. Yesenin walked over and embraced him. "It's all right, Lump," he said soothingly. "We are Chekists. It is our way. If it's any consolation, Korchagin's driver was reporting to me. Korchagin will probably get this apartment. If you play your cards right and testify well I'll bet he keeps you on. You can still have your little room up there and he'll probably get the Daimler too. I know you love that car. At my interrogation I'll have a word with him about you. We go back a way and I'm sure he'll look after you. Now, listen. I'm going to the office to turn myself in. They'll be here in a couple of hours and they'll seal the place. Don't touch any of my papers. I've already burned what's important but if they think you've taken any documents they'll drag you into it as well. I want you to have all the food in the cupboards and the icebox, all the tinned stuff and the caviar and the sausage and cold cuts. Fill up a suit-case and take it to your mother."

"Thanks, boss," sniffled The Lump.

"Also, in my stash behind the bookcase in my study there is an enve-lope with twelve hundred rubles."

"I can't take your money, boss," said Brodsky miserably.

"Well, if you don't take it, whoever tosses the place will pocket it and spend it on booze and whores or gamble it away. I'd rather you have it and buy something nice for your mother, and use the rest to get yourself some nice girls down at the Hotel Druzhba, or maybe that motor scooter you've been wanting. Goodbye, Lump. Take care."

"Goodbye, Madman," said the Lump, giving Yesenin a final hug.

Yesenin decided to take one last walk through the streets of Moscow. The sun was rising high and the ice cream vendors were on every corner. It was a fairly long walk to the grim yellow façade of the Lubyanka, but he took his time, and the people crossing the street did to avoid him did not annoy him at all. *Bet it's Korchagin who arrests me,* thought Yesenin with a tired smile. *Bet he says to me, "You always had the look of a man who might be guilty someday." Well, I always did, didn't I?*

They met him at the top of the central staircase in the Lubyanka, before he could turn left to go to his office. He felt the hand on his shoulder. He turned expecting to face Korchagin, but instead he was confronted with a tall, massively built NKVD officer with the face of a gorilla, accompanied by a second *gaybist* unknown to him. With some surprise Yesenin recognized the big man as Captain Joseph Vlasic, Stalin's personal bodyguard and chief of security. Vlasic saluted smartly and Yesenin returned the salute. "Colonel Ivan Vasilievitch Yesenin," rumbled the captain, "I present the compliments of the General Secretary of the All-Union Communist Party. Comrade Stalin has requested to see you. Now. A car is waiting."

VI. The General Secretary

Yesenin entered the anteroom of Stalin's office in the Kremlin and received a pleasant little nod from a little bald-headed man behind a desk, as if Yesenin were an everyday guest in the inner sanctum of the Father Of The Peoples. "Ah, Ivan Vasilievitch! There you are! Let me inform The Boss that you have arrived." He picked up a telephone. This was Comrade A. N. Poskrebyshev, Stalin's long time secretary, a man of tested loyalty. Stalin had allegedly tested Comrade Poskrebyshev's loyalty by arresting his wife and sending her to Karaganda for ten years, yet

Poskrebyshev continued at his post. This episode was whispered through the corridors of the Kremlin as an astounding example of Party loyalty and discipline in action on both the part of Stalin and his little secretary. Yesenin was the *gaybist* who had arrested Poskrebysheva and dragged her screaming from her apartment, and even a hardened Bolshevik might have wondered at the cheerful greeting he received. Yesenin was in on the secret, of course. Stalin had disposed of Poskrebysheva as a favor to his old comrade, so that Alexander Nikolayevitch could carry on his long-standing affair with a Kremlin typist free of his wife's objections. Yesenin handed over his pistol to Vlasic without being asked and also the dagger from his boot. "Go right in, please, Comrade Colonel," said Poskrebyshev.

"Marina Antonovna, please don't take offense, but I would appreciate it if you would not interrupt the General Secretary and myself," Yesenin whispered under his breath. "Meetings with Himself are always a bit tricky."

"He will never know I am here," simpered Marina.

Stalin's office was stark and simple. The wooden floor was uncarpeted. There were no armchairs, only straight-backed chairs with worn upholstery. Stalin did not work at a desk but at a long table beneath two framed photographs of Karl Marx and Vladimir Ilyich Lenin. Files, books, and reports were stacked neatly in ordered rows along the table. To the dictator's right was a bank of five telephones. Telephones were a status symbol, and most top Communist bureaucrats wanted at least ten phones on their desk for show. Yesenin himself had three, but Stalin had only the ones he actually needed. There was a direct line to the Lubyanka, another to the Moscow military district headquarters of the General Staff, a third to the offices of the Central Committee, his intercom to Poskrebyshev in the outer office and Yezhov downstairs, and a single open line to the Kremlin switchboard. The General Secretary himself sat behind the worktable, puffing meditatively on his famous Dunhill pipe that he held to his lips with his curved, withered left arm.

Stalin was dressed in his usual simple uniform with the buttoned pockets and the high-topped boots, no insignia at all of any kind on the collar or epaulettes. This one was summer white. He was studying a list. Without looking up he gestured to a chair. "Take a seat, please, Comrade Colonel," he said. "What about Belinovsky?" he asked without waiting for Yesenin to sit down.

"You're asking me?" returned Yesenin in surprise. "I don't know Belinovsky."

"But you've seen him?" asked Stalin, looking up. In the afternoon sunlight the man had the face of a rat, his moustache thin and grizzled like an old rat's muzzle and his chin dewlapped and wobbling, but the yellow eyes were the eyes of a ghoul, glowing the with bestial fury and hatred of all life, hungering to rend the flesh of men. Yesenin noticed he was wearing reading glasses.

"I've seen Belinovsky a few times in the corridors here, heard some speeches of his at the Praesidium, yes," said Yesenin.

"Does he have the appearance to you of a man who may be guilty someday?" asked Stalin.

Yesenin shrugged, "That was just an aphorism I cooked up on the spur of the moment. Look, *Vozhd,* you know perfectly well looks have nothing to do with it. We're all guilty. I sometimes wonder why you don't just line up the whole Party and shoot every third individual. That's how Lenin got the trains to run on time."

"But it's so much more *fun* this way," admonished Stalin gently. "Ah, well." He made a mark by Belinovsky's name and laid the list aside, and took off his reading glasses. "I took the liberty of pre-empting the usual channels and saving us all some time, because eventually I would in any case have been called upon to decide in this Galinskaya matter."

"Actually, I would have requested for an appointment myself in any case, Comrade General Secretary," said Yesenin. "I wanted to ask you something."

"The interrogator wants to interrogate me?" exclaimed Stalin with a chuckle.

"Not interrogation, Comrade General Secretary. More a request for enlightenment. I must confess I am puzzled by the manner in which you have proceeded. You clearly have known for quite some time that I murdered Marina Antonovna Galinskaya in my apartment on New Year's eve and then secretly disposed of her remains. Yet you waited seven months, and then took the unusual step of having your underling Yezhov assign me the task of investigating her disappearance. Why did you do that?"

Stalin smiled benignly "Do you know why men seek power, Ivan Vasilievitch? I will tell you. They seek power not only so they can destroy what they despise, but so that they can create. Create using live human beings as building material. Experiment with people. I have never understood the fascination men like Podichevsky have with chess. What is the fun in simply picking up a piece and moving it to another square, where it obediently stays until you are ready to move it again? You can't make a wooden chessman laugh or cry or love or hate or confess. You can't torture it or humiliate it, or reward it. What is the fun in having puppies or kittens who never climb out of their box and run around getting into things? I assigned you this investigation purely out of curiosity. I wanted to see if you would run away or brazen it out. You brazened it out. That impresses me. What were you planning to submit by way of a report?"

"A forged cable saying that she had defected and been killed in a subway accident in New York," Yesenin told him.

"Not bad," said Stalin. "Why not accuse someone more to hand?"

"I might have accidentally accused someone you wanted to keep around for a while. I didn't want to trip you up or embarrass you," said Yesenin.

"Good thinking," said Stalin approvingly. "I confess that I was annoyed with you when I found out that you killed her. She was very pretty to look at and very pleasant to be with. You're a useful man and I wasn't going to have you shot or even demoted, just send you off as a camp commandant up in Kolyma or the Soloveichiks or Tunguska for a bit. Maybe Karaganda if you like the ladies. I wouldn't get rid of a useful man simply because he broke a pretty thing. But then I heard something that made you an interesting man as well as a useful one, and interesting men are far more rare than useful ones. I heard that you were talking to yourself, conducting long conversations with the spirit of this dead woman. Tell me, was she really answering you back? It sounded to me as if she was."

"Of course!" sighed Yesenin. "You planted microphones and recording devices in my apartment. Yes, Comrade Stalin, she answers me back."

"Is she talking to you now?" asked Stalin curiously.

"No, Comrade General Secretary. Before I came in here I asked Marina not to interrupt our conversation."

"Do you think she would talk to me?" requested Stalin.

"I am afraid I was never very interested in politics," said Marina.

"She says she's not interested in politics," Yesenin told him.

"How delightful!" exclaimed Stalin clapping his hands like a small child. "A ghost who is not interested in politics!"

"Comrade Stalin, I am still uncertain whether this voice I hear in my head is in fact the ghost or spirit of Marina Antonovna Galinskaya, or whether I am simply insane. It is more than likely that I truly do deserve my cognomen of The Madman."

"Don't feel badly, Ivan Vasilievitch. We live in an insane epoch. It doesn't matter where the voice comes from, the important fact is that you hear it," said Stalin. "An NKVD officer who hears voices! How perfect! Yes, yes, Ivan Vasilievitch, you are definitely my next Inspector General for the People's Commissariat of Internal Affairs!"

"I beg your pardon?" asked Yesenin, stunned.

"Beria and I are going to get rid of that grotesque dwarf downstairs," confided Stalin. "He's served his turn. I'll want you to get very cozy with Beria, of course, for the time will come when he as well has served his turn and must go. Then who do you think will step up in his place?"

"You want a People's Commissar of Internal Affairs who strangles women and hears voices?" asked Yesenin incredulously. "In God's name, why?"

"Ah, now, remember, God does not exist," said Stalin, wagging his finger in admonition. "I ought to know. I studied in for the priesthood in a seminary. As to why, let us take a look at three People's Commissars, past, present, and future. Yagoda, Yezhov, and Beria. All hand picked by me. Each one worse than the last, if I do say so myself. Each one more cruel, more devious, more cunning, more sycophantic, and more wicked than the last. But they all have the same problem. They are all vicious and evil, but sane. They know perfectly well the nature of the state they serve and the risk that their high position places them in. Eventually, any sane man in that position is going to start plotting against me, as the only way to save himself from me and from whomever I have picked to be his successor. A madman like you, however, would be too consumed by his inner demons to worry about petty intrigue. You would be intent on playing out the great melodrama, reliving over and over and over again this one episode of your life that you can never undo. You have an existence as a person outside the structure of the state. Put more simply, you are a man with a hobby. Your lovely ghost. Not only does she constitute the central aspect of your existence, but since such things are rather difficult permanently to conceal, word will eventually get around and other sane plotters will stay away from a madman whom they dare not trust. What a superb way of keeping you loyal! There is also a great advantage to me from the propaganda point of view in having an NKVD commissar who is known to be insane. I tell you to do something, it turns out it is a mistake or is excessively unpopular, I can overrule and countermand you with a shrug and say, 'Eh, what can you expect? Useful chap, that Yesenin, but we all know he's a bit touched in the head. Hears voices, you know.' Besides, I think it gives you a truly Russian quality."

"I don't understand, *Vozhd*," said Yesenin.

"This ghost business gives you a tortured soul. All true Russians have a tortured soul."

"Er, I am honored by your offer, Comrade General Secretary, but I am afraid you don't understand," said Yesenin. "I murdered a woman. I must turn myself in to the proper authorities and confess."

"Ivan Vasilievitch, this is not a Dostoevsky novel. Or even a Kolchin novel. You are not Raskolnikov and I am not Porfiry Petrovich. Socialism has a much more enlightened attitude towards these things, at least among useful men. I *am* the proper authority, and you just confessed," said Stalin. He pointed his finger at Yesenin. "Don't do it no more, *karasho*? I have problems enough with Beria raping women all the time without you strangling them as well. So, there are all the legal formalities observed. Go home, but before you do tell the Lubyanka seamstress to start sewing general's stars on your uniform."

"I assume you don't want me talking to Marina in public? Or telling everyone about the conversations I have with her?" said Yesenin. Stalin took off his glasses.

"Fascinating!" he exclaimed. "Why do I get the impression that you are about to try to blackmail me, Ivan Vasilievitch? What do you want?"

"The chess master, Boris Podichevsky, and his secretary, Nadezhda Morozova?"

"Yes, your conversation with the lovely Nadia was monitored. Very gallant of you to let her sleep on the couch. They are both to be arrested, of course, for espionage and plotting defection."

"Let them go to Vienna," said Yesenin. "Let those two kittens get out of the box and run off into the grass. You don't really need them. While you're at it, give General Rodrigo Diaz his passport back and let him go home to Spain, to die like an *hombre* in his own land with his bullet wounds in the front. There will be benefits from that. He'll be good propaganda, I promise you. The lefty press will eat it up when he finally ends a life that has no meaning to him without Marina, and he won't begrudge you that life, Anarchist though he is. Otherwise I'll talk to Marina anywhere I please. Eventually I'll become too much of an embarrassment and you must either shoot me or lock me up in the cackle box. You want me to play with as a toy, *Vozhd*. OK, you've got your new toy, your new Inspector General. But that's my price. Let them go."

"Very well. I will let them go. On one understanding between us," replied Stalin softly. "Every dog gets one bite, Ivan Vasilievitch. You just had yours. You will never try anything like that again with me. Not ever again. Not now, not twenty years from now, if I let you live that long."

"I understand, *Vozhd*. Thank you." Shaken and bemused, Yesenin stood up, saluted, and shuffled to the door. In the doorway he turned back to the dictator who had replaced his spectacles and was already studying his death lists again. "Comrade General Secretary?"

"Yes?" asked Stalin looking up.

"You never asked me why I killed Marina."

Stalin shrugged. "I didn't ask because I don't care."

"No, of course not. Tell me, Comrade General Secretary, did you ever hear or read a poem by an Englishman named Wilde?" asked Yesenin. "Kolchin made reference to it last night, and I have been trying to remember it. Something about how each man kills the thing he loves?"

Stalin took off his glasses again, and spoke:

> *"Yet each man kills the thing he loves.*
> *By all let this be heard.*
> *Some do it with a bitter look,*
> *Some with a flattering word.*
> *The coward does it with a kiss,*
> *The brave man with a sword."*

"It is from *The Ballad of Reading Gaol*," said Stalin. "I spent many years in exile in Siberia, Ivan Vasilievitch, and I didn't spend all of them reading Lenin and Marx. Now go."

           *   *   *

Yesenin got back to his apartment that night and found everything undisturbed, except that all his food was gone. The Lump had not taken the envelope of cash behind the bookcase. Yesenin summoned Volodya the porter and sent him out with money to buy some tea and bread and cheese from a nearby black marketeer, and while he was waiting for the man to return Ivan Vasilievitch carefully searched his apartment. He found the microphones hidden in his study, his lounge, his bedroom, and one carefully concealed in the light on his balcony. He ripped them out, and traced the wires through a small hole that disappeared into the floor, presumably into a room somewhere downstairs. Yesenin knew at least some of the other apartments in government mansions were monitored, but he figured he would be exempt because it was known that he never had anyone up to his place except for the occasional paid woman.

When the food came Yesenin made himself tea and ate the bread and cheese. Then he spoke. "Marishka? Are you there?"

"Yes," said Marina.

"What must I do, Marishka?"

"You know what you must do, Vanya." And he did know.

In August the Master Boris Podichevsky went to the tournament in Vienna along with his wife, his former secretary Nadezhda Morozova, whom he had married in properly businesslike civil ceremony the day before his departure. The Master won every single match, checkmating Sir Angus Robertson in eighty-four minutes and forcing Velasco Gomez to concede in ninety. He then shocked the chess world by announcing that he was remaining in the West. The bride and groom would be settling in England. Numerous articles attacking Podichevsky's overrated playing style, his plagiarized strategies, and "bourgeois flamboyance" appeared in *Pravda* and *Izvestia*.

In September of 1938, the new Inspector General of the NKVD found it necessary to do a tour of the Finnish border posts. Having completed his inspection of the crossing on the Leningrad-Hammerfors highway, General Yesenin got back into his powerful armored Daimler touring car, which was driven by a lumpish person. Instead of turning right and heading back toward distant Leningrad, this Lump swerved left and before the startled border guards could react, he smashed through the barriers and was roaring down the road into Finland. That night Yesenin was in Helsinki. The next night he was in Stockholm, and a week later the General was sitting in a room in Whitehall smoking pack after pack of Lucky Strikes and spilling his guts to Sir Angus Robertson and his colleagues in MI6. The only discordant note came at the end of the interrogation when Yesenin asked, "How could any people so bloody stupid as to put milk and sugar in tea end up ruling the biggest empire in the world?"

VII. By A Distant Sea

Some years after the end of the second war, an old man of foreign extraction came to live in the little village of Peel, on the Isle of Man in the Irish Sea. He called himself John Basilson, but although he spoke educated English quite well everyone knew he wasn't English. The old man had a surprisingly generous government stipend that took care of all his simple needs. He lived in a small cottage in the village and kept to himself, tending to his garden and playing classical music on his phonograph. The local police inspector was a retired Scotland Yard man, and he told his friend the vicar he remembered seeing Basilson a few times during the war, coming out of Whitehall. "He was one of the cloak and dagger lads," confided the inspector. "Handled some foreign desk for MI6. Presumably his country of origin."

Basilson held himself aloof, always polite and helpful, even willing to play Father Christmas for the local children, but he discouraged excessive curiosity about his provenance and his past. As the years wore on the locals became used to his presence. Every few months or so, he would get visits from the mainland. These visitors were occasionally men of military bearing wearing neat suits and ties and bowler hats, carrying briefcases, but mostly the old man's guests consisted of an odd lumpish-looking fellow, exceedingly ugly, and a married couple, an older man and his quiet, attractive middle-aged wife. When the lumpish fellow came the local off-licence could count on Basilson dropping by for a case of imported vodka. When the married couple came it was the best cognac, tea, and sweets and cakes for the couple's three children, who would run up and down the street playing with the local urchins while the man and his wife sat in Basilson's garden and talked. Often Basilson and the man would play chess. The foreign lady, it was noticed by those who saw her in the village, had a rather noticeable scar under her left jaw.

There was a third, more infrequent visitor to the old man's home. Every now and then, very rarely, someone would report that they had been passing by at twilight and seen the old foreign gentleman sitting in his garden with a beautiful young woman wearing an oddly old-fashioned green evening gown, a fur hat, and boots, of all things.

In 1964 John Basilson was found dead in his home of a heart attack, and it was of this mysterious young woman that the vicar and the police inspector spoke as they stood by his newly filled grave after the funeral. There had been no clue as to Basilson's religious affiliation, or indeed any clue to his past at all anywhere in his cottage, but the vicar and the entire village had liked the reclusive old man and the church committee gladly agree to allow him burial in their grounds. The churchyard stood hard by the sea, on a beetling hill over a small strand like those which line the Manx shoreline the whole island round, and the sea wind and the sound of the breakers soothed the eternal sleep of those who rested on the small ridge above the rocky beach. "No, no addresses of anybody," said the inspector. "Our office was quietly notified some years ago that if anything were to happen to old John we were to call a certain number in London. We did, and two chaps from Whitehall cleaned out his place this morning. Wish I'd been able to contact the chess fellow at least. I'm sure he and the family would have wanted to be here. But that young lass I saw him with a couple of times, her especially. Always curious about 'er, professionally speaking, I mean. How did she even get here? The others, the chess player and his family and that lumpy chap, they all came to Peel from Douglas ferry terminal by taxi. But I never saw no taxi bring 'er or take 'er away. Maybe she was his daughter. Lovely looking girl, though. The most beautiful dark eyes I ever saw, even though I was just at a distance passin' by 'is house, and a smile that seemed to light up the twilight."

The vicar looked down onto the beach below him, and his blood ran cold. About a hundred yards distant, walking away from him, he saw the very young woman under discussion. Her oddly out of date evening gown looked even more archaic now, like something the vicar's mother might have worn, and the boots and the fur hat were an oddly exotic and foreign affectation. Beside the young woman was a tall man wearing a green uniform of some kind, with a visored, blue-banded cap and blue shoulderboards. They were holding hands and walking away towards a headland. Although he could not see the man's face, something about his posture and his gait looked horribly familiar. The vicar looked down at the newly dug grave, as if to make certain the occupant were still there, and when he looked up again the couple had disappeared from sight.

"A lovely lass altogether," said the inspector reminiscently. "I wish I could have met her."

"No, Fred," said the vicar. "No, somehow I don't think you want to meet her. At least not just yet. Come up to the house. I could do with a drink." Before the two of them went up to the vicarage for their drink, they both paused and looked back at the curious epitaph that John Basilson had requested be engraved upon his headstone.

Yet each man kills the thing he loves.
By all let this be heard.
Some do it with a bitter look,
Some with a flattering word.
The coward does it with a kiss,
The brave man with a sword.